DAYS OF DISTRACTION

DAYS OF
DISTRACTION

A NOVEL

ALEXANDRA CHANG

ecco
An Imprint of HarperCollins*Publishers*

FIRST EDITION

Designed by Suet Chong

Library of Congress Cataloging-in-Publication Data

Names: Chang, Alexandra, 1988– author.
Title: Days of distraction : a novel / Alexandra Chang.
Description: New York : Ecco, [2020]
Identifiers: LCCN 2019016988 (print) | LCCN 2019020621 (ebook) | ISBN 9780062951816 (ebook) | ISBN 9780062951809 (pbk.)
Classification: LCC PS3603.H357273 (ebook) | LCC PS3603.H357273 D39 2020 (print) | DDC 813/.6—dc23
LC record available at https://lccn.loc.gov/2019016988

ISBN 978-0-06-295180-9

20 21 22 23 24　LSC　10 9 8 7 6 5 4 3 2 1

For my family

CONTENTS

I.

SAN FRANCISCO

When I read the book, the biography famous,
And is this then (said I) what the author calls a man's life?
And so will some one when I am dead and gone write my life?
(As if any man really knew aught of my life,
Why even I myself I often think know little or nothing of my real
    life,
Only a few hints, a few diffused faint clews and indirections
I seek for my own use to trace out here.)

—Walt Whitman, "When I Read the Book"

People think I'm smaller than I am. For example, my feet. In fact, I wear size 8.5 or 9. According to Google, these are the most common sizes for American women. Average is good, I reason. It means that wherever I end up in this country it will be easy to find someone whose shoes I can borrow.

Everything in our house smells of mildew, even with the dehumidifier running. In the morning, while J still sleeps, I take out the full tank of water collected from the overnight air and dump it in our front yard, a place full of sand and desert plants. The fog hangs low over the street of families and retirees. To the east, Sutro Tower juts through the clouds. If I walked west to the end of the block, then up the long, zigzagging stairs to the top of Grandview Park, and if not for this early fog, I'd be able to see all of the Sunset with its rows of pastel houses and, past that, the vast green of Golden Gate Park, where in the northwest section, the all-female herd of bison roam their paddock.

I've come to cherish this ritual. In front of our small yellow house, watching the water pool dark, then sink into the ground. I know where I am and what I am doing.

But now we are preparing to leave this all behind.

This is the place and time in which the most average person is average in their own special way, or learns to believe it. The ordinary can be powerful. The flower, the sidewalk cone, the clouds in the sky, the sunset, so many sunsets and skies, new shoes, a haircut, overheard pieces of conversation, pets and food, for sure. Anything is up for curation, if that's the story you want to tell. People you've never met can reach into the snippets of your day-to-day life, add it all up to make meaning. At least that's how it feels. Here, now. I know there are people who choose to opt out. Though not many in this city, the center of pressure, where an office of somebodies came up with the notion of people being brands. Sharing and shouting isn't the issue so much as the corruption of living in real time. People experiencing everything at a remove through the eyes of a consumer (actual or potential), a future audience to judge. Some are adept at this anticipation; they gain massive followings. I do not fall into this category. I am on the other side. Those long stretches of getting lost in a giant, sticky web of other people's earlier moments. It's true not everyone lives like this or that. Only almost everyone I know.

I write about gadgets for people with money to spend. I consider this my first real job. It feels good to have one place to go five days a week, to see the same faces, to receive a steady paycheck. It's been a year and, among many other things, I've learned that journalists love to gossip. I'm not immune, I love it, too. Maybe gossip isn't the right word—we merely enjoy talking about each other. What's that if not some form of affection? I don't understand or like the reporters who don't do it. They're the less driven ones, the ones too oblivious or too precious for the job. The ones who want to be friendly with everyone, as if that doesn't also make them untrustworthy to most. It's part of our work description: Trading information for information. Leveraging vulnerability to gain trust. Determining not only who knows what, but also how to coax those people into telling. Our office is its own microcosm of drama. It gives me almost everything I need to feel a part of the world. My title is Consumer Technology Reporter.

"Everything we do in life matters," said the tech billionaire to the famous portrait photographer. The photographer chose an angle to make the man's head and hands look disproportionately gigantic. A leader. A genius. He was already a very large man. He stared off into the distance, making a pensive expression. The photographer asked him to elaborate. "How we communicate and interact with society matters," the billionaire continued. "How we travel on this very planet Earth matters. We have to realize that no *matter* how small or large our actions, everything we do *matters*. The moment you forget that, the moment you put that aside, your life becomes erratic, chaotic."

Weeks later, the photographer gave a short talk about his experience working with the *titans of tech,* in which he drew attention to this particular man as the one who rose above the rest. Exceptional, the photographer said with a quiver in his voice. The most authentic and soulful person he had ever met.

I tell Tim the plan. He is a senior writer, my deskmate, and I think, too, a friend, who might help. How, I'm not sure, except that he is in a better position than me. He squints his eyes at the news. He wears clear-framed glasses and a slicked-back undercut, which make him appear much younger than the father of three children that he is.

"You know you could stay. Let him go alone, establish yourself. Are you two getting married? Where are these grad programs anyway? You could end up in the middle of nowhere, then what're you gonna do? You're young. You're up and coming. The editors like you. You're at the cusp of your career. What's gonna happen if you follow this guy, especially to the middle of nowhere? Might be a different story if you're getting married. My wife, she followed me here, but we were already married. You're not too young. How old are you again? Jesus, you're young. I mean, I got married at twenty-four, and my wife was twenty-one at the time. That's how it is in the South, though."

"I don't want to get married," I say.

"You wanna go to the middle of fucking nowhere for a dude you don't even wanna marry?"

"I mean I don't like the institution of marriage in general."

"Oh yeah, yeah. Very San Francisco of you. Look at Adam over there. He's with his girlfriend sixteen years. No plans for marriage, then he just shows up one morning, knocking his desk so we can hear the click of that ring on his finger, like 'Hey, look at me, I got married. Happy me!' That's gonna be you soon enough."

"That's not the point," I say. "What do I do jobwise?"

"Okay. Here versus the middle of nowhere. Pretty easy, if you ask me."

"Where's the middle of nowhere? Why do you keep saying that?"

"Fucking Michigan or Indiana."

"It's possible he could get into school here or in New York City."

"You better hope so."

Tim looks back at his computer, where columns refresh themselves in his custom social deck. The words tick down at a steady speed. He is one of those, the ones adept at cultivating a following.

"So when would you move if you move?" he says, still staring at his screen. He clicks, smirks at something.

"Not until summer."

He continues clicking, then begins typing, faster, faster, moving his right hand back and forth between keyboard and trackpad. I go back to looking at my emails. Conversations between us often end this way, abruptly and without ceremony, the courtesy between deskmates. Many minutes later, he turns to me and says, "Here's what I'm thinking. Don't tell the editors yet. Wait. Until you know for sure where, or if, you're even going."

OH (office, two interns):
"Where'd you learn to make this?"
"From a photo one of my friends posted on Instagram."
"Is your friend a chef?"
"Yeah."
"Do you have a lot of chef friends on Instagram?"
"Yeah, a bunch."
"Wait, are they really your friends? Or just people you found on there? Like, do you really know and care about them?"
"Oh, sure. They're my good friends and I care a lot about them. They just don't know I exist."

J works in a lab with scientists and mice. The lab breeds genetic deformities into the mice—bad eyes, basically. He observes the rodents, how they handle their disabilities, which ones can lead "normal" mouse lives, which ones become too ill. The goal is to make discoveries that will translate into curing eye diseases in humans. As someone with severe myopia, I should appreciate these small sacrifices for the greater good. He tells me there are protocols for how to humanely kill the animals. These protocols vary based on size and age. One option is to put the mice into a chamber and overexpose them to CO_2 until they pass out and die. This is the most standard procedure, and relatively efficient (five mice at a time), but they struggle for a couple of minutes before dying and it is terrible to watch. Another is to euthanize the mouse with an overdose of chemical anesthetics, like the pound does with un-adoptable strays and lost animals never retrieved. This is painless when administered correctly, but gets expensive and time con-suming to perform with each individual mouse. Then there is the option to decapitate the mouse, if it is small enough, with a pair of very sharp scissors. This is cheap and fast. J has to lay a sheet of plastic and paper towels on his lab bench to catch the mess. Yes, small sacrifices for the greater good. This is what he wants to do for the next five or so years. It's something I can believe in, in concept, but I would never be able to get my hands bloodied. His title is Research Associate II.

In bed, we talk of the future. Maybe we'll get to stay. Maybe we'll go to New York City. And then . . . But what if . . . How about . . . We excite and exhaust ourselves with hypotheticals.

I tell J what Tim suggested.

He wraps his arms tightly around me and says, "You're not going anywhere."

"Exactly. I'm staying right here, and you'll go somewhere else."

"No! You know what I mean."

"Right, that I'm not going anywhere and then you can come back to visit me in this house."

He squeezes me tighter and I try to wrestle myself free.

"You think you're so funny," he says.

"I am the funny one in this relationship!"

"Hey, stop wiggling so much. Be nice."

I tuck myself into him, the way it feels right for both of us, my head on his chest and legs wrapped around his. We lie quietly for a while. He says, "Good night, little sweetheart," and falls asleep. His body twitches. I'm not little, I tell him in my mind. My legs are thicker and stronger than yours. I close my eyes and listen to the movements inside him. It does not matter how many times I hear them, it is like receiving dispatches from another realm.

I, too, should apply to graduate school, according to my mom. About J, she doesn't question whether I will follow him. ("You will cry if he is far away," she says matter-of-factly.) If I am also in school, however, we can both be doing something productive and respectable at the same time.

"You can change jobs, go really work in technology. At a tech company that can pay a lot. Marketing. Or finance. Management. These writing people doesn't respect you. They don't pay what you deserve. You have knowledge about technology now. Business school likes that."

"I don't want to."

"Why not? More money."

"No. I don't want to work with those people. They're all weird and have social problems, too! Have you ever talked to one of them? You feel like you're dying inside! Everything is, 'How can *you* benefit *me*?' I just want a fair raise and to somehow keep this job. I hate it when you tell me to do something that doesn't make any sense and that I don't want to do at all!"

"Geez, calm down. Why none of my kids care about making money? How did you become like this?"

"Sorry, Mommy."

But something in her voice tells me she is at least a little proud.

Hundreds of thousands of clicks on my stories, the data states. On some, more than a million. The charts do not capture how many of those millions scroll down past the first paragraph, or even the headline and photo, but that doesn't affect ad revenue or the amount of praise one receives from the editors. Everybody gets excited when a story trends on Google News or goes viral. Once a week, the digital side posts a list by the office entrance of the most-clicked-on pieces. Writers gather around to stare; they trace their fingers down in hopes of reaching one of their own. It is meant to breed healthy competition, they tell us. I am consistently middling, with the occasional bump, which is better than being at the very top one week and off the list the next. Those writers have no sense of their value.

In the car with Jasmine, a staff photographer and my closest work friend. We're headed down the 101 to some product launch announcement in the South Bay—me to write, her to shoot. She's driving, smoking a cigarette, blowing the smoke into the car even though her window is open. It's her car, so I don't say anything even though I am sick and coughing.

"The other night I slept with a guy," she says. "A white guy."

Me: "Uh-huh."

"Tell me if I was being overly sensitive, but after we had sex, we were lying in bed and he goes, 'Man, I could really go for some Chinese food.'" Jasmine turns to look at me as she drives and smokes. "Like, what the fuck, right? So I say, 'What the fuck, man?' And he goes, 'What? What did I do?'"

I nod. I worry that she might swerve out of our lane on the highway and we will crash to our deaths. I point at the road ahead. She scoffs, flicks her butt out the window, and lights a new cigarette.

"So, what do you think? What would you do if somebody said that?"

"I think I need more context. Like, what time was it?"

"There's nothing more to say about it. Is that racist or not?"

"Did he end up getting Chinese food?"

"Fuck no!"

She fumes, smoke swirling out of her nose, like a dragon. I shake the thought, knowing she'd be upset if she knew I had thought it. I already know I haven't said what she wants to hear. And to myself I say: That would never happen to me.

Our little house is sparsely furnished, not many steps up from a college dorm. We are, after all, only two point five years out of college. The kitchen/living/dining room walls are lavender and the bedroom walls are mint green. The colors don't bother us anymore. We have a short white couch and two white chairs, a small wicker coffee table, and a small TV, all free hand-me-downs from J's parents and grandparents. There was one splurge: a round, solid oak dining room table with pedestal feet, bought off Craigslist from a young family for $100. Once in the little house, we realized it took up too much space. We preferred to eat our meals on the couch, in front of the TV. We pushed the table against a wall, and now it is stacked with books and papers and jackets and random junk accumulated over time. The backyard is bigger than our house, and wild. There are tall grasses and weeds, two trees: one leafy, one peach, though the peaches never sweeten in the fog. When we first moved in, J tried to hang a hammock between them, but the trees were too far apart. The hammock was boxed up and returned. There is a lot of unused space back there, which is sacrilege in this city. But the rent is a steal, so we don't feel too bad.

"What are you doing?" J asks this Sunday morning as he hand-grinds coffee beans in the kitchen. He is the type to delve into side interests and hobbies. Currently, he has the coffee and mountain biking and bike building and cooking and mushroom growing. He bought the grinder after a week of research into third-wave coffee rituals. He wants to do it right. He wants to make the perfect cup. Me, on the other hand, I don't have hobbies. I focus on one thing at a time. I like coffee, however it's made. What I like more is to make plans.

"I've created a spreadsheet of all the schools you're applying to with checklists for all the documents you'll need and emails for professors to contact," I say. "And I want to rank them for likelihood, like on a scale of one to five. Will you tell me what you think?"

The coffee beans crunch loudly in the machine, so I shout the names of the schools to him. For some reason there are two schools in Pittsburgh, though neither of us has ever been to Pittsburgh or knows anyone in or anything about Pittsburgh. We like the sound of it, though, two solid smacks of our lips. He shouts back numbers, though he refuses to go above three, which I often bump to three point five or four. The goal is to have a range. When I shout the names of the Bay Area schools, he stops grinding and tells me, quietly, that they are probably ones or, more likely, zeros.

"Why do you think that?" I ask.

"I'm not competitive. I'm not that smart," he says.

"Don't say that. There's still a chance."

He shrugs. He walks over with a full cup. "Here you go. Thank you for helping me."

I nod. "Thank *you*. The coffee's really good."

OH (bus, two young women in blazers):

"I don't understand."

"What's not to understand?"

"Okay. You eat more, it turns into added weight in your body. But what happens when you lose weight?"

"You eat less and you lose weight."

"But what happens to the weight? Where does it go?"

"You burn it for energy."

"But where does it, like, go?"

"It goes away in your waste, like urine and sweat and breath."

"Is it shit out? Or is it shat? Shitted? But what you're saying is that you eat yourself? And that's how people lose weight? They eat themselves?"

"Well, not really. Fat's just stored energy and then fat shrinks when you use it."

"So, what I'm hearing is that it's a form of cannibalism? Self-cannibalism? That's hella creepy."

Every morning, we scan East Coast tech news. One of us starts a thread, and we circulate story pitches. Our editors green-light some, tell us to toss others. We prioritize the news, rushing those pieces, then move on to stories with longer lead times or embargoes, and finally, if we can, work on our evergreens, the ones that are more in-depth, or random, or "fun," and can go up whenever they are done. All of this involves, for the most part, not moving from our desks.

Which is why I now have a standing desk. Everyone has been talking about how much healthier it is to stand than to sit—less back pain, lower blood pressure, reduced risk of heart disease, reduced risk of cancer, improved mood, etc., etc. I used to stand a lot. It helped that Tim also stood a lot. We stood next to each other for a month, boosting one another up on our accomplishment. One day, Tim sat after lunch. He said his feet hurt. I continued to stand, but then worried it appeared to him that I was making a statement about his sitting by my standing, so then I, too, sat. We avoided eye contact. The following morning, we stood, but again, after lunch, Tim said his feet hurt. "Don't worry about me, I'm old," he said. "You keep going." But again, I sat and he did not seem unhappy or disappointed with my choice, and eventually, we both gave up and went back to sitting most, if not all, of the day.

There is something unnatural about standing for hours with nowhere to go, without moving any part of one's body except one's hands and fingers to type, while the rest of the room sits. It draws too much attention. It is performative.

The first editor nodded vigorously: Absolutely. You deserve a raise. He was the one who divulged the fact of my being the lowest-paid writer in the room. Then he left for public relations. Good luck! The wheels are in motion! he said upon departure. We got a new editor who said he hadn't heard, he didn't know what to do, maybe I should talk to somebody higher up? The managing editor above him wrote, I'm in Hawaii, let's have a chat when I return, then he returned, was *swamped,* and would be in touch at an indeterminate date. After one month of waiting, I gathered enough courage to walk across the hall and into his office as he ate lunch at his desk. He looked up from his sandwich and waved toward a chair. "Everything is in flux," he said. "I want to make this a priority, but things need to settle down. I can't say exactly why, but this isn't the optimal moment in time."

I left dissatisfied, but curious. I told Jasmine everything. She said she'd overheard talk about *something* being a big deal, but she didn't know what. Tell me when you find out, she said.

I told Tim everything. He shrugged. I gave him a look.

"I want to tell you, but I was sworn to secrecy," he said.

"I won't say anything, I swear."

"Don't, seriously. This time I really can't. And it's any day now, so you'll find out soon enough."

"What's the difference between now and a few days? Please."

He shook his head. "Fine. I'll tell you this much: All those old rumors about a certain somebody leaving? They're finally coming true."

He was right. Days later, the managing editor's boss—the publication's editor in chief of more than a decade—resigned, though word was that corporate had pushed him out, with a replacement lined up to start in the new year. An outsider.

People are frantic. Everyone waits anxiously for the coming changes. As for me, the weeks continue to pass, as though my request has vanished.

How does one measure the space a person inhabits? How can one be sure of how much or how little one takes? And what is the best way to maneuver given one's perceived size and status?

A young white man holding neon orange and green Nerf guns larger than his torso yells on the Muni platform: "I love my fucking job!" The man walking with him, nearly identical, slaps his back three times and laughs. The second man has small Nerf guns sticking out of his jean pockets. Upstairs, a busker sits on a tarp and plays a guqin, the sound reverberating far down the long white halls. I hear the music before I see him. A sad, slow, lonely sound. He is hunched, gray-haired, wrinkled, frighteningly thin, in a plain navy sweater and navy slacks. His fingers move like arthritic dancers. He reminds me of a grandfather I do not know, or of my father, in a too-close future. Through wet eyes, I take out my wallet and place all the cash I have into his empty instrument case. It is not much, but it is something. Almost nobody carries cash these days. I wonder how he makes enough to survive in this city. He looks up and nods.

J and I are representative of the Sunset neighborhood's history: Irish and Chinese. Though the Irish are dwindling.
    "What are you writing?" he asks beside me in bed.
    "That the Irish are dwindling in the Sunset," I say.
    "What's that for?"
    "I don't know. Documenting our lives. I guess because I don't know what's going to happen next and it's comforting."

"Hm, cool," he says. "So, like a diary."

"No, not like a diary," I say, though I can't explain, yet, why not.

Then again, J is third-generation Irish. We watch *Hell on Wheels,* an American Western set in the post–Civil War 1860s. Whenever the Irish characters are discriminated against on the show, I feel more connected to J. I want to say something about it, but when I look at him, it does not appear that he identifies with the beaten Irish man on the computer's screen.

When we go to Davis, we say we are going home. But when we return to San Francisco, we also say we are going home. Our sense of home is knit even tighter, because our homes in Davis are in the same neighborhood. And so now, for the holidays, we are leaving our home together to go home to our homes down the street from one another.

Because I like to and because it is only an hour and a half's car ride away and because he is nice and will drive me, because I do not have a license and cannot drive myself, we go home together often. At least once a month. On the way there or the way back, we like to stop at the Pacific East Mall in Richmond. We grocery shop at 99 Ranch Market and eat at the noodle place or the Szechuan restaurant. Going there reminds me, too, of a kind of home. The handwritten signs on neon paper in shop windows, children running up and down the fluorescent-lit corridors, the sounds of familiar dialects, the overflow of items in bins and on shelves, the scuffed linoleum floors, the shopping carts with their errant wheels.

My mom texts, telling me to pick up a bottle of ning chiao. My brother appears to have a cold. Actually get three. Just in case.

In the medicine/herb store, I approach the shopkeeper and ask for ning chiao. What? she says. What *something something* . . . ? I repeat, Ning chiao. She shakes her head and says she doesn't have it. I text my mom back. Impossible, she replies. They have. I scan the packed display cases and walls until I find the small, familiar green-and-white label, and point to it.

"Ah, yin qiao!" The shopkeeper laughs as she rings me up.

J walks over with a bag of peanuts.

"Together?" the shopkeeper says in English.

"Yeah, together," he says, and hands her cash. He is one of the almost nobodies left who do carry physical bills. He is old-fashioned in this way, and in others, like not having Facebook. (And for both, I admire and begrudge him.)

"You don't have to buy the medicine," I say.

"It's okay."

"Yín qiào," says the shopkeeper, emphasizing the inflections.

"Mmm." I nod. "Yín qiào," I imitate.

Good, good, she says. She gives me a thumbs-up and waves us goodbye.

As we walk back to the car, he asks what that was about. I explain that I was saying the name in Shanghainese, the only way I knew how to say it, and that since I couldn't communicate in Mandarin and she didn't understand Shanghainese, there had been some confusion.

"They sound that different from each other?"

"Yeah," I say. "I could only understand some of what she was saying and couldn't explain anything."

"That must be annoying."

"It is. But mostly I feel embarrassed. Like how could I have lost it all so easily? How did that happen?"

"At least you're really, really good at English," he says. "That's more than me and it's the only language I've ever known."

I laugh and squeeze his knee. Silly boy. But his comment does make me feel better.

There is a tree in the house this year because my mom has a renter, an international university student from China whom we plainly call "the student." My mom wants to give the student the full experience of an American Christmas. The tree is plastic with lights embedded in its branches. She has hung some old ornaments I haven't seen in a few years, including a golden bell I once believed Santa had gifted me from his sleigh, and encased photos of each of us—me, my sister, and my brother—on various Santa laps. The staircase is wrapped in multicolored lights and decorated with big red felt bows.

"What do you think of all this Christmas spirit?" I ask my sister in our shared room, on the same bunk beds we've had for as long as we can remember, longer than we've been in this house.

"Mommy went all out for the student," she says.

"But isn't the student going to Disneyland with her friends? It'll be just us for Christmas, right? I don't want to spend it with her. It's awkward. Mommy acts weird."

"Yeah. I think she's leaving tomorrow."

"As long as it's not as crazy as last Christmas, I guess then I'll be okay."

"It won't be," says my sister. "It wouldn't be possible."

We are quiet in our respective beds, me on top, her on bottom.

"Do you think all of the decorations are really for the student?" she asks.

"Maybe. It's an excuse, at least."

She doesn't say anything, but I know she understands. Our mom is doing exactly what she wants, now that nobody is telling her otherwise.

In his parents' home office, I edit J's application essays. Cut a run-on into three short sentences. Correct typos and grammatical errors. Rearrange passive sentences into active ones. Move paragraphs around for better flow. But I do not understand the scientific terms, the stuff about "mutations on cerebral angiogenesis" and "context-dependent signaling" and "intracellular accumulation at the expense of secretion," so he must sit there explaining his research until I minimally understand. It's only then that I learn he's not studying eye diseases, but something entirely different—the genes responsible for preventing hemorrhagic strokes. I am baffled at the last two years I've thought (and told people) eye stuff, eye stuff. He says that his research is hard for him to explain, and that when he tried I didn't seem interested.

I apologize. He says it's okay.

He says he wants to learn how to be a better communicator and writer. He wants to know what I'm doing, so he knows what to do the next time. I show him the edits and try to explain why I made them, why the structure and sentences now offer more clarity. But there's also the issue of taste and style, I say. This, here, isn't incorrect grammar, but this other option, I think, reads better. There are many different ways to say the same thing. He is easy to edit because he accepts all of my suggestions.

"Okay. Was the essay really bad, though? You keep muttering."

"No, it isn't *that* bad," I say. "And I don't."

But as J watches me continue deleting, typing, copying, pasting, I notice myself. I repeat "Let's see" under my breath over and over, as though I want to visualize some future, altered version of what's in front of me. Let's see. Let's see. Let's see.

With my family, I also play editor and logistics coordinator. My mom asks me to revise her self-reported employee performance evaluation. I've done this every year since she got the job, in a university finance office, ten years ago. And her cover letters and résumés before that. The same goes for my brother and sister, plus college applications and now the occasional class paper. We go through their yearly FAFSA forms together, determine which loans to accept and reject. I have long filled out applications and written statements to whatever government or official entity required them. My father never learned how to use a computer, despite having bought the earliest ones for my mom and us to use. So when I was growing up, he would dictate whatever he needed written. My job was to type and smooth out his words.

My brother says he's read a scientific study that determined there are only seven types of human faces. We are out to dinner at a Mexican restaurant, the four of us: my mom, my sister, my brother, and me.

I discreetly point at a man with wide-set eyes and thin lips.

"What kind of face does that person have?"

"I don't know. I can't remember the specific faces. But isn't it fascinating? When you think about it, there isn't much variation. There probably are only, like, seven types."

My sister points at a woman with a high forehead and a pointed chin.

"What face does that person have?"

"I'm not sure. What I'm saying is people don't really look all that different. Like, when you look at them, they all have the same parts—eyes, nose, mouth, whatever. We aren't as unique as we think we all are."

I point at a man with a sharp nose and hollow cheeks.

"What about that person?"

"I don't know!"

"What are you talking about?" says my mom after looking up from her phone.

"Stop looking at your phone during dinner," I say. "You're more addicted than us!"

"Are there two people in this place with the same kind of face?" says my sister.

"Which ones are they?"

"Whose face is what?"

"Can you point them out?"

My brother slams his hands down on the table. "You guys are so annoying!"

My sister and I cackle from the joy of teasing him.

"Don't be so mean," my mom says, though she, too, is laughing. "What is he talking about?"

"Didi's just saying we all have the same kind of face."

You can't choose your family . . . but if I could, I'd still choose this one, mine.

Okay, maybe with some tweaks. Like us all being in the same place, or vicinity.

Though in many ways it has been easier this last year, with my dad in China. I hate to admit it. I am the most attached to my family, its past and its potential and its ideal forms. I am the oldest. I hold on the most. I worry the most. My brother and sister don't call him nearly as often. I text them reminders every week or so. Call Daddy if you haven't. My brother makes up excuses about not knowing how to use the calling card or, more often, does not respond. My sister says once every few weeks is enough. But now I hand them the phone, with him on the other end, so they take it. I hear them going "Mm-hmm," "Yeah," "No," "Okay," and the longer silences, meaning he's telling a story or lecturing or making requests. Then they hand the phone back to me and he talks about a stabbing at a Chinese elementary school (what I figure is his third telling). A man entered a playground and stabbed children in the face, hands, and bodies, until a teacher—also stabbed—tackled him to the ground. Luckily, no fatalities. Not like at Sandy Hook a week earlier. If somebody who worked at either of the schools had a gun, he starts, well then.

But I stop him. "No, nope. I don't think so!"

"Don't be impatient with me, young lady," he says. "Let me finish."

Next, "There are crazy people everywhere. Avoid crowds. Avoid parades, concerts, malls, movie theaters, anywhere where lots of people gather. Do you know what to do when you hear shots? Run to the nearest store or building and find cover. Duck low. Don't run into the streets. Hide. Do you understand?"

"Yes, Daddy," I say.

"Okay, that's that. Second on the list. I remembered something I want you to bring me when you visit. An At-A-Glance daily diary. You know the ones I use?"

"Yup. I will when I come. What about you? Are you eating?"

"Yes, I got noodles from the cold noodle lady, so that will last me a few days."

"That's not enough. Just try to eat more, okay? And drink less, please." I wonder momentarily why I am telling a grown man how to eat and drink, but then again, that man is my father.

"I'm drinking only Chinese medicinal wine, so it's actually good for me. Oh, and there's a new beer I found. German stuff. Good shit. It's only a dollar a can!"

"Just don't drink as much of it, please!"

"Okay, okay. Now, what's your mother doing? Let me talk to her, too."

When I point at the phone and move it toward her, she shakes her head and shoos me away. Now I am the one coming up with an excuse: she's busy, in the shower, cooking, shopping, out for a walk.

"Busy, busy, everyone busy going nowhere," he says. "Relay this message: I want to talk to her. Tell her to call me."

"Okay, Daddy, I will," I say. "Merry Christmas! Love you."

"Love you more," he says.

It used to be the other way around, years and years ago. When the four of us left for China, my dad stayed behind in San Francisco. It felt as though we didn't have a physical father, only a phone that carried a familiar voice, telling us what to do, how to behave. Until, like a Chinese American Santa Claus, he would make trips from the States to visit us. He'd bring suitcases of stuff we wanted, stuff he thought we should have: Tommy Hilfiger shoes, Calvin Klein jeans, Gap sweatshirts, Esprit T-shirts, Nintendo Game Boys, and books. Baby-Sitters Club. Chronicles of Narnia. Wayside School. The Boxcar Children. Dr. Seuss. Shel Silverstein. My brother, sister, and I would scoop it all up. Our American belongings reminding us of where we were from.

Then there were the years in Davis when we stayed here and he made trips back and forth, on a schedule all his own. Though as time passed, he would stay with us for longer and longer durations.

But whatever now is, there is a sense of permanence. Him, there. Us, here. None of us have visited since he's gone. I planned to at one point, even got my ten-year China visa. But then work happened, or something else. I couldn't take vacation time, I didn't feel like I had the money for the trip, I missed a good deal on flights. Now just isn't the right time. But he is always asking and his list of requests grows.

He left on Christmas last year, in the dark morning, in a shuttle headed for SFO, for a plane to Macau. My parents' interactions had appeared to be okay to decent that month, but we all knew that between them, things moved cyclically and no state lasted long. One night while out with J, I got a call from my dad telling me to come home right away. Book him a one-way ticket to China—this was the last straw, the straw that broke the camel's back, he wasn't taking anybody's shit anymore, she was the lit fuse and he was the exploding dynamite, she says they're divorced and wants nothing to do with him, so be it, let's see how she likes it, this was final, it was his way or the highway—look into Shanghai, Zhuhai, Macau, Beijing, Hong Kong, and find the cheapest ticket for the soonest possible date. He hung up. I called back and made my pleas—it had been a while since he'd gone to China, how would he find a place to live, what would he do there, how would we get in touch, shouldn't we slow down a little—to which he said, I've survived this long, haven't I? Don't worry about me. Worry about yourself. Just do as I say, now. And again he hung up. So I went home and did as I was told.

They did not speak a word to one another in the days leading up to his departure, but on the day of, she came with us to stand outside the house to send him off. Another, the most recent, goodbye.

J has pointed out that I'm the only adult person he knows who continues to call their parents Mommy and Daddy.

But so does my sister. (Although my brother switched to "Mom" and "Dad" at some point.) Perhaps it means something deeper—a stubbornness or unwillingness to change, a desire to cling to childhood. Or it is, more simply, what we're used to, and doesn't mean much at all.

My mom says she's making all of our favorites for Christmas dinner. Chicken in tomato sauce for Didi. Lion's head for Mei Mei. Shanghai-style braised pork belly for me. And lots of veggies— bok choy, Chinese broccoli, tomato and egg stir-fry, mushrooms with fried tofu.

"What about for you, Mommy?"

"Me? I'm just happy all my kids are home for me to spoil. Now come over here and help me clean and chop."

At home, our San Francisco home, J does the cooking. He gets back from work before me and by the time I'm home, the food is ready, or close to. He makes carnitas. He makes braised beef and onions. He makes stir-fried basil eggplant and tofu. He makes chana masala. He makes potatoes au gratin with leeks and Gruyère. He bakes shortbread cookies with little dot illustrations, indented with chopsticks: a dog, a baseball, a scorpion, smiley faces, our initials in a heart. When he has time, he pickles various vegetables and attempts to grind his own mustard.

I do have one consistent kitchen chore, which he can't seem to get right: I measure the rice and water for the rice cooker by the finger method I learned from my mom. After rinsing the rice, stick your index finger in until it hits the bottom of the pot. Take note of where the top of the rice meets your finger. Add water. Stick your index finger so the tip now touches the top of the rice. You want the top of the water to meet the same spot on your finger as the top of the rice previously did. Basically, equal layers of rice and water. It sounds complicated, but it is easy. It also yields consistently balanced and uniform rice.

J walks the block over to our house. He comes in with a bag of Verve coffee from Santa Cruz, where he and his family—mom, dad, and younger brother—rented a beach house for the holidays, as they do each year. And each year they invite me. I went once and experienced so much guilt and disconnect over what felt like choosing them over my own family that I have never gone again.

"For me?" my mom says as she takes the coffee. "Sorry, I don't have anything for you."

"Oh, no, that's fine," he says. "It's my pleasure."

"See, he gives me something for Christmas. So good," my mom yells to my sister, who is on the couch looking at her phone, and whose boyfriend has not given our mom anything for Christmas.

"Geez, if you really needed a present just tell me and I'll tell him to get you something next time."

"I don't need! You need to train him better, like your sister."

"Jing Jing's the bossy one. She probably bosses him around all the time."

"Yeah, ha ha, she does," says J.

"What? No, I don't! Tell them I don't."

"Oh right. No, she doesn't."

We all laugh.

"Wow, I feel bad for you, man," says my brother. "My sister's pretty crazy."

"Well, what about you? Did you get your girlfriend's mom anything?"

"I don't have a girlfriend."

"I thought you did," my mom says. "The one lives upstairs from you?"

"We're just talking and hanging out."

"Didi is, like, super casual about women. They're, like, just talking."

"Ah, how my son end up like this? So bad!"

"Yeah, you have two sisters who are telling you what to do and you're probably just a typical college bro," I say. "Don't mistreat women!"

"Oh my god, all I said was that she's not my girlfriend. Ling

Ling's the one who has the bad boyfriend who doesn't give presents. If I had a girlfriend, I would obviously give her mom a present."

"Yeah, right."

"Don't bring it back to me!"

"Okay, we're going out. We're leaving now!"

"Bye, have fun!"

One of the reasons I love J is because he can handle, even likes, my family.

At some point between year two and year three of our relationship, he started calling me Jing Jing.

"Jing Jing," he'd go, teasing. My name was all wrong in his mouth: the emphasis in the wrong spot, the *J* soft and mushy instead of pointed and sharp, as it should be.

"Don't call me that," I'd say.

"It's just for my family," I'd say.

"You're saying it wrong."

"It's Jing Jing. You're saying 'Jing Jing.' Do you hear the difference?"

No, he could not and he still can't.

It's year five and now he calls me by this name most of the time. I've gotten used to the way he pronounces it. I think of it as the version of me that is particular to him. And he says we are family, too.

We go to Mishka's, a local coffee shop, where my sister used to work. The barista taking our order remembers me and gives us a discount. We've already run into three people we know from high school. Davis is small and slightly suffocating like that. It was not somewhere I wanted to stay, or live in again. But UC Davis is still an option, since it is, technically, our home. We are here to submit the last of his applications. We divide the list up and load the documents into their designated portals, until finally we are done. It's done. We'll end up in one of those places.

Our friend Becca walks in as we are congratulating ourselves and clinking our coffee mugs.

"You guys are sickeningly cute," she says. "It's too much. Planning your future life together. I need a boyfriend! Help me find a boyfriend, please."

The next twenty minutes are spent under the seduction of Tinder swipes. We get excited every time we see somebody we know—since the app is based on location, a few guys from high school have shown up. Their chosen photos speak to how much or how little they've changed: band nerd shirtless and ripped on the beach; soccer jock still doing his soccer jock; our mutual friend drinking beer, a photo from the other night's hangout. Pass, pass, pass, Becca says.

"Do you really want to be with a Davis kid?" I ask. "Why do Davis kids always glom together? What is it about them?"

"You realize that's what we are, right?" says J, a Davis kid, meaning he was born here and spent his whole life up until college here.

"No," I say. "I am categorically not a Davis kid, so no."

"Didn't you come in elementary school?" says Becca, also a Davis kid.

"The middle of sixth grade!"

"You hate being associated with Davis, even though it's where you're from," says J.

"No, I'm not from here!" I say, in part proving his point.

"Whatever, you're two Davis kids who've been together forever. Wait, is that who I think it is?" Becca shows us a cute punk kid turned clean-cut hipster, standing in front of a brick wall with his hands in his skinny-jean pockets.

"I had the biggest crush on him sophomore year," says Becca. She swipes right. It's a match! "Technology is the fucking best."

Open-plan offices are conceptually cool, but they do not work cool. Everyone is visible to everyone. Just another way to breed competition, plus worry, disturbance, and procrastination. If you don't wear noise-canceling headphones, then you are bombarded with office noises: the typing, the chewing, the groaning, the mumbling, the complaining, the tapping, the squeaking, the bickering . . . Then, too, there's the ever-present anxiety about somebody flying over to talk, and if they approach from behind, it's unexpected and frightening, and if they approach from ahead, you have to watch them coming across the space as your anxiety and anticipation build. What do they want? And what is the best position in which to talk—do you stand up once they've arrived? Do they squat as you sit? Do you stare up at them from your chair? And how best to end the conversation—do you say see you later, though you can technically see them at all times across the open expanse? Do you say goodbye? Do they walk away with no formalities? Do they make a grand exit?

To avoid answering such questions, there is the work chatroom: Parley. Even though we are all physically in the same room, it's quieter, easier, and more efficient to communicate through the screen, through Parley.

When I first got my work computer, I'd misread it as Parsley. (Which I still consider a better software company name.) Then, I thought it was Parlay, as in, to take one thing and transform it into something better. It didn't take long, however, to realize it was "par-lee." *Did you see what so-and-so said in Parley? Get on Parley, we need to talk. The business people are going crazy on Parley right now. Why isn't anybody responding to my question in Parley?* The original definition is: a discussion between opposing sides, or enemies, over the terms of a truce. This offers a decent analogy for office communication.

Especially true of our publication, which is divided down the middle between web and print. We are all on the same floor, but web people sit in a room on one side and print people, plus management, sit on the other side. Doors, the restrooms, and a long hallway divide the two sides. The Berlin Hall, everyone calls it.

J dislikes that I have Parley notifications on at all times. It is constantly buzzing, during dinner, during TV time, and especially these days, as our group prepares for the yearly Consumer Electronics Show (CES) in Vegas. The problem is my guilt. It never seems as though I'm doing enough, and if I do more, respond faster, I think, maybe somebody important will notice, and I will be lifted out of this wait.

Nobody likes to go. All of us complain during the weeks ahead. CES is four long days of Las Vegas product porn. We are bombarded with pointless gadget after pointless gadget in the crowded convention center, we wait in lines to get into rooms with who knows what kind of announcements, we take countless meetings with overeager PR people, we type up stories on dirty carpeted floors, we go to pseudo-parties at night, we test our luck in casinos, we drink too much, and we get very little sleep. As Jasmine says, "It's a nightmare hellscape, but at least we're in it together."

Yet beneath our snark is desire. We want to find the next piece of technology that will make us better, give us purpose, fill our voids. We are looking for what we can show the world and say, here, this is the future, and the future is bright.

The senior gadgets editor, Corey, and I meet up to attend a few meetings together. Afterward, he tells me he's sick of the booth babes and the way women are being used to sell products at the convention. He says I must feel grossed out. He points out that during our meetings, the men rarely look at me as they talk, even after he explicitly tells them that I am the reporter. Have I noticed? No, and I think he might be wrong. I distinctly remember making prolonged eye contact with a young male product manager showing us the company's new flippy laptop-tablet hybrids. But maybe Corey is right and the executives mostly address Corey. Maybe I don't notice because I spend my time taking notes and examining the product that I am supposed to write in detail about, while Corey sits there drinking coffee and eating the free snacks and making jokes. Now I wonder why he even accompanies me to these meetings in the first place.

Jasmine and I, plus another reporter named Elizabeth, decide to go to a tech party. And though they are not ever quite what we want from a party, we are lured to them by their offers of free food, free drinks, free swag.

From the pedestrian walkway over the strip, Las Vegas looks how it always looks, neon in the night, vibrant and lively and loud. But the scenery is in contrast to every person we pass—men, men, almost entirely men—who look, well, like they're here for a tech convention. Dressed for the office, practical shoes, with lanyards around their necks. Then coming toward us from the opposite direction is a group of thirtysomething-looking ones, rowdy and swaggering, an aged fraternity party. One jumps in front of me and makes fingering gestures at my crotch. He scampers off grunting. "Don't go near him!" another one yells. "He's got diseases!"

The horde whoops and laughs.

I turn.

I see their grotesque backs.

"Fuck you!" Jasmine yells.

I start yelling, too. Fucking assholes! A few turn around and see me flipping them off.

Jasmine jogs after them and throws something at one of their heads, a full water bottle. I run after her. The bottle misses and thuds on the pavement, a dull sound. The dicks look back at us and laugh some more.

Elizabeth has not moved from the spot of the encounter. When we walk back to her, she can't stop saying, Wow. Wow. Wow.

"Fucking impotent jerks," Jasmine says. "A curse of ten thousand years of sexlessness on all the fuckers."

"You're so brave," says Elizabeth. "I don't even know what I'd do if it was me. Do you think they were here for CES? I doubt anybody here for CES would do that."

Jasmine and I look at each other, like, is she serious? Then Jasmine conveys to me, with a flutter of her eyelids, what do you expect, she's not like us. Yes, sometimes we are this good at understanding one another. When our similarities align in a sort of power.

Another tech company party, another white man. This one introduces himself as vice president of something or another, and asks if Jasmine and I are sisters. He asks if we'd like to see his room, and when Jasmine points at me and says, "She's taken," he pivots and asks if Jasmine alone would like to see his room, and when I point out his wedding ring, he says he and his wife are separated, that she's not in Vegas anyway. He says that clichéd line we all know, one not worth repeating. This is when Jasmine and I decide to stop going to these fake parties, to stop doing anything besides pure work for the remainder of the trip.

Now, Corey again, in the publication's rented office—if it can be called that; it is more of an enclosure, a shed, placed along one of the convention center's pavilions. He is talking to me about his longest, most serious relationship while we eat a quick lunch. He and his girlfriend had met online. She moved in with him, scolded him for using his iPad in the bathroom, took his dogs on walks, and then broke up with him a year later. It's so hard, he says, when you put so much effort into a relationship, into this other person, and they end it like that. He snaps his fingers. Feels like such a waste of time, he says. J and I have been together for five years. I don't call him my boyfriend anymore because it sounds too trite—now I just call him J. I don't really know what to say to Corey. He seems to want relationship advice, or maybe a sympathetic ear. So I nod. I want him to know I'm listening—I will get this raise, somehow, eventually—and I say, That really sucks, Corey, I hope you find somebody, I really believe you will. I remark that there are plenty of single people in San Francisco. He shakes his head and looks down at his salad. Corey is always trying to lose weight. Well, yeah, he says, just not age-appropriate ones. But maybe in Vegas? he says, more hopeful. Whether he means being age appropriate is less of an issue in Vegas, or there are more people his age in town, I don't bother asking. I don't want to know. He is fifty-four.

The convention center is a sensory deluge, and in it I have found nothing to give me hope, and still I post. I post about an app-controlled massage pillow, an app-controlled oven, an app-controlled blood pressure monitor, an app-controlled fork . . . I write about a gross number of smart and 4K TVs. (But, but, look how beautiful the images are up close!) In a room lined with televisions the size of my refrigerator, I run into Tim. We don't notice each other until we are in each other's faces, attempting to move through the stream of other bodies.

"How're you holding up?" Tim says.

"Fine," I say. "You?"

"So sleep deprived and hungover," he says. "Wild night with the new EIC."

"Wait, he's here?"

But then the bodies surge and Tim is pushed along in the opposite direction, waving goodbye.

I run a hot bath and order a load of room service: chicken fettuccine alfredo, four-cheese quesadilla, chocolate cake, coffee, and tea. When the food arrives, I push the cart next to the bathtub, climb in, and eat while submerged in the steaming water. Yes, I could live this part forever, enjoying life on the company dime.

At the airport and here comes the newest editor (the one who claimed he didn't know how to get me a raise). He pulls me aside and says, "You did great coverage. Let's talk when we're back in SF."

See, somebody noticed.

Today, I turn twenty-five. A gigantic bouquet wrapped in burlap is delivered to the office under my name. At first I think it is a gimmicky gift from a startup and am embarrassed. But then I see, on top of the bouquet, a handmade card in the shape of a heart cut from thick green folder paper. *I can't wait to spend forever with you,* written in J's sloppy scrawl. One of the plants I think is a magnificent flower turns out to be a small head of cabbage. I show any coworkers who ask.

"I guess you have to go with him, then," says Tim, with his signature sarcastic tone.

"This is one of those rare moments when I think having a boyfriend could be fun and nice," says Jasmine. "But it doesn't take long to remember, oh yeah, men are terrible. Don't look at me like that. I mean *most* men, not *your* man."

The new EIC has been shipped from NYC headquarters, and on his first day, he shows up with a celebrity. They walk into the office to craning necks and not-so-casual stroll-bys. The new EIC believes in celebrity covers, in well-known faces selling newsstand copies. This is giving people what they want: an actor goofily embracing a robot. The EIC himself is very young for his job, thirty-two, and he wears beautifully tailored suits and leather oxfords. He slicks his hair back with pomade so that it shines under the office's fluorescent lights. His skin looks like molded wax. The publication's parent company bred him to take over the website and sent him here to us. The old-school San Franciscans resent the pressure to dress better.

The actor happens to be up from LA this week for a premiere of some indie flick (why else SF?), so the new EIC has invited him in for an up-close look at *where the future is fulfilled*. The celebrity asks to meet Tim, who, having written a mega-viral magazine feature about the safety pitfalls of AI technology, has become a momentary celebrity in his own right. I wonder if Tim will ride this wave of acclaim straight out of here and into a more lucrative, higher-status job. The new EIC grips Tim's shoulders, seeming to have the same thought and hoping to anchor him there with praise. Our best guy. Our star. The kind of sharp reporter who digs up the deepest, buried scoops. The stories you didn't even know you desperately needed to know.

As the celebrity and Tim talk, I roll away to the farthest edge of our shared desk and hunch over my laptop. Another kind of person might leverage the proximity to introduce themselves to the celebrity, or cozy up to the new EIC. This is what a fellow consumer technology reporter, Kevin, is now doing. Tim tenses. He is not a fan of Kevin. Kevin is all Southern California positivity and good vibes, though he's originally from Nevada. He talks brightly and loudly, his speech littered with clichés and curse words. But more importantly, Tim does not respect Kevin as a reporter, especially after Kevin failed to do much in Vegas, according to Tim. The celebrity greets Kevin with practiced, fatigued poise. Kevin asks to take a selfie. Then he asks if the EIC and the celebrity want a photo together. Nothing is real unless it is documented, captioned with a mini essay about having "the best job ever," publicized to everybody—meaning whoever happens to follow Kevin's social media feeds, which is a lot of people, because Kevin is also one of those natural promoters—to see and to like and to judge. And here I am, on my phone, quietly doing all three.

The newest editor and I meet in the cafeteria, at one of the steel dining tables. He sits at the head, so I sit at the corner next to him.

"Like I said, great coverage on the Vegas trip," he says. "I just want to check in to see where you're at."

I worry Tim may have told him something about my leaving, but then he says, "What are you thinking long term here? Do you want to do tech news forever? Go into features? Essays? Something else?"

"Oh, long term I'd love to write more features and essays," I say. "I like the speed of news writing, but it would be great to take on bigger stories, maybe broader tech and society pieces, or even science stuff."

"Great. I'd be willing to work with you on your pitches, help you expand out of the gadget scene, if you want?"

I nod. "Yes, definitely. Thanks!"

"Sounds good, we've got a plan," he says, and slaps the table. But before he gets up, I ask whether he can also talk now about the possibility of a raise.

"Oh," he says. He chews on his lip for a while and bites off a piece of dry skin. I start to bite my own lip. "You haven't heard anything from the higher-ups?"

"No, nothing new," I say.

"Hmm, well," he says. He shifts in his seat. "They're probably busy, then. Give it time. Here's my advice: focus on the writing. As it is, you just don't have a strong personality or voice coming through. In your writing, I mean. Think about Tim. When you read his pieces, doesn't matter what they're about, they're distinctly him. Sometimes I read your stuff and I'm like, this is clean, easy to edit, smart, but a highly intelligent algorithm could do it, too, and probably with fewer errors—not with the tech we have today, but it's not too far off. You wouldn't want to lose your job to a robot."

The editor laughs. I surprise myself by laughing a little, too, as though on cue.

"Upping your voice is how you'll stand out. I'd suggest pitching the print side, too. They have to know you before giving you more, especially with the new EIC. We all need to stand out in order to stick around now."

"Okay," I say.

"Anytime you want advice on a pitch, I'm here." He slaps the table again and says, "All right, back to work."

"You look off," Tim says when I return to our desk. "Was it bad news?"

"No," I say. "He offered to work on pitches with me."

"That's awesome. He wants to help you out. Good sign. Take advantage of it."

i hate him i hate him i hate him, I text J. he basically lectured me and called me a robot. and it had NOTHING TO DO with a raise, like i thought it would.

He replies with a crying-face emoji. You're the cutest robot I've ever seen.

I reply with a frowning face. No.

Jk. You're the cutest, smartest, most
deserving person

that's better

But then I remember, I laughed automatically when the editor laughed. Like a robot.

I started in the newsroom at twenty-three. I was the youngest staff writer in the room until a couple of months ago, when they got a new fresh-out-of-college boy for the Business vertical. It had meant a lot to me. It still does. I felt I'd achieved something meaningful in landing a job here. I compared the speed of my rise with others', I looked at their employment histories on LinkedIn, I made timelines for how soon I could move up to a senior or editor position. I am nowhere close to the best-known tech reporter my age—there are places that brand their writers with big personalities and those people become huge names—but I don't want to be famous. I just want to quietly move up. I have a decent reputation, plus the backing of the publication's reputation. Some people here say I have a lot of potential. The last three young writers with potential who came through my position left for the *New York Times*. I thought I wanted to do whatever I could to follow that trajectory. But now, well, I don't know if it's possible, if it is in conflict with the other plans, like where J and I will go. Or if I even have it in me to be a part of this for much longer.

My mom wanted me to have stability and safety, to avoid having to experience any "very bad, sad years" as she calls that time of our lives when she supported us on her two part-time jobs and, I now realize, credit cards left unpaid. Better yet, I could lift the whole family out of this perpetual state of minor discomfort. I wasn't doing a great job of it, despite having worked since fourteen. Before this, I was part-time at another tech publication, proofreading e-book guides for Luddites with titles like: *Smartphone Camera Basics: Shooting Tips Your Way* and *Switching from PC to Mac: Don't Worry!* and *How to iPad: The Future at Your Fingertips.* I was also an assistant to a rich woman in Pacific Heights. And I commuted to Berkeley once a week to help out with admin work for the university's engineering department (though I majored in rhetoric). There were other gigs scattered here and there, whatever I could land to make some extra cash. I couldn't quite settle, and it unsettled my mom.

"Why not go work at a big company?" she'd often say. "Google or Facebook. Then your future is good. Writing on the side."

But I didn't listen. Now I wonder, would I have been happier if I had?

When the first editor here interviewed me, he walked us past the newsroom, where dozens of people sat at their desks typing with what looked at the time like fury and passion, and into a bright, window-lined space.

"This little room was the publication's first office," he said. "Rented out from another company. Now we just use it to have meetings and store all these extra gadgets." Boxes and bins lined two gigantic shelving units. An electric bicycle rested in the corner. On the wall, a black square clock that looked more like an art piece displayed the time in a grid of illuminated letters: IT IS HALF PAST TWO.

"Cool," I said. I didn't know the publication's history. I didn't know anything specific about technology, but I figured I used a smartphone, a computer, and the internet better than the average person. I wanted to write; it didn't matter at the time about what.

He sat on a low leather couch, and I sat across from him in a matching low leather chair. He slouched lower and lower as the interview progressed, until he was practically lying down on the couch, his legs splayed forward in the space between us. I tried to look at least mildly comfortable. I uncrossed my legs and leaned forward.

"Let's say I assign you an explainer on dual-core versus single-core processors. What would you say is the difference?"

"Dual-core processors are faster because they have two times the processing speed?"

"Well, not really. It's faster because—" I didn't understand what he said next. "I bet you if I asked that of anybody out there, not one would give the correct, technical answer. What I need on my team is somebody to fill in the knowledge gaps."

I said I was a quick learner.

"So who are some tech reporters you admire?"

I listed some names I'd only recently learned, names that accompanied the articles I'd read to prepare for the interview. He nodded approvingly. "I like his work, too. Really contextualizes tech use for the everyman," he said. "Yes, that guy always has the sharpest reviews." When I mentioned admiring the desk for which I was interviewing, he said, "No need to flatter us." But he smiled and added, "I have a feeling we'll be working together soon."

"It's not a lack of confidence in oneself preventing people from going after jobs where they don't meet all of the qualifications, but a lack of confidence in other people's abilities to view them as capable of doing the job, and therefore hiring them," said the leadership expert, who had surveyed one thousand people to come to this conclusion. "The main barrier is not a mistaken perception about themselves, but a mistaken perception of what is a real requirement or rule, of how processes like these truly work, and this is especially a problem for women."

In an attempt to show versatility, I pitch a story to a senior magazine editor about a startup that's genetically engineering plants to make them glow. The company uses a gene gun to shoot custom DNA sequences (based on glowing marine bacteria, coated on nanoproduct) into plant stem cells. The editor accepts the story and says I should turn it into a two-page piece about technological developments that will save the environment, the idea being that these plants will be able to replace streetlamps and whole cities at night will eventually be lit with leaves. After I interview the founder, however, it becomes apparent that the plants can barely glow at all. They are dimmer than a weak night-light. The photos on their website, he relents after I press him, were all taken in a pitch-black room with extremely slow shutter speeds. But we're making progress! he promises.

The editor for the piece is severely disappointed in the development, and says that the story will now be a two-hundred-word sidebar in the Front of Book and that I should still include a line at the end: "In the future, our streets could be lit by glowing trees!"

It's not technically a lie—we don't say how far into the future, and "could be" is not equivalent to "will be."

Tim says of my career, "That's an okay step."

J sends me photos of the mice he works with.

Something for your not-diary, he texts.

The cutest photo is of a little brown one sitting inside a bottle cap, tiny nose tucked into his chest, looking as though he's fallen asleep.

I text back: Please don't tell me he's dead.

No. It's just knocked out.

It's going to die later today though, he adds, with a crying-face emoji.

I don't ask who is going to do the killing. I know it is him.

Every day I check the forums where soon-to-be graduate students post updates on the schools from which they've heard back. I trawl the archives for the last five years to estimate when the Bay Area and New York City schools will respond to J, and every hour (or less) I reload to see if somebody has posted an interview invite for this year. If he hasn't gotten one, a rejection is inevitable.

"Don't tell me," he says. "I don't want to know. I want to have a healthy day-to-day life."

"This isn't *unhealthy*," I say. "I just want to know as much as I can about what's likely to happen in the future. Like here, it says that the UCSF program sent—"

"No, don't tell me. I'll just wait until I get the official email."

"Fine," I say, and strike through UCSF on the spreadsheet.

J sulks in the kitchen.

As long as I've known them, my parents have bought lottery tickets. I don't. Then, at least, I am completely certain I will not win. The certainty is more manageable for me than the cycle of hoping/not knowing and losing and hoping/not knowing and losing. The poor man's tax, I've heard it called. Or worse, the stupid tax. But what the people who say that don't understand is: when in all aspects of life the odds are entirely against you, it can be worth paying for even a tiny increase in hope.

Many women are addicted to online shopping. One editor spends hours browsing clothing sites and adds item after item into her various shopping carts—shoes from Zappos, blouses from Madewell, dresses from Nordstrom, jewelry from various indie artisanal de-signers on Etsy, bath products from Lush, paintings and vases from One Kings Lane—until they are full of everything she wants to buy. Then she exits out of the tabs one by one, click, click, click, goodbye goods. "It makes me feel like I shopped without having spent any money," she says.

The challenge arises when the sites save the items in her cart after she's closed the tabs, those damn cookies, and what's worse is when they send her emails telling her she "left something be-hind . . ." or to "take another look!" so that when she returns, she's reminded of the many things she had previously wanted and feels reinvigorated by that wanting, thus purchasing said items after all.

J receives his first acceptance, from UC Riverside, and is soon after invited to interviews in Pittsburgh, Nashville, Davis, and Ithaca. We celebrate by going to dinner at the brewery down the street. He drinks several beers and smiles all night.

"I feel like I can finally breathe," he says. "Are you upset, though?"

"Huh, why? I'm really happy for you. Those schools are good!"

"But there aren't any here or in New York City."

"It's not the most ideal situation, but whatever. It feels good to know, at least. We'll figure it out." I hold up my glass. "Next stop, one of those places!"

I call my dad in China to tell him the news. He asks whether I've told my bosses. I say no, I don't want to jeopardize my raise—assuming somebody is considering it—or my job for that matter, by telling them I'm leaving when I don't even know where yet, and it's still not for a while.

HIM: You have to learn how to negotiate. Be firm. These people respect that.

ME: What people?

HIM: The white men. You go in there and tell them your dad knew Bloomberg, back in the seventies. They all want to be Bloomberg. You tell them that your dad is making some calls to get you a job with Bloomberg. See what they say.

ME: No, I'm not going to do that.

HIM: Just as a joke! See how they respond. They'll be impressed, I'm telling you. You have to know how to handle these people.

ME: No, Daddy!

HIM: I really did meet Bloomberg. I have some friends. I can make the calls. You just tell me when.

ME: No, seriously. It won't help anyway. They just keep saying wait.

HIM: When was the last time you talked to them? Did they say when exactly they're getting back to you about this raise?

ME: No.

HIM: Did I ever tell you when I was working for my buddy Ken Lansing at the camera store, this was in New York, nineteen seventy . . . six, I think, no, nineteen seventy-five, so I was twenty-six, around your age. I told him, 'Look, Ken, I'm not taking less than thirty dollars an hour. I've been here six months and already I sell the most cameras. The customers love me. I'm your best salesman. I'm not taking anything less. If you don't pay me what I deserve, forget about it. I'm outta here,' that's how I said it. Fuggedaboudit, like the Italian New Yorkers. You know what he said? He said, 'Okay, you got a point. I'll pay you what you're asking.' He paid me thirty dollars an hour after that, plus commission. Yep. Yep, your father was doing well back then. You're how old now? Twenty-five, right, but twenty-six according to Chinese lunar year, which means you're twenty-seven soon, so almost thirty. How much are you making an hour right now?

ME: Definitely less. Like way less.

HIM: Jesus! This was nineteen seventy-six! You're making less than I was making thirty-some years ago. Take inflation into account and—okay, so this is what you have to do. You contact your boss and you tell them everything you've accomplished there, and everything you're doing. Make your value known. Figure out a number that you want and ask for more than that. Drive a hard bargain. That's how you negotiate business—

"Jobs are replaceable. People you truly love are not," writes a successful and prominent journalist in the article online titled "Why Developing Serious Relationships in Your 20s Matters," though also: "I'm not suggesting, mind you, that you settle down in your twenties. I don't envision you in a ranch home in the suburbs at twenty-six, feeding your toddlers Cheerios and pureed organic carrots and carting them to and from soccer practice in the family [Missouri: Suburban; SoCal: Prius]."

—and that's how you do it. Take it from this old-timer. You know why people like me? Because I have style. Mention Bloomberg, see what they say!

ME: Okay, okay, Daddy. What about you? Are you eating food?

HIM: Yes, yes. I ate dumplings this morning. Why do you always have to ask if I'm eating?

ME: Because I feel like if I don't remind you to eat, you won't. You said you were going to try to gain weight back, but I don't believe you.

HIM: Look, I ate dumplings. You know, I've always been skinny. Some people get old and fatter. Other people get old and skinnier. That's me.

ME: Are you drinking water and tea?

HIM: Aiya. Yes, yes. I'm drinking so much water. Tea all the time, too. I've had three cups today. Do you remember when Ling Ling and Didi would say to you, 'Stop being so bossy, you're not my mom!'? Ha ha ha.

ME: Yeah, yeah. Just please take care of yourself.

HIM: Okay, okay. Now you. Remember, be firm. Be bossy at work, not with me. You helped your bonehead. Now help yourself. And tell him I say hello and congratulations, bonehead!

What I leave out, to prevent the conversation from going for an hour longer, is that now is the worst time. With the new EIC, the office froths with rumors of who's rising up, who's being poached from where, and more importantly, who's out versus who's safe. Occasionally I hear sniffling in the bathroom stalls. Fewer people eat in the kitchen. More stay at their desks, in front of their computers. The idea is to appear too dedicated to the work to enjoy food.

I know what my dad would have said. Focus, work hard, and it will pay off. He often speaks in platitudes and idioms when I seek advice, and when I don't. He did that for years—worked hard. Seven days a week working on cars in his shop, gone before I woke up and back in time for a late dinner. ("We're more like Europeans," he used to say. "They never eat before eight.") I don't know how he can believe the words he says, when it did not, in the long run, pay off for him.

My feet are flat and wide. I wonder if it would have been better to have bound feet, like my great-grandmother's. Little things that could fit inside a mouth. At Nordstrom Rack, I try to put on a size 7.5 boot.

J, whom I am supposed to help shop for an interview outfit, walks into the aisle and finds me struggling.

"What are you doing?" he asks.

"Nothing's cooperating," I say, breathless from the fight.

He calls from Pittsburgh. "It's so cold here!"

He's getting along great with the professors. (He is far more impressive in person than on paper, we both know.) He says there are a lot of bridges. And everywhere the graduate students take them, out for dinner and to the bars, sports paraphernalia on the walls. So many people wearing jerseys. Penguins. Pirates. Steelers. Sounds like a fantasy novel to me.

"People don't say 'yinz' as much as I expected," he says. "And they don't really like it when I say it, but they're all super friendly. I don't think I've ever talked to this many strangers before. Plus, it's super cheap to live here. And one of the professors was really excited you're a writer. She said she could probably help you get a job at the university press."

"That sounds boring," I say.

"You never know! Dude, it's so cold here, though. It would be hard. But I've seen women wearing these full-length fur coats. I bet you'd look really good in one."

I spend lunch looking up neighborhoods and apartments in Pittsburgh. There's no harm in imagining, for now, running away to a life of wearing fur and loving sports.

I won't lie. There is a thrill and rush to the reporting, to the deadlines and the potential scoops. In my second week, a major company bought a startup for an enormous sum of money, making the young founders ridiculously rich. I'd recently seen a friend from high school who worked at the bank that managed the startup's funds. I texted him and asked if he knew anything interesting about the acquisition. He replied that he did. Would I want to know how much each major player made from the sale? I checked with my editor, who checked with his editors; they all said absolutely—it was a huge scoop. Did I think the source was legitimate? How much was the source willing to put on the record? My friend thought it would be easier than this. That he'd give me the information and I'd publish it, no complications. But no, there was much more to negotiate, and as we did, he grew increasingly worried about his letting this secret out. Would he be traced back as a leak? Would he lose his job over it? What he had considered a fun little thing to do had turned into a threat. He wanted to take it back. My bosses said: Do what you can to keep the source on board. I told my friend not to worry. It wouldn't be traced back to him. We wouldn't reveal his or the bank's name. We would say, "a source with knowledge of the startup's finances," was that okay? Would that make him feel safe? He said that he also didn't want my name attached to the story. His bosses might one day see that we were friends online and figure it out.

After I agreed, he gave me the percentage breakdowns. One of the founders was halfway to becoming a billionaire. Another was a comfortable hectomillionaire or centimillionaire—terms I had to look up, for people whose net worth is more than $100 million. The rest of the dozen or so employees had become instant multimillionaires. The amount of money was obscene and intoxicating. I gave up the numbers and the byline to another reporter. And though I received no public credit, the adrenaline from obtaining the information, and the internal approval from the editors, kept me happy for some time.

Also: When I interviewed the VP at a tech giant and before we started, he sat at the table with this sad, pleading look and said, Be easy on me. I hadn't considered how much power I held until that moment, and then I became filled and thrilled by it. I was pleasant during the interview, not because he asked, but because that's how I always am when I interview people. Smile and nod. Repeat what they say to nudge them into further talking. I've learned most people want the opportunity to monologue.

Afterward, I wrote a scathing piece. He sent me an email with a link to the article and a single word in the subject line: ouch.

I showed the email to Tim.

"Good work," he said. "It matters when it hurts them."

I was proud, but now I don't know of what exactly. How did it matter? The company is still thriving. He is still an overpaid executive. And here I am, sitting at the same desk, eating a free, stale bagel for lunch. Proud of my dignity and integrity? Or maybe, more likely, and only, the recognition and attention afforded by others.

It is just a keg inside a fancily decorated refrigerator, which sends out a tweet each time someone gets a drink—there is a built-in motion detector—but still, we call it the Beer Robot. Everyone has a beer on their desk as they type. I don't know what to do because I've forgotten my Pepcid AC, which I usually carry in my bag for these occasions. It doesn't seem appropriate to drink without antacids and glow red in the workplace. Everyone would think I was wasted. But then again, it doesn't seem appropriate to withhold from drinking when everyone around me is drinking. They might ask me why I didn't have a beer. I would have to explain. They might think I was a square and judging them, which I was not. Or perhaps they'd think I was sober, which also seemed to undermine those in the office who struggled with addiction. Or—

I stop myself. Tim stares at me. "Damn, sorry. I didn't realize it was going to be such an existential question for you," he says, then chugs his beer. I go get a cup and fill it one-sixth of the way, and keep it by my computer to show I'm having a good time.

J has long wanted to cure my Asian glow. He says he'll make a compound that can activate alcohol digestion in the stomach rather than letting it travel straight to the bloodstream, which is what it currently does in my body. I am missing the necessary enzyme to break alcohol down, although "necessary" doesn't seem quite like the right word. The best part, according to J, of creating a product to cure this problem will be the late-night infomercials he's envisioned. They will feature *before* shots of sad, flushed Asian men and women and *after* shots of happy, pale, but still drunk, Asian men and women. Imagine the music! The sound effects! The funny faces everyone will make! The dance choreography!

There is a decent market for a cure, but not all Asians will need it. Take, for example, my dad and my brother and Jasmine, none of whom get Asian glow, either because they were born with the lucky—better descriptor than "necessary"?—enzyme, or because they drink with such frequency their bodies have adapted.

Jasmine and I go out after work, and I stop in at a Rite Aid to pick up the Pepcid AC. She texts the new photographer, a guy she's recently hired, though she's known him for years through the photography community, which is apparently very close-knit and dramatic and incestuous.

"Wait, so are you—"

"Just tell me what you think of him," she says.

By the time we get to the bar, the other photographer is there, sitting at one of the high tables. He looks like your standard hipster San Francisco white guy—beard, beanie, beer in hand. I try to think of a nicer, more special way to assess him for Jasmine. *Artsy and tall* is the best I come up with.

The three of us spend the night doing what comes as naturally as breathing: complaining about our jobs. Jasmine goes off about how incompetent the editors and writers are—Not you, though, she hedges—how they expect her not only to go and make photos for so many of their stories but also to clean up after their stupid mistakes in the CMS, without any acknowledgment or thanks for her catching their fuckups. She says that without her, the publication would be sued up the ass for copyright infringement. It's too much work. That's why they needed another guy. She waves at the guy, who lifts his glass. I get tipsy and talk about how the editors always tell me how great I am at my job, that my stories are smart and my copy clean. They make me edit other writers' posts when they're busy, and you don't even want to know what that raw copy looks like. Plus, they all pretend like they have nothing to do with my salary, even though they're all technically my bosses.

"Is that supposed to motivate you?" Jasmine says. "Just ask again for your raise already! It's all you fucking talk about."

"This is temporary for me," the other photographer says. "I already know I won't be here for long. I need to do something more creative with my life."

Jasmine glares at him. "You said during the interview you were stoked for this job."

"Well, I was. At the time. I do really appreciate you hiring me. I need the money," he says, and smiles.

"You." She points at him. "You just got here, so you better commit to something for once and stay until I say so. And you." She points at me. "You stop using your boyfriend as an excuse and figure out your shit."

When drunk she is not completely ineloquent, but neither is she kind.

"There's no right side up, there's only upside down," the man outside the corner store says over and over, pacing.

One of the employees walks out. "Hey, buddy, what's going on here?"

"There's no right side up, there's only upside down."

"You make a good point."

While J is gone, I am afraid of the dark and ghosts. When I wake up in the middle of the night and need to pee, I lie there in my half sleep wondering if I can hold it until morning, if it is worth getting up and going through the dark spaces to the bathroom. There are more embarrassing fears than this. Like of aliens and clowns and mind control by radio waves. I curse Nickelodeon's *Are You Afraid of the Dark?* The answer to which was a resounding yes for '90s children nationwide. Don't be ridiculous, I tell myself. Still, I turn on the bedroom light, then the living room light, then the kitchen light, then the bathroom light. And when I turn off each light behind me, I walk faster toward the lighted areas, until I am back in bed, head under the blanket, having a very difficult time getting back to sleep.

In an all-hands Editorial meeting, the managing editor who is ignoring my request for a raise says the n-word. He says it, several times, in reference to song lyrics relevant to a Culture desk story published on the recent history of how rappers come up with their rhymes. The room stills. It freezes. It becomes too hot. The air dries out. Jasmine coughs. I look at fellow consumer tech reporter and nonwhite person Kevin, who looks at me and raises his eyebrows as if to say, *Is anybody going to do or say anything?* I blink a lot and my mouth goes dry. Kevin cocks his head and looks as though he is about to speak, but the moment passes. Our new EIC is going on about how he wants us to write more day-two stories with analysis and opinion, not just the day-one news pieces with the facts—our stories can stand apart from the rest with smarter contextualization, because we're smart, this publication is smart. That's what we're known for.

I fidget with the seam of my jeans and stare at the bright spines of old magazines on the lowest shelf of a bookcase. The editors pitch stories. Some are approved, others not. I am worrying about what has been said, worrying that somebody else is worrying about what has been said. Then I realize there are no black men or women on our editorial staff. Not one. Why hadn't I noticed this before? Am I stupid? There is only Kevin (Latino) and Jasmine (Asian—Chinese) and Mo (Asian—Indian, and the social media associate, who seems to have been on his phone this entire time, as he always is) and me (Asian—also Chinese)—we are not white. There is one black woman in Sales/Marketing, whose name I don't know, because nobody in Sales/Marketing ever speaks to anybody in Editorial or vice versa, and they are definitely never invited to each other's meetings.

How had I not noticed? I worry that somebody else in the room is just noticing this at the same time as me, that they are looking at the few of us who are different in the same way that we are looking at ourselves in that moment, as painfully not-them, as other. Or worse, I worry they are not noticing anything amiss at all.

I ask Jasmine if she thinks the managing editor said the n-word because he's of another generation and hasn't met enough people different from him—basically, is he too old and too sheltered? He is a white man in his forties, like most everybody here—and doesn't know that it is violent and offensive for him to say that word, even if he is quoting.

"None of them know shit" is Jasmine's response. "And they don't give a shit, either."

"But maybe—"

"Nope."

"But—"

"Stop trying to come up with excuses. The answer is: nope."

Kevin is more optimistic, because he is Kevin, the positivity guy.

He says, "I'm going to send him a note politely explaining that it is inappropriate for a nonblack person to say the n-word. I'm going to send him a really great article that contextualizes the use of the word historically and is a sort of explainer for people. I think he'd appreciate that."

Word spreads. Or more accurately, words spread. Fast, as usual, in the newsroom. Mo is taken to the gadgets room by the managing editor and the EIC. We peek over our screens to watch them sitting there on those couches, talking with stern looks, all three of them very straight and stiff. We refresh Twitter on our screens to keep abreast of new commentary, takedowns, and words of support. Mo's tweets now have hundreds of retweets and likes. The longer the words remain, the more attention they get; the numbers tick upward, not like the countdown of a bomb, though we all still sense the buildup of an impending implosion. ("Twitter's blowing up!" one writer says.) A chorus of voiceless voices responds: This editor should be immediately fired! Disgusting! and Not to defend the guy or anything, but wasn't he just quoting? Maybe I don't get it and WOW, IT'S 2013, HOW IS THIS STILL HAPPENING and cool for putting him on blast instead of just handling it with him in person like a decent human. just saying.

Mo exits the room and returns to his desk, avoiding eye contact with us all. He clicks and taps. We refresh and watch. His earlier tweets vanish. In their place, he's written,

I have spoken with the editor in question and he has apologized. (1/5)

I, too, apologize for sharing a private editorial discussion on a public forum. (2/5)

It was not my intention to harm the editor, only to share my
concern over the use of a historically degrading word. (3/5)
I know that the editor did not mean harm and am satisfied with
his apology. (4/5)
My hope is that any continuing discussion will exclude attacks
on him or the publication for which we work. (5/5)

Half an hour later, the managing editor and the EIC exit the
room. They retweet all of Mo's new tweets.

"I'm going to quit, say good fucking riddance to that place," I say,
entering our house. I throw myself dramatically on the couch.
"Wherever we're going, I'll find a job there. Or I'll get somewhere else to hire me remotely. Like, how likely is it that *this* guy
is going to give me a raise? Unlikely to never happening. You
should tell me more about this university press thingy in Pittsburgh. God, I need a new job! Can I just quit? Or should I wait? I
have no money! Hello? Are you listening?" I look up at J.

"Huh?" He turns from the stove. He pulls his earbuds out.
"Were you talking to me? I was just listening to this crazy *Radio-
lab* episode. What were you saying?"

"Nothing, blah. Just work drama."

"Okay," he says. "Do you want to tell me again?"

"No. Not really. I was just venting."

The next day, I ask Kevin if the managing editor responded to his
email. He says no, but he believes it still made a difference, even
if small.

Tim says it's terrible, a real bad look, but then also, why didn't
Mo say something during the meeting, instead of live-tweeting it?

I had the same thought. But for reasons, I think, different from

Tim's, so I don't say anything. It only occurred to me later, after reading Mo's original, now-deleted tweets. In one, he wrote: a white boss says this word and not one person in the room even blinks. because hey it's just a word? i can't even.

It bothered me that he had implied none of us had cared. And seeing him, in that moment, on his phone, he'd looked to me like he wasn't paying attention. Why was he framing it as though he was better than everyone else? Why was he presenting himself in this way online, when in person, in that moment, he'd said, like us, nothing at all?

We convene in corners and nooks. We whisper. We go for walks around the building to speak more freely. Jasmine and I head to the vintage clothing store two blocks from the office. As we push through hangers of overpriced blouses, a cloud of indignation thickens around us.

"It's total bullshit," she says. "Same shit all the time, all the places. White man does something shitty and racist, and who apologizes publicly? The person of color. I can't believe Mo fell for that."

"Yeah," I say. I mention my concern over Mo's one particular tweet.

"I mean, he's not talking about you. He's talking about the whites. They didn't blink."

"But he implied us, too."

"Don't take it so personally. What I'm pissed about is that he fucking deleted it all and apologized. I mean, now he's made it worse for sure. Caving to them."

"But he kind of had to, right? He's the social media editor, so he represents the public voice of the site."

"This site should be publicly against racism!"

"I know, I know. I'm sure they made him do it, though."

"Made him?"

"Like, maybe he thought he'd lose his job if he didn't apologize."

"The other guy should have lost his job. You think that's the first time he's done something like that? No fucking way. I heard him use the n-word on multiple occasions to describe people who take public transit! He was complaining about people who drive to work. He goes, 'People who use public transit are the n-words of commuting.' What in the fuck? I drive to work. You know why I have to drive to work? Because I live all the way in Oakland and have to go all over the place to take photos for this damn job. And my car's a piece of shit I can't fix because I'm broke. He has no fucking idea about anything, living in his nice-ass Noe Valley house, acting like he has some marginalized experience because he takes the BART? Puh-lease. And do you know how many times he's said something to me thinking I was you?"

"Wait, really? How many? When? What does he say? What do you do?"

"At least two or three times. He goes, 'Nice article today!' I just look back at him, like, you idiot."

"You're joking," I say. "So he thinks *I'm* being rude to him."

"Who cares, he sucks."

"Jasmine," I say, "I know that, but—"

"Oh my god, stop worrying," she says, and laughs viciously. "I tell him I'm a *photographer*. And he always tries to backtrack like he meant, nice *photos* for the article!"

"Oh." I stare back at the clothes on the rack. "Okay."

"You worry so fucking much about what they think of you," she says, "when they're not even worth it. And they don't give a fuck about you."

Her words sting, but they also feel true. "Yeah, you're right," I say.

"We should just kill all men and all whites, then take over this place."

I wonder if she means this place, as in the publication, or this place, as in the country or the world. Before I can ask, she holds up a dark purple piece with a black collar and says, "Do you think this is too sheer for the office?"

"No," I respond. "With an undershirt, it would be perfectly professional."

The school in Nashville is the only one that exclaims Partners more than welcome! in their email invitation. On the way there we have a layover in LA. I see a famous actress in front of me in the Starbucks line. I text J, who is waiting at the terminal. He doesn't know who I'm talking about, so there is nobody to corroborate my excitement. Then, when we get on the plane, I see the woman again, sitting next to her less-famous actor boyfriend in first class. We are on a plane with a university baseball team and end up seated in the middle of many rows of them. "Did you see Reese Witherspoon is on the plane?" they say to one another.

"It's not Reese Witherspoon," I tell them. "It's ———."

"Ohhhh. That's cool, too!" the one next to me says, then puts on his headphones and promptly falls asleep.

It is somewhat comforting to encounter these young "all-American" men, in their baseball uniforms, mistaking one famous white woman for another.

Imagine: August 17, 1982. My mother arriving at the Nashville International Airport, technically the second American city she's seen. She had connected from Chicago, where she'd spent four hours walking up and down the various terminals, fascinated by the people, the language, the food. She'd ordered a Chicago-style hot dog. It looked like a too-large, overstuffed bao bun. Why pickle and tomato? She felt very American as she took her first bite; she liked the way it tasted—very salty, kick of acid, the pepper's heat—even though the useless tomato slid out onto her lap. As she stepped into the arrivals area, scanning for her host family, she wondered briefly what she would eat in Nashville. More hot dogs? All she knew was that the people coming to get her were a husband and a wife and a daughter, and that they were American, which to her meant white. Smile a lot, her best friend had told her. Shake their hands firmly. Americans like that. Call them Mr. and Mrs. Erickson.

She could tell them apart from the rest only because they held a sheet of paper with her name on it: Lei. All three were waving. The parents told her to call them Robert and Susan. The young daughter, Jeannie, wrapped her arms around Lei. We're so happy you're here. Lei mirrored their greetings. She was nineteen and eager to learn. They took her home, showed her the bedroom she'd have for herself—a room twice the size of the room she shared with her sister in her former home—and told her to make herself comfortable. The house sprawled on forever. The bathroom she would share with Jeannie, and only Jeannie, not the whole family, had pink tiles and smelled of something unfamiliar and sweet.

Everybody behind a counter calls me "sweetie" or "darling" or "honey," like we are intimates at home. And though it is harmless, even friendly, it gives me pause.

On the bus, the Vanderbilt graduate student acting as tour guide points out the window at the giant houses with wraparound porches and tall pillars holding up wraparound balconies. They all have huge entrances that suggest somebody important walks in and out each day. We pass one flying a Confederate flag in the front lawn.

"Oh, Tennessee was part of the Confederacy," the graduate student says. "So we still get a bit of that here."

There are some laughs, some scoffs. I whisper to J, "A bit of racists? Is that like a pinch of salt?" He shrugs.

Another guy on the tour, a few rows ahead of us, says, loud enough for all to hear, "What's that supposed to mean?"

The white tour guide mumbles and rubs his hands together. He points out the window at a coffee shop. "And this here is where the hipsters go," he says. "Any of you from the coasts and big cities will love it. Why don't we stop in!"

"I wonder where my mom lived," I say to J as we walk around the nearby Belmont campus.

"Look at that," he says, pointing to a Victorian garden with intricate white gazebos flanked by bronze deer.

"This is insane. I can't believe this is the first American city my mom saw."

"Doesn't the campus look like it's from a movie?" he says.

"Yeah, one that takes place in the South, where guys wear cowboy boots and girls have debutante balls, and everybody goes to the honky-tonk on the weekends to dance." Only a day earlier did I realize that "honky-tonk" was not the same as "honky" and that white people were not offended by the hyphenated word "honky-tonk," that in fact, it seemed that white people quite enjoyed honky-tonks, as I stood there in that crowded, entirely white room pressed between J and the bar, staring up at a band in matching denim, flannel, and red neck bandannas, who sang energetic songs about being born in the back seat of a Greyhound bus and tailgating and loving you when you're anywhere and that tomorrow's the day we're gonna fly, when I said to myself, Nope, this is not going to work for me.

"How weird do you think it would be to come from the biggest city in China to this?"

"It already feels weird coming from California."

I text my mom: Did you really like Nashville?

She replies: Yes. Everyone was so nice.

One's early experiences in a new place are the most charged. They imprint the deepest and have the most influence over how one relates to that place. For example, San Francisco is my city of origin, it is the beginning of everything for me. It is where we lived as a family, where I learned to speak and think. I love the city, especially our neighborhood. My dad's old mechanic shop was on 9th Avenue. Now it is owned by a dealership. Whenever I walk by, the chemical smells of motor oil and grease and solvents take me back to being a kid, reading magazines in the front office, eating Skittles from the candy machine, sweeping the dust from the shop's floor for a dollar.

That day I moved back after college, I walked alone down Irving Street, toward the Outer Sunset, toward the water of Ocean Beach. As the cross street numbers increased, so too did the number of Asian businesses and restaurants, especially the Chinese. There were Chinese groceries and Chinese travel agencies and Chinese housewares stores and Chinese banks and Chinese day care centers. The vast majority of the population walking the streets, coming in and out of stores, was Asian, and I was overwhelmed, my eyes watered as a well of feeling pushed its way up from the bottom of my stomach into my throat. I was so happy to have returned to where I felt I belonged.

The same can be said of a relationship or a job. If the present (or envisioned, imagined, predicted future) appears low on fuel—as it does, for example, at my increasingly shitty job—memories of a vibrant past can act as reserve energy, propelling one forward on the same path. The beginning has that special power. But if weak, it can also eliminate any possibility of a future.

Later that evening in the hotel room where the university has put us up, I tell J I do not want to live in Nashville for five years. He says he understands. He says the professors told him that they have a difficult time recruiting students from the coasts.

"It's why they invite partners. To convince us with their Southern hospitality," he says.

"It didn't work," I say.

"I feel off from eating all this fried food anyway."

We spend the last day eating up more of it, walking to the various neighborhoods, and it is a nice trip, because we know we will not return.

I read the bit I've written about my mom's Nashville arrival to her. That isn't real, she says. She does not like hot dogs. The daughter's name was Jane, not Jeannie. The bathroom was big, but she doesn't remember how it smelled.

"But I like Chicago-style hot dogs," I say. "And Jeannie sounds cuter, more Southern."

"So you are writing made-up stories now?" she asks. "What about journalism? The truth?"

This is separate from that. Some made-up stories and some real, but they all come from the same person, and they will, I hope, all add up to some kind of truth.

I request, receive, and read a copy of Sheryl Sandberg's new book *Lean In* and am now asking, in Parley, if any editors want to run a review. I'm inspired! I'm Leaning In!

Sure thing, says one of the Business editors I've never worked with before. Can I turn it around by 3 P.M.?

A rush job, but I agree, because I have asked for it, plus I thrive on deadlines. It's one of my favorite feelings—the pressure of time creeping up on me, and pushing myself to meet it. The editor asks if it will be a positive or negative review. I reply,

Mostly positive, but I'm aware of the criticism and will address those concerns. Interesting, he responds. Could be a good contrarian angle, then.

What I liked from the book were the reminders to overcome internal barriers. To ask for more. I wanted to believe that the cause of asking, going for it, leaning in—whatever you wanted to name it—could lead to an effect of success.

When I'm done, I tell the Business editor the draft is ready in the CMS. He says okay. The next morning the review is up on the site's home page. The language and substance are shockingly altered. Where I hedged, he made firm statements. Where I made room for criticism, he shut it out. He did not ask if his edits were okay, he did not tell me when it would go up, and he gave it a cringe-worthy headline: "Why You Should 'Lean In' to Sheryl Sandberg's New Book."

When I ask him in Parley about it, he writes: Your review was serviceable. But I felt it needed a strong, opinionated, and distinctive take to make it stand out, especially since so many others posted their reviews last week. I made edits accordingly.

Clicks come to mind. As does the term "devil's advocate."

Whatever belief I had in the power of Lean In™—at least for my given situation, because here I am qualifying my not-so-strong, not-opinionated-enough takes—is diminishing.

Facebook. Work. Facebook. Work. Facebook. Work. Facebook. This is the typical routine. Sometimes a coffee, bagel, or tweet.

Tim messages in Parley: So . . .

I tense. I look over at him next to me. He points at his computer screen, so I look back to mine.

Let's go for a walk in 5? Get some coffee.

We don't take breaks together. We have other friends in the office for that, largely based on hierarchy and/or age. He and the senior writers and editors. Me and the staff writers and photographers. For five minutes, I sit beside him, anxiety bubbling. Outside, after checking behind and around us so many times that I lose patience and ask him to please hurry up, he tells me those rounds of layoffs everybody has been anticipating—they will start soon, as soon as the next day. Biggest news: The managing editor is out. Also most of the magazine's Art department, and at least a handful in Web Editorial, possibly more, to "eliminate redundancy" and "bring in new blood." The Berlin Hall will be no more. All of Editorial will move to one side as the website and print staffs merge under the new EIC.

"You're okay," he says. "That's why I'm telling you this. I don't want you to worry when it happens. There are important people here who want you to stick around." I ask if he's one of those important people. "Let's just say I've been asked for my opinion and I put in a good word for those I know do good work. I don't do that for everyone."

When I ask him who else is getting let go, he says he's not 100 percent sure; we'll all know soon enough. He asks if there are any updates about my boyfriend's graduate school prospects. I tell him we have options, but none are here or in NYC.

"That's unfortunate," he says. "Are you sure you're still moving with him?"

"Yes, for the last time!"

"Look," Tim says. He taps erratically at the edge of his coffee cup. "The timing is really off. You're going to end up asking for too much. You want to stay on remotely, right? That could happen. But that *and* a raise?"

The sun is too bright. The cars are too loud. The street is too crowded. Kevin walks out of the building just as we're heading in. "Coffee! Just what I was thinking!" His face is all grin and radiating sickly cheerfulness.

Tim looks at me and says, once Kevin is out of earshot, "For example, that guy."

Sheryl Sandberg writes an email thanking me for the kind review. It is surprising that she takes the time. Does she have ulterior motives, a grand PR plan, or is she genuinely this sweet?

Again to the South Bay to visit a startup that's raised more than $2 million on Kickstarter for an activity monitor that does not exist. Palo Alto is bright and beige, manicured lawns and wide clean streets of expensive cars and storefronts. Jasmine drives us to the startup headquarters, an apartment in a bright beige complex with perfectly clipped bushes and tall trees. A sign proclaims STANFORD WEST. It's the kind of place that wants to remind you of other places, but then it's hard to come up with where exactly you've seen it before. A mirror college town with money somewhere. A certain type of person finds it incredibly comforting. We deem it terribly depressing. The founder greets us at the door in leather flip-flops, too-long jeans, and two tight polo shirts, the white collars both popped. Inside, it smells of cologne and cheese. Beige curtains against beige walls, as though nothing matters beyond consistency.

"It's no Apple garage, but it's what we've got," the founder says.

This is what the publication's status in the land of tech journalism affords me: an exclusive interview and the first up-close, hands-on look at a sought-after device. The single prototype is ugly, but Jasmine manages to make decent photos using colorful processing chips and wires as props. During the interview, she tries to photograph the thing on my wrist, but it looks absurdly huge. We use the founder's wrist, but she whispers to me that the man's skin is too pale, reflecting too much light in contrast to the black activity monitor. She giggles indiscreetly. When I ask when he expects the working devices to be available, he says, "Soon. Things are coming up, but we'll solve them. There will be more problems, guaranteed, but we'll overcome them. That's the fundamental code to a successful startup."

Back in the car, we talk shit. The activity monitor is ridiculous. We are only covering it because it has made money, and that money is funding an illusion. Shouldn't we be doing something more important, not just telling people to buy, buy, buy, fueling the capitalist machine? Then her car makes a strange rumbling sound somewhere in the rear. The passenger-side window no longer rolls up.

"We might break down, but that would be a good excuse not to go back to the office," she says. "Then again, I really need the money to get this shitbox fixed."

J designed and built a bike for my body, my exact height, the reach of my legs. He got it powder coated a deep turquoise, put on particular wheels for smooth, comfortable road riding, and attached a strong light to the handlebar. I am, however, very scared of biking in the city. A week hardly passes before the local blogs post another two-paragraph news piece detailing the cross streets of the latest accident or fatality, the victim's name, a grainy photo of the scene from some corner store's camera. I will only bike if he's there guiding me. We ride down Judah to Ocean Beach and I don't hit or get hit by a car. It feels good. My legs pumping, then the coasting, how easy it is to glide together, slow enough to look around, fast enough to have the sense of efficient movement. I do nearly crash after getting my front wheel stuck in the Muni light-rail tracks. J comes hurrying back to help. Ride more off to the side, he says, waving his hand. Behind me.

Heart beating fast, I follow his path.

"It's a new era in China," my dad says on the phone. "New president. This guy cleaned house. He was doing that for months. Anyone corrupt, or anyone he didn't like—out. He's consolidating his power. Let's see what he can do with it."

"Sounds like my workplace," I say.

"What's going on at your work is small fish," he says. "This is on a much grander scale." He talks some more about political movements in China, but I only half listen, scrolling through Facebook and Twitter as he talks.

"Okay, that's that," he says. "Second on the list. Do you know which U.S. president was the first to visit China while he was president?"

"No, who?"

"You don't know? You have all these gizmos and gadgets, you should use them to learn. Know history, that's the most important—"

I look it up on my phone as he talks. "It was Nixon."

"Exactly. He messed up big time. But what he did for U.S.-China relations, that's why I like him. So that's that. What's new with you?"

"Nothing, nothing at all."

"Still no news, huh? Did you do what I told you? Bloomberg is on the line."

"No. Not yet."

When it comes to our country's political drama, J is much better versed than I am. Did you hear that *blah blah blah* said *blah blah blah's* platform on *blah blah* is totally *blah blah blah*? That's what I hear. I shake my head. No, wow, huh. Sometimes I think that I need to be more interested in what the powerful people are saying about the other powerful people. Then I look in the mirror and shrug. Statistically, it's very unlikely that I'll ever become a powerful person, so why bother?

J says if we move somewhere cheap, then my current salary plus the lower cost of living will be the equivalent to, or maybe even more than, if we remained in San Francisco and I got a raise.

"Or I can just say, 'Fuck you guys, I'm leaving and I'm not going to work for you anymore unless you pay me better and value me,'" I say. "Worst thing that happens is they say no, and then I'll be free of them."

"Then what?"

"Then I find another job."

"Do you really want that, though?"

"Yes. No. I don't know."

"Maybe it's because you're hanging out with people who hate their jobs. Maybe you should just listen to Tim. He sounds like he knows what's going on."

"Tim's on another level. And it's not like they hate their jobs. They just have realistic, somewhat cynical outlooks on the whole thing. I'm naturally attracted to that. They're the most interesting kind of people."

"Yeah, well, Jasmine's more than cynical. She's crazy."

"No, she's not," I say. "She's just really opinionated."

"Crazy opinionated," he says.

"Don't," I say. "You don't really know her. And you don't know what it's like to be in that place every day, where all these old white men sit in their fancy offices and boss everyone around, and you're so fucking underpaid and underappreciated and nobody gives a shit about you. You don't even think what that editor said is that big of a deal! And you think Jasmine's the crazy one?"

"I never said I didn't think it was a big deal," he says, slower. Sometimes I imagine he treats my outbursts like he does the angry mice he works with. With care, with gloves.

"Well, you didn't say you thought it was, either. You probably think it's great that he didn't lose his job over a *little mistake*."

He looks at me like he doesn't know me. I sense it, too, that I am channeling somebody else, that I am recycling or regurgitat-

DAYS OF DISTRACTION   69

ing somebody else's words as my own—as my own pain—and directing it toward him, as representative of someone or something else. But is it not all connected?

"I'm sorry," he says. "I agree you're underpaid. I know that's stressful. And I think what the managing editor said is wrong."

I look out the window of the car, at the passing pastel houses as we head up the hill back to our own pastel yellow home. The tower. The sand.

"I know," I say. "Sorry for yelling. And anyway, he's losing his job after all."

Kevin messages me in Parley: Can you meet in the kitchen?

How does the time pass? We've never spoken for this long, but misery loves company, as it's put, and he's just gotten let go. He says that management told him he wasn't a fit culturally. Culturally, he repeats. He says a buddy of his at the National Association of Hispanic Journalists said it's enough to make an official complaint against the publication. But to whom is the complaint made? An association that has no control over what a private company can and cannot do? And will it get him his job back? Will he have to hire a lawyer? Culturally! He can't believe it.

"I'm thinking of leaving journalism for good," he says. "Work for a nonprofit or go back to school. Everyone says journalism is dying anyway. It's toxic. I've always wanted to get a Ph.D. in history or English."

"Nooooo."

"Isn't that what your boyfriend's doing?"

"Biology, not the same. I mean, I'm not saying it's not a good idea, only that there might be better ones, like trying to find another job."

Kevin looks mournfully at his hands, all positivity drained from him. So this is what he really looks like, I think, and for a moment, I find him attractive.

"At least they're giving me ten weeks' severance, which is like fifteen K, so that plus my savings, I can survive for at least six months if I move out to a cheaper place. The Sunset's cheap, right? Do you know of any apartment openings? Maybe this is a blessing. I don't have any responsibilities. I've always wanted to write a book. I can do that in the meantime," he says. Some light returns to his eyes. "Or I can learn a new language. And yeah, maybe I really will go back to school. Anything's possible! I'll show them."

"That sounds great!"

"We'll have to stay in touch."

"For sure!"

Afterward, I hurry back to my desk and calculate Kevin's yearly income. He makes—no, made—about double my salary. I tell Tim. His eyebrows jump up above the frames of his glasses.

"Holy shit," he says. "It makes even more sense why they let him go."

"Is that the only reason I'm here?" I say. I rest my head on my desk and close my eyes. "Because I'm cheap labor?"

Tim rolls over to my side of the desk and pats me awkwardly on the shoulder. "No, no, no, no."

A list of all the things I could do with an extra $15,000: Pay off nearly all of my remaining student loans. Pay my half of the rent and utilities for seventeen months. Pay my mom's rent, so she doesn't need to have the student renter. ("But I like the company," she says. "It's lonely without you guys here.") Visit my dad, no problem. Buy all of my brother's and sister's textbooks and school crap for the next three years. Buy J seven new fancy mountain bikes—ha ha, no, I wouldn't do that.

"So Tim was right and you don't have to worry," J says when I call him from the alley behind the office. He has left me again, this time for an interview in Ithaca, some below-freezing cold place in upstate New York.

It's true. All it might take is a shift in perspective, a state of mind, to allow a situation fresh air. But this is harder done for the person in it than said by someone outside.

And each day another set of people goes. The rest of us hold on tight.

Every day, I Gchat with my mom while at work. Today, she writes, What can you do? That's the job you chose.

I start talking to other writers about how much Kevin got paid versus how much I got paid versus hey do you want to tell me what you get paid? Some of them happily do and some do not. One woman tells me she thinks contractors tend to have higher salaries than full-time employees to make up for the lack of benefits. When I tell her that Kevin was FTE and I am a contractor, all she says is, Oh, I see. Are you FTE? I ask. She avoids eye contact. She fusses with her hair. I can tell she is deeply uncomfortable with my questions. I don't care. I feel like I've shed a layer of tact and social sensitivity, and underneath is all rough, abrasive matter. I ask again. She says things like, she doesn't know who makes these rules. It doesn't make sense. She's sorry. Was there anything she could do to help? Could she take me out to lunch?

Jasmine rages about the layoffs, especially Kevin's. She says it's very likely Mo will soon go, too. Not like he'll have any trouble finding a job—every other job listing is for a community manager these days. That's why she's been running the publication's Tumblr, so she can put social media experience on her résumé. The hustle never ends. Doesn't matter that any teenager on the street knows how to post pictures online. Not that *we* need to really worry. We won't get fired. Nope. That wouldn't be a good look for the publication. Not a good look at all. The only two women of color in a room so devoid of women of any kind. And two Chinese girls, as if that's good enough. Ha ha. We're lucky now, aren't we? So fucking lucky.

I point out to Jasmine that when she was in charge of hiring a new photographer, she hired another white man.

She is silent, smoking.

"Yeah, I regret that," she says. She lights another cigarette. "Fuck dating white guys."

An editor comes to talk to us about the old days when he worked as a newspaper reporter. He wants to teach us a lesson about deadlines. "Back when I was at the *Chronicle* they'd ask me for six inches of copy on something that wasn't even on my beat, something I knew nothing about, like new Muni regulations because the transportation reporter was out, or some housing bill, because the housing guy was out. And they'd ask for it in twenty minutes, so they could get it in the morning paper. The printer had a schedule, you know? And you know what I'd do? I'd give it to them in eighteen minutes."

Tim and I sit there, me staring, him shaking his foot incessantly.

The editor goes on about how news reporters these days don't understand how easy they have it with web. How deadlines matter to fewer and fewer of us. How back in the day reporters hit *the streets,* talked to *real people,* didn't just sit at their desks silently sending *emails.*

Then the editor pauses. "Why do you look like that?" he says to me.

"Oh, that's her death stare," says Tim. "That's when you don't want to mess with her. She's scarier than she looks."

"What?" I say. "No, I was just zoning out."

The editor laughs and throws his hands up. "Okay, just don't kill me." It is 3:30 P.M. by the time he leaves, tapping his watch to remind us of the 4 P.M. deadline.

I glare at Tim.

"Don't worry. Guys like him will be irrelevant in no time." Everything he says these days is ominous, as though he is an office fortune-teller.

At the ceremonial groundbreaking of the Transbay Tower (later to be known as Salesforce Tower), architect Cesar Pelli says, "We have designed a tower appropriate for the city. The tower will be svelte but dynamic, elegant, and very gracious. The gateway to the city and the tallest building in the city side by side. It's a fabulous combination."

"When this transit tower is complete it will have the impact of transforming the city skyline with the tallest structure west of the Mississippi," says Mayor Edwin Lee.

He calls it "a place for innovation and inspiration."

I hear someone in the office say, "San Francisco is going to the bros."

J gets accepted to Cornell in Ithaca, New York. It feels like winning the lottery.

"Let's go," I say.

"Are you sure? Even though you've never been?"

He had only good things to say about the place, it is the best school for him, so yes. "Absolutely," I say. "Let's get out of here."

It is a huge relief to stop waiting on this one decision.

We look up housing in Ithaca, click through images of two- and even three-bedroom apartments and houses. We envision living someplace close to a waterfall. "You can have your own office," says J. "We can go on hikes all summer," I say. Everything will be so cheap! We'll get a dog! And a cat! Our future begins to take shape in our collective imagination, and we are as excited as children with new toys.

Every round of layoffs calls for an all-hands meeting in the cafeteria, and at this one, the new EIC gives a speech about how we are reshaping the website into something better, something indispensable to our readers, and how each of us is an important piece to the puzzle of making this happen. Occasionally the EIC calls out individuals for praise, to inflate ever-shrinking morale. Today, he references a story about an in-depth look at a company's interface redesign, a story I wrote.

"And *this* is the type of story that will get us recognized as the best tech publication in the field," he says. "Really good work, umm . . . yes, good work!"

The EIC does not remember my name, or worse, does not know me at all. People look around, trying to figure out who wrote the story. Tim waves at me to say something. I slide down in my seat and refuse to look up.

"It's okay," Tim tells me afterward. "Other editors know you wrote that story."

"So is now the time to tell somebody I'm moving to Ithaca?"

"Where is that?"

"Upstate New York."

He shakes his head. No. No. No. No.

The rich white woman whom I previously worked for had a husband who was a venture capitalist, a term I'd never heard before I met her, and which she could not explain. She did, however, keep abreast of the Silicon Valley social scene. Mark Zuckerberg and his girlfriend, Priscilla Chan, got engaged, she told me one day as I organized her closets. She said that she had looked up Priscilla and had very quickly determined that I was much prettier. So much prettier that Mark Zuckerberg should, in fact, be marrying me, not Priscilla, who looked to be a bit on the bigger side, nearly as tall and certainly as thick as Zuckerberg himself. Zuckerberg might be a smaller-than-average man, though—it was hard to tell from the photos—but either way, it would not be a problem for me, since I was a small, cute woman, she continued. She had the misconception that Priscilla was an opportunistic, vengeful vixen, from the way the Asian woman had been characterized in the movie *The Social Network*. Honestly, she had been a bit surprised when she finally saw Priscilla's photo and learned of her successful background—fluent in many languages, first in her family to graduate from college, medical school at UCSF.

"You two share so many qualities, but of course you're much prettier," she repeated.

I did not know which of her comments was most important to address. I was fluent in one language. I was the first in my immediate family to graduate from college, but I was nowhere near medical school. What exactly was she trying to say? I had spent the duration of her speech focused on managing my facial expression, on not moving any muscle in any direction. To look as blank and still as possible. I coughed and apologized. I said I didn't think the woman in the movie was meant to be a portrayal of Priscilla, specifically, since the character did not even date Mark Zuckerberg's character, but that I had found it nonetheless shallow, annoying, and stereotypical.

"Yes, that's it! These men don't understand anything," she said. "Now I only wish there was a way for you to meet Mark Zuckerberg before they get married."

I reminded her that I had a boyfriend.

"Oh, sweetie, you don't know if that's going to last."

I went back to organizing one of her large walk-in closets, intent on not ripping her things into small pieces. And to a certain extent, it worked. I continued to work for her for months after. We drank tea together. She ordered me expensive lunches every day. She called me her friend. When I left, she hired another Asian girl to replace me.

I've seen Mark Zuckerberg a few times in person, but never close enough to examine the pores in his skin or the pupils of his eyes, so I'm not certain he has either. Two times he's been on a stage shilling a groundbreaking new product of Facebook's, usually clapping and looking wide-eyed and lost, a sad, wild animal. One time he was in his glass cage corner office, which made him appear to be on view for the Facebook employees to walk by and admire, a creature whose presence would inspire. I asked my PR guide of the day if we could get closer to the office to see what he was up to and she said sure. There was Zuckerberg, sitting at his desk, on his computer, typing. He looked calm. He didn't notice his new audience. I wanted to approach the glass, to knock on it and wave, to startle him into that familiar frightened look, but my PR guide took me by the shoulders and said we had to get to a meeting with some lesser animal who was going to tell me about another groundbreaking new product. As we walked away, I looked back to catch a last glimpse of the Zuck in his natural habitat.

Now here he is again, talking about a Facebook phone and something called Chatheads. Or Chat Heads. Whatever they are, you can chat with them—that's the gist. And here I am typing like a maniac. It does not look like a terrible phone, but who will buy it? He has a deluded sense of his audience's relationship to his platform. Nobody loves Facebook like that. It's more of a shameful and sickening addiction, like eating scoops of jam directly from the jar.

On our afternoon walks, Jasmine smokes. I cross my arms. Sometimes she takes a photo of me with her phone. I try to shield my face. I tell her I don't like the way I look in photos, uncomfortable and upset. "That's who you are, though," she says. "Trust me, at least when I'm holding a camera."

I tell her about an idea I have. I want to get all the contract permalancers together and write a joint letter to the EIC—and all those who are in charge—and tell them we want to be converted to full-time employees. We want benefits. We want job stability. We want scheduled evaluations and clearer processes for pay raises. We want transparency. I say there are so many of us, if we all voice our dissatisfaction together, it has to do something.

"Interesting," she says. She hesitates. She corrects herself. "Yeah, it's a good idea. I just don't think it will do anything."

"But shouldn't we at least try?"

"It will be a lot of work for nothing."

"What are you worried about?" I ask, surprised and hurt that the one person I thought would support the idea 100 percent is flinching.

"I'm *not* worried," she says, stomping on her cigarette butt.

J is stoned and listening to me vent. He is baking a dozen cookies and saying, "If anyone can rally them, it's you," and "Ha ha, this cookie looks like a dolphin," and "Do you think my calves are getting bigger? I'm doing calf exercises just to make them bigger for you!" and "Aren't you glad that you won't have to be in that office much longer?"

"Yes to all of the above," I say.

"I love the sentiment," says a copyeditor. "But I'm grateful to even have a job here. I applied for years before I got in."

"Now just seems really unstable. People are being fired, and I don't feel comfortable asking for more," says a video editor. "Maybe after things settle?"

"Have you talked to contractors at other publications who've tried to do the same?" says a fact-checker. "Could you gather more information before we decide what's next?"

"I'm totally on board if others are on board," says a home page editor.

"If you're so unhappy, why not leave? Wait, are you doing this *because* you're leaving soon?" says a Business reporter. "Some of us actually want to stay on, you know. We aren't in the same position as you. Don't drag me into this."

If there were an app that let me see the world as J sees the world, I'd pay more than two dollars for it and would give it five out of five stars. I would become one of those people who walk around with their phone always out, pointing it in all directions, looking through the screen to see how differently J and I perceive the spaces around us. How augmented is his reality from mine is the question I would like answered.

Stressful events occur in groupings. At least that's how it feels now, my mom on Gchat:

Your father called me five times yesterday!

why?

I had to call him back to make him stop calling
He says Didi told him he got MIP again

why would Didi tell him that?

Who knows. Didi doesn't think

so what did daddy say about it?

why was he calling you?

He says now he has bad dreams about you guys

He worries Didi is going to get arrested or worse

And that ling ling is doing badly in school too

Hanging out with wrong crowd

Always with negative thoughts

He thinks everything is negative

He lecture me to lecture them

Do this do that. He drives me crazy!

ok, so he just had bad dreams?

so he's fine otherwise?

Yes, he's fine! I'm the one not fine

Tell him not to call me

Call you if he has these thoughts

You need to take care of him, not me

ok ok, i'll talk to him about it

Why does he call me?

We are divorced TWELVE YEARS!!!

OK I SAID I'LL TALK TO HIM

Good. Thank you.

And now a senior editor is telling me that she knows the tech industry has a diversity problem and that tech publications, too, have a diversity problem. But what can they do when so few women apply for the jobs? Women need to try harder, just put themselves out there, do well in the interviews, not be their own biggest obstacle. Like you and me, she says. Like Sheryl—Lean In™! Once you start hiring based on diversity, everyone in the newsroom is going to feel uncomfortable, like women are only diversity hires and not the ones who deserve the job based on skills and abilities. And where does it stop? Will we need to start hiring Asians and African Americans and Mexicans just because they are Asian or African American or Mexican? What about gay people, who are also sorely underrepresented? Will you ask them if they're gay during the interview? You could get sued! And who will you hire if you have a bunch of diversity candidates—the woman or the minority or the gay guy? What do people want when they call for diversity? Wasn't trying to find good people in itself good enough?

I don't know what to say. I shake my head and drink my tea and point to the kitchen door, like I've gotta go. She stares at me. Finally, I come up with "It's complicated."

"So complicated," she says, nodding.

I walk back to my desk. I wonder what it is about me that makes her say we are alike, as though our experiences are one and the same, and how she expects me to respond, and if I have met her expectations. A dark feeling spreads its fingers inside me. Have I made myself this accommodating? A harmless vessel for their confusion and rage? They must see me as soft and small and unthreatening, because I have never suggested otherwise.

I'm having dreams about my teeth falling out again. In my dreams my teeth hang on by a little piece attached to the gum. They are a bit painful, but mostly uncomfortable. I try to shove them back in place and hope they heal, but I end up spitting them into my palm. They're cracking and crumbling and I worry that no dentist will be able to glue them together and put them back in my mouth. And yet, I am relieved because the pain and discomfort have ended. I hold all of my broken, rotten teeth in my hands, mildly sad to have lost them.

According to some Chinese interpretations, this means misfortune will strike my family, or I will have a long and happy life, or I will soon acquire land. According to teethfall ingoutdreams.org, these dreams symbolize anything from "feelings of insecurity or vulnerability regarding a recent event that disrupted your life" to "an indication that you're in the process of growing, discovering and developing aspects of yourself that were previously hidden or neglected." Or there's Freud: it's about castration and anxiety around sexual performance.

Jasmine says nobody would say shit like that to her, she's made herself *very, very* clear to everyone. She fights with people at work. She yells at them if she is upset or annoyed. "The point is to make them scared of you," she says.

It occurs to me that Jasmine is more talk than action, but I try to suppress the thought. We do not address my failed attempt to get people to write a letter or petition, or whatever it was, although I'm sure she's heard. Instead, we talk about how she's been seeing a therapist to deal with her anger issues. Her therapist suggested that during moments of feeling ungrounded, she start describing the physical characteristics of her surroundings. For example, the desk is made of wood; the keyboard of this computer is white and gray; there are three pens—one black, two blue—on the table; a notebook is open to a page of notes written in blue ink; the carpet is gray with flecks of red; there are one, two, three, four . . . eight windows in this room; my shirt is army green; Tim is typing next to me; his shirt is a medley of bright colors in triangular patterns; he is looking back at me with his clear-framed eyes—

"Are you okay? Are you crying?" He is rolling over in his bright blue office chair, yet again.

"No, I'm fine."

I look back at my computer and do not wipe my face, so he rolls back to his side and leaves me alone.

I apply to other jobs, without disclosing the specifics of where I'm moving. "New York," I say. One place says they'll hire me for the SF or NYC office. I clarify. I meant *upstate* New York, would that be okay? They say absolutely not and tell me I've wasted their time. Guilt-ridden, I start including Ithaca in my cover letter. Out of the dozen or so jobs, two places get back to me. One offers an even smaller salary than what I am now making. The other offers a negligible pay bump, but is a super-niche site very few people have heard of, let alone read. That seems more embarrassing than doing nothing at all. I despair.

J rubs my back, tells me it will all be okay.

Every day I play out the "if . . . then" game with myself. If I impress the editors, then I will get the raise. If I get a raise, then I will stay at this job. If I move to the middle of nowhere, then I will have no leverage. If I get my raise before I move, then they can't take it back. If I stay at this job, then I might hate myself. If I leave this job, then I might also hate myself, plus no money. If I don't move wherever J goes, then I am abandoning him. If I abandon him, then all I will have is this shit job. If all I have is this shit job and no raise, then I might as well follow him and have no job and no raise. If I move to the middle of nowhere with no job and no raise, then . . . what?

Tim asks me to get coffee again. He says that I might be the luckiest person in the office. I feel very far away from the statement. The new managing editor is, listen to this, *from Ithaca*. My first thought is *Too late*.

Corey, who has somehow gotten promoted amid the newsroom turmoil, takes me to a conference room and tells me he's heard. Nothing is secret in the newsroom. He only wishes I had said something to him sooner. He is my boss, after all, and we need to trust one another. I try to look calm. It occurs to me that I might lose my job for rabble-rousing. Part of me would be relieved. I steel myself for the blow. I wonder what Kevin said when he was let go. "Totally get it"? "No problem, bro"? "It's cool, it's cool"? I try to come up with a more dignified reply. Another part of me wants to cling to what I know: Please, please, please don't make me go.

And as though he's in a cliché-ridden movie, he says there's good news and there's bad news. But then he doesn't pause to ask which I want to hear first. He just keeps talking.

"So. I know you're moving. The good news is that the new managing editor really likes the idea of having somebody in Ithaca. Who knows why. Guess he's attached to the place. You can work remotely with the East Coast team. You'll be a one-person Ithaca bureau," he says, and laughs like I've won a prize.

I say I still want a raise. I try to be firm, like my dad said. I tell Corey about my other job offers, but my voice comes out splintered. I am not convincing.

"You're incredibly valuable to us as a reporter," he says, as though some supportive words are equivalent to concrete change, money, and power.

I tell him that if I don't get a raise, I may consider going freelance or just leaving, period.

"You know we don't have piles of money lying around," he says. "This is journalism we're talking about. This isn't the kind of job where you make piles of money. It's about loving the work, putting your heart into it."

What about the piles going into the remodel of the office? What about the piles used to hire all these new people from other places, assuming they all got pay bumps to come over here? What about the piles used for *his* raise? What about the piles . . .

"Let me get back to you. You take this time to think things through, too."

"What was the bad news?"

"The bad news was that I wouldn't be your editor anymore."

I leave the room.

"What about this?" J holds up a pot I've never seen. "Will we use it in Ithaca?"

"No. Delete it," I say. Delete, delete, delete to the years of collected crap.

We pack the necessities, belongings with which we can't part. Boxes of books for me. Bigger boxes of bike stuff for him. We both look at each other's possessions and ask, Are you sure? Yes, we're both very sure.

The rest, nearly all of it, goes to Goodwill or on Craigslist. More people have entered our house in the last two weeks than in the last two years. No fewer than three times, I locked myself in the bedroom while J handled the sale. A woman named Diva took the dining room table. "Beautiful! What a steal! What a find!" I heard through the wall.

Now there is a box of leftovers. We discuss its fate. The garbage can is overfull; the lid hovers precariously over our trash.

"Somebody might like this stuff," says J. "I'll put it outside."

"No way. Who?"

But he doesn't listen. He is stoned and writes ads under the Free section.

> Old corkboard, one crumbly edge but still functional. Comes with a secret message!!!! For the stunning price of $0, get it today. Drive up to the FREE box at 10th and Moraga.

> Have you ever wanted to own an XXL Microsoft Phone branded baseball-style shirt? Never worn, very stylish. Comes with a shitty matching baseball cap for the truest Microsoft fan.

> Greasy stovetop teakettle, black. It boils water even though it is not clean.

> Never before used . . . PAPER! Only a little yellow from age, this lined notebook paper is available to the lucky first caller. (But don't actually call, just pick it up.)

I laugh and laugh. I tell him he could have a great career in copywriting.

We watch from our window the people who come to take our stuff. In two hours it is all gone. And I feel a little sad to see it go, all the accumulated items that added up to make this place what it was, a home.

The last few weeks pass without progress. People are fired, including two contractors who wouldn't get on board with organizing. I try not to gloat in public. New people enter. I don't bother getting to know them. The office layout is shifted. Everybody is moved across the hall, except me. I lose my desk. I work alone on the couch in the spare-gadget room. A leftover employee among leftover devices. I find it funny and sad that this is where the publication began, where my time at the publication began, and where it all ends. Sometimes I get visitors, like Jasmine and Tim. But even they, in this climate, are trying to prove themselves to whoever is paying attention. I do very little writing. Nobody seems to notice. Sometimes, in the afternoons, I sit with my laptop on the floor of the corner office that once belonged to the deputy web editor (since let go). I imagine how it would have felt to step into this office each day. Probably very exciting and empowering at first, then normal and comfortable, then like it wasn't enough. I stare out the window at the passing cars and people. They look like they're busy. I find a sublet in Ithaca. I map out our cross-country drive. Back in the gadget room, I spend hours organizing the shelves of gear and smartphone cases. I put a bunch of cases in my bag, thinking: They owe me.

On my second-to-last day in the office, Corey comes in.

"Wow, it looks way neater in here."

"I've been busy," I say.

He tells me he's gotten approval for a 4 percent raise. "That's all we can do," Corey says. "It might be a different story if you stay in town, but I know you have your mind set on going." He says we'll check in again when I get to the Ithaca bureau. ("L-O-L," he says out loud without laughing.) "And to clarify and reiterate, we'll have to hold your pay until then."

After he leaves, I calculate what this 4 percent "raise" means for me, then spend all afternoon sitting on that couch, wishing they would have let me go with severance instead. Then I remember I would not have gotten severance—that is a benefit limited to full-time employees, which I am, infuriatingly, not.

We sit on the fake wood floors of the empty house and eat sandwiches from the market down the street. J spills crumbs everywhere, but it doesn't bother me. We brush them out the front door. I remember one more thing. On the bottom of the wall, where it meets the floor, in the smallest print I can manage, I write: *JJ was here.* Like I have in each of the houses I have left before—the first one in SF, the two in Shanghai, the two in Davis, and now here.

"Those are my initials, too" he says.

"I know." We smile at one another.

"What if it gets painted over?"

"Doesn't matter. They'll still be there, underneath."

II.

ROAD TRIP

What one carries from one point to another, geographically or temporally, is one's self. Even the most inconsistent person is consistently himself.

—Yiyun Li, *Dear Friend, from My Life I Write to You in Your Life*

Gail Borden
Public Library District
www.gailborden.info

Rakow Branch Checkout Receipt

Customer ID: **********3859

Items that you checked out

Title: Days of distraction : a novel / Alexandra
Chang.
ID: 31113016543930
Due: Saturday, October 31, 2020

Title: The only story / Julian Barnes.
ID: 31113015991809
Due: Saturday, October 31, 2020

Total items: 2
Account balance: $0.00
Saturday, October 3, 2020 12:06 PM
Checked out: 2
Overdue: 0
Hold requests: 0
Ready for pickup: 0

Please remember to return materials on time;
others are waiting to enjoy them as well.

Sign up for text message alerts -
www.gailborden.info/text

Rakow Branch Checkout Receipt

Customer ID: **********3869

Items that you checked out

Title: Days of distraction : a novel / Alexandra
Chang
ID: 31130165439620
Due: Saturday, October 31, 2020

Title: The only story / Julian Barnes
ID: 31130159918608
Due: Saturday, October 31, 2020

Total items: 2
Account balance: $0.00
Saturday, October 3, 2020 12:06 PM
Checked out: 2
Overdue: 0
Hold requests: 0
Ready for pickup: 0

Please remember to return materials on time;
others are waiting to enjoy them as well.

Sign up for text message alerts -
www.gailborden.info/text

In Davis, his parents give us one of their cars, in better condition than our old car (also from his parents) and roomier, for the cross-country drive. A box-shaped car that we fill to the brim with boxes.

Each day I'm home, my mom talks about my leaving. The anticipation of it—of my being across the country—bears down on the time we have together, now.

"When will you come home? Thanksgiving?"

"Probably not. The flights are too expensive."

She reminds me that she's going to Australia in December to visit one of her sisters. Will I come home or stay in Ithaca?

"I don't know," I say. "Either way, I won't see you. Maybe spring, then."

"Geez, that's too long!"

What is the longest we've gone without seeing each other? A couple of months is the answer to a question I have not had to ask before. But people leave behind their families all the time. They leave for all kinds of reasons. She did once. My dad did, more than once. This is nothing in comparison. No oceans or languages or barriers to cross. Just one country. From one edge to the other.

We play Ping-Pong at his family friend's birthday party. It is crowded with people we don't know, and many little kids run around chasing each other, squealing and screaming. One boy stops at the table to watch us.

"You're a lot better at Ping-Pong than your brother," he says. "Can I play?"

J and I both stop and look at each other. I don't know what to say. I want to cry.

J goes, "You're right, I'm terrible. I bet you could beat her." He hands the boy the paddle.

The boy and I hit the ball back and forth until he gets bored, only a few minutes in, and runs away.

"Do you think the world's going to be a lot better when all these kids grow up?"

J says maybe.

"No. The answer is no. Because the world is going to beat their innocence out of them, and they'll end up hurt or hurting like the rest of us."

"Are you feeling okay?" He approaches.

"I'm feeling very high-strung, or is it on edge, or maybe it's in pieces."

My dad is talking about the virtues of East Coasters in comparison to West Coasters. The former, according to him, possess all the good qualities as people: hardworking, direct, genuine, honest, trustworthy. New Yorkers, he says, are his favorite people.

"It's not really New York, though. It's upstate New York."

"That's the real New York. It will be good for you. People on the East Coast aren't lazy, they aren't so carefree and loosey-goosey about everything."

"I'm not like that, either."

"That's because you were raised by someone like me," he

says. "You belong on the East Coast. But look at your bonehead. Just your typical California boy, laid-back and goofy."

"Those can be good traits, too," I say.

"Yes, to a certain degree," he says. "Tell him from me: Drive safe and don't smoke so much marijuana."

"He doesn't smoke and drive!" (At least not across the country . . .)

"No, in general, if he wants to do well in school. He needs to cut back. Tell him."

"Okay, I will." (I do not.)

"You'll have to FaceTime me every day," my mom says as we leave.

"Every day! That's too much."

I am, however, comforted by the availability.

They gave me a card with a cat meowing *Goodbye* on its cover. Inside, names and short notes. *We'll miss you terribly! Good luck! Safe travels! Keep in touch! Take pictures!*

One note in red ink: *I'm still mad at you for leaving. This place is going to suck even more now. <3, Your only real friend here.* Unsigned, but it's Jasmine, of course. And Tim's: *You can still do a lot in the middle of nowhere.* I keep the card in the glove compartment, but take it out several times to look at it, studying each individual's handwriting, whose handwriting I realize I've never before seen. Some slanted and optimistic, some heavy and pointed with intensity, some letters so small they withdraw into the paper. My coworkers are finally revealing hidden parts of themselves to me. I take a pen from the compartment and write the date in the corner—May 29, 2013—so my future self will remember.

Correction: They're not really my coworkers anymore. Just people I used to work with.

What does that make me? An ex-journalist? An unemployed person? A trailing partner?

"You do technically still work there," says J.

"I'm going to quit. I've decided. It was like having Stockholm syndrome. I'm out, I can now see clearly. I'll find something else."

He laughs. "You *were* pretty miserable."

Now that we're on the road, the wind blowing through the open windows, I tell myself, Cut loose from whatever it was you were living in before! Look at the beautiful sky! Onward!

We talk about everything we're excited to do: Visit our friends in Portland; go through Montana, a place I've never been and which he says is beautiful; figure out what Midwesterners eat; see all of the country's landscape; etc. To finally have a vacation and be free of any responsibility, except to end up at his grandmother's upstate New York hometown for his great-uncle's ninetieth birthday. But that is not for many days. We have time. All the time to do as we please.

Then Ithaca. What will Ithaca be like?

"There's no better redneck than an upstate New York redneck," the new managing editor told me. "And make sure you get snow tires."

Since he asks where the term comes from and because he is driving and I am doing little but sitting beside him, I conduct a bit of research on my phone. The first use of "trailing spouse" appeared in print in the 1981 *Wall Street Journal* article "Problems of Two-Career Families Start Forcing Businesses to Adapt," written by reporter Mary Bralove. (An amazingly strange last name.) "By far the majority of those 'trailing spouses' are women. The Catalyst report finds that wives tend to relocate for their husbands' careers. In most cases, such moves are decided by whose salary is higher," she wrote. It's true we are moving for his academic career. But I am not a wife. I am not moving because J's salary is higher. Although it is also true that I do not currently have a salary to speak of.

That word—trailing—evokes a rolling suitcase bumbling along behind somebody, its wheels getting stuck in divots, its body toppling over as it runs into bumps along the path, a deadweight that needs constant pulling, adjusting, and care.

"You're not a suitcase or deadweight," says he.

"Right, so then I'm not a trailing spouse or partner or whatever." The if-not-that-then-not-that logic does not quite add up, but it doesn't matter—the point is, I'm refusing to be either.

"Moving is one of life's top-five stressors," one of the former coworkers told me at my farewell drinks.

"What are the other four?"

"Death of a loved one, divorce, major illness or injury, and job loss," he said. "This, according to the experts."

"What qualifies somebody to be an expert in life stressors?" I yelled. "Like, how we're all *experts* in when the next iPhone is coming out?" I was drunk. It was over.

Am I truly experiencing two of life's *greatest* stressors? There must be, I believe, as a nonexpert on the topic, greater stressors than these.

I take it back. I won't quit. I will work for them remotely. I will be the Ithaca bureau. It will be different. Or, at least, it won't be exactly the same. For one, I won't have to be *physically* around them. So that could be better. What do you think? I ask J.

"I think it would be good for you to take a break from thinking about it."

"A break from thinking? How? Tell my brain: Now, stop. And then magically it works?"

"Enjoy the views!"

"What views? There's nothing new out there."

On the road for only four hours; everything outside looks like someplace I've seen before.

According to a Pew Research study conducted between 2011 and 2013, 73 percent of Americans say that on a scale from 0 to 10, the importance of working hard in order to get ahead in life is a 10 or "very important." Only half of the rest of the world agrees. The other half has other priorities. Like what, I wonder, and should I have them, too?

"A good traveler has no fixed plans and is not intent upon arriving. A good artist lets his intuition lead him wherever it wants. A good scientist has freed himself of concepts and keeps his mind open to what is," wrote Laozi, way back when.

Now J is sighing his big performative sighs.

I deign to look up. "What? What is it?"

"Are you looking at your work chat?"

I shove the phone under my thigh. "No," I lie. (They're having another all-hands meeting next week. More layoffs.)

"I saw! Stop doing stuff on your phone. How about it's your turn to drive?"

"Perfect," I say. "Sounds perfectly wonderful to me."

I am in the left lane going five below the speed limit when a truck begins to tailgate and flash its headlights behind us. He is speaking to me in code. I feel like I might throw up.

J tells me to change lanes so the truck can pass.

That's not possible. I would if I could but I can't.

J goes: "Now. You're clear. Now. Clear. Okay. Now."

It is early afternoon in somewhere, southern Oregon. Not likely high traffic, but from this, my, vantage point, the cars on the wretched freeway are bumper to bumper. We continue on for several more minutes, the white truck taking up the whole rearview mirror, until, finally, it merges into the right lane. The driver flips us off as he passes. My hands are clenched and wet on the steering wheel. When there are no cars in sight, I pull over onto the shoulder. I have lasted thirty-seven minutes total.

"For somebody who likes to be in control of everything, it's weird you don't want to drive," says J.

"I have more control over here, telling you where to go. It's impossible to know what's happening from over there. It's precisely because I don't feel like I have control that I can't."

He shakes his head.

"Don't! It's not like you're teaching me how, and I'm just supposed to do it?"

For the next hour, we do not speak.

I got my learner's permit (for the second time) specifically to help drive across the country. Though I have obtained a document approving me to do so, in the legal sense, I have not been imbued with the ability to maneuver a car, in the literal sense. There were a few times in a parking lot across the street at the junior high with my dad. Those drives were short and smooth. Then the few times when friends in high school and college, being dumb teenagers, asked me to be the unlicensed designated driver, and being a dumb teenager, I consented. I drove across small college towns or on winding country roads with people in the car singing and screaming, windows rolled down, their white hands petting my face. Their beer breath warmed my neck. Don't be a bad driver, they said. Don't be a stereotypical Asian driver, and a woman! I never checked the mirrors or looked anywhere except ahead. It felt like playing a video game I knew I couldn't win. It felt like driving wild animals to their death. It felt like driving myself to my death.

My dad has said that I have driving in my genes, thanks to him. My younger sister and brother both got their licenses at sixteen. But I hate the way my brother drives, like a maniac, or a teenager, which he is.

"Well, he gets it from your mother," said my dad.

"How do you know I wouldn't, then?"

"You're more like me."

According to the National Highway Traffic Safety Administration's 2006 data, Asians experienced a rate of 4 motor vehicle fatalities per 100,000 population—the lowest among all ethnicities and races. Whites had a 12.5 per 100,000 fatality rate. The discrepancy between the rates suggests that Asians in this country are no worse drivers than other, and are, possibly, the safest drivers. Then again, this data only really states that Asians do not die as often in car accidents, whether we are bad drivers or not.

In Urban Dictionary, "asian driver" is given its own lengthy definition with thousands of up-votes:

this is being posted as a public service, learned from years of experience.
some other sure signs that can help you spot an asian driver are
    1 they make a left turn from the right lane
    2 both hands on wheel in death grip
    3 head never moves from straight ahead posistion ex: like
checking mirrors
    4 red and gold thing with tassels hanging from rear view mirror,
blocking yet even more of thier already severly limited field of view
    5 flower pattern seat covers and doillie things near rear window
    6 NUMEROUS dings scrapes and dents on bumpers and doors,
tire sidewall is completely scrapped off. this is caused by MANY
botched attempts st parrallel parking
    if ever involved in accident with asian driver, be forewarned . . .
they will not speak english.
    Quoted with its racism and xenophobia and typos and all.

I watch him drive. He looks calm. His lips are closed, but a little slack at the corners. He looks like a man who knows what he's doing and doesn't have to think about it. He looks like he's meditating with his eyes open. His dark, dark eyes. Dark like a well, the pupil drowned out. Framed by those long, dark lashes and strong eyebrows. The sun gives his auburn stubble a pretty glow. He's so good at driving, it's like watching somebody who is scared of nothing at all. He is beautiful.

    I reach over and clasp his upper arm between my hands.

    He looks over. "What?" he says.

    "I'm sorry I got mad. I just don't like driving."

    "That's pretty obvious," he says, and smiles.

What I am is an excellent directions woman. I point and say, Turn here, exit there. He is the one who drives but does not listen, or at least does not comprehend, until I yell, Here, here, here, more frantically jabbing the air. He is also the one who swerves and goes, "Ha ha, see, no problem. We made it!"

Our high school friend Becca, who does not yet have a boyfriend despite her Tinder matches, works on the socks team at a clothing company. She is in charge of creating the graphics files for dozens of sock designs, ensuring each pair matches its designated style and color in the database, that the file containing said pair of socks is the correct size and format. Her bulldog bites the toes of men's shoes while the shoes are on the men's feet. That's what he does to J when we stop in at her apartment.

"Bad dog," J says, shaking his foot, only further enticing the dog to bite.

"Good boy," say Becca and I, patting the dog's butt, laughing.

"I'm not sure I like it here," Becca says of her life in Portland. "All I do is work these annoyingly long, tedious days. And I hate the people at work. They only care about their image, they're all, 'The last time I went to Tokyo this' and 'Cool whiskey bar that, have you been?' And I'm like no, I'm not fucking made of money! They all dress a lot better than me, too. Everything's *vintage* or made by some *local* designer, which just means *expensive*. And not to be harsh, but it's like, their entire existence is made for Instagram! It's making *my* life miserable."

She takes us on a tour to eat the best doughnuts and the best biscuit breakfast sandwich and the best ramen and the best pizza in Portland, and quite often the world, according to the advertisements in the dining establishments' windows.

In the middle of the night, on the air mattress in Becca's living room, J swings his arm onto my shoulder, waking me up. I push him off and tell him to stop, but he appears deep in sleep, an innocent. His mouth is open, his eyes slide side to side behind his eyelids. I move closer to him and watch him breathe. I bring my fingers to his chest and lightly graze the hair there. Where are you? What are you dreaming?

He wriggles and mumbles nonsense.

"What is it?"

"Those moves are very good."

I repeat: "What? Where are you?"

"Where are I?" he says.

His pillow is on the floor. I pick it up and move it to his head. Eyes closed, he grabs the thing and shoves it between his legs, then smiles gigantically.

While J goes mountain biking in the hills, Becca tells me she's read a novel by a Chinese American writer about growing up Chinese American in Massachusetts during the 1970s. I remind her I have also read the book and was the one who recommended it to her.

"Is that what it was like for you in high school?" she asks.

"Not really. I mean it was the 2000s, so . . . but yeah, there were similarities."

"Wow. I feel like I know you so much better now."

She tells me that Asians have it really bad—*the worst*—in her opinion. I can't tell if she is saying this to pander to me for the suffering she thinks I may have experienced in high school as her friend, unbeknownst to her, and that I may still experience today, or if she really believes what she's saying. Whatever it is, I tell her she is wrong. Or, it's more complicated than that. First of all, there are differences between the experiences of East Asians and Southeast Asians and South Asians. As for me, East Asians have it pretty good.

Being light-skinned. The model minority myth. Though used as a tool against other races, it just goes to show how East Asians have privileges. Etc., etc.

But, she says, her family in Ohio really, really dislike Asian people. Like the time she took her cousins to San Francisco's Chinatown, they wouldn't shut up about how disgusted they were by it all—the people, the food, the smells, the cheap trinkets—isn't that really terrible?

I say yeah, that's racist. Your cousins sound racist.

She nods enthusiastically. She hates her cousins. She says they're terrible people.

But, I say, the Chinese in America don't typically face police brutality. And we have high rates of college attendance, low rates of incarceration, no history of enslavement.

But, she says, she's never really seen firsthand as bad of racism as how her cousins behaved toward Asians in Chinatown.

It feels like we are doing a sort of dance, the steps for which I cannot and do not want to master, so I end it by retreating to the conversations I know how to have, and am left with a nagging sense of having failed at something.

In high school my closest friends were a group of seven white girls who, amazingly, called themselves the Milk Club. I was not allowed in the Milk Club. Not, as far as I could tell at the time, for racial reasons, but for sociohistorical ones. They had formed the club in the seventh grade and I did not know all of them until tenth. There were never new members. Too, the name did not have overtly racial origins, but practical ones, since each girl got a carton of milk at lunch. It's a catchy name, with a strong ring—I have to admit, their branding was powerful. Everyone knew of the Milk Club. The name itself had cachet and hype. It is surprising to me that none of them have gone on to be famous, or at least social media stars.

I spent the last two years of high school with the Milk Club, was allowed to partake in their many traditions: sleepovers, dress-up dinners at Denny's, Secret Santa, extensive listicle- and chart-making. (But not the notebook—from the official written document, I was excluded.) At one of those sleepovers, the topic of my going to China for a couple of weeks came up. The host's mom was in the room with us. Why are you going to China?, she asked. Her family is from there, the girl replied. They are?, the mother said. She appeared genuinely confused. Her brow furrowed; she stared at me, an examination. Then came the apology. I'm sorry, I never saw you as Asian until just now! We all had a good laugh about it. I felt a kind of relief. I had passed, been accepted, blended in—at least with this one woman. It took a few minutes for the initial shame to kick in. Then years for it to curdle inside me, mixed with other instances like this, to really make me sick.

Andrea Freeman writes in her journal article "The Unbearable Whiteness of Milk: Food Oppression and the USDA": "Early milk promoters associated the whiteness of milk with the putative purity of racial whiteness. . . . An agricultural history of New York from the 1930s asserted: 'A casual look at the races of people seems to show that those using much milk are the strongest physically and mentally, and the most enduring of the people of the world. Of all races, the Aryans seem to have been the heaviest drinkers of milk and the greatest users of butter and cheese, a fact that may in part account for the quick and high development of this division of human beings.'"

The people I used to work with have gifted us several audiobooks so we can better pass the time. J wants to listen to a zombie apocalypse novel. No matter how hard I try to pay attention, I become drowsy. The characters' voices sound relaxed and bored, like they are giving a lecture on how to file taxes rather than recounting global horrors. *Malnutrition, pollution, the rise of previously eradicated ailments* . . . I fall asleep within minutes. I cannot stay awake for this end of the world.

For the last several years I have said to him that I do not ever want to be pregnant. It's not that I don't like children. I love them. I want to adopt. There are so many babies who need homes that it doesn't make sense to me to make another baby of our own. Truthfully, the impulse was selfish at first. I don't want to carry anything in my uterus, and I don't want my body to blow up and my bones to lose density, and I absolutely don't want to deal with the pain of giving birth and the possibility of my vagina tearing into my asshole.

After speaking to scientists working at a showerhead company, of all places, who said my generation's children would likely be the generation to deal with the apocalypse, I felt more justified in my not wanting to bring any more babies into the world. I can't tell others to do the same, and I am happy to raise some of their children to have the wherewithal to make it through a world on the brink of annihilation. Who knows how exactly yet, since I'm fairly certain I would be among the first to go in an apocalyptic situation. I don't know how to do anything except think and talk. I am legally blind without my contacts or glasses. I can walk relatively fast for extended periods of time, but I can barely run. My only postapocalyptic survival skill is being with J. So when he looks a little teary, and very upset, at my no-baby ranting, I stop and say, Who knows. I could change my mind. It is changing all the time.

Between our appetizers of wings and our entrees of tall burgers and onion rings, I notice that all the other couples in the four booths lining the wall of the diner are Asian/white—Asian woman, white

man. My awareness of our likeness to the other couples shakes
me out of whatever we had been discussing. I tell him to look.
He laughs, ha ha, like it's a happy coincidence. It seems to be more
than that, and more sinister. It troubles me that others who look at
us, for example, the waitstaff, might think so too.

This isn't the first time. The racial matchup was so common in
San Francisco, it was easier to ignore, unless, that is, we had to
walk directly by a pair where the man had the exact same coloring
as J, the pale skin and the brownish hair, both with a tint of red.
And this did happen more than once or twice. At least five times. I
would grip his arm and glance at the man, then the woman—who
sometimes, but not as often, in my opinion at least, would look
very similar to me—then back at the man. I would push J along
in order to pass faster, to distance ourselves faster. I didn't like to
think about how our relationship, which I felt was singular, could
be lumped into a "type." Then there was the eerie feeling that
came with seeing a mirror couple, the questioning of how they
came to be, if their lives were parallel to ours, if their experiences
were similar, and whether one of us could be swapped with the
other without anyone noticing a difference.

I ask if he's listening and he says yes, though he has not said anything in response. This is one of his worst qualities, the way he
chooses silence in certain conversations, so not only do I feel idiotic and crazed, like I'm talking to myself, I also have to do the
work of speculating what he's thinking.

"I don't know," he says.

"What don't you know?"

Another annoying silence.

"I guess I don't get why it's bothering you so much now," he
finally says.

"I'm not *bothered*," I say. "I'm just thinking about it right now and I'm explaining to you what I'm thinking and how I feel. There are so many Asian-woman-white-man couples, and it's like, why? Are all of the white men fetishizing the Asian women? Or are Asian women more prone to dating white men, and why? Or something else? Why don't we ever find ourselves in a place with all Asian-man-white-woman couples? Or Asian-woman-black-man couples? Or black-woman-white-man couples? Or Latina-woman-Asian-man couples? Or—"

"Maybe you just notice them because you're Asian and I'm white," he says. "Maybe they just love each other and race doesn't have anything to do with it."

I burst out with fake laughter. "Yeah, right. Sure."

"Okay," he says.

"What?"

"I don't know," he says. "I don't really want to talk about this anymore. I want to listen to this book."

"Fine then," I say.

J taps the phone screen for another chapter of the apocalypse— *The human mouth is packed with bacteria, even more so than the most unhygienic dog*—and I fall asleep, frustrated.

I'll take this out for you. That was our line as *courtesy clerks*. I'd gotten the job, at fourteen, thanks to a stubborn persistence. After packing the food into paper bags and placing them into the cart, no matter what: Here, I'll take this out for you. It was to be presented as a statement, not a false offer but a genuine commitment, to lift the burden of having to answer a half-hearted question off of the *guest*. Still, there were certain conditions where we expected a No, it's all right, or an I can handle it, or No need, or I'm okay. And this was one such condition: a husband and wife, of able body, shopping together. And yet they smiled with all of their teeth. They let me push the cart out for them.

The husband chatted nonstop, about the dry heat and whatever else was on his mind. It was summer in the Central Valley and I was sweating in a dark purple polo and black slacks, grocery uniform. The wife walked several paces ahead down the parking lot.

"Do you go to Davis High?" the man asked. "My son's a sophomore there. His name is David ——. Do you know him?"

"I'm a sophomore, too," I said. "But I don't think I know him."

"He's a bit of a nerd, antisocial type," he said. "Takes after his mother more than me." He waved toward his wife's back. "I tried to get him to play sports, but he wouldn't have it. Sits in front of his computer all day, doing God knows what, *boo bee bloo beep*." The man cracked himself up. I laughed a little, too, out of customer service duty. "You're a nice girl," he said. "I'd really like you to meet my son."

I thanked him and said I would ask my friends if they knew David. This was my job. Be courteous and kind to the *guest*.

"Terrific," he said as I loaded the groceries into the trunk of his car. His wife sat in the passenger seat. The man stood watching me. It was my job, but there were also certain conditions where I anticipated help, and this was one of them. None was provided. I shut the trunk, and the man said, "Great talking. Keep my son in mind. I'd really like to find him a nice Oriental girlfriend, and you fit the bill."

He got into his car. I pushed the cart back to its bay next to the store, slamming its metal body against its identicals.

Somebody once asked me to identify the emotions that most strongly affect my life and the actions I do or don't take. I couldn't name them at the time, but now I've thought more about the question. Here is the answer I've come up with: revenge and regret and fear and guilt.

When I wake up, there is tea. We are at a Starbucks drive-through window.

"All rested, sleepyhead?"

He offers me the cup.

"No being grumpy on our fun road trip, Jing Jing."

He smiles wide and squinty-eyed. He is smiling more often than not. But he really does have the sweetest smile, all big and genuine; it almost convinces me that he's right. At the very least, I can forgive him his wrongs.

The only way to remain awake is to listen to music or look at people driving around us. Since he is well into the book, I stare out the window. I look for couples. Are they having fun? Where are they going? Are they having their own little disputes? (*No farting with the windows up! It is my strong belief that men should wear shorts only when working out, never else! You always forget to pack the important shit, like napkins!*) Or how about that lone woman, in the lane over, with her window down, swaying her head and shaking her shoulders to the booming sounds of some song. I can't hear the music exactly, since our windows are up. But the bass beats pulse toward us, heavy and fast. She looks around fifty—in a yellow tank top, tanned arms. She catches me looking at her and exaggerates her dance moves in my direction. I laugh. She waves her hand out the window. I wave back, then she speeds past. I wish I could know where she's headed.

Ithaca will be the farthest from California he's ever lived. In fact, he's never lived anywhere else. Same with me, except when my family moved from San Francisco to Shanghai for two years. That's when my dad stayed behind. But that was different in many ways. It was China. I was a child. I didn't understand anything and I was highly adaptable.

The China I remember most is like this:

The apartment in Pudong. The tadpoles had sprouted legs, which meant they needed to be tossed. My sister and I poured them into the alley gutter, crying for the lost swimmers. There were too many. They drained away with the waste.

A woman held her baby, her arms outstretched, pleading and repeating to those who passed: Please take her. My mother watched from the window five stories up. She petted my brother's head and said, Would you like a little sister today?

In summer, the air was thick and heavy, the dragonflies flew low by our thighs. It was enough to smother the wails of our losses. The alley was empty of people at night.

Back then, I didn't understand the reasons for either—our departure or his staying put. For years, my mom said it was because she missed home and family. My dad said it was because he had to take care of things and to work. When we returned, he no longer had a car repair shop and we no longer had a house. They took us to an unknown town, Davis, and said here's where we'll live. We accepted because we had no choice. The explanations and stories shifted based on time and speaker. Money. Business mistakes. Greedy relatives. Lawsuits. Separation. Stress. Her mistakes. His mistakes. I still don't know what truly happened, but at this point, does the truth really matter.

As for Davis, the beginning was not great. The sixth grade teacher introduced me as an immigrant from China. Though it was not entirely true, neither was it entirely false. I didn't correct her. My sister and brother were placed into ESL classes until they could distinguish between "a stove" and "an oven," though our mom never used the latter. The teachers made them name never-eaten dishes on a cartoon Thanksgiving table. I seemed to escape the classes out of age and luck, but none of us could escape Davis. It reminded me of the movie *Pleasantville,* of that 1950s TV town Tobey Maguire's character escapes to. A made-up place in a made-up movie, far removed from my experience. I cried often in the first weeks; I wanted to go back—to San Francisco, or even China seemed like a better option at times. I fell asleep fantasizing about what life would have been like somewhere else.

One of my junior high teachers once said in class, Davis is full of the kind of liberals who claim they want to make the world a better place, but who will fight to the death to prevent a homeless shelter from being built in their neighborhood.

Davis, too, was the place of my family's tectonic shifts. Divorce. Poverty. Domestic disputes. Charged, simple terms I hated, still hate, to use to describe those days. But I'm getting used to them. Both their ability to quickly summarize and their inability to capture beyond a shallow essence.

But Davis is where I met and found J, who is listening intently to this story of his. *Fear is primal. Fear sells. That was my mantra.* "Fear sells."

I hit pause on the phone. "What's this guy talking about? What's happening now in the book?"

"He's selling a vaccine," he says.

"For what?"

"For—wait, do you really want to know? Should I explain everything you've missed? Are you going to listen now?"

"Uh . . ." I think for a while. "No, I guess not. It only sounded interesting for a second."

"It is interesting! I wish you'd stay awake and listen to it with me."

"No, no, it's okay. I don't want to." I press play again and go back to staring out the window or sleeping.

In Montana there are big mountains and fast-driving semis. I remember something a friend who grew up in the countryside once told me: If you want to fit in with rural people, wear camo. So much of it in Montana. At a highway rest stop we see a family of close to a dozen, various ages, each wearing at least one piece of camo. A teenage girl with her ponytail looped out the back of a camo baseball cap. A little boy in camo shorts. One man in a camo T-shirt, another in a camo button-up. A woman in a camo zip-up jacket. An old man and woman—grandparents—in matching camo sweatpants, and so on.

There are two opposing reasons animals in the wild have camouflaging abilities, a pop-science article tells me. One is to go unnoticed while hunting. The other is to hide in order to avoid being caught. When a tawny frogmouth senses danger, it fluffs out its feathers, freezes, and looks like a broken tree branch. Aristotle long ago noticed that the octopus "seeks its prey by changing its colour as to render it like the colour of the stones adjacent to it."

As we travel deeper into the country, how best to hide myself? Will J's presence provide a sufficient cloak? Where and when and how will who or what come out to attack?

He turns twenty-six. We celebrate at what looks like the fanciest restaurant in Butte. A group of men in suits sit at the table behind us, talking about regulations and meetings and numbers. There is thin green carpeting throughout. The candles on the table are fake.

J says he has a fantasy about us one day retiring to the Montana mountains. He grew to love the area after his family's vacations here during his childhood. All day they hiked, swam, and fished. All activities I am not wholly against. But I can't imagine living in Montana, at all, ever. Or, rather, I strongly dislike my imagination of living in Montana.

"I want to say nice things because it's your birthday, but I'm never living in Montana."

"Why not?"

"How many Asians do you think there are? Like none?"

He looks it up on his phone. "Says here that Asians make up zero-point-six percent of the population. So no, I guess it wouldn't be that fun for you."

"Zero. Point. Six." I glance over at the men eating behind us.

"And you don't like the outdoors much, either."

"It's not the outdoors that are the main problem, although yes. I'm not in love with this whole camping, living-on-the-ground thing—but it's cheaper for the trip, so whatever."

Another drawback: tent sex needs to be very quiet so as not to disturb neighboring tent sleepers. But all of these camping materials—what were they thinking?—with the smallest of movements, the stuff produces the loudest, scratchiest noises.

I know this much about driving: It is not okay to close your eyes while on the highway, or under any circumstance, really, but I'm not behind the wheel, so the rule need not apply.

We don't only date white men and women. But we are only dating white men and women right now. My sister is with a tall man with fluffy brown hair and a significant nose. My brother is "talking to" a rock climber with cropped blond hair. They are both young, so I think maybe they might not actually end up with a white person. Me, on the other hand, I have been with J for my entire adult life, and here I am in this car, so it seems that I will end up with him, a white man. J does not like that, again, I'm pointing this out.

"It's as if being white is the one thing that defines me," he says.

"Well, it's definitely a *big* part of what defines you," I say.

He used to wear a shirt that had a stylized logo of the words STOP RACISM! printed on the chest. I told him to stop wearing it. It made me very uncomfortable to be seen with him when he was wearing the shirt, and even if I was not with him, the thought of him being seen in that shirt at all made me uneasy. I couldn't explain why and I still can't quite explain it. Maybe I was worried that people would think he was with me because he was trying to stop racism? Maybe I was worried he was actually dating me to stop racism? Maybe it had to do with me knowing he would never stop racism by wearing a shirt that said STOP RACISM? Anyway, he can't wear the shirt anymore because I threw it out when we moved in together. The act was a relief at the time. Now I feel mildly guilty for tossing something he liked, and with not at all a bad message.

It's not that I didn't think of our races when we first got together. Or haven't thought of our races since. Of course I did and have. At first they were ghostly thoughts. Really, he wants me? How could this be? Why not her or her or her? Or is it *because* I'm—so ghostly was that thought it could not be completed. Those weren't our problems. He wasn't like that. We fell in love like young people do for the first time—fast, reckless, absolutely, and hard. But unlike most, we remained in love. In college, I made a list of all the couples we knew who believed they would stay together. I crossed each one off after they broke up. We are the last ones left.

When we talked about race, we did so mostly from a distance or as a joke, like something that could not touch the depths of this combined entity that was "us." But I know we do not and cannot exist outside of it. I know I am guilty of avoiding, or not completing, the conversations. That might still be our problem.

From an OkCupid FAQ:

Q: Are you saying that because I prefer to date [whatever race], I'm a racist?

On an individual level, a person can't really control who turns them on— and almost everyone has a "type," one way or another. But I do think the *trend*—that fact that race is a sexual factor for so many individuals, and in such a consistent way—says something about race's role in our society. . . .

. . . you can actually look at people who've combined "white" with another racial description. Adding "whiteness" always helps your rating!

My sister once dated a ginger. A real serious ginger, bright orange hair and skin a landscape of freckles. J's mom saw her and her boyfriend walking downtown together in our hometown when they'd come back for a winter break. After spotting them, she called J and said, "Those girls love gingers!" When he told me this, I responded, "You're not a ginger, are you? You're just very pale."

There is a long line of cars attempting to enter Yellowstone. We sit in ours from way behind, confused, craning our necks to see what's taking so long, until finally, we spot them: the bison. Giant creatures walk along and across the road, at least seven of them, slow and plodding. Wild and closer than the ones we'd seen tucked away in Golden Gate Park. We approach with caution. One gets so close on J's side, he could open the window, stretch himself out to touch the beast.

"They're huge," he says. "Huge and scary and gross and magical."

"Don't touch. Keep the window closed," I say.

Their fur is matted and dreadlocked, falling off in patches. They are unkempt and free.

We are in front of bubbling yellow ponds. It smells of sulfur all around us.

"We're in the land before time," he says. "Let me get a photo of you. Pretend like you're falling in." I do and he laughs.

"You know that's the title of those cartoon dinosaur movies."

"Then we're in a cartoon dinosaur movie. Look at how cute you are in this picture. I think it's my favorite picture of you ever."

"No! I look gross. I haven't showered in four days!"

"Even better," he says. He leans in and takes a huge, disturbing sniff of my dirty hair. "I love the way you smell."

Yes, waiting can be rewarding, sometimes. I forget. Old Faithful is one example, even with the huge crowds encircling the geyser's hole and the sun bearing down on us. (J burns immediately.)

"Any minute now," says a father to his daughter.

"But you've been saying that forever!" she cries.

She's not wrong. Compared to a grown man who has spent many more minutes alive, ten minutes would feel like much longer—possibly even like forever—to a small child.

Wow, wow, wow, everyone says together when the geyser blows and a thousand photos are taken.

Wall Drug, we see the signs for miles. As the billboards increase in number, and the distance in miles on them drops, our excitement grows.

REFRESHING! FREE ICE WATER and HAVE YOU DUG WALL DRUG and THE EXPERIENCE . . . PRICELESS, they announce.

"We *have* to go," I say, and J agrees.

We are suckers for the ads, our anticipation built up so high that when we park alongside the long, low building with its awning of brown shingles and bright yellow wind flaps, it looks like a castle of mystery and intrigue. I hate ice water. And yet I want ice water.

The place is packed with Western kitsch and tourists speaking different languages—Japanese, German, Mandarin, French are the ones I recognize. The halls are lined with photos of Wall Drug devotees and their signs, staked across the globe, painted with the number of miles from wherever they stand to this destination.

J orders a vanilla soft serve and it melts down his hand. He licks at the escaping droplets. He puts a cowboy hat on my head. "Perfect," he says. He tries one on himself, but it doesn't fit. Almost no hats fit him, his skull too long from frontal bone to back, so they look like they float slightly above him. He tries on more hats. His freaky skull provides ample entertainment. In the backyard we climb a gigantic dinosaur play structure and take a photo with a plastic Mount Rushmore replica. It looks so real that we do not regret having skipped the faces carved into the Black Hills. How could it be more fun than what we just had?

Nothing but fields for miles. Over the car speaker someone says *Because Americans worship technology. It's an inherent trait in the national zeitgeist.* I take twenty photos of him looking out at the middle of the country. Then close-ups of his face, of the hair growing down his neck, of his thick forearms, of his hands on the wheel, of his skinny calves leading to feet against the gas pedal.

"Why?" he asks. "Is it for that thing you're making?"

"Yes," I say, even though at first it was not.

Bugs smash into the window and grill and the RocketBox on the roof—the whole face of the car is deeply freckled in yellows, blacks, greens, and grays. At a gas station I try to squeegee the splattered bug bodies away, but many won't budge, glued on by the sun's heat.

"Looks like you've been traveling a long way, little lady," says a deep voice.

I see the man at the pump next to me. He is thick and tall and ruddy.

"Yeah, ha ha ha ha."

"Looks like you need a hand with that." He takes a step toward me.

"Ha ha, no, I'm okay! Ha ha." I grip the squeegee handle. Would this work as a weapon?

"Little lady, I—"

J walks up with two Snickers bars and a gigantic bottle of water.

"What're you laughing about?"

The man retreats and waves at J. "Nice car you've got!"

"Okay," says J. I get into the car. J stands outside watching the man pull out of the gas station, then he gets back inside.

"That guy was weird. What'd he say that was so funny?" J asks.

"Nothing was funny."

Why do I laugh, then? Out of discomfort. Better yet, defense. I add it to my short list of survival skills. If you make people believe you're strong and comfortable enough to laugh in the face of danger, maybe then they won't eat you alive.

Here we are on a tiny dirt road that Google Maps insists leads to a campground. There is nothing in sight and it is growing dark.

"Might as well see where this takes us," J says. "An adventure!"

We make more turns down little roads. No cars pass. We see no sign of human life. Along the edges of the pastures are wooden fences, primitive and spare. Any animal could squeeze through, though there is, also, no evidence of animal life.

I start to sweat and my stomach grumbles. I worry something will jump into the path and we'll hit it, or the path will end in a ditch, or we'll get lost and not find our way back out. I feel like I'm in a horror movie. I don't want to get stuck out here.

J says not to worry. He is not worried. Right then the Google Maps app dings and tells us we have reached our destination.

"Where? There? That?"

Beyond is a metal gate blocking off more pasture, which rises up into a hill. At the bottom of the hill are two pickup trucks, one tent, and a gray porta-potty. It is not a campground, as far as I understand campgrounds. It is nothing recognizable.

"I guess we could pitch a tent here?"

"There?"

"Okay, I'll check it out first."

J puts the car in park and gets out. I lock the doors and watch him walk the hundred or so feet to the gate, behind which the trucks are parked. I look at my phone. No signal. How will I reach anyone if something happens to him or to me? Strangers. The wild. The type of strangers in the wild. I look in the glove box for something blunt. A metal flashlight. Knocking on the window. A jolt. J's face. I unlock the doors, then relock them once he's inside.

"You're so paranoid," he says, back in the driver's seat. "It's fine, but definitely a hunting site. It could be fun?"

"Nope, not going to work," I say.

He turns the car around, not without disappointment, and we go to the unadventurous, cookie-cutter KOA we'd previously passed, where there are lots of other people and other cars, and where I relieve myself into a toilet inside a solid concrete structure.

I wake up from a nightmare in some tiny town, South Dakota. I want to call my mother. But it is too late, or too early. So early it is dark, and she is this wide country away from me. This is the most humid night in memory. Mine, at least. Mosquitoes hit their bodies against the tent's mesh window, waiting for breakfast to venture outside. I think about the trip my mom and I took to Yosemite two years ago, just the two of us, a mother-daughter trip. But why did we go to Yosemite? We wanted the natural elements, but we were so out of our own. The whiteness around us put me on edge, as it does now.

I shake J awake.

"It's so hot," I complain.

"Maybe don't use that below-freezing sleeping bag, then."

He doesn't understand that I need the weight of the sleeping bag to protect me from overexposure in these unfamiliar places. Like a dog that needs her tight anxiety jacket when she's around perceived danger.

Some people have hardly suffered in life. Like him, who sleeps so soundly. He's experienced so little external pain. That should be a good thing for a loved one. But then why am I lying here in the dark resenting him for it? Stop with these bad thoughts, I tell myself. Or think of nothing. Or just don't think.

Everybody drives slower in Minnesota. Windmills sprout from all the land. Do the two have anything to do with each other? Anything is possible, but not all is probable, a fortune cookie once told me.

I fall asleep again. This time, when I wake up, the car is pulled over and I can see the red-and-blue whirl of lights in the rearview mirror.

"What—" I begin.

"I was speeding."

The officer comes up to the driver's side window. I gape at him, then wipe the sleep spit from the corner of my mouth. J says, yes, around eighty, we are on a road trip, moving across the country, New York, California, yes.

"Thanks, motherfucker," says J as he rolls the window back up.

"Don't! He might hear you and get mad."

"Whatever. I don't care."

The ticket is for thirty-five dollars—and no points on J's license. Mail in a check by this date. The cop says to have a nice day and drive safe.

"Very sorry, sir!" I say. We watch him drive off ahead of us.

"I fucking hate cops," says J.

"I mean, fine. But you *were* speeding. And you *were* being very antagonistic for no reason. And *look* at how lucky you are."

"Well, if you were awake maybe I wouldn't have sped. Don't fall asleep anymore when I'm driving. It defeats the whole purpose of this trip."

"Well, I'm wide awake now with both eyes on the speedometer."

J glowers at me, then starts driving. The adrenaline from the encounter wears off. I pinch my forearm to keep my eyes open. Still, all I see outside are bland fields.

"I don't care if the dead find me," he says without feeling.

"When we listen to music instead of this book, I stay awake better."

"No. It's almost done anyway."

In Madison we eat fried cheese curds for the first time. Squeak, squeak they go against our teeth.

A white busker on the street yells to J: "Mister, you've got a beautiful wife!"

J replies, "Thank you!" and squeezes me close.

"Do you want dessert? Let's go all out," he says.

"Okay," I say.

"The pot de crème," I tell the waitress.

"What?"

"The pot de crème," I repeat.

"Oh, you mean, the pot de crème," she says, and walks away.

"Wow," I say. "Cool, cool, cool."

"She definitely understood you the first time. What a snob."

When she returns, J says, "Thank you for the pot de crème," in an even worse accent than mine. She smirks. We stifle our laughter.

Day seven and we are making very good time. I've gotten to know this car like I would a person. All its strengths, flaws, and quirks. Some people might not understand its appeal, given its size and shape (big, boxy) but it is, in fact, incredibly practical. It is sturdy, reliable, strong, and it takes us from place to place. The car, I have decided, is very much like J. Minus the big and boxy frame; he is more lithe and triangular.

I get an email from Tim.

Subject line: Shit's hitting the fan here.

Body text: Corey got fired.

I send Corey a text: Are you okay? I just heard.

He doesn't respond.

There are cows and clouds outside, looks like blue skies for days.

J is afraid about one thing during the trip: that his bikes will be stolen. It's not totally unfounded. He's had several of his bikes stolen, because they are worth a lot, worth stealing. Each time we go for a ride in a new place, there is a long process of unlocking and relocking the bikes to and from the car rack. It is a mysterious, intricate process, with many locks, like taking apart and putting together a brainteaser puzzle. I am not to help, because I would not be a help, so instead, I busy my hands with my phone.

Jasmine now:

"So guess the fuck what. There's this new unofficial minority group at work. They get drinks and commiserate about how hard it is to not be a white guy in the office. And they don't even ask me to go with them and I'm, like, one of two women of color left here. *And get this.* Steve is in the group. There's a fucking white guy in the fucking *minority* group."

I am in Illinois. I don't want to care. I am far away from the office, and yet, as Jasmine speaks, I can see it. I can see these people huddling together, whispering, socializing. Leaving Jasmine out, because she's too much for them.

"Why Steve?"

"Didn't you see he came out as bi on Facebook recently?"

"No. So you're not still seeing him?"

"Fuck dating white guys."

"You've said that before," I say.

"This time I mean it. I seriously fucking mean it."

And this time, for the first time, I look over at J and wonder.

After I hang up, he asks, "So, how's Jasmine?"

"Good, good."

"No work drama?" He raises his eyebrows and looks over at me.

"Eyes on the road, buddy," I say. "And, sure, there's always work drama. You really want to hear it?"

"No," he says. "No, I don't."

"Okay, then don't ask."

"Somebody is being moody."

"Yes. That somebody is me."

Why is it bothering you now? One, you have the time. Two, traveling into unknown parts of the country is giving you raw skin and fresh eyes. Like a newborn with sensory overload, but what you're overloading on is this sense of race, the colors that stand out against an increasingly white background. And all you can feel and see is this difference, wary and on edge of what could happen wherever you go. And here beside you is somebody who does not understand.

In kindergarten. The boy who sits across from you, in a fury over your taking a crayon he wanted from the shared crayon bin, says, Your nose is flat and ugly. You're stunned into silence. How have you never noticed this about your nose? It is the first time you see yourself in the eyes of this person, and from then on you are constantly aware of how you might appear in those eyes. Your mom advised: *You* tell him his nose is big and pointy and ugly.

But you didn't. His nose was not, and you were too scared and wounded to retaliate.

Seventh grade history class. Mr. Hannah is teaching Chinese culture from a textbook. He looks only in your direction. You try to look away, but have a habit of holding eye contact with people who look at you. He has a reputation among the students for being creepy, though students say this of many male teachers. Which does not make it any less true, only less of a distinguishing quality.

He decides, midlesson, to improvise. "Tell us about the language," he says to you.

What about the language? You've forgotten so much in the year back.

Him: "How about the words that mean different things but all sound the same?"

You think for a while. "Like, māo and máo? One means 'cat' and the other means 'hair'?"

He goes: "Ha ha ha ha ha! I can't tell the difference. They both sound the same."

The class responds: "Ha ha ha ha ha!"

He says: "You know, Chinese people name their children by throwing pots and pans down the stairs. Ching bong bing chong ding dong."

He goes: "Ha ha ha ha ha!"

The class goes: "Ha ha ha ha ha!"

You go red.

Him: "Isn't that true? What's your Chinese name?"

You say you don't have one.

Him: "Wow, that's too bad. It's sad when we lose touch with our heritage."

He moves on.

What you meant was: You don't have a Chinese name for him

to say or know. You are protecting a piece of yourself from people like him. At home, you tell your mother about what Mr. Hannah said. She is furious and yells that she will call the school to complain. Bring her the phone. She's getting the man fired. You protest. You don't want her to make it worse by drawing it out, by bringing more attention to it; it's already so embarrassing. You want to forget. She listens because you are adamant.

Why, again, hadn't you listened to her?

Then there was the time in high school when a boy asked if all Asian women had black nipples. He said he'd seen it in a porno. That one you didn't tell your mom.

Looking back, I don't know why that guy couldn't have just watched more porn videos featuring Asian women—there are so, so, so many, after all—to locate the answer to his question, instead of asking me. This, I tell J.

"Well, I mean, your nipples aren't black, but they aren't pink," he says.

"That's not the point! And whatever, your nipples are so pink and pale they're practically invisible; you look like one of those nipple-less Barbie dolls," I say.

He sidles up next to me in the tent and says, "Why, thank you."

"I meant it as an insult," I say. But now he's latched onto me, smiling goofily, again.

Maybe there's a sculpture of a wild animal out front—a bear, a moose, a hawk—or maybe there's an American flag, or there could be a parking lot of pickup trucks with bumper stickers with seemingly innocuous statements like CHANGE . . . and WORK HARDER, then upon closer inspection, beneath, YOU MAY LIVE TO REGRET: VOTE NOBAMA and MILLIONS ON WELFARE DEPEND ON YOU, or maybe there's a look on the hostess's face, or the way she says, *Over here,* or possibly there's a room packed full of older white customers eating slabs of meat, or maybe there's a waiter who doesn't come to the table for twenty minutes and the white people seated afterward have already gotten their appetizers, or there's all of this mashed into one place and this makes you feel both incredibly visible and sickeningly invisible at once, both so inside your own body and so outside of it, or maybe it's all nothing, it's all a coincidence, a slip of the mind, a confluence of small signs that don't intentionally mean to add up to anything, certainly not *this.* Maybe it's all in your own head. Nothing exactly terrible happens, and you're back on the road.

Also from Pew:
- Looking at all married couples in 2010, regardless of when they married, the share of intermarriages reached an all-time high of 8.4%. In 1980, that share was just 3.2%.
- About 36% of Asian female newlyweds married outside their race in 2010, compared with just 17% of Asian male newlyweds.
- White/Asian newlyweds of 2008 through 2010 have significantly higher median combined annual earnings ($70,952) than do any other pairing, including both white/white ($60,000) and Asian/Asian ($62,000).
- Mixed marriages involving Asians and whites were even more stable than same-race white marriages.
- More than four in ten Americans (43%) say that more people of different races marrying each other has been a

change for the better in our society, while 11% say it has
been a change for the worse and 44% say it has made no
difference.

Which is to say, the data bodes well for us. But from where does
the data originate? Who agreed to answer the survey? And who
are these people who think it's been better for our society? Like,
how? I, for one, would firmly be in the "has made no difference"
category.

The zombie story is long over. Now we listen to country music
because it's the clearest station on the radio and is fitting for the
drive down the empty I-90.

"What are you thinking about?" I ask J.

"School," he says. "What are you thinking about?"

"Nothing really," I say. "What about school?"

"I'm nervous that everybody is gonna be way smarter than me,
and that I'm gonna fall behind," he says. "Then everybody will
find out I'm dumber than them."

"That's not going to happen," I say. "I'm sure you'll be fine.
You're smart and you work hard."

"I hope so."

When I told people back home that he was going to start his
Ph.D. in biochemistry at Cornell, they said, Wow, he must be a
genius. To avoid appearing cruel, I learned to nod, rather than
laugh maniacally like they'd told a very funny joke.

The laughing was not nice of me.

No, it was not, he agrees.

Real beds make you feel like a real person. I am not built for sleeping in a tent, on the ground, for this many days.

"Please let's get a hotel," I say in South Bend, Indiana.

Atop the scratchy floral bedspread and happy, I turn on the TV, flip through the channels until landing on a familiar episode of *Law & Order*. A woman has been stabbed and murdered. The detectives hunt for a man. J asks if I want to explore. I decline. He goes out into the night. If we were in San Francisco, I'd have to go to sleep by now, and then I'd have to get up early to go to the office. I'd have to write two to four stories about new gadgets. I'd have to avoid thinking about whether the work mattered. I'd have to listen to Jasmine or whoever complain about work. I would have to listen to myself complain about work. Other reporters would cover the important stuff: the Google bus protests, the privacy breaches, the tech tax breaks ruining the city.

It was good we left.

On the TV, the Chinese American psychiatrist says, "You know, most animal species aren't monogamous."

J returns with food from Steak 'n Shake. "These are the blandest fries I've ever eaten," he says. "But oh my god, this burger. And they were the friendliest counter staff ever."

"Can I try some?"

"You said you didn't want anything."

"I just want a small bite, just a taste."

"I knew you'd say that, which is why I got you this."

He pulls a second burger out of the bag.

"I don't need a *whole* one!" But I do. We eat our burgers in bed watching another episode or three of the *Law & Order* marathon, then fall asleep with grease on our breath.

A tech journalist acquaintance texts saying he's heard I've gone freelance. I reply asking where he'd heard.

Is it not true?

well it's not official. who told you?

The rumor mill ;)

It doesn't matter. The point is, am I interested in talking to somebody about a gig for a major social media company that shall not be named? First, I must sign an NDA.

Ok, I text back, curious.

The role is to aggregate and curate stories for a newspaper app they'll soon launch. There are many categories, including ambiguously named ones like Cute, Exposure, Well Lived, and Score. They're hiring a curator for each category and they want to know if I'd be interested in leading Tech.

J and I stop at a coffee shop in a town outside of South Bend so I can do a trial under the instruction of the editorial lead from the media consulting company contracted to manage the app's freelancers. The trial involves me sending him a batch of what I consider the top dozen or so technology stories posted from various sources across the site. It takes half an hour.

The editorial lead emails back: I'm really liking your selections. Are you able to dive in and start doing this on a daily basis, ASAP? And, I guess a less practical but nonetheless relevant question, did you enjoy doing it?

"You're funny," says J, who has been waiting patiently. "We're not even done with our road trip and you're getting a job. But how exactly is this better?"

First, the pay—it is more than what I was earning per hour in San Francisco. The work will take, according to the editorial lead, four to five hours a day, though slightly less on Saturdays, which I will also need to work. But I know I can do it faster and bill for the allotted time. No writing involved. Each day, I must keep an eye on tech news and upload stories into the app. What they want is my ability to distinguish important from fluff, necessary from superfluous, good from mediocre.

Do I enjoy it? It is easy and mindless work. I'll have a source of income as soon as we get to Ithaca. All of this gives me a sense of peace and direction. So sure! I really enjoy it. Sign me up.

Can we go any faster? Can we totally skip Ohio? (I think of Becca's cousins.) Let's arrive a day early to upstate New York. We drive nine hours that day. And by "we," I mean "he." I'm tired of the road. I want the destination. I want to start this new life. None of this journey stuff, the experience, the unknown. I stare out the window, fall asleep, dream of nothing.

"Wake up," he says. "Look." I do. "It's like Gotham or something," he says. "It's so dark and industrial and sad."

The skyline is tall, bleak buildings lit yellow from within. I almost expect gray smoke to rise from their tips and plume into the gray sky, for the clouds to smother the city with rain and lightning. But it is quiet, we watch it pass. It occurs to me, not sadly, that Cleveland is likely a place I will only ever pass and never go.

Durhamville, a tiny Erie Canal town with a population of less than six hundred. It has a post office, a fire department, two churches, an elementary school, and a bar.

"How do people live here?" I ask.

"I was thinking the same thing," he says.

The house is big and old, full of J's relatives, Irish Catholic stock, who are all there for Uncle Bill's ninetieth birthday. Uncle Bill sits in a big brown leather chair, smiling at everyone and giving two thumbs up to all questions. He rarely speaks. A woman goes up to kiss him on the cheek. He smiles, asks, Who are you? Everyone chuckles. With me, he takes my hand in both of his and shakes it gently. In this grasp I feel safe and innocent.

The others I don't know about. Some avoid speaking to or looking at me, but that's okay, because I don't want anybody here to pay much attention, to pick away at the pieces of me that are different. J's parents had warned: Somebody might say something.

I stick to his grandparents, who are visiting from California. While J catches up with long-lost aunts and uncles and cousins, his grandmother takes my arm and leads me away on a tour. The hallways and staircases and rooms seem out of my dreams. One leads to another through narrow halls, small doorways lead to tiny, hidden rooms. Decades-old wallpaper peels at the edges. J's grandmother takes me to Uncle Bill's old bedroom and tells me it is the same as he had left it in his youth. His books and baseball cards and trinkets are on a small desk, looking well kept, with the exception of the dust. Against the wall, a twin bed covered in an old patchwork quilt. I take it in. It is a room that feels mystifyingly familiar. It is a room of the American imagination.

J's grandmother says Uncle Bill has lived here his entire life, only away for a few years at war. "And the last fifteen years he's had to live downstairs due to his mobility," she says.

She takes my hand again, her skin soft and cold. She says, "You can write about this one day."

I clasp her hand back and nod.

J's blood is from this place so inherent, yet so strange, to me.

I have a recurring dream that takes place in my first home in San Francisco. In the dream, my family has moved back into the house without the permission of the new owners. I am whatever age I am in the time of the dreaming. My brother and sister are small children. My parents are still together. I am anxious that we will get caught in the house that is no longer ours, but my dad says that if we stay put, they cannot kick us out. The house is filled with our old furniture, but it has strange hallways and doors I've never seen. I sit in my parents' closet beneath my mother's hanging clothes, like I used to as a kid. Then I remember that we have cats and that nobody has fed them. When I go into the garage, where we keep their food bowls, they come scurrying out from the dark. They are frail gray shadows of their former selves. I curse myself for forgetting them. I pour the kibble into their bowls until it spills over and they eat, ravenous.

What if his grandmother never left Durhamville? What if my parents never left Shanghai? What if his grandfather never left Ireland? What if his mother never left Philadelphia? What if my dad never left New York? What if my mom never left Nashville? What if they hadn't chosen Davis? How many improbable moves did it take for us to reach each other? How many miles? How many decisions made by those before us, to carry themselves from one place to another, from the familiar to the new?

III.

ITHACA

In order to confirm our own existence, we need to take hold of something real, of something most fundamental, and to that end we seek the help of an ancient memory, the memory of a humanity that has lived through every era, a memory clearer and closer to our hearts than anything we might see gazing far into the future. And this gives rise to a strange apprehension about the reality surrounding us. We begin to suspect that this is an absurd and antiquated world, dark and bright at the same time.

—Eileen Chang, "Writing of One's Own"

At first, everything has a hint of the ancient and crumbling. On the way in, we pass an incredible number of cemeteries, littered haphazardly and crowded with old tombstones. Reminders of how long people have lived here, have walked these parts and died in these parts. It is quiet; the living people appear to move slower. The humidity has followed us here and been amplified. It weighs everything down. Through the car window, J points out the sidewalks curbed with long granite slabs instead of the usual cement, an unusual feature I should appreciate. But all of this eventually leads to open-air shopping plazas of big American business: Walmart, Home Depot, PetSmart, Lowe's, McDonald's, etc. The transition from old to new is seamless. Those recognizable corporate names give Ithaca a grander status, as though it's not a college town but a small city. Somebody explained to J, who now explains to me, that people from surrounding areas come to Ithaca to do their shopping. It is the destination for those within an hour's drive, and the people who come down from the hills aren't as "nice" or "cultured" as Ithacans. But to me, upon first glance, it looks very much like the places we passed in the middles of nowheres.

"I'm not going to say you deceived me," I say, half joking.

"No, you'll see. It's going to be great!"

The couple's apartment is modern, clean, and well furnished. The air is thickly sweet. We wander from room to room, turn on all the lights, hold up the framed photos of them—two attractive blonds, always smiling, arms wrapped around waists—in front of trees and mountains and old buildings. We peruse the bookshelves full of self-help and business books, smell the candles left in each room, and test out their mattress. (Just the right amount of give.) On their fridge, in script font against bright colored backgrounds, quote magnets: *Home is where the heart is. (joseph c. neal)* and *Be the change you wish to see in the world . . . (gandhi)* and *What would you attempt to do if you knew you could not fail? (unknown).* I read them to J and we laugh at their cheesiness. A bottle of wine left on the dining room table is accompanied by a note on a piece of mono-grammed paper. *Welcome to Ithaca! Local beer also in the fridge* ☺

"The bathroom is tiny," he reports.

"How bad?" I find him sitting on the toilet in a closet-like room. "At least close the door."

"I'm suffocating now," he cries.

I stand in the living room and examine the put-togetherness of the place. The house oozes its positivity and there is no escaping its reach. "If two grad students can afford to live like this, then yeah, I could definitely get used to it."

"We'll need a bigger bathroom, though," he says from the other side.

"Maybe even two. We can dream big here."

The next-door neighbors appear to be having a party, with porch drinking and pop music. We sit out on our—or rather, the couple's—respective porch, drinking our welcome wine. One of the neighbors waves at us. We wave back. The guy starts walking in our direction, and I wonder if he will invite us over, if it will be that easy in this new place to meet new people, make new friends, settle down. If this is the nature, the advantage, of living in a small town.

The waving guy stops a few paces away. "Oh, sorry. You're not who I thought," he says, then turns around and walks back to his party.

"I was worried for a second," says J.

"You wouldn't want to go?"

"Not really, no. I just want to hang out with you."

"Okay," I say.

We go back inside and into the couple's bed. The strangeness of the space is exhilarating. Afterward, I wonder if it is rude or inappropriate to be using their bed, but then it seems ruder and dirtier to use their couch or floor.

J goes out to run errands and explore while I begin aggregating. I want to explore, too, but I am trapped on my computer. The social media giant wants three batches of articles per day—morning, midday, evening. In between, I am to keep my eyes on the feeds and input "high-impact breaking stories." Today, the biggest tech-related news: Edward Snowden comes forward as the NSA leaker; Apple unveils a slew of new products at WWDC; tech companies deny involvement in NSA's PRISM surveillance system.

In other news: jury selection begins for George Zimmerman's trial; six now dead in gunman's rampage in Santa Monica; a new report (yet another) states record-high carbon levels could result in a disastrous rise in global temperatures. Those I don't input into the channel. They go into the "Fear" part of my brain.

Not Corey on the phone, but Tim, who has now been promoted to deputy editor of both web and print, proving the system does not stop its forward trajectory. I tell him I'm quitting. Or, I mean, I'm going freelance. I have stuff lined up. (The vaguer, the better.) The important part is, I will no longer write for the publication.

"Are you sure?" he says. "I want to do right by you. You know that, right? But the way things are . . ." He doesn't end the sentence. There is no justifiable end and he knows it. We hold a moment of silence for its death. Then I say yes, I am sure. I understand.

"Let me know if I can help in some other way, okay?" he says. "I want you to continue contributing. Whenever you want. Promise you'll keep in touch."

The part about asking for a raise the final time, with Corey, that wasn't exactly true. I was not stoic or firm. I cried, and not a few elegant tears. I shook, had a hard time breathing. I told him I'd been waiting so long, fucking six months and now *they'd* waited me out long enough that I was physically leaving and didn't have leverage. He had his palms on his knees; he nodded down at them. He was ashamed, but of my outburst or its cause, I don't know.

Jasmine told me she'd heard what happened, which means, of course, Corey told people. They all think I'm weak now. All the effort to hold it inside, wasted. I don't want to work with people who think I'm weak. Even Tim. We were being polite with one another, when both of us know that I'm going to ghost.

At night, J falls promptly asleep, naked and sticky with sweat. I am awake, staring at the ceiling, telling myself, What's done is done is done is done. But the wet heat is unbearable. I get up and go into the kitchen, turn on all the lights. I open the refrigerator and freezer doors, then lean into the cold. With my phone propped against a box of frozen corn dogs, I swipe through people's former lives until I am shivering, until I have forgotten where I am.

Day three and I have barely left the couple's apartment. In bed, tunneled into my laptop when J returns.

"Hello?" he calls from the front door. "How's the work going?"

"It's boring as hell," I call back.

I get out of bed to greet him. I remember I have legs.

He is carrying several full grocery bags into the kitchen. "How do you feel about burgers for dinner?"

"Burgers are a thing I don't yet feel bored with. You know what? Hell is, probably, at least, interesting. This work is as boring as the I-90 in the middle of the country."

"Sad," he says as we put away the food he's bought. "I thought that might happen."

"Why didn't you save me from myself? Why didn't you tell me not to do this?"

"But you wanted to take it, so I thought you'd like it."

"What? You just said you thought I wouldn't."

"I really have no idea what I was saying, I was just saying stuff like usual."

I laugh. He tells me about the places he's seen in Ithaca, how beautiful it is now that it's not frozen and covered in snow like it was during his interview, how the DMV is miraculous with no wait time, how he wishes I could go out with him. Soon, I say. Once I get the hang of this work, I'll be able to step away.

"And it's not that bad, really. I just feel like a sellout. But at least I'm going to make money. How else am I supposed to survive?"

"You can always ask me for money." He wraps his arms around me from behind. "I'm getting my summer stipend soon, and it's coming in a lump sum!"

I swat him off. "It's too hot for touching in this place. And no, I can take care of myself."

"We take care of each other," he says, and smiles.

We take an evening walk to one of the downtown waterfalls a few blocks away. Another defining feature of this place: all the water—the lake, the creeks, the gorges—and its proximity to everyday life. Here, it is raging, loud and white against dark rock cut jagged and deep from millennia. The sound of it is overpowering. The mist cools our faces.

"This isn't boring!" I yell over the water's crash.

What if I had my own channel? It could be called: "Some Snippets of Asian America" or "Pickings from a Particular Past" or more plainly, without alliteration, "What I Found in My Searches." Maybe I should have listened to my dad long ago: the past offers answers for the present and future. That's what I want from it. And to fend off this sense of restlessness, that's what I will do. I will aggregate in parallel. An ambiguous, one-word title could be: "Distractions."

For example, here, from *Asian American Society: An Encyclopedia:*
Just as white male desire for black women operated as an undercurrent to race relations during the pre–Civil War period, white male desire for Asian women helped change attitudes about interracial marriage. Of course, complexities and differences abound. In the case of white-black relations, attitudes slowly and unevenly changed in spite of the desire of many in power to maintain the status quo of sexual access and property accumulation. In the case of white-Asian relations, attitudes began to change because enough of those in power wanted to facilitate access. In her study of anti-miscegenation laws, Peggy Pascoe argues that legislation following World War II adapted to suit the desires of returning U.S. soldiers who wanted to marry women that they met while serving in Japan, Korea, and other Asian nations.

And this, a pamphlet from the Chinese American Citizens Alliance in 1926, the time of the Chinese Exclusion Act:

It is a well-known fact that the Chinese male population of this country far outnumbers the Chinese female population and that the Chinese male resident here, desiring to marry, must in most cases go to China to seek a wife of his own race, the number of Chinese female residents here being too restricted to supply the demand. Such being the conditions obtaining, under the law as it now stands, most of our Chinese-American citizens must of necessity remain unmarried or if electing to go to China, there to marry, must either give up their residence and virtually give up their citizenship here or live separate and apart from their wives, who are debarred from admission to the United States under section 13 of the immigration act of 1924.

The only solution of the problem, the immigration act remaining unamended, would be the marriage of the Chinese-American citizen resident here to a woman not of his own race, and this is not only undesirable and inadvisable from the viewpoint of both white and Chinese, but contrary to the laws of persons of the Mongolian race being prohibited in the States of Arizona, California, Idaho, Missouri, Utah, Wyoming, Mississippi, Oregon, Nebraska, Texas, and Virginia.

The first night of chess, with the couple's glass set, he won three games in a row, after which I gained a sense for the game, developed a strategy, and beat him. I continue to beat him and each round moves faster. On the fourth night he throws up his hands and quits. He says, "This isn't fun anymore. You're crushing me."

The face of a Chinaman is matter-of-fact and stolid. There is no flash of fancy nor gleam of imagination. But there is intelligence; curiosity and ingenuity are seen in every feature.
—L. T. Townsend, *The Chinese Problem*, 1876

In tech news: Apple executive testifies in court that the company did not collude with publishers in setting e-book prices; Google to use high-flying balloons to provide internet to remote areas; Edward Snowden in Hong Kong, says U.S. spied on Chinese civilians.

Whenever the phone cuts out, which is often, I call my dad back. When I blame it on the calling card, he says, No, something must be going on. They're probably listening. They're monitoring us. When I ask who, he says, The Chinese government, the NSA, who knows who else. He's a person of particular interest to them.

In other news: Rupert Murdoch files for divorce from Wendi Deng. Plus, much more horrible events I am avoiding.

A long time ago, my mom showed me an image of Wendi Deng with her two young daughters, a baby in her lap and a toddler by her side.

"What took you so long?" she asked. She had been calling my name from upstairs, while I had been in my room typing aggressively into AIM chat boxes. I was fifteen. I was busy.

"I was doing homework," I said.

She was lying in bed with the magazine and pointed at the woman on its cover. "This woman is very, very smart," she said. "Do you know who she is?"

"No." I examined her wide mouth, her large white teeth. The daughters looked lighter, their hair a cardboard brown. "Some rich Chinese lady?"

"Yes, she is very rich. She married a very rich man. Rupert Murdoch. Do you know who that is?"

"No."

"Would you do that? Would you marry a really rich white man?"

"Hmm. Maybe, if I liked him." I had a crush on a white boy who played bass in a band, and whom I was certain I would love forever as long as he continued to play in said band and invite me to his shows. But I was also still in love and AIM chatting with a Korean American boy from science camp, who at the summer's-end talent show had sung and played church songs on his guitar. It seemed, above all else, that I needed to be with a musician.

"She met him when she was a low-level employee," said my mom. "And then she married him. What is that called? She was very ambitious. Very strong in will. Opportunistic. Some of these Chinese women are very opportunistic. They see what they can get and they do whatever to get it. Now you see she lives a really good life."

"With a really old, ugly man." My mother had turned to a spread of Wendi and Rupert, side by side, him wrinkly and age-spotted, her lithe and radiating glamour.

"He will die and she will have everything."

I hugged and kissed her. "Don't worry, Mommy. I'm so smart, I'm going to be the rich one," I said.

"Ha ha, yeah. That sounds good, too."

I felt no kinship with Wendi Deng. It was the first time I'd heard the adjective "opportunistic" used to describe a person. It seemed to have a slightly sour connotation, the way my mom said it, though the more familiar "opportunity" was a word enveloped in the good—seize the opportunity, make your own opportunities, a rare opportunity—having to do with fortune, luck, and winning. Yet being opportunistic, a not entirely positive trait, was paired with intelligence and could lead to a "really good life," and though, even then, I knew it was not a path I would take, I knew, too, that it was not my place to judge what others were willing to do for such a life. There were women I admired and in whom I saw more of myself: during the Olympics, I liked to watch Michelle

Kwan skate; at night, occasionally, it felt special to see Connie Chung anchoring the news. They were, however, all peripheral figures.

Activist Grace Lee Boggs, in response to a question about how being born Chinese affected her outlook on life (from *Hyphen* magazine):

> I think being born a Chinese female helped a great deal to make me understand the profound changes necessary in the world. . . .
>
> Because I was born in the United States, there was more opportunity for women in the United States that was very different from China. And as a result, [my mother] felt very envious of me for the opportunities that I had and this created a lot of tension between us. I don't know whether that exists for Chinese or the Asian families that are coming here to the United States today. So that being born Chinese was not so much a question of being discriminated against because I was Chinese, though there's some of that, but a sense that I had a different outlook on life. I had the idea, for example, from my father that a crisis is not only a danger but also an opportunity and that there is a positive and negative in everything.

Not only a danger but also an opportunity.

I had a similar idea from my father, though I had not thought of it before as particularly Chinese.

It is difficult to parse which parts of me come from my family, from being Chinese, from being Asian American, from being American, from being a woman, from being of a certain generation, and from, simply, being.

It was the German Nietzsche who originally wrote, "Out of life's school of war: What does not destroy me, makes me stronger."

And then its variants made their way into the modern popular lexicon. But even he could not have been the first to have had that philosophy. It is as possible that the idea originated with the ancient Chinese.

Some superstitions passed down from my parents:

    If your ears burn hot, then somebody is thinking of you.

    If you sneeze three times or more in a row, somebody is talking about you. The more sneezes, the more talk.

    Shake your legs while you sit and you shake all the money out of your life's pockets.

    For each grain of rice you leave in your bowl, your future partner will have a freckle or mole on their face. ("But doesn't that mean you both didn't finish your rice, because you have so many? Why is it bad?" "Just finish your rice.")

    Killing spiders is killing your ancestors.

    Don't write in your own shadow. (Consequences unclear.)

    Behave. People are watching you. (Perhaps not a superstition so much as a warning.)

Everybody here wants to give lengthy directions. Drive until you get to [street name], make a left, when you see [landmark] you're about halfway there, then at [another landmark] make a right, which is at [another street name], keep going for a while until you see the house with [mildly distinguishing feature]. We're the house a few doors down from that, at [number][street name], that has the [even less distinguishing feature].

It's okay, I try to interrupt. I can find it, I try again. It's fine, no worries. Until I give up and, not listening, allow them to speak at me. When we get in the car, I enter the address into Google Maps and let it, instead, do the directing.

"It's because not everyone has a smartphone," J explains.

"In what time are we living?"

We come up with the idea for a make-believe blog called *That's So Ithaca*. So far, dentists' offices in houses. How people talk about Wegmans, the grocery store on steroids, as though it is a theme park. A man in a tall hat and cape asking if we want to see some magic. A sedan entirely covered in green ITHACA IS GORGES and ITHACA, NY, 10 SQR. MILES SURROUNDED BY REALITY stickers.

A week in, and it honestly feels like we've already seen it all—it's that small.

"It reminds me of Davis," I say.

"In a good way, right?"

"I mean, it's a little stifling and monotonous."

"But isn't it also quaint and cozy? And there's really good coffee."

He has been putting all of his coffee-making skills to use with local Gimme! beans—maybe even better, he claims, than his favorite beans in San Francisco. Maybe the best. He loves Ithaca already; he fits right in.

On our walk to a nearby apartment, I read to J another one of my finds:

"Did you know that interracial marriage was banned in California up until 1948? That's a year before my dad was born. That's not long ago! And in the western states it was more a fear of Asian men stealing white women. So this article from the *New Republic* says, 'The weirdest aspect of the anti-miscegenation movement that Pascoe documents is the widespread belief that the child of a racially mixed marriage is inferior to the average person of either race. . . . Fear of the "half-breed" seems to have deep roots in human psychology, and to be connected with ata-vistic concerns with "impurity" and the "unnatural" that continue to resonate . . .'

"Et cetera, et cetera . . .

"'It also helps to explain why the first successful post-Reconstruction challenge to the laws did not come until 1948, when the Supreme Court of California, in a case called *Perez v. Sharp*—a suit by a black man and Mexican American woman (classified as white) who had been refused a marriage license—invalidated the state's anti-miscegenation law. By then the eugenics movement had faded, and the political grounds for the anti-miscegenation laws of the southern states did not exist in California, so the court could invalidate the law without worrying about too great a backlash.'"

"Huh, interesting. Who's Pascoe?"

"A history professor at University of Oregon."

"Do you think our kids would have chicken legs like me or thick legs like you or something in between?"

I punch him in the arm. "Be serious."

"No hitting," he says. "But seriously. Eugenics, besides being creepy, doesn't make biological sense. In mouse genetics when you cross two inbred lines, the babies have this thing called 'hybrid vigor,' where they're healthier and stronger than either of the parents. In the old lab, we had these tiny, mean, athletic mice that would try to bite whenever I handled them. And then we had these big, fat mice that were really mellow and nice. When we mated the two, their offspring were these big, strong mice that were pretty nice."

"Okay. But you're equating mice and people."

"Well, that is the basis of modern science. That mice are model humans."

There is a street festival outside. Booths and music. The smell of barbecue. A group of kids on scooters and bikes trails next to us.

I smile at them. Some laugh and ride past. One little girl stops and asks if we want to have some food.

"It's okay, thanks, though," I say. "We have to be somewhere soon."

"Where?" she asks.

"There." I point to a duplex down the street. "We might move into that building."

"Cool! Then we can be friends and play," she says. She bikes away. I tell J that I feel good about living here.

The man from the property management company walks up to us. "To be honest," the guy says, quietly, on the stoop, "this is an iffy neighborhood. I know it's tough to figure out neighborhoods when you're coming from out of town."

"What do you mean?" says J.

"Oh, just that I think you two would be better suited to living somewhere uphill, or on the other side of downtown, like Fall Creek. That's where I live. We can just skip this unit."

I look over at J, who looks at me. We telepathically communicate.

"No, that's okay," I say.

"We'll look at this one," J says.

"You sure? Okay then." The guy, whose whiteness has now become blinding, crosses his arms. "I'll wait out here." Behind him, a banner hangs on the nearby park's fence: CELEBRATE JUNETEENTH!

We walk, quietly, through the unit. I try to like it, but it has been poorly maintained—the carpets look like they haven't been replaced in decades and there are mold stains on the walls. Back outside, the white man says, "What did I tell you? I'll send you our better listings," and hands J his business card.

We walk back through the celebration. J throws the card in a trash bin.

"Let's *not* live in Fall Creek," I say.

"That's where the sublet is; that's where we're living right now," he says.

"Oh," I say. "That's, like, a ten-minute walk away. What the hell."

Is this an Ithaca thing?

> A festival held annually on the nineteenth of June by African Americans (especially in the southern states), to commemorate emancipation from slavery in Texas on that day in 1865.

Back at the couple's apartment, I tap another article, read more. "In essence, Juneteenth marks what is arguably the most significant event in American history after independence itself—the eradication of American slavery," states the *Smithsonian* writer. "Today, 39 states and the District of Columbia recognize Juneteenth, although most don't grant it full 'holiday' status."

"Huh, never heard of it before," says J. "Wonder why we didn't learn about this in school."

And that guy. Is this an Ithaca thing?

No. Of course not. It only feels more acute in conjunction with the place's newness and unfamiliarity.

J turns off all the lights inside the apartment. I ask what he's doing. Just wait, he says. He goes outside and returns with his palms cupped together. He opens his hands and inside is a blinking greenish-yellow dot. The first firefly I've seen in real life. It hovers up into the living room. We coo together as it blinks about. He calls it our magic lightning bug. He is trying to show me what is good here.

And now, just as I am learning how to take longer breaks from this work, he goes. He is one of the few selected for a summer rotation, before most of his cohort arrive. For this, I feel proud, as though his success is partly mine. He starts in a lab that studies how intestines develop their winding shape, using chicken embryos as models. No more mice. I want to remember accurately what he is doing with his days.

"So, you're alone now," says my mom. "How are you?"

"Good. Just working and looking for housing and stuff."

I sit at the couple's big dining table, round, like our old dining room table, but polished and used for its intended purpose. I stare out the kitchen window. In the neighboring backyard, a handyman sands, methodical and slow, a plank of wood. He moves from one end to the other in small circular motions.

"Your new job is good?"

"It's freelancing."

"How much it pays?"

"Thirty dollars an hour, but it's part-time."

"Then is it enough?"

The whir of the sander is muffled by the distance and the walls, but I can see the spray of fine wood dust coming off the plank, gathering in a thin layer on the stone beneath. I want to be that man, the one deeply involved in a singular task.

"Supposedly there are graduate students who support whole families on their stipends."

"You will let him take care of you?"

"No. This job is plenty. It's cheap here. I'll probably even save money."

"It's good, then?"

"It's good because it's easy."

"That's not you, though, taking things easy."

Or I want to be the plank, waiting still and patient to be smoothed out. Or the wood dust, falling away from its former self.

"It could be. I can be laid-back. I can be happy with just this."

"Yeah, right. You? Your boyfriend can help you be a little more laid-back. But you need to keep busy, or else who knows." My mom laughs. I laugh, too, even though I wish she were not right.

"I want to retire when I'm fifty-five, find a nice guy, get a fun side job for a little bit extra money," she says.

"What kind of side job? Isn't your job already fun and easy?"

"Not that fun. Faculty can sometimes be demanding. Why don't you say anything about me finding a guy?"

"I don't know."

"You don't want me to date. You think I have to be with your father."

"That's not true. I don't think you should be with him at all."

The handyman has stopped sanding. He wipes at his forehead with the back of his gloved hand. That is one thing I do not want to be, the dirty glove.

"Have you talked to your father since you got there?"

"Yes, on Father's Day."

"Good. Have you sent him his social security money this month?"

"Yes."

"And he has enough? He's not spending it all on drinks? You should tell him not to."

I have the urge to hang up, or punch something. "Yes, okay? It's all fine."

"Okay, I just want to make sure!"

"You tell me you don't want anything to do with him, but then you ask me all of these questions, and it's very *annoying* to me!"

"Geez, okay, okay."

The handyman has left; he has taken the plank of wood with him. My mom and I both don't say anything for a while, then she asks what I'm having for lunch.

"Frozen corn dogs. Ha ha."

"Yuck. You eat craps when your boyfriend doesn't cook for you, huh? You should cook if you're so bored. Or go for walks. *Exercise.* Hi, yes, you need to email the form. The ID number need—"

"What? Okay, I guess I'm hanging up now. Okay, bye then."

"Can I talk to you later? I'm busy now."

I go through the couple's drawers. There is a handmade scrapbook of the guy as a high school teen. One section is dedicated to photos of him playing water polo. Somebody has written in bold letters captioning them throughout: GREAT SHOT! and THE BIG GUY and ATHLETE OF THE YEAR!!! He looks a lot like J did in high school—chlorine-bleached hair, triangular molded body, sunburned pink skin. I call J, excited about the coincidence of them both being former water polo boys, but he does not pick up. Everybody is busy but me. Or, I am busy, but not in the same way. I spend the next hour, between work, reading a box of old birthday and holiday cards, then I flip through some notebooks on their shelves, though most are blank except for the first few pages of meaningless, irrelevant notes, then I recheck their bathroom cabinets, testing bottles of lotion and perfume, pretending that I am them, living here. Then, I remember that I do. Live here, I mean.

Wafted by wind and steam, the Chinese are pouring into this country as the frogs did into Egypt. Like their prototypes, they not only cover the face of the ground, but find their way into dairies, laundries, and "dough-troughs." But they are not a plague, at least in my opinion; and the fact that they continue to come, still finding ready employment and good wages, proves that the labor market is not yet over-stocked. . . .

Some of them will become rich, all will make a living, and many will possess themselves of homesteads and settle down as permanent occupants of the soil. The negro, if too thrift-less to prevent or oppose this threatened invasion, deserves to decay away before a more energetic race. . . .

. . . I shall have something to say about the Japanese. The refugees from that island kingdom, who lately sought asylum in this country, are making a good beginning. They have gathered their first harvest, and have tea plants more than an

inch high. A promising class of their young men are studying
English and the useful arts.

—*New York Times,* "The Chinese Question,"
August 11, 1869

The Pacific railroads have a perfect right to employ Chinese
labor, as have all other people. It is not a crime to do so, but
a most natural and prudent thing. These railroads, however,
employ all the skilled white labor they can get, and only use
the Chinese for the hardest kind of drudgery such as white
Americans no longer care to undertake. But they are not
called upon to defend themselves in this connection. They are
entitled to go into the labor market precisely as all the rest of
the world does, and take the cheapest they can find. We all do
the same thing. The Chronicle does it even while vilifying its
neighbors for acting on its own ruling principle. The work-
ingmen do it. The people who are trying to get up boycot-
ting organizations do it. And therefore we have a right to say
that those who seek to make the employment of Chinese by
any one a cause of offense are either hypocrites or fools. The
laws of political economy are such that cheap labor will always
command the market while it is procurable. That is why we
are justified in demanding the exclusion of the Chinese. In a
nominally free country, where no man has the least right to
abuse his neighbor or to threaten him for employing whatever labor element he chooses, it is impossible to prevent the
Chinese from interfering with white labor so long as they are
suffered to come here.

—*Daily Record-Union* (Sacramento), Saturday, May 13, 1887

Excerpt one: Pit minority races against one another to benefit
white supremacy. The creation of the model minority.

Excerpt two, eighteen years later: This model minority no longer benefits white supremacy. Therefore, no more allowed in this country.

A few blocks down the street is the tiny Gimme! Coffee shop, reminiscent of San Francisco, because everybody inside sits with their laptops. Plus there's air-conditioning (not very San Francisco), so I, too, sit there for hours, aggregating. I also scroll through Petfinder for a dog and Craigslist for an apartment, send emails to strangers, sell ourselves as a nice, responsible couple. My boyfriend is a graduate student, I write. I work from home as a— I wonder how best to describe what I do, but cannot come up with a term that is correct and not nonsensical or long-winded, so I simply leave it as is: I work from home.

The first time I saw a young couple's home, I was an undergrad going to a friend of a friend's housewarming party. It was in an unimpressive gray complex on the north side of campus. I trudged up the carpeted stairs expecting to see an average college apartment, the kind of place where kids play beer pong and put their feet up on wobbly chairs. The awe hit me hard. It was a stunning adult space, glittering with touches of the couple's life together— potted plants, paintings on the walls, nice rugs. Plates of cheese and crackers rested on the coffee table. A bright woven blanket was draped effortlessly on the back of a big gray couch. The hosts poured wine into glass glasses. Their youth made it impressive— that they could saunter effortlessly ahead of the rest. I wondered how they afforded it, if their parents were rich, or if there was another way to access this life that I had yet to understand. They were an interracial couple, too, a white woman (and though I still thought of myself as a girl, and we were the same age, I saw her as distinctly older) and a brown Latino man. Hand towels, red-and-white checkered, hung from the silver oven's handle. I watched the host wash his hands, then wipe them on one of the towels. That small gesture seemed to convey all I wanted at the time. An adult domestic life with quiet, sweetness, and peace.

There are typically two paths available to the child of an unhappy marriage: unknowingly repeat the same offenses as your parents or deliberately go far off in the other direction to prove you will not be them.

In the couple's kitchen, I look through their multilevel spice rack. Things I've never considered using: dill weed, sage, celery seed, white truffle salt. "Why don't you cook for him, since you're home?" my mother said. But the thought of cooking exhausts me. It was a grand enough gesture of love, wasn't it, to follow him here?

"When you have the idea for what you want, you obsess and just do that without listen to anybody," my mom says. "That's you."
    She says I did the same thing with J.

So, too, did Salvador Roldan and Marjorie Rogers. The year was 1930. Like many people who want to get married, Salvador and Marjorie met, liked the look of one another, fell in love, and decided to spend their lives together. They went to the county clerk of Los Angeles County for a marriage license. The county refused. Salvador was Filipino American and Marjorie white, British American, and California's anti-miscegenation statute had been in place since 1850. Originally, it banned marriages between "negroes and mulattoes" and "whites," but in 1880, the state revised the statute to include "Mongolians," in response to the influx of

Chinese immigrants. Salvador and Marjorie brought their application to court. The basis for the case was a simple one of technicality and misclassification: Salvador Roldan argued that Filipinos did not fall under the category of "Mongolians," but rather that of "Malay, Malaysian or Brown Race," which was not listed in the statute, and therefore, legally, he had the right to marry Marjorie. The court agreed, and in its long-winded way officially determined, three years later, in *Roldan v. Los Angeles County*:

> In 1880, in a group that would compare very favorably with the average legislature, there was no thought of applying the name Mongolian to a Malay; that the word was used to designate the class of residents whose presence caused the problem at which all the legislation was directed, viz., the Chinese and possibly contiguous peoples of like characteristics; that the *common* classification of the races was Blumenbach's, which made the "Malay" one of the five grand subdivisions, i.e., the "brown race," and that such classification persisted until after section 60 of the Civil Code was amended in 1905 to make it consistent with section 69 of the same code. As counsel for appellants have well pointed out, this is not a social question before us, as that was decided by the legislature at the time the code was amended; and if the common thought of to-day is different from what it was at such time, the matter is one that addresses itself to the legislature and not to the courts.

Salvador and Marjorie were married, though not as happily as they would have been years prior. One week later California revised its statutes to include "Malays" as another race banned from marrying whites.

The white-haired woman behind the cash register swivels in her chair by pressing her puffy hands against the scuffed, dirty burgundy countertop, then opens her mouth. "Look at my teeth," she says. "This one's loose." With a middle finger, she wiggles a gray upper molar. "Says she'll take me to the dentist soon, my daughter." She grins wide. Her hair is wavy, tall, and thin. Patches of pink scalp show through the cotton candy–like wisps.

"Oh, that's good!"

"This tooth will fall right out if she doesn't!" She coughs into the hand she is using to hold my change, which she thrusts toward me. "See you next time, honey."

Slotted for *That's So Ithaca*. This town is a giant Reuben sandwich from an eager old white woman with loose teeth.

On the phone with my dad, I say it's scary not to know what I'm going to do, though I hope I'll get used to it.

"You think that's scary? That's not scary. What you really need to be scared of is number one, the U.S. or a European country waging war with China. Number two, terrorist attacks. That's why I'm always telling you: avoid crowds. Number three is the destruction of the earth through global warming. Without Mother Earth, none of us matter anymore, none of us will be around, none of us can survive. That's what's truly scary. I'm glad I won't have to live to see it happen. But you need to be prepared for all that."

"Okay, okay, Daddy. I have to go help cook dinner."

"What's for dinner?"

"Pasta and salad."

"When you visit me," he says, the way he's started many sentences, "I'm going to ask you to bring me some special foods. Tabasco sauce, pepperoni, cheese, just something hard like Swiss or cheddar, and let's see, what else, a good leather cleaner and conditioner, the stuff they have here isn't high quality, it's all toxic. Check where it's made. Don't get anything made in China. I need to clean my bag and boots. And those things your mother uses, the dusters, what are those called?"

"Swiffer duster," I say.

"Yeah, bring a few of those."

"Okay, well we can talk about it again when I'm actually coming. I need to settle down here first," I say.

"How's the bonehead liking school?"

"I think he likes it. He's busy. He's at work from, like, seven to six or seven."

"Good. Working hard is good for someone like him. Tell him that he needs to be serious about what he's doing, study, prove himself, and he'll be fine."

"Okay."

"What about you?" he asks, as though he's forgotten what I've just told him and his lecture about my being scared. Then I have the fear that he is losing his memory.

"I just said," I say. "We just talked about it. Don't you remember?"

"Right, right. You're worried about work, yes, I heard you. I meant, what about you and New York. You like it?"

"It's fine. But I really have to go now. Love you," by which I mean it's time to hang up now, meaning we've talked for long enough, meaning I'm done with this conversation, meaning I'm tired and need a break. And yes, also, I love you.

I grew up hearing his stories of survival. He beat tuberculosis as a child through willpower and a diet of pure onion and garlic. His father threw him out of the third-story window of his home. He landed with only scratches and bruises, thanks to his resilient body, plus tree branches slowing his fall. He and his brothers jumped on and off moving Shanghai trams so as not to pay the fares. They would narrowly avoid getting hit by cyclists and cars. As a taxi driver in New York, he escaped several mugging attempts. He had a gun is how. In Hong Kong, he fought off robbers in his apartment by throwing one off the balcony. That man died. It was an unfortunate circumstance. He had asked them to leave; he had warned them. All those Hong Kong boys made fun of him for not speaking English or Cantonese. The fights were numerous. Six months later, he spoke better than them all. In San Francisco, he raced cars on the hills and spun out, almost crashing to his death. Yes, he and his friends were reckless and wild, but they knew how to be young and alive. Just like in life, he bounced around, but he always walked away. Even with a full mouth of shattered glass.

Some stories I knew to be true. Some I considered plausible. And others, I brushed off as gross exaggeration. But every time I wondered, How did I, so cautious and fearsome, descend from somebody like him?

For the first three weeks, thunderstorms that last a minute or longer, raging and gray, then sun and bright sky, like nothing happened. J comes home soaked and laughing, as though from another planet. There is rain up the hill on campus and sun in the flats is how. Microclimates like back home. I think of romance movies, where lovers drench themselves making out in the rain in T-shirts and dresses. I never understood why. It seemed impractical, cold, and uncomfortable. Turns out they were living somewhere I didn't know about until now, where water comes down when it's hot, a respite.

"Your upper lip is the first place that gets sweaty," says J. "It just pools there like little lakes. Like the Finger Lakes."

"Don't look at me." I lie in the couple's bed in front of a small fan in nothing but my underwear and hope that this lack of movement means that I am conserving energy or power or hope, or something like that.

Our routines have flipped. In the mornings, he gets up early and bikes up to campus before I am out of bed. I listen to him leave and feel a bit smaller. I have nowhere specific to go. No people expecting my presence. I don't have to shower or change out of pajamas or put in my contacts or do my makeup. It is a little lonely. But in some ways it is also freeing.

Like this. Alone, in bed with curtains shut, during the middle of the day. I have never had this much control over my time. I open an incognito window on my computer (somehow that little added privacy comforts me). I type in a porn site's URL, one that J showed me back in college, and which I have remained loyal to because it is what I know and it fulfills its purpose. I am not sure what I'm looking for—my preferences aren't consistent. Something has to fit the mysterious workings of my moods in that month or day or hour, approved by instinct. I start and stop several videos. Too close up. Too much noise. Too aggressive. Too fake. I land on an amateur video of a couple, about our age, an Asian woman and white man, both French. Normally I hate porn that involves Asian women, but this one feels different. The video starts like a vlog, with them walking around, going to cafes, shopping, doing couple activities. They talk, they laugh, they tease, they peck each other on the cheeks. They appear to be a real couple. And their being French seems to transport them into another realm, where—though I know it not to be true— they are unscathed and untouched by the same problems. Then it cuts to their bedroom. I watch the woman, keen to dissect whether she is enjoying herself. After five and a half minutes, I am convinced. I close the computer and take off my underwear.

It is the Chinese way to sit still, enjoy each day and each period of life—serene in the knowledge that an all-wise Providence is working out a plan of which each of us is a part.

We can't hurry the slowly grinding mills of the gods; and we do not wish to. . . .

I—that flustered, worried, defensive little Hollywood flapper—found happiness when I ceased to worry about time.

No one can give me what belongs to some one else; and no one can take away that which is mine.

—Anna May Wong,
Los Angeles Times Sunday Magazine, 1934

And yet, I sign into Parley. No matter my better impulse telling me not to. Old habit, routine, a desire for the near past.

Jasmine pings me and a flashing tab appears: YOU'RE ALIVE.

As I'm typing a response to her, Tim pings me: So . . .

Jasmine:

YES! i am very much alive! how is it over there? is it terrible?

it's okay, the weather is fucking weird, but it's really pretty

ITHACA IS GORGES

right. ha. ha. ha. don't lie, you miss me

sorta . . .

but mostly because i have no friends here and have literally met nobody except old people showing us houses

get their numbers!

you can clean their dentures and eyeglasses

Tim:

what's up?
Back to work?

not really . . .

Why not? Why are you in the work chatroom then?

it accidentally signed in

Do you want to do some reviews? The new gadget guy's looking for more freelancers. Or what are you up to right now? I have a couple newsy things you could whip up.

ah, not right now, sorry

What are you doing with yourself?

just moving and stuff

Jasmine:

they'd appreciate that

ugh, let's just chat on gchat, I don't want to be on work chat anymore

idk why I came on here anyway

because you're worried people are going to forget you

Tim:

i'm doing some freelance work too

That's right. For who?

just some stuff here and there. anyway, i have to go do something right now. ttyl!

Alright. Happy to hear you're keeping busy.

Instead of moving to another platform to chat, Jasmine calls. We talk about the office, by which I mean I listen to her talk about the drama of which I'm no longer a part. She updates me on the layoffs, new hires, restructures, resignations, redesigns. She says the other photographer (her ex) isn't getting along with the art director, one of the EIC's newest hires, that the two are clashing over aesthetics, that her ex is too precious about his creativity, and that he constantly pushes against what the art director wants. Jasmine says the art director has approached her, since she is still technically her ex's direct superior, to ask her to handle him. I ask what that means. Will he be let go? She says she's not sure, except that his fate is in her hands, then releases a movie villain's cackle. I stretch out my legs on the couple's couch and wait for Jasmine to stop laughing before I tell her that I think it would be best if we didn't talk about the office anymore. It's hard for me to listen to what's going on there. I need some distance. I am still upset about how things went with the contractors, how we failed to present a united front, but I am careful not to say I am upset with her specifically. She is silent on the other end.

"Are you there?" I ask.

"Okay," she says. "You want distance. Sure. Distance. Don't

worry about it. You're over there. New life and all. I'm the one who has a lot of *work* to do."

She hangs up. I stare at my phone's home screen, part of me waiting, wanting it to do or say something, but it does not.

From the book *Chinese American Voices: From the Gold Rush to the Present:*

A Letter Writing Campaign to Discourage Immigration (1876)

The Chinese Six Companies is asking our fellow clansmen not to make the long sea voyage to the United States so as to avoid bringing trouble on the community. The reason we have been subjected to all kinds of harassment by the white people is that many of our Chinese newcomers are taking jobs away from them. And yet, if we take a look at the wages of the Chinese workers in the various trades, we can see that they are shrinking day by day. This is also due to the large number of our fellow clansmen coming here. If up to 10,000 people come here, even if they do not take away 10,000 white men's jobs, they will still drive down the wages of 10,000 workers in various trades. It's inevitable. If this trend is not stopped, not only will the white men's harassment continue, causing a great deal of trouble for our community, but even skilled Chinese workers will have difficulty finding jobs and will lose their livelihood. If it is hard for the Chinese who are already here, imagine how much worse it will be for the newcomers.

Therefore, in an effort to prevent disaster before it strikes, the members of the Six Companies believe that the best course of action is to have each person in California write a letter home exhorting his clansmen not to come to America. And who would doubt such advice when it originates from a kinsman? This is much better than our posting thousands and thousands of notices. If the trend should cease and fewer clansmen come here, first, further trouble from the white people would be avoided; second, wages will stop shrinking; third, there will be no worry about newcomers being detained. Everyone will benefit. Just a single word from you will do a world of good. For this reason, we are urging every one to write home.

The Chinese Six Companies
15th day of the 3rd month, Guangxu 2nd year [April 9, 1876]

I do the thing you're not supposed to do. I cut off all my hair. Ten inches, and now the ends don't even graze my chin. It's not as dramatic or drastic as it might appear to others. The driving force: this heat. But still it feels like shedding something from myself, like all the old emotions lived in the ends of my hair and are now gone. When J comes home, he says he likes it. He is one of the only straight men I know who prefers short hair on women and doesn't say something like, *You look like a soccer mom.*

More additions for the *That's So Ithaca* blog, accumulated on my own:

A full-face-tattooed white man walking and peeing in daylight around the perimeter of the addiction services building. Buddha statues decorating front yards in, of course, Fall Creek. The nets beneath bridges above gorges, to prevent jumpers. Restaurants with names like Spicy Asian and Asia Cuisine. Granted, the food at both is quite good.

What do you do all day? I ask him. Why are you always late? What's it like in lab?

He says he's running experiments. He takes photos of the embryos' intestines at various stages of development. They twist and turn in incomprehensible ways. He speaks words I don't understand and can't repeat because they have no meaning to me. He says there is also a lot of waiting in lab.

"So while you're waiting up there," I say, "I'm waiting down here for you."

He looks at me apologetically.

I ask if he likes the work. He says he does. He says it's challenging, but also fun. He feels like he's doing something important and meaningful with his time.

"That must be nice," I say.

He is silent, not knowing how to respond.

I read an interview in which an actress says she loves the fact that she has no boundaries. Her openness to life is worth the few bumps along the way. I'm the opposite. I, at all costs, avoid life bumps. When we're together, I'm less afraid of the world and its dark corners. But now when I'm alone, which is the vast majority of my days, I find myself double-checking everything, wondering what I've missed.

And yet, everything is coming together. We have found a place to live. In an effort to interact with locals, I have applied to, and gotten an interview for, a job at a museum. J's mom sends us an email with a photo of a fluffy white poodle with the subject line: Puppy obsession. She explains that she and her husband want to buy us a dog and have found the perfect one back in California. We've come all the way across the country, so our dog will do so, too, despite my certainty of there being many available dogs in upstate New York. But they want to give this to us, J says. Let them, it's easier.

And I know it is a sort of blessing, that the hardest part about interacting with his parents is accepting all of their gifts.

"Sorry I can't give you more nice things and money," says my mom each time I tell her J's parents are giving us another this or that.

"No, I don't want you to," I say. "I want to get *you* more."

She laughs. "Yes, you should. That's what grown-up kids are for."

There was our first Christmas in Davis when I helped my mom pick out presents for my sister and brother. I was eleven; they were eight and five. My dad was away, in China again. My mom said we could spend eighty dollars on each of us, a lucky number. We hunted toy store sales, big-box stores, and drugstores. Puzzles, books, hair accessories, figurines, Pokémon cards, nail polish, etc. We did a good job; the gifts beneath the tree looked plentiful. For me, I waited until the post-Christmas sales. We went to the mall, and I spent hours rummaging clearance bins and racks until I finally picked out a brown wool sweater with suede elbow patches from Ann Taylor. It was thirty-five dollars and my most treasured piece of clothing for a decade. She asked, This is all you want? Nothing else? Nothing else, I said. She hugged me close and said that I was good, that she was sorry it was this way. By the following year, we stopped bothering to keep up appearances.

The next house is run-down, but it is a house, a true stand-alone house with a bright blue metal roof and dirty white vinyl siding. It sits at the bottom of a steep hill, like a San Francisco hill, on the "wrong" side of downtown, in an old neighborhood gradually being overrun with college students. ("You're how old again?" the owner asked us. "Oh, good. I want to avoid renting to kids.") The wood floors are real and worn, with rectangular patches of cement and plywood randomly placed across the living and dining rooms. The kitchen has a big white '50s electric stove, old beige tiles crookedly lined halfway up the wall behind a chipped enamel sink. There is a built-in breakfast nook with a stained glass light fixture hanging from the pitched ceiling. It is the oldest house we've seen, and very simple, but also very big and inexpensive.

We move things from the couple's apartment to the house at night, after J comes back from lab.

"I'm going to start a business," he announces. "It's going to be called Crispy Chicken. I'm going to specialize in CRISPR techniques in chicken embryos, so labs like ours can order mutated embryos from my company."

"I have no idea what you're talking about, but it sounds super creepy."

"Crispy Chicken, though! Isn't that the best name for a company?"

"For a restaurant, sure."

"'Crispy' would be all caps, like CRISPR, but no R at the end and actually a small Y, so CRISPy Chicken."

"But then is that really clear? Is C-R-I-S-P the same as C-R-I-S-P-R? Doesn't the acronym stand for something?"

"You're not being supportive of my business idea."

"No, no, you should totally go for it. I one thousand percent support this."

"Don't start off our new home with lies!" he says, and pushes open the front door. "Look at all of this space!"

When he's gone, I set up the bedroom. We have upgraded to a king-size mattress, and there is space for more: a dog bed and crate (already ordered), two side tables (Craigslist?), and dressers (antiquing?). I draw up a layout of the downstairs and start arranging imaginary furniture: couch, coffee tables, TV, chairs, cat tree—

"Wait, we're getting a cat, too?" says J upon seeing the plan.

"Aren't we?"

"Let's wait and see how the dog goes first."

"So much waiting and seeing," I say. "When we get the cat, the cat tree goes here."

In tech news: A bunch of the major companies announce quarterly earnings results. They're all making billions in revenue. They're also buying smaller companies so that they can make more. Hooray for them.

Across the country, protests in response to George Zimmerman's acquittal for murdering Trayvon Martin.

The city of Detroit files for bankruptcy, estimated $18–20 billion in debt.

Despite the Senate passing a comprehensive immigration reform bill, the House refuses, refuses, refuses to vote.

Afong Moy is a native of Canton city, about seventeen years of age, and engaging in her manner; addresses the visitors in English and Chinese, and occasionally Walks before the Company, so as to afford an opportunity of observing her astonishing LITTLE FEET, for which these Chinese ladies are so remarkable. Afong's feet are Four Inches and an eighth in length, being about the size of an infant's of one year old. And to add to the interest of the exhibition, the shoe and covering of the foot will be taken off, thereby affording an opportunity of observing their curious method of folding the toes, &c., by actual observation prove the real size of the foot beyond a doubt. She will be richly Dressed in The Chinese Costume. And in order to give the audience an idea of the language and cadence of her country, will sing a Chinese Song. . . .

. . . Various Chinese curiosities will be shown and explained to the company, and every pains taken to gratify the curious, as to the manners and customs of these singular people. . . .

Admittance to the whole, 25 cents; Children under 10 years, half price.

—*New York Times,* July 9, 1836

The first Chinese woman to arrive in the United States. As spectacle.

In China, we used to amble through the alleyways, from school to our apartment, beneath the fluttering laundry strung above our heads, the cyclists chiming their bells as they passed, the gray complexes barricading their paths, and one of the other children said, Your country is so beautiful that it's the only country we'd name "beautiful country," and we told him, Yes, it's beautiful there, but it's beautiful here, too, sweeping our arms at the place around us, when we passed a woman hunched over, draining the blood from a chicken's neck into a pink plastic bucket, the creature's limp head resting in her red-soaked hands, and we screamed and laughed and laughed and ran the rest of the way home, pointing out all the ugly-beautiful things we saw.

I have the brilliant idea to build myself a desk. In the evening, J takes me to Home Depot so I can buy my materials. When he leaves the next day, I sand and stain the wood all on my own, then lug it inside and upstairs into the office. I screw in metal hairpin legs. The desk goes against the wall with the window. I put my laptop on top of it and bring up a dining chair from downstairs. I sit there for a while, aggregating. I am sweaty and I feel deeply accomplished; it's beginning to feel like a real home office.

When J gets back, he places his hand on my desk and shakes. "It's wobbly." He says it in a voice like he's had a rough day and is taking it out on the desk.

"It wasn't when I used it today," I say. "I'm only typing on it, so it's fine."

"I really hate wobbly desks," he says. He hands me my laptop and turns the desk over to examine my work.

"Stop," I say. "I said it's fine. Just leave it alone."

"It's not sturdy. Wow, you really didn't attach these well," he says, shaking the legs. "And the planks aren't tight together, either." I leave the room, insulted. From downstairs, I can still hear him drilling.

He comes down many minutes later. "All done," he says. "All better."

When I don't respond, he says, "You're welcome."

"I liked it the way it was," I say.

We are both quiet for a while. I look through Instagram on my phone. One of my former coworkers has posted a photo of a new meeting room furnished with dark pink lounge chairs and mid-century modern coffee tables, captioned: Working in style! #worklife #interiordesign #blessed. I groan. J asks what's wrong.

I show him the photo. "Is this supposed to be ironic or what?"

"Maybe you should unfollow them," he says.

"No. They might notice. It just makes me feel like I'm wasting time here. I don't know what I'm supposed to be doing."

He is silent.

"Say something," I say, annoyed.

"I feel like you're mad at me." I look at him. He continues, "I wish I could be with you more, but it's hard. I feel a lot of pressure to do well in lab. Everybody's always working."

"Yeah," I say. Now I am the one who feels bad. I have the thought that I am an unnecessary burden on him. That I am being selfish. If I were a cheerful and happy girlfriend, his time in graduate school would be seamless and productive. I do not want to be the suitcase that he must drag behind him. "I'm still getting used to this new life," I say.

I order a million home items online to ship to our new, *permanent* address. Afterward I feel, if not better, then at least subdued.

No husband of mine will say, "I could have been a drummer,
but I had to think about the wife and kids. You know how it
is." Nobody supports me at the expense of his own adventure.
Then I get bitter: no one supports me; I am not loved enough
to be supported. That I am not a burden has to compensate for
the sad envy when I look at women loved enough to be supported. Even now China wraps double binds around my feet.

—Maxine Hong Kingston, *The Woman Warrior*

Now I consult my sister. "Do you remember when we first moved
to Davis and how sad we were?"

"What I remember thinking was that every cat was a stray. I
kept asking Mommy and Daddy, 'Can we keep this one? What
about this one? Can I take this one home?'"

We laugh for so long, I start crying and can't stop. I can hear
her boyfriend in the background, "What's so funny?"

"And I thought people in Davis were way too friendly," she
continues. "The first day of school, these six white girls all sat
around me and said they wanted to be my friend, and I was like,
Oh my gosh, this is scary! Who are these people? What do they
want from me?"

I choke back my laughter and tears.

"Have you made any friends?" she asks.

"No," I say.

"Don't sound so depressed. It's still pretty early. Why don't
you try joining a sport or something? Physical activity could be
good, too, you know."

"That's what everyone keeps saying, but when have I ever
been athletic?"

"True, but you could change," she says.

"Well, I'm going to meet my dog soon."

"Wow, okay, maybe you're sadder there than I thought."

"No, no. I'm trying to get a job at a museum, so hopefully I'll meet people there. And here's another positive: I went downtown the other day and had a full conversation with a stranger and she was really friendly."

"Who?"

"Well, she was a barista—"

"Oh my god. Baristas are paid to be nice to people!"

TALKS WITH CHINESE WOMEN

It seemed strange to hear this old Chinese woman speak of "America, New York, London, France," for in general they know nothing of the outside world, and very little of their own country.

She had been very happy with her kind missionary friends, and had been brought up as a good Methodist. At the age of fourteen, however, her mother claimed her in order to arrange a marriage for her. All this time her feet "had been neglected," and allowed to grow to their natural size; but now she and her mother determined, even at that age, to begin bandaging them, for they knew no man in a respectable position would marry a large-footed woman.

"Did you suffer, Amah?" I asked in horrified tones as I looked at her feet, now three inches long.

"Oh, yes," she answered quietly. "I thought the pain would kill me, and I could neither sleep at night nor enjoy anything during the day for months and months; but every day I asked my mother to pull the bandages tighter, and would sit in the door-way and watch the children playing and other persons coming and going, while I could only rock myself to and fro and moan."

— *Lippincott's Monthly Magazine,* January 1901

I find myself at the running shoe store, asking for recommendations. The clerk tells me to take off my flats and walk from one end of the store to the other. She crouches, watching the movement of my feet. She asks me again to walk back and forth. I feel awkward and exposed. Afterward, she declares that my feet overpronate. This means they roll inward beyond the ideal and I need stability shoes to prevent ankle and shin pain on runs. She says it's a good idea to go a half size up, given the width of my feet and swelling during runs. Why can't my feet be normal? I ask. The clerk says this is perfectly normal, plenty of people overpronate, but she is a salesperson who wants to make me feel good, to convince me to purchase the shoes. And though I know this, it works and I do.

The tag on the lavender stress-relief tea bag says: *Let things come to you.*

At the interview for the museum position, the director, a white woman in her forties named Rebecca, worries that I'm both over-qualified and underqualified—I have a college degree and years of work experience, but have never worked in a museum. The place collects and displays pieces of local history. I tell Rebecca I'm very interested.

The temperature-controlled basement holds all the archives in cardboard boxes. The items too large for boxes, like a shovel from the nineteenth century or a little rocking horse with no eyes, sit on a row of shelves labeled LARGE ITEMS. There is a box full of old dolls in plastic bags, labeled DOLLS, EARLY 20TH CENTURY and a box of TOILETRIES, 1920S where I find a gigantic, pristine tampon in bright pink paper wrapping. Then there is an entire wall of stuff that has no home. My main job would be to enter new items into the archives spreadsheet—including an item title, estimated origin date, location of use (if relevant), and donor (if known); re-organize all the boxes in the basement—stuff has been misplaced or mistakenly lumped together over the years (I tell her about my time with the rich lady to prove I can sort objects); and help around with whatever else she may need, like writing thank-you cards to donors and making event flyers on the fifteen-year-old computer. She says I can come in whenever I have time, but not more than five hours a week, given the budget. The pay is eleven dollars an hour.

"We're not much of an operation. It would be just you and me," she says. "And the volunteers, but they do their own thing. How does that sound?"

I say I'll take it.

For days, I am anxious the dog will die during his flight to us. But there he is, alive in his crate, offering relief and entertainment. On the first night, he follows us from room to room, up the stairs and down, but when we try to touch him, he backs up and tucks his tail between his legs, staring so wide we can see the whites of his eyes. I read online that this means he is in the beginning stage of flight. He proves the internet correct when we walk toward him and he skitters out of the room. But a minute later, there he is again, standing there with his eyes on us, watching.

"Come, puppy," I say. "I get you."

Jing Zhang, Jing Zhang, the schoolkids in China used to tease. My name backward. Nervous, nervous.

Dark outside. J still at work. The dog stares at the basement door, his tail tucked as he slowly backs away.

"What is it now?" I ask.

"Don't scare me," I say. "We're all alone."

"Aren't you supposed to be a form of protection?"

I walk to the basement door, turn on the lights, open the door

slowly, see only the stairs, hear nothing. I realize the dog is looking not at the basement, but at a backpack J has left on the ground.
I pick it up and shake it. The dog stumbles back into a wall.

"You're worse than me," I announce.

The teachers found peace in their offices during recesses and lunch.
They let me in because I was American. Chinese students were
allowed only for punishment or chores. The math teacher didn't
like me. She spanked me in front of the other teachers. Out of jeal-
ousy, my mother corrected. It was a gentle smack. Qiào pìgu! They
laughed and laughed. The first of many days that I was ashamed of
myself in that new country.

The drawing teacher, on the other hand, let me sit at her desk
and read her books. The animals in them made unrecognizable
sounds. The dogs went "wang" and the cats went "mao" and the
ducks went "gua."

"What about the fish?" she asked.

I thought for a while, searching for the answer.

"I'm only kidding," she said. "The fish don't make noises anywhere."

In tech news, a blur, and I no longer care. I click and input the
stories with no use of my mind. Perhaps this is the best job for me.
I am, as that one editor once called me, a robot.

There's a dead tree on our street. I only know it is dead because I
am stopped on the street, needing a break from running with this
dog. All the other trees are heavy with dark leaves, and the dead
one is totally leafless. I must have passed it before and not paid
attention. What else am I now noticing? That I despise running.
That the dog trots like a horse and likes to move in inconvenient

zigzagging patterns, distracted by smells and things beyond my senses. That I have never before been this silent and alone.

I go to the historical museum on slow news days and the weekends to scan photos and file them accordingly. An hour or so, here and there. But it, too, turns out to be a lonely job. Rebecca sits in her office with her door closed.

But where does this photo go? It's not in Tompkins County as far as I can tell, and there is no date stamp. Only *Dr. Kin Yamei (May King)* scratched into the corner.

I knock on Rebecca's office door, with the excuse of a legitimate question.

She yells for me to come in.

I show her the photo. "Where would something like this go? Do you know what the historical tie is to this place?"

She glances at the photo but barely looks. "Oh, I don't know why we have a lot of the stuff we have. All these directors coming through, in and out and in and out, taking all sorts of donations—and now look! It's piling up, collecting in these boxes for years! Just start a box of miscellaneous stuff and we'll figure out what to do with it later. Or we'll let the next director figure it out—ha ha! Could you close the door on your way out?"

I take the photo home with me and tape it on the wall in the office, above the no-longer-wobbly desk.

I like her expression, serious and calm and dismissive, as though she has been interrupted in the middle of her work. As though she is saying, Can't you see I'm doing something important? What are *you* doing? Hanging on the wall above her desk is a scroll of four large Chinese characters. A potted plant sits at the left corner of the desk. There is a flower. Chrysanthemum?

I call my dad and attempt to describe the strokes of each character, but we get nowhere. He tells me to text him the photo, but I
worry it will take too much off of his prepaid cell service.

"It's fine," he says. "Call me back in five minutes."

When I do, he says, "It's an old saying. Maybe from Laozi or
Kongzi or Mengzi. It says you are humble to serve without expectation. You are to serve without any expectation of getting anything in return. Some people serve and expect something, but you
shouldn't if you are humble and have decided to serve."

"All that in four characters?"

"Something like that. A saying like that. I could be totally off
track. But I think I'm on track. Ask your mother and see what
she says."

My mom and I text:

    It's something about a hero, a female hero.
    I don't know what the third character means.
    It's ancient Chinese characters.
    So this person in the picture is a writer?

                        no she was a doctor

    I'll look it up.
    The name is Bian Que and living in Lu
    country, famous physician.

                      no her name is Kin Yamei

    Her idol is Bian Que.
    The banner says, hero Bian from Lu
    country. Look it up.

                      Bian Que is a woman?

    No, he's a man. Not female hero, I was
    wrong about that.
    Where you find this?

                        at work

    You like your work?

The freelance job?

no, the museum. they're both fine,

kinda boring

See. I told you.

Bian Que was the first known Chinese doctor, alive between 401 and 310 B.C. So Yamei Kin was a Chinese doctor who looked up to the original Chinese doctor. Makes sense.

A quick search, trying to figure out Yamei's ties to upstate New York—why her photo is in these files. She was an orphan by three in Ningbo, China, and was adopted by American missionaries, who brought her to the United States as a teenager. She was the first woman of Chinese descent educated at an American university, and that university was Cornell. But it was Cornell's medical campus in New York City, before it was called Cornell—back then it was the Women's Medical College of the New York Infirmary. She graduated at the top of her class in 1885. She later had a brief stint in upstate New York, where she sent her son, Alexander Amador Eca da Silva, to middle and high school. Not a very Chinese name for the son of a Chinese woman.

We decide to sign the dog up for a training course at a local pet store. He is seven months old and he knows one command: sit. And only after repetitions of the word, only very slowly, as though he does not trust that what comes out of our mouths has anything to do with him.

"It's clear he understands what you're asking," the trainer says. "He's choosing not to listen. He needs more practice listening and responding."

"Ha ha. Like somebody else I know," I say, elbowing J.

"Huh? What?" he says. "I didn't hear you."

"I said—"

"Just kidding, I heard you." He laughs. "Did you see that, boy? It's not that hard!"

At the Fall Semester Welcome Barbecue, the most Asians and Asian Americans I've seen since arriving in Ithaca. But to each one I introduce myself as just the girlfriend, no relation to the cell biology or any other science or university department. Just the trailing girlfriend. I don't intend or want to, but I can hear it, that grating self-pity. It's either that or what I've said, but many afterward appear to avoid me.

But there are other partners, too. We are introduced to one another, cordoned off at our own table as the scientists mingle. The ones who have been around a while dole out their woes and advice.

"I almost never see him," one woman says. "Sometimes he'll come home for dinner with the kids. Then it's back to lab until three or four in the morning, sleep for a few hours, and he's gone again by seven or eight. Seven days a week."

"You have to get him to commit to one weekend, or at least one Sunday, a month together," another says. "Take a trip somewhere."

"For me, I have to sit in the lab if I want to spend time with her," a man says. "So I bring her dinner and watch stuff on my computer while she works."

"Do you think they really need to be there that much, though?" one asks. "Can't they figure out a more efficient way to work?"

"I just wish he would spend more time with his kids."

"No, that's just how it is. That's the culture. Look at them, they're all like that."

"Or if they're not, they're not dedicated to the work. And you'll be stuck here for years."

"Right, exactly. We need them to work hard so we can leave sooner."

There is sarcasm and resentment and bitterness in their voices. Many of them appear to be stay-at-home parents. They all sigh and roll their eyes and nod. They look at me and the new partners like, Don't worry, you'll be us soon enough. I get up and excuse myself.

"I was hoping to make friends," I say to J, back in the car.

"You didn't like them?" he asks.

"It's not that I don't like them," I reply. "I just don't want to be like them."

Yamei Kin married Hippolytus Laesola Amador Eca da Silva, a man of Portuguese and Spanish descent (which explains her son's name), in 1894, when she was thirty years old. By then she had already received her medical degree and practiced medicine in China and Japan for seven years. Was she the first Chinese American woman to marry a white man? However much I search, I can't find confirmation.

I go to J's lab for the first time, on a Sunday, and sit with my phone as he works. ("It will only take fifteen minutes," he said. It has, so far, been thirty-eight minutes. We are supposed to go on a hike. I feel bad for the dog waiting in the car.) One of his Chinese labmates, an older postdoc, comes to talk with me. He asks if I speak Mandarin, and I explain that no, unfortunately, I used to, but I've forgotten. He shakes his head and says he's worried this will happen to his son, who was born here, and although he speaks both languages at three years old, he may give up on Chinese after he enters preschool. He wants to put his son in Chinese school, but it's only for two hours each week. The labmate asks what my parents speak at home, and I say almost entirely English to my siblings and me, though there was more Shanghainese in the house when we were kids. Still, none of us felt comfortable speaking in Shanghainese after a certain age and we always spoke in English to each other. He looks more at ease upon hearing this. He explains that they speak only Mandarin at home. Also, the son has no siblings, will likely never have siblings, so this should help keep their family language to Mandarin. He is concerned for me; I have a very Chinese face, but now, as we speak, he says he realizes I'm not really Chinese at all. I should relearn Mandarin. It is inside, he says. You just have to find.

There's an old journal somewhere in my grandmother's house filled with pages written in Chinese. My mom says that my grandmother, when she was alive, would talk about the journal. She was proud and sad. The beautiful penmanship. The detail of the prose. I was eight and full of potential when I'd written those lines. And now what? So much has been emptied out.

I remember one entry in particular, because I had written it with the intention of showing off. I'd described a trip to the zoo and each animal I'd seen. How the turtles' eyes were like sesame seeds (a simile stolen from somewhere else) and how the ponies' braided tails whipped back and forth like clockwork to keep the flies away. Or maybe it had been a trip to a temple and the descriptions were about the buildings, the incense, and the Buddhas carved into the walls?

I thought I had retained at least this, the memory of what had been written, and only forgotten the medium, the language. In trying to remember, however, what's frightening is that it's become clear I've forgotten both.

That same labmate shared with me his theory that the world will end due to increasing levels of stress. People will compete and never relax and always try to innovate and achieve until they are so high-strung that the world collapses. A place like this—he pointed down at the lab's shining linoleum floors. This breeds stress. Take care of your boyfriend. Then he walked off.

The details of such an ending were sparse in his telling. I doubt it will happen like that. Much more likely, a drug-resistant bacteria takes us down, or rising sea levels and heat render the earth uninhabitable. But it's an interesting theory, hustling toward death.

When I tell J, after he is finally done with work, he says, "I think he meant stressed people hate each other and it causes conflict, like war."

"Is that how you feel in the program?"

"Not yet, no," he says. "But I see people like that all of the time."

It seems fitting that I should talk to you about peace, because my nation is the only one in the world which has lived up to your doctrine. Perhaps it is fitting, too, that a woman should talk to the peace delegates, because it is woman who has kept man from becoming altogether a brute.

—Yamei Kin to Peace Congress in New York City,
October 1904

Some mornings he says goodbye, but often he forgets. Some days I'll text, You didn't say bye and he replies, I thought you were sleeping.

And many nights when he returns, he is the first person to whom I've spoken that day. Sometimes I try calling, but he is too busy to talk. So when he is home, what I want to do is talk and talk. I want to hear voices, his and my own. But he has spent a long day working and interacting and talking with people in lab. So when he is home, what he wants to do is cook and listen to his podcasts and rest. So neither of us is much satisfied with the other. Or maybe it's mostly me who is not.

"What do you think?" I ask the sleeping dog.

He lifts his head to look at me.

"I'm sorry to wake you, but you can't just sleep all day and ignore me."

He tilts his head, a sign of intelligence.

"I know, it's not fair, is it? Sometimes you want attention and I'm busy. And now I want attention and you're asleep. But look, I'm making up for it."

I massage his whole body, like the dog trainer taught us. It relaxes and soothes them, the trainer said.

"See. We understand each other just fine."

I have located a three-hundred-page biography of Yamei Kin, compiled by an institution called SoyInfo Center, which touts itself as "the world's leading source of information on soy, especially soyfoods." Their tagline is "Soy from a Historical Perspective." Their book on Yamei is one of dozens about various regions, figures, companies, and ingredients important to soy. But I'm less interested in that than I am in Yamei's life. Here's what I've gathered so far:

Yamei Kin and Hippolytus Laesola Amador Eca da Silva married at the British consulate in Yokohama, Japan. He was a musician and a linguist. A year later, they move to Hawaii, where she works as a doctor, and they have a child, Alexander. A year after that, she leaves Hawaii for San Francisco with Alexander in tow. No husband. But the husband follows two months later. Then Yamei leaves with her son for Los Angeles, where she gives her first lecture on missionary work in Japan and China.

The *Los Angeles Herald* reported in February 1902:

The women of China are supposed to represent a type of the oldest and least progressive women of the civilized countries. But even in China the new woman is slowly but surely gaining a recognition. Recently the empress dowager gave a reception to the ladies of the foreign legations in Pekin and the wife of Minister Conger delivered a spirited and telling speech. And now courtesy may be returned in kind, for we have a real Chinese new woman in our midst. To be sure, she is partially a product of our American life and institutions, but nevertheless it is to the Flowery Kingdom that credit should be given for having furnished us this entertaining and unusual illustration of what the Chinese new woman may become.

As for Hippolytus, there is little mention beyond stating that Yamei, "weary of her husband," leaves her son in the care of a friend and takes a six-month work trip to Japan.

To pass the time, I click around the map on a travel site, searching for the cheapest plane tickets to various locations. I've saved up enough money from aggregating to afford a last-minute trip to nearly all of Europe, and most parts of Asia, including China, if I find cheap or free places to stay.

In J's rare spare time, we do have one new shared hobby: going to estate sales and antiques stores, of which there are many in the area. At one, the man showing us around tells us about his dead mother.

"She lets me know she's here from time to time," says the man. He's wiry and thin. He has the kind of sun-damaged face that makes it hard to pinpoint an age, and a sharp desperation to his speech, like we're the first people he's seen in days. A real possibility. "After she died in the fire—you see, the store used to be three times the size, now we just got the little storefront for the fancy stuff and this barn for everything else—after she passed away, I didn't leave the house for seven years. I couldn't step outside, not even to get the mail. You want that coffee table there? That's a nice one. I'll carry it down for you. I got it. I got it. I'm stronger than I look. My mom, she keeps watch over me. She flickers the lights to let me know she's in here. Dad doesn't believe me, but I know it. I know she's speaking to me. She's watching over me."

We offer twenty dollars for the table, but the man says he only wants fifteen. He tells us to stop by anytime. He'll show us around the local farms and places, he's got the time.

"We will," I tell him.

"We are not going on a tour with him," J says back in the car.

"What? Why not?"

"Dude, that guy was crazy."

"He seemed nice. And he could show me around, since I have no friends."

"You don't want to be friends with a crazy person," says him.

"Maybe he's just sad and lonely."

"You always think crazy people aren't crazy."

"Maybe then that means I'm crazy."

He laughs and pats my knee. "Oh, Jing Jing."

"Don't condescend," I say.

This bee has been hovering by the bedroom window for three long minutes. Does it badly want to get inside? Why? There's nothing going on in here. I tap the glass to scare it away, but it is not deterred. Perhaps it is studying me as I am studying it.

On Instagram, another one of my former coworkers, this time the younger-than-me Business reporter, stands in front of a wall with the words THE WALL STREET JOURNAL: DIGITAL NET-WORK. Accompanied by an obnoxiously long comment that be-gins with "Some personal news" and goes on to detail his new reporting position, how much hard work it took for him to get there, and the many, many thanks to the many, many people (appropriately tagged) who helped him get to where he is today. Forty-seven minutes ago, seventy-eight likes.

I close out the app. Yes, I should unfollow them all. I should not spend so much time on other people's lives. Instead, I spend the afternoon looking up journalism job listings in New York City. Just to look, I say to myself.

Another tech reporter with whom I'm acquainted, but whom I never liked—he was the type to push his way to the front at a product announcement, as if being a few minutes ahead got him the scoop—sends me an email asking if I can talk about the aggregation work I'm doing. He wants to understand why the company has decided to use humans, instead of algorithms, and how this affects what shows up on the feeds. He says he's heard from some that it's a biased process, that certain topics and sources are off-limits. Is it true? He's working on a feature. Can I talk? Can I answer some questions? Provide some insight?

I read the email a couple more times, but do not reply. I don't want to be his source and it bothers me that he has found me doing something I'm not especially proud to be doing.

The tea bag says: *The purpose of life is to know yourself, to love yourself, to trust yourself, to be yourself.*

By when is one meant to achieve this purpose?

The SoyInfo Center biography is lengthy and dense, a collection of nearly five hundred documents compiled over thirty-five years. In the index, under "Important Documents #1," is a short list of page numbers. I go through to check each one for more about

Yamei's personal life, but they are all about her work in relation to bringing soy and other agricultural plants from China to the United States. In one letter, she writes on pai ts'ai: "It is especially prized for its sweet 'buttery' flavor which I have heard characterized of certain varieties of lettuce. It is not eaten raw or for salad purposes: but when dropped into boiling hot water after being cut up in fairly large pieces it makes a staple green vegetable. The rapid growth struck me as being valuable, for if in the same time as is necessary for growing lettuce, one can obtain a good green cabbage, it will be undoubtedly as popular here as it is in China."

At the museum I watch the decades-old computer boot up its home screen pixel line by pixel line. I have not seen anything like it since the '90s, or maybe ever. Rebecca has left a folder of receipts on the desk, with a sticky note: *Please tape these on individual pieces of paper for the accountant. Thanks!* Sticky note is her preferred mode of communication.

The inefficient and antiquated process of it all drives me mad.

My recent major accomplishments have been to teach the dog to *lie down* and *leave it* and *where's J?* If J is home, then the dog runs straight to him. If J is not home, the dog runs to the window and stares outside.

In the yard, busying myself. Do the weeds know they're dying when they've been pulled out? Or are they unaware as they slowly wither? Technically, they're still alive when they're in my fist.

She is typically Chinese in appearance. There are the pale complexion, the dark hair, the small dark eyes twinkling with fun. Small in stature, but alert and active in body and mind. Dr. Kin wisely retains her Chinese dress.

"I am a pioneer," she says, "and know a pioneer's difficulties." But her example has made the way easier for others to follow. . . .

"You must make your own plans and carry your scheme to success."

—*Altoona Mirror,* 1911

There had been many other plans and goals. As a kid, I'd have fantasies of playing flute concerts in front of thousands of people, being applauded by them all, though I was a shit flutist. Same goes for pretty much every activity I tried. Brief obsessions that lapsed when I realized I would not succeed. Tennis, guitar, gymnastics, ribbon dancing, watercolor, swimming, or whatever else I thought had potential. I was also very into parrots at one point, but I didn't know how to be "the best at parrots."

Now a text from the reporter, who has gotten my phone number from somebody: Did you see my email? I just have a couple questions.

Again, I do not reply.

Buzzing, buzzing, my stupid phone. I hold it close to my face and see a missed call from a long string of digits, my dad's Chinese phone number. It is two in the morning. I put the phone back on the side table. A few minutes later, the buzzing again. J grumbles beside me. This time I pick up.

"Call me back," my dad says, and hangs up. He never calls because it costs much more for him than the calling card does from my end. It must be an emergency. I put on my glasses and get out of bed.

"What's going on?" J mumbles.

"Nothing," I say as I walk out.

In the office, I dial the calling card number, then the account number, then my dad's number, but get an error message. The number does not exist. I hang up and try again. And again. When my dad picks up, I speak quietly into the phone. "What's wrong, are you okay?"

"Hi, Jing Jing," he says. He sounds cheerful, too cheerful. "I was just thinking I hadn't heard from you in a while. I was walking back from the store with my case of beer—you know they said they can deliver now, straight to my door? And it doesn't cost extra. I might take them up on it. Save me the trip. I was walking back and I thought, How long has it been since I heard from Jing Jing? It's been longer than usual, right? How's the weather there? It's starting to get cold, isn't it? The leaves must be changing colors, yes?"

"Daddy, it's two in the morning here."

"Oh, it is? Sorry, sorry. I must have calculated the time difference wrong. Ha ha, sorry, you know I'm getting old. Sometimes I can't think straight."

I strain to hear background sounds, but there is nothing to distinguish his location. "Are you sure you're okay? Where are you right now?"

"I'm fine. I'm in my apartment. Don't worry about your old man." I can hear him gulp and swallow something. "Have you met real New Yorkers yet?"

"What? Daddy, is something going on?"

"I said I'm fine! You're the one who sounds sick. What, are you catching a cold?"

"No. It's the middle of the night. You woke me up."

"Oh, right, sorry. Sorry to bother you. Go back to sleep, sweetheart."

"Okay. Can you please just take care of yourself?"

"Don't worry about me," he says. "I'm watching this TV program now about the Tang dynasty. You know, that was the most progressive dynasty, especially for women. I would say it was my favorite dynasty."

"Okay, Daddy."

"'Okay, Daddy,'" he imitates. "You sound so grumpy. What, you're not happy to talk to me?"

"I just want to go back to sleep."

"Okay, okay. Let me ask you this. Are you proud to have a father like me?"

I close my eyes. I can feel a headache starting. I try to take even breaths.

"Hello? Did you hear me?"

"Yes," I say. "Sure. I am."

"Okay, good. Say hello to your bonehead for me. Love you. Sleep well. What did you used to say as a kid? See you later, alligator."

"Right. Bye, love you."

"Don't love me too much," he says, and hangs up.

I sit there for a while. Now Yamei Kin's face on the wall looks pitying and judgmental. Really, what are you doing?

I go back into the bedroom. Light from the streetlamps outside is coming through the window. J has left the curtains open, because he likes to wake to natural sunlight. I close them, because I want to sleep in. When I get back into bed, J scoots up against me in the dark, wordless. He puts his arm around me for a while, but I can't bear his touch. I push him off and tell him to give me some room. This wakes him. "So mean," J whimpers. I pull the blanket over my head, curl on my side, and stay like that until late morning, long after he has left.

I was nineteen when I was able to put a name to my father's scent. It was during a party and I pressed myself up against J. He kissed my cheek, his stubble rubbed against my skin, and the smell of him brought me straight back to my father when he'd kiss me good night as a child. I had always thought it was a cologne, but this on J was not cologne. It was a mixture of beer on his breath and some kind of deodorant, but mostly it was the beer breath, that warm, malty, human scent. I was torn between feeling closer to J and feeling further from them both.

It occurs to me, too, that I see J as little as I saw my dad as a kid, and the thought irritates me. What greater loneliness and longing is there than living with someone you once knew so well, and who is now hardly around?

"Where are the numbers?" Tracy Chou, a software engineer at Pinterest, asks in a blog post directed at tech companies withholding employee diversity data (including the one for which I am freelancing). How many women are working in tech, in engineering roles in particular? "The actual numbers I've seen and experienced in industry are far lower than anybody is willing to admit." She offers Pinterest's numbers: eleven women out of eighty-nine engineers. She says this is on par with the gender ratio of those graduating with CS degrees. "We have to be thoughtful about sourcing candidates and building the right culture, and we invest in deliberate efforts to connect with women in the community."

I post it on the app's Tech channel. A half hour later I receive an email from the contracted editorial lead: Hey, I got a complaint from HQ about that piece, so removed it. They didn't love the critique. Plus, it's not news, per se, and they want to keep it to hard-hitting news. Otherwise, great job with the picks today!

People like to holler at us, from across the street, from out of the windows of their cars, from their porches, or just as they walk by.

"Best-looking dog this side of the Mississippi!"

"How much did she cost?"

"Do you have a license for that wild animal?"

"Two walking works of art!"

Before I can process or respond, the hollerers speed away. I wonder if they are satisfied with the exchange. Me, not so much. The dog tugs us both forward, unbothered.

I used to pray neurotically before bed. Dear God and Buddha, please keep my family safe and healthy and happy. I pray that Daddy is safe, safe, safe, safe, safe, safe, safe, safe, healthy, healthy, healthy, healthy, healthy, healthy, healthy, healthy, happy, happy, happy, happy, happy, happy, happy, happy. I pray that Mommy is safe, safe, safe, safe, safe, safe, safe, safe, healthy, healthy, healthy, healthy, healthy, healthy, healthy, healthy, happy, happy, happy, happy, happy, happy, happy, happy. I pray that Mei Mei is . . . I pray that Didi is . . . I pray that the cats are . . . Please keep all of us safe, safe, safe, safe, safe, safe, safe, safe, healthy, healthy, healthy, healthy, healthy, healthy, healthy, healthy, happy, happy, happy, happy, happy, happy, happy, happy.

It helped assuage that sense of chaos I had as a child. Now? Not so much, it appears.

Instead, I open Find My Friends several times a day to track each of their whereabouts. To know where they are is a comfort. Though my dad is missing, and J is always in one spot—the campus lab.

My brother texts a compilation video of Jeremy Lin getting smashed, tripped, hit, and ripped on the basketball court without any flagrant fouls called for him. "He got a lot of Jeremy Lin . . . almost decapitates [him]," says the announcer in one. Then, Lin is slapped so hard in the face his nose bleeds. He continues to run for a few seconds before touching his nose and becoming visibly frustrated. A whistle is finally blown. Then, he's hit as he approaches the hoop. "Did he get hit in the face again?" The announcer's voice, with a snide lilt. "Looks like it," the other responds. *Oh, just the usual.* Then another smack against his nose. Then he's whacked in the head. He falls. He curls on the ground. He gets on all fours. He rises. He winces.

I remember my dad on the ground, in front of the toilet. My mom would make him green tea in his favorite mug—the brown ceramic one with the two finger-size handles, like two ears on either side—and place it on the vanity. Close the door, he'd mutter if he noticed us watching.

"Daddy's a little sick," she'd say. "Go back to sleep."

My sister and I get into it on the phone. I'm telling her she needs to call our dad more, and she is saying she does call him. She's also busy, she has class and homework and she works on top of that. I'm saying what's a phone call? What's a half hour a week, can't she make time for that? I'm sure she's watching tons of Netflix and sitting around with her roommates and not always super busy doing something important. So just call Daddy during one of those times. She says it's more like an hour or longer. I say, So what? She makes a loud, wordless noise and then screams, "You're so controlling!"

My mom now: "You can't push her like that. You're always on your father's side, but Ling Ling doesn't have the same relationship."

I think about the times when I was away at college and all of them would call me to recount a fight from each side. Mei Mei's stuff out in the yard. Running away or being thrown out. Months of silence between her and our father. Once, they didn't talk for half a year, despite living under the same roof.

"Why don't you tell Didi to call more?" says my mom.

"Because he doesn't listen!"

"That's true," she says. "Maybe he learned the best way."

Chinese are imbued with the consciousness that each of us is only a link in a long life chain. The important thing is the family. What does it matter that one link shines more brightly than another?

—Anna May Wong, *Los Angeles Times Sunday Magazine,* 1934

My brother says everyone's families are fucked up in their own way. Ours is nothing special.

What a wise stance for being twenty years old, I think.

When I ask if his future family will be fucked up, he says oh yeah, it for sure would be, which is exactly why he's not having one.

Now the reporter is calling, making me both hate and admire his persistence. He reminds me of what I once chased, what I could have been. I answer the phone. He launches into small talk, faking a longtime friend catching up—How have you been? Where are you living? Whoa, that's a big change. What have you been up to?—that morphs into digging for the information he wants—I mean, what are you doing for work? Did you see my email and text? I give him short, clipped answers. I tell him yes, I saw his email and text, but he's mistaken and I don't know what he heard, but he must have gotten some bad information. I can't be of help.

"Oh, really? But somebody reliable told me you're working for Facebook," he says, in a condescending tone.

"Who?"

"Somebody who assured me you're doing that work."

"Well, I'm not. Who was it?"

He changes his tactic to bullying. "Are you sure? What's the big deal? I'm guessing you signed an NDA, but you won't even talk off the record? This could be a big story. It's Facebook, it's not like you're loyal to them, are you? Come on, what's the harm?"

But I don't budge. "No," I say. "I don't have anything to say."

I hear him typing in the background. Then he is silent for long enough that I think about hanging up on him. Finally he says, "Fine, get in touch if you change your mind?"

"Don't worry, I won't," I say, and hang up. Why so much anger? I ask myself. But here's a novel idea: a form of technology that would allow me to kick this reporter in the shin from across the country.

J asks if it's such a good idea to quit only four months in. I tell him it's not a big deal, since it was a freelance gig, not a real job. I didn't like it anyway. I will never put it on my résumé or ask them for a reference. It was soul sucking and I was a sellout and now at least I am not, technically, lying to that reporter. I'll find other work.

"But wasn't it good for you to have something consistent to do?"

"What are you saying?"

"Work to keep you busy. You've always needed work as long as I've known you."

"Well, maybe I'm evolving. Maybe I want to become something beyond work. Or maybe I deserve a break. And besides, there's still the museum. Don't worry about me," I say. "When have you ever had to worry about me?"

He looks at me with suspicion, then shrugs and says okay.

Here, in part, an answer about Yamei Kin and her husband, from the *San Francisco Call* in August 1904:

Superior Judge Hunt at yesterday's noon hour granted a divorce in a case that has probably never found its equal in this city. It will probably shock certain women's organizations which, according to the husband's testimony, listened for a long time to the lectures of his wife, who was then the only Japanese woman holding a degree as a doctor of medicine from an American college.

The plaintiff in the case is Hippolytus Laesola Amador Eca da Silva and the defendant Yamei Ken [*sic*] Eca da Silva. He was a Chinese interpreter employed by the Government. She is a graduate of a New York school of medicine and became sufficiently versed in the ways of doctors and women to gain a hearing before the clubs of her sex. Her husband was not "up to date," according to his testimony yesterday, and she, declaring herself a "new woman," left him. . . .

When she returned to San Francisco Da Silva met her and asked her to live with him again, but she declined on the ground that she had lecture engagements to fill in the East.

It's unclear from the sentence whether the article's author or her husband mistakenly calls Yamei Kin Japanese, instead of Chinese.

But this much is clear: She wearied of him. He was not up to date. She declared herself a new woman and left him. She had better things to do than to live with him.

"You always need a backup," says my dad, now sounding his composed self. "Like in war. That's why Chiang Kai-shek lost. No backup. And why the Americans lost in the Korean War. Well, technically, that war hasn't ended. Because there was nobody to back them up to begin with."

"I thought you were talking about a backup plan for my work."

"Both. You need a backup plan and backup power, like a generator when you lose electricity."

"Okay, I get that, but as for war, I don't like to think of my life like that."

"You can learn from war, though, how to think abstract, strategize, win. You know what I always say. My way——"

"Or the highway."

He laughs, that familiar high-pitched, breathy sound, like a cool breeze. "That's right. You know, I will always back you up. I hope your bonehead does the same." He pauses to think. His talking has taken a slower pace over the last couple of years, though he still talks as much, if not more. "There's a very old Chinese book you could learn from, I don't know the American title. It's written by a famous general about war."

"Yeah, *The Art of War*. I've never read it. The only people I know who love it are white guys."

"You better catch up and learn then. That's *your* history."

Instead of reading it in full, I look up Sun Tzu quotes.

"Appear weak when you are strong, and strong when you are weak."

"Great results can be achieved with small forces."

And this line of thinking again: "In the midst of chaos, there is also opportunity."

But upon further research, all appear to be diluted renderings. The closest thing I can find to the third is this, from an official translation by Lionel Giles: "Amid the turmoil and tumult of battle, there may be seeming disorder and yet no real disorder at all; amid confusion and chaos, your array may be without head or tail, yet it will be proof against defeat."

Watching J dance and wrestle with the dog, laughing and laughing. I have never felt more comfortable with another person. And our beginning was so strong. He was my first everything, including the first to whom I explained my entire family situation, and he is still the only. Of course I love him, despite this place, despite our differences, despite these changes. I could die now knowing that I have loved and been loved. I don't need a backup plan, do I? We are not in the same situation, Yamei Kin and I, now, are we.

                                       ·

He finally agrees to a kitten. More life, more anchors to this place. We go to the local SPCA and ask a young volunteer if we can bring the dog inside to test his reaction to cats. She agrees to our, as we soon learn, dangerous experiment. J takes the dog into a room and holds his leash tight. The volunteer and I carry kittens toward the room, but most fight back. They flail and scratch at us as soon as they see or smell the dog, and we all retreat. Two kittens make it into the room. The dog whines. He wags his tail. He does not look like he wants to kill. We bring the kittens closer. One shits right there in the volunteer's arms. The other, a black one with a white patch on his chest, does not bristle or flinch. I crouch and inch him closer and closer, until the dog nudges his nose against the kitten's face and licks the kitten's ear. The kitten looks at the dog, then looks away.

    "Wow," the volunteer says. "This one isn't scared at all."

So he is the one we take with us in a little cardboard box.

    "We're a happy family," J sings during the drive home.

In the matter of singing, it is worthy of note that the Chinese learn by ear; with but little practice, they sing the more common tunes and words with commendable accuracy, and take such pleasure in the exercise.

                  —L. T. Townsend, *The Chinese Problem*, 1876

But J and I have this in common: We can't control our pitch and we remember lyrics to almost no songs at all. We sing, but what comes out of our mouths does not merit the praise of that verb.

J also sings "Ebony and Ivory" to the cat and dog. This, however, makes me uncomfortable.

"Why?" he asks.

"They aren't races," I say. "They're pets."

"I just meant that they're literally black and white," he says. He starts to sing again. "And they live, dog and cat, in perfect harmony."

I go out to the bars with people from J's program, even though he stays home. He's had a long week of twelve-to-thirteen-hour days and isn't interested in staying out late with people he's seen at school and in lab. But he says, Go, have fun, I know you need to get out of the house. I kiss him on the forehead and leave.

But the scientists are hard to have fun with. They talk mostly of science, and to me they say things like "Is all of California that liberal?" and "What exactly do you do all day?" and "Are you considering graduate school?"

Two drinks in and I have determined my night's goal: find weed. I know J will appreciate it, too. It used to be a nightly activity for him in San Francisco, and now we've gone months without it. He will be happy with me if I can find it, all on my own, as he had done many times back home. (Wait, is that why things haven't been great in Ithaca? Because we haven't had weed? What an easy fix!) I squeeze through the crowd, weaving through, searching for the right kind of person. Then, while scanning the outdoor patio, somebody says beside me, "You look like you're ready to pounce."

I turn and see a tall man with long dark hair and a cigarette in his mouth wearing a white T-shirt that suggests toned muscle underneath. Yes, this could work. I ask if he smokes. He looks at me like I'm an idiot. He waves his cigarette in front of his face. "Do you want one?"

I decline, and clarify that I mean weed—does he smoke weed and would he know where I could get some. I reclarify that I don't mean at this very moment, but more generally, to buy. To buy sometime soon. He nods and puts out his cigarette, then asks for my phone. Good job, I tell myself. This isn't so hard. He has a nice face. Somebody comes from somewhere to slap him on the back. A small thrill. The exchange is over quickly; I say thanks and go back home, feeling accomplished.

The next morning, in bed, I tell J about the weed guy, who put his name in my phone as Rob. J, like I predicted, is happy and asks when I will make the call.

"Call him? I'm not calling him! I'm going to text."

"Hm, okay. Whatever works." And like on all Saturday mornings, he leaves for the lab.

Alone, I wonder how quick I need to be about initiating the transaction. I figure the sooner the better. Hey, this is the girl from the bar last night, I type out. Then I realize he may have met many girls at the bar last night. I try not to think about the fact that he looked like a guy who would meet a lot of women at a bar. Then I begin to hate myself for describing myself as a "girl" to some random guy, so I delete the whole thing and retype: Hey, I asked you about weed last night. Can you meet up? I'm free whenever.

Then I delete the last sentence, so as not to sound too desperate. Rob texts back that he can meet in a couple of hours.

I call J and update him on the entire process. "Shit, I wrote 'weed' in a text, is that really bad? Do drug dealers hate that?"

J laughs. "It will be fine. Okay, I need to go back to work." He is always calm. Laid-back. Not worried.

"Wait, wait, wait. What if he calls the cops? Or what if he's a psychopath? Should I bring the dog, just in case?"

"Sure, bring the dog. I have to go."

"Okay, but if I go missing, the dog will be wandering around and somebody will call you and then you'll know something bad has happened!"

But he hasn't heard this last plea because he's already hung up.

The drug dealer and I decide to meet at the Gimme! Coffee shop. On the way there, I rub the money in my pocket until it is warm. I think about a time in San Francisco when J went out with his labmates and didn't come home when I'd expected. He wasn't responding to texts or calls. It was past midnight on a weekday, unusual for him, and I worried. I tracked him on Find My Friends and watched his little blue dot move around the eastern parts of Golden Gate Park. Finally, after I'd envisioned all sorts of horrible scenarios, he texted that he was fine. He returned soon after and said he'd had an adventure. He'd gone into the park to find some-body who would sell him weed. (Why? Why didn't you just ask your usual person? J shrugged and said he wanted it that night.) He walked up to a group of bros, skinhead types, J called them. But they refused him, saying he looked like a cop. He'd started to bike home when a guy playing his guitar in some bushes called after J. The guitar-playing guy talked to J for a long time, about a friend who had been killed on the nearby street. The guy asked if J would watch his belongings while he went to do something for his friend. J said sure. (Why? I asked again. And all J could say was, He looked like somebody who would sell me weed.) The guitar-playing guy walked into the middle of the street and spun in circles, playing his guitar and singing. After he was done, he returned to J and said, You want weed? Follow me. The two of them biked for a while, through the park and out to some commercial building. (Did you know where you were? Again, he shrugged and said, Sort of.) They got off their bikes behind the building, then the guitar-playing guy threw J up against a wall. Are you a cop? Are you a fucking cop? J shook his head and said no. The guy patted him down. Okay, the guy said, satisfied. How much do you want? When the exchange was complete, the guy jumped on his bike and sped off.

What if he stabbed you? What if he robbed you? Weren't you scared? I asked.

J said he was surprised when he got pushed and patted, but the guy was harmless.

I told J to never, ever, ever do that again.

He laughed. Don't be mad, he said. He held up the bag of weed. It turned out fine.

I arrive early and sit on the bench outside, waiting. The dog pulls like crazy whenever somebody walks in or out. I am too early. I wait for a long time and am certain Rob won't show up. I consider going back home. I consider texting Rob that I've changed my mind, or that I got sick, or something came up and I can't make it. But I need to decide quickly or else I might run into him as I'm walking back. A father and daughter approach, interrupting my thoughts.

"Is your dog friendly?" the father asks. I say yes, and ask if his daughter wants to pet the dog. The daughter is pressed up against her father's legs, shaking her head, but he holds her tightly in place and says it's okay. He explains that his daughter is afraid of dogs, and that he, too, is a little afraid, because of the many wild street dogs where he'd grown up, but that he is trying to overcome this fear with and for his daughter. Go on, the dad says, and begins to nudge her toward the dog. The daughter tucks her chin into her chest and squirms, closes her eyes. The dog pulls forward. Both father and daughter shrink back. But the leash is tight, so the dog does not reach them. The father laughs. "See, he wants to meet you," he says. "Go on, it's okay." It seems he is speaking as much to himself as to his daughter. The father reaches a hand out to the dog, slowly, cautiously. "See, it's okay." His voice wavers, but he lets the dog sniff his hand, then leans farther in and pets the top of the dog's head. It reminds me of a time my father carried me down into our San Francisco home's pitch-black crawl space. Don't be afraid, he said. There's nothing to be afraid of in the dark. Then he let go of my hand and wandered off somewhere I could not see. Come back, I said. I cried. I closed my eyes, as though the darkness I put myself in would be more bearable than the darkness beyond.

But this daughter opens her eyes. I loosen the dog's leash. Child and animal are face-to-face. She pets him as cautiously as her father did, then smiles. "He's soft," she whispers. The dog licks her face and she giggles. The father picks up his daughter and thanks me, and as they walk away, I can hear the little girl excitedly recounting to her father—"Baba, the doggy licked me, Baba, did you see?"

This is when Rob walks up and says hi.

I barely recognize him. Only the hair—dark brown, just past his shoulders, with a hint of wave at the ends, reminding me of my own hair before I'd cut it all off—and the certainty from the night before that he had an attractive face. He looks at me, then at the dog, then back.

"You brought a dog," he says.

"A very friendly dog," I say, but he is already scratching the dog's ears as though they know each other, a gesture I find both endearing and invasive.

Rob says we should go to the park across the street. I don't like the idea, but it is the middle of the day and light out. I have just witnessed two people overcome a fear together, so I go.

We sit at a bench and I let the dog off leash to wade in the creek. We watch him for a minute, quiet and adjusting. Any resolve or determination I had the night before has vanished. I stick my hands in my coat pockets and rub the bills again. I want Rob to direct this interaction. But he, too, looks uncomfortable. He crosses and recrosses his legs, then asks me a series of questions: how long have I been in town, why have I moved here, where did I move from, what do I do, what do I think of the place? He seems to become calmer the longer I talk, the longer I answer his questions. He interjects occasionally, saying that he's a local, he went to college in California, too, at Pomona. He misses the West Coast. He hopes to move back there one day, but for now, it's easier to be home. As he relaxes, he stretches his arms out along the length of the bench. I resist flinching away from the one resting behind me. I call the dog back and make him lie beside us, to bear witness.

Rob tells me he lives down the street with some friends, all townies. He works up on campus—a "chill" job, where he helps run a few undergraduate leadership and scholarship programs. His mom is a fairly popular professor in the plant science department, and knows a lot of people, which is how Rob got the job. He says all he had to do was tap into the "Ithaca Filipino Network." I ask how big of a network that really is. He laughs and says it's small.

"Do you just deal on the side, then?" I ask.

"No," he says. "This is a one-time thing. We always have enough in the house, you know? I just thought it was funny, the way you asked. And I didn't feel like I could back out after you texted. But then, before I got here, I started worrying you were an undercover cop or something. I'm pretty paranoid in general, though. This all worked out. Right? You're not a cop, right?"

"No," I say. "I was worried you were, or you were going to call them."

We share a laugh, about the absurdity of our shared fears, and what I think, too, is the absurdity of two Asians working for the Ithaca Police Department. I realize he is the first person I've met in Ithaca whom I've had an easy time talking to, and I surprise myself by saying the thought aloud.

Rob smiles. "Don't worry, Ithaca will grow on you." He pulls a sandwich bag out of his pocket. "I just assumed you wanted an eighth?"

I nod and hand him the money. The dog whines. We talk some more, to dissipate the awkwardness of the transaction. Before we part ways, he gives me one of the bills back.

"Friend's discount," he says.

We sit next to the bedroom window with J's pipe and blow the smoke out of the screen. Each time, he lights it for me, because I can't seem to do it without burning my finger with the flame. We get into bed and I turn off the light on my side table. He protests a little, but I keep quiet and leave the light off. We lie next to each other, touching one another's arms and stomachs and necks and chests, until our eyes adjust to the dark and I can see the outlines of his face. Every movement of ours feels like fate, like destiny. We are perfectly timed because time relaxes for us. Afterward, I go sit on the toilet and feel my whole body pulse in the dark. I think about how content I am, but also how stupid I've been, how stupid I will be once this high wears off. What's wrong with me, I whisper. I want to hold on to this feeling that everything is good, or at least okay, but already it is slipping away. When I return to the bedroom I find J lying with his eyes closed and a smile on his face. What are you thinking? I ask. Nothing, he says. I'm just happy.

For Halloween I dress up as a mad scientist among scientists. I wear an old lab coat that J brought me from his workplace. On the chest pocket is written in Sharpie YING YING. I cover the name with a sticker of the history museum's logo. Somebody asks me if the sticker is part of my costume, to which I reply, No, it's just where I work, it is just covering somebody else's name. I don't want anybody to think that Ying Ying is my Chinese name—however similar it is to my Chinese name. If "Matt" or "Casey" or "Erica" had been written on the coat, I probably would've left it and joked that it was my scientist alter ego. Later in the night, when I am drunk, I find a Sharpie, rip the sticker off, and scribble over the name until it is all blacked out.

A graduate student in a mouse costume is talking to me about the difficulties of committing to one lab. Though I don't understand the science, I've learned the social workings of the department, the rumors surrounding professors and their work styles, the hierarchies and competitions, which students are rotating where, who is excelling and who is flailing. J has gained more confidence as the months have passed. The professors love him, they fight over him, and he has his pick for which lab he'll join. (A happy shift for J, who lacked so much confidence coming in.) This woman whom I am speaking to is having a more difficult time. She came straight from undergrad, and wasn't accustomed to the lack of instruction, the lack of worksheets and assignments. She tells me she misses her textbooks, the things that told her, Do this, then that, memorize this, then you'll ace the test. One prominent professor already made clear to her that she would not be welcome in his lab. The rejection was so painful and shattering, she left early and cried the rest of the day. And this is where the discussion of our parents begins. The woman, too, is Chinese American. Both of her parents are medical doctors. When they ask how the Ph.D. is going, she feels compelled to lie. She has to find another power lab to join, to make them happy, to make them proud. I wonder if she is confiding in me because she expects some shared experience, or sees me as an older-sister figure—she seems incredibly young—or if I am simply the one there at the right moment to hear her out. I say that sounds tough, that perhaps she should consider a lab that interests her more, rather than one with perceived status, because then she might be more committed to the work. She nods and says it's something to consider. Then come the questions: Were your parents strict? Were they disappointed you didn't go into medicine or science or engineering or law? How did you tell them what you wanted to do? How were you able to deal with them? No, I told her. They weren't disappointed. They definitely didn't let me do whatever I wanted, but they didn't expect I would go into science or engineering or medicine. Maybe law and business were suggested more than I wanted to hear, but in the end they let me pursue what I wanted. Did you have to play an instrument? Only until I was thirteen, only until I didn't want to anymore. Was it hard for them to say "I love you"? To hug you? To show you affection? Not at all. She looks as though she's thinking very hard. Wait, are your parents American? she asks. Yes, I say. She lights up. Oh, okay! That's why you were so lucky, because they grew up here, too.

I know then, despite our similarities, we are vastly different. No, I say, very slowly. They are immigrants, who came here in their twenties. They are naturalized Americans. Oh, she says. What do they do for work? I tell her my dad is retired and my mom is an accountant. She nods. I guess they just weren't really Chinese parents, then, she says. I almost say to her, You mean, they weren't *your* Chinese parents? They weren't stereotypical Chinese parents? But instead I cough and say, calmly, lightly, jokingly, Well, they are Chinese and they are my parents, so they are Chinese parents. She laughs. You know what I mean, she says, with what I think is a touch of condescension. This is not a battle I want to fight. I feel something akin to pity, but alongside it, anger. I think of her doctor parents funding her life, of her use of the term "lucky," of our different understandings of what that means. Why does she need to reaffirm these markers of her experience, a valid and real experience I know to be true, as *the only* qualifiers—and why to me, who certainly knows exactly what she means? Maybe it feels safer. Maybe it is a scientist's mind at work. Maybe it is better to be exceptional in this way than to be something else, something less familiar. And now we turn away from each other, likely both bitter with the other.

What would somebody like her want to hear? Perhaps a very simple scenario: junior year, for every minute I was late home, I had to study an hour for the SAT. Or maybe a story with more of a physical effect: the one time, a blooming bruise on the skin covering my ribs, how it fascinated me with its red and purple whorls. Or would more confusion and violence satisfy? How they cursed each other out in Shanghainese and threw whatever they could get their hands on. How my sister and I had to pull them apart. Me pulling my mom and my sister pulling my dad, and yet somehow us all toppling onto one another on the couch. I don't remember what my brother did or where he was, only that later, the police arrived, and the three of us stayed in a bedroom refusing to be questioned, how we did not come out until it was quiet. Are these the sad stories that you want?

The tea bag: *Act, don't react.*

An hour deliberating over an email to Tim, to ask if he has any work for me. We haven't spoken in months. He writes back ten minutes later:

> Do you want to do a roundup review of mechanical pencils? No rush,
> it's evergreen.

Yes, sure, okay. Anything to make me feel like I'm doing something with myself.

Also in the email:

> Remember what I said? That the adjustment period for moving
> across the country to follow your partner is about six months. He has
> to forgive you for everything you do in that time period. That's what I
> did for my wife . . .

I must have made my situation sound bleaker than I'd intended.

That said, less than two months left to do and feel anything and whatever in that ellipsis.

When we first graduated, J worked at a bike shop, the same one that employed him as a high schooler and whose owner also ran a Bible shop next door.

"What was the point of going to college if I'm back here doing exactly the same thing?" he said. He cried and smoked a lot of weed in those days. I now understand better how he felt then.

In January 1937, Pardee Lowe wrote of his successful marriage to a white woman in *Asia* magazine:

MIXED MARRIAGE
A Chinese Husband and American Wife
Are Put to Test

Commencement time for me meant no hilarious celebration, despite the fact that I held under one arm a diploma from an internationally famous graduate school of business and in the other a wife who had just rejoined me after a year abroad studying music. The absence of parental approval and the withdrawal of our monthly allowances signified all too conclusively the objections of our respective families to our sudden marriage of the year before. And the problem of unemployment loomed before us; the depression was then at its worst, and jobs, it seemed, were not to be had. . . .

Not only my own future was at stake but my wife's. Strange had been our romance, partaking of all the qualities of fiction. Even the gods in their Olympian detachment must have smiled at the singularity of our union, the product of fortuitous circumstances and inalterable fate.

This is more like us, I think.

The weather is turning, dropping fast. More of my hair is falling out than usual; I find it everywhere in the house, and sometimes hanging from the dog's butthole as he shits. My mom says it has to do with the seasons.

"People lose a lot of hair in the fall and winter," she says. "Then it will grow back in the spring."

"I'm not a tree," I say.

"Yes," she says, "you are like the trees. Needs sun and water and vitamins."

Two ginkgoes shed all their leaves yesterday and today they're totally naked, the ground beneath them a thick pool of yellow. The white dog wades in.

At the crowded coffee shop, where I am pitching random ideas to editors in hopes of getting more work. A white woman who looks to be in her midthirties asks if I mind sharing a table. I nod. I mean, no, I say. I don't mind.

Days have passed during which I haven't spoken in person to anybody but people behind or in front of registers, or J, but even then, barely. But she is an extrovert, clearly, which brings it out in me. Though I stutter at first from nervousness and excitement, we talk for a while, pleasantly. When I mention what I'm doing, she lets out a yelp of recognition, as though we are two friends bumping into each other at a party of strangers. She's a professor in the journalism department at the liberal arts college in town. She used to work as a producer at a morning TV news station in a nearby city, but realized that it didn't suit her personality. Waking up incredibly early in the mornings, having to chase some small story down, it was tiring and often felt meaningless. I say I felt the same about my work. She says she's found meaning in teaching, even though she's training some students to be the next generation of morning news producers. Not that it would be any good for them. Almost nobody watches TV news anymore. There's no stability or money in it. That's the past. The present, the future, it's all online. I say sure, but there's no stability or money in that, either. She asks if I have any interest in teaching.

"We could really use a person like you," she says. "Somebody who can bring a different dimension to our students that we don't have with our current staffing. We don't have tenure-track positions right now, but we're looking for lecturers. It's easy, you just tell them what you know, make some activities and exercises, that's about it."

Yes, she does make it sound easy. I hadn't considered teaching before, but now I picture myself standing in front of undergraduates, clicking through PowerPoint slides, waving my arms to emphasize takeaways, asking important questions. The students look back with attentive, curious faces, hungry for knowledge. Yes, that could be meaningful.

Then the woman leans in toward me and asks, "How do you like Ithaca?"

I want to be positive, so I say that overall, it has been pretty nice.

She leans farther in, and looks like she's about to tell me a secret. "How do you feel about the lack of Asians in town, though? The last time I visited California, I noticed there were so many Asians everywhere. I was like, wow! It almost felt like traveling to a different country."

A significant shaking and bumping take place inside my brain and body. I can't say I'm having thoughts, exactly, only reactions and feelings. Disgust. The sense of having been tricked. Distrust. A strong desire to escape.

She laughs and says she didn't mean anything by it. She loved California—amazing people and amazing weather.

"Honestly, Ithaca is also wonderful," she continues. "You're actually quite lucky to have ended up here. It's incredibly diverse in comparison to the rest of upstate New York. The two colleges attract a lot of international students. And Tompkins County is very liberal. Places just outside of Ithaca—have you heard of Free-ville? Or Spencer? Or Owego? I could never live in those places. It would be so weird and uncomfortable not seeing people of dif-ferent ethnicities and backgrounds walking around. That isn't my kind of place. They're also much more conservative and closed-minded," she says, still leaning toward me. Her breath is sour, like something is rotting inside her. I look away. She keeps talking. "I just meant it's not California, so you must be adjusting. But really, you lucked out. Ithaca is really a paradise on earth."

"Yeah, it's fine." I pack up my computer and down what's left of the coffee. What's fine exactly? Ithaca? The adjustment? Her remarks? "I have to go pick something up now, sorry."

"I hope you're not offended. Please know that wasn't my in-tention!"

"Oh, no," I say, and stand up. "The table's yours now."

"It was so nice to meet you," she says. She hands me a business card. Associate professor. "Definitely apply to the lecturer posi-tion. Email me when you do and I'll put in a good word!"

I walk back to the house, the whole way thinking of things I could and should have said.

Maybe it meant nothing. Or it meant something. She was being sympathetic in order to bond. Or she was making a statement, nothing more or less. Is this what was meant by a "different dimension"? Oddly, yes. Upsettingly, yes, she's right. This town has been an adjustment.

For example, how my body does not know how to respond to this drastic change in climate. Or how haunted Ithaca feels with its narrow streets of old houses. Or because it's tiny and I have walked to all the places I can walk to, seen everything I can see. Or that J is so busy, living a full life, while I plod in circles in the house and my mind. Or the dead squirrel I saw, so pristine and still, its eyes so open that I thought it was simply taking a rest, staring up at the sky, but then the dog nudged it with his nose and my whole body felt its death radiating out, like death could touch me. Or the creeks that rise so high and rush so opaque and brown, you begin to wonder what's being swept away underneath.

And yes, the whiteness. The whitenesses. The kind the woman distanced herself from. And the kind she inhabits. I thought I had grown accustomed to at least one, from time in Davis, time in the workplace, time in life. But maybe I have not.

When I get home I look up the college's journalism department page and see that, as expected, the faculty is entirely white, with the exception of one black male professor who teaches sports journalism.

"You speak of the yellow peril, we speak of the white disaster," said Yamei Kin to a New York audience in 1904.

After I tell him about the encounter, J asks if I'll apply for the lecturer position. I say nope, not going to happen.

"Just because of what that professor said about Asians in Ithaca?"

"I'm trying to prevent and avoid certain situations when I can."

"Who cares what she said? It can be to your advantage."

"That's one way to look at it."

"I bet you'd be good at teaching. And it doesn't seem like you like what you're doing now anyway."

"But I don't want to see her again. I don't want to interact with her. I'm the one who cares about what she said."

"You probably won't have to, though. Don't you think it would be better to at least try?"

"Yes, I would have to. She'd be the reason if I get hired, and it would be irritating and demeaning to be around her."

"I just feel like you complain about your work now, so you should try to do something different. And it sounds like they want someone like you."

"What does 'someone like me' mean?"

"Someone with a tech journalism background."

"Sure, okay. But that's not only what she meant. I just don't want to be some walking form of proof that she's a good white person. She's the kind who would see me and make little comments about how she helped get me there, as if I should be forever grateful to her. And she'd be constantly trying to prove how good she is. Like, she'd come to me to make herself feel better. And it would have nothing to do with me and everything to do with her."

"It sounds like you're overthinking what she said. You're taking a hard lens to it."

"What do you mean, a hard lens?"

"Like, you think what she did is really bad and that she's bad."

"I'm not saying that everything and every person is either good or bad. There are obviously gradations and variations. I'm not saying she's the worst person, or that she was blatantly racist. But what she did comes from that same line of thinking."

"To me, it just seemed like she was being nice and thought you'd be a good fit because you worked in online journalism, and the Asian comment was just something she noticed. I mean, California is way more Asian than here."

"Wow, yeah, okay, great! Let me just go work for this nice, observant white lady, who definitely doesn't want anything from me, like for example filling some diversity quota she just realized she needed to fill or whatever! As long as she's nice and I get something out of it, then nothing else matters."

"Okay, then."

We both go quiet.

"You don't get it," I say.

He doesn't respond.

"I just wish you would try. Or maybe you'll never understand and that's fine. Just trust that I'm upset for a real reason and support me."

"I do support you. But I'm also telling you what I think. Do you want me not to be honest with you?"

"No. That's not what I said. I just don't get why you're arguing with me, your girlfriend, and defending some random person you don't even know, after I tell you that she made me feel weird and bad. It feels to me like you're defending her because she's white and so are you."

"I don't think so. I'm not arguing. I have my own thoughts, too. And I don't want you to feel bad. But I don't think you should feel that bad from what she said."

"Oh. My. God. Really? We're going to keep doing this?"

Our conversation, or whatever it is, goes in a few more spirals, and both of us grow fatigued. And in the tiredness, the silences between our words extend further. There are distances neither of us wants to traverse, as though going from where one stands to where the other stands is to break from an essential part of oneself. And if both of us remain as firm in our positions, then what? Is it possible both of us are in the right? I doubt it. I won't go there.

Fuck dating white guys, I hear Jasmine say. This is the longest she and I have gone without talking since we met. I realize I miss her. I miss the past. I fantasize about running away. Booking a flight back to San Francisco. Getting up and walking out the door, taking the bus to New York City and staying there. Him doing something more terrible than this, him cheating on me or worse, so my departure can be justified and understandable to everyone outside of us. A life with somebody who would understand, without the trouble or difficulty. Or a life alone. A life with my own direction.

. . . With the impetuosity of youth, we were eager to solve the mysteries of the universe together, to seek hand in hand the attainment of perfection in a world of imperfection. These mysteries and aims were to be eternally symbolized for us in the symphonies we heard, in the historic spots we visited and in our growing interest in each other. . . . Within three months from the time of our first meeting, we were secretly engaged.

Then, followed months of heart-searching discussion on the problem of the marriage of diverse races. I was truly a product of environment. From infancy to young manhood I had lived in an atmosphere poisoned with the bitterest racial prejudices and antagonism. . . . As a result, like all my kind, I suffered from the twin diseases that are ineradicable from Chinatown, pathological race consciousness and what I call "Americanitis," a condition in which all of one's traditional heritage becomes anathema and all that pertains to the western world seems perfect.

He finds me upstairs in the office and approaches. He touches my arm. I refuse to react.

"Alexandra?"

"What?"

"I'm sorry," he says.

I don't believe him. "I don't believe you," I say. "Sorry for what?"

"Sorry for not supporting you and listening to you," he says. "I know I don't understand, but I'm going to try harder. I just don't want you to be miserable at home, doing work you don't like. You're always talking about how much you hate Ithaca. It makes me worried."

Now I feel guilty and ashamed. Why?

"I'm not miserable. I don't hate Ithaca," I say, unconvincingly. He holds me.

"Spending the last two hours on Vine *was* an excellent use of our time," I say to the kitten, who is curled into a shrimp shape on my lap.

Was it this morning or yesterday that I brushed my teeth?

> Being of a proud nature, I did not wish my *fiancée* to rush blindly into a mixed marriage without a true picture of the situation. To forewarn her, I implored her to read all the books obtainable on the subject of interracial marriage. She did and found the trials and tribulations of such unions numberless; their joys, few. Yet, undismayed, sure of herself, she refused to turn back.

Oh, that's what I should have asked him to do. I send him this article and a long list of others, collected in a haze, then text: Did you see the links I emailed?

He writes back: Yes, but don't have time to read them right now. I will later.

> Do not think that I overstress the horrors of race prejudice. One cannot be indifferent to the sufferings of one's own people any more than one can ignore a severe personal injury. . . . But my wife, who had never yet personally experienced any instances of race prejudice, was amazed, insisting that I was foolish, that I magnified the dangers.

The dog and the cat sleep in the same position, on their backs and feet up, as though in peaceful surrender. They know something I don't. I could watch them forever.

And now, high alone, I am thinking about texting the not-drug-dealer Rob. But I don't know what I would say besides "hey," so no, my sober part tells my high part, Don't.

> ". . . Under this pressure our marriage will doubtless crack wide open. In case it does not, your cross will be a difficult one to bear. You will be denied the right to choose your place of residence. Personal services will be extended grudgingly. The majority of your people will stare at you as at a circus freak. Still others, race glorifiers, will despise and curse you for committing the most unpardonable of mortal sins—

marrying a 'Chinaman.' These experiences will sear your soul."

I stumbled on recklessly, mercilessly, intent on enlightenment. I have often asked myself, Was I cruel? Perhaps. Yet the greater cruelty, I was convinced, lay in leaving her in ignorance.

I collect some more articles and attach them, replying to my previous email to J.

Stoned thoughts, numbers, approximately, 261 to 272: Do white people ever wish they weren't white? And if so, why? Out of guilt or something else? Do they ever wish they were Asian? And if so, why? Misunderstood desire? To steal and to plunder? A self-hatred rooted in . . . what?

One late October night, however, we were brutally dislodged from our false sense of security. We drove into a sumptuous Southern California autocamp. In answer to our request for a night's lodging there came back the laconic reply, given to the accompaniment of a slamming door and a muffled oath, "All taken!" The cabins were untenanted. The camp was practically deserted. Yet, the realization was bitter, we were not wanted. My wife became intensely angry; for it was her first experience with racial prejudice in its extreme form. As for me, my face flushed fire as a flood of bitter memories came rushing back.

That was not this. This doesn't mean anything. She didn't mean anything by it. You didn't mean it. This doesn't have to mean something. This doesn't mean anything, if you don't look at it that way. What does this mean, then? This means nothing. What do they mean, then? What they mean is that you mean nothing.

He once told me he loved me because I was loyal. Loyal!

Couldn't that be translated into a form of narcissism? I love you because you love me.

Then again, I guess I do, too. Love him because he loves me.

"But maybe the me he loves is not the me I am. And vice versa, the true, deep-down him that he is is not the him I love," I say to the dog and cat curled here beside me in bed.

"Does that make sense?" They follow me everywhere. They are the best listeners.

Stonehead, my mom called him.

"It's 'stoner' or 'pothead.' And he's not one, I swear," I said, laughing.

"Pothead, stonehead, bonehead," she said. "All the same!"

"Actually, yeah, you're kinda right."

On the phone with my sister—who has forgiven me—we are asking ourselves, yet again, and this time more seriously on my end: Why are we with white men? Is it because we've been taught all of these years from all of this white American media that whiteness is the epitome of attractiveness? And even though we are aware of it, have we internalized it so deeply that it can't be rooted out? (That might have something to do with it.) Or are we subconsciously trying to climb social and political ladders? Are we fitting into this stereotype of the gold-digging Dragon Lady Asian wife? (We hope not!) Or was it that, where we grew up and went to school, white people were more readily available? (Must play a role.) Or, my sister muses, are we trying to ensure that our kids are part white? (I am probably not having kids, I say. Okay, she says.)

"I've thought about that a lot lately—am I dating a white guy to make sure that my future kids are also white, and have it easier? Is that a form of survival?"

"Well, are you?"

"I don't think so? But I don't know! Maybe it's subconscious!"

We laugh for a while. It is funny. It's all too funny. We survive through the laughter.

She asks if I remember how everybody obsessed over our cousins when we were young. Yes, I say. Those beautiful Eurasian faces. She says she used to think the mixed-race white and Asian girls in high school got along better with the popular white girl crowds. Maybe it was simply because they were white passing. Their proximity to whiteness gave them white privileges.

"I had no idea back then that a lot of white people can't even tell when somebody is part Asian," she says. "And if they're the ones who can't tell, I guess that's what matters, so maybe that's why."

"But I always think mixed-race white and Asian people look more Asian," I say. "The Asian genes are so dominant. In that way, we can't be erased!"

"Yeah, but that's just how *you* see it," she says. "And even though they look Asian, they're treated differently. I feel weird about saying they look better, or more attractive, because saying that makes me feel like I'm saying that looking whiter is better."

"Yeah," I say. I tell her about not-drug-dealer Rob, and how he is mixed-race Filipino and white, and how yes, he is also hot.

"Ha ha! See. Anyway, it's just something I've wondered."

The notion that interracial relationships with white people could solve the problems of racism—that, we don't even consider.

What I'm wondering, though, is: What would be different with an Asian man, or another person of color? How much easier would it be? What kinds of conversations and pains could we bypass? What kinds of cultural aspects and perspectives of the world could we share?

"I've been with more people than you," says my sister. "And not only white people."

It's true, I've only ever been serious with J. He was my first boyfriend, first everything, which, too, has its advantages and drawbacks. But I have the impulse to defend myself.

"I *saw* and *sorta* dated plenty of nonwhite people in college," I say.

"You sound like Didi," she says. "And that's when you were like, what, eighteen? Nineteen? So then why didn't you date them more seriously?"

"I don't know," I say. "I guess because I was eighteen or nineteen."

"Anyway, in some ways it was easier. But we had other problems. I mean, look at Mommy and Daddy. It's not like being with somebody of the same race or ethnicity solves everything, either."

"True, true," I say. "But do you think Daddy was happier with Mommy than with Sharon?"

"Oh yeah," she says. "I forget he had another wife before, and a white one. Thinking about them from before creeps me out. Wait, are you asking because of this guy you met?"

I laugh. "I don't know," I say. "But it is a question I've been asking myself."

"Do you ever look at me and think I look like a stranger?" I ask.

"Huh? No," says J.

"Oh."

"Why? Does that happen when you look at me?"

"I mean . . ." I hum a short tune. "There are also times when I look in a mirror and I'm like, what the, why? That looks like a stranger, too. Does *that* happen to you?"

He looks at me, worried. "No," he says, slow.

"Never mind, maybe it's just me!"

It was not that bad, he said.

Unquestionably bad:

On May 4, 1983, Thong Hy Huynh, a seventeen-year-old Vietnamese refugee, was stabbed and killed on the science quad of the Davis Senior High School campus, in between class periods, in front of an audience of around one hundred students. The murder was said to be the culmination of a months-long "feud" between a group of Vietnamese boys (all immigrants, refugees, newly arrived in the country, newly arrived in this idyllic little college town—Huynh had been there all of three years) and a group of white boys. The feud, unsurprisingly, was caused by the white boys tormenting and bullying the Vietnamese boys. In the middle of this particular murderous dispute, the white boy, with violence and racism in his heart and mind, went to his car to get a hunting knife, and stabbed Huynh in the torso.

"This might have been a conflict between human beings without the immigrant aspect being a factor," said the principal days later at an assembly. "But I don't want to downplay the possibility of conflict between the mainstream and new people."

"They were loners—they stayed by themselves," one student said of the Vietnamese boys. "They always tried to ignore the hassling. I guess the only people who get bothered are the people who make themselves outcasts."

Of the white boy, it was said that he had "a thing about showing off in front of his friends."

The following week, on the same day as Huynh's memorial service, during which his mother cried for forty-five minutes and collapsed, leaflets from a group called the White Students Union of Sacramento circulated on campus, urging white students to stick together. For what purpose exactly, it was unclear. Two years later, the white murderer was convicted of voluntary manslaughter—a lesser charge than murder—and sentenced to a measly six years in juvenile detention, after the judge heard pleas from the mothers of both the victim and the murderer.

It's too lenient, it's not enough time, said Huynh's mother.

The school put up a plaque, which is still there today, in the science quad among perennials. I have seen it. We walked by the plaque nearly every day in high school, but most of us never noticed or paid much attention.

Another outcome of the murder: Friendship Day. It was—and still is—a monthly event meant to bring high school students closer, to break down social barriers, and to build, as the name calls for, friendship. And yet, the day itself was, like Davis, so white. A group of select students acted as Friendship Day facilitators. To become one, you had to go through an interview process. It was common knowledge, however, that it was largely a popularity contest. If you were close to an outgoing facilitator or the Friendship Day coordinator—a well-liked white male AP U.S. history teacher—the chances of you becoming one increased exponentially. It was no surprise then that facilitators were predominantly white. There was an occasional outcast—a dorky kid or an international student—among them, there as if to prove the system wasn't what we felt it to be. Facilitators, too, chose who to invite. I knew a boy who went to four Friendship Days in one year. My senior year, I went to two, and on one occasion, my friend group made up at least half of the attendees. We didn't need to be there. And we didn't ask, Who isn't here because we are? It was innocent. We were having fun, and for a good cause. Inclusion and exclusion worked in these veiled ways.

Not that the day did much to address racism. It started with a clip from *The Breakfast Club,* followed by a conversation about stereotypes. A fine movie and activity having nothing to do with race. There was a doughnut-eating contest to the song "Roxanne," where students attempted to eat a small Entenmann's powdered doughnut each time the Police sang the name. Perhaps the most "compelling" activity was when the group responded to yes/no questions, and those who answered yes had to cross the room to the other side, then make eye contact with somebody on the opposing side. Questions like, Are you an only child? Do you have a 3.5 GPA or higher? Do you sometimes feel lonely? Again, I don't remember any questions related to race. (J says the only ones he remembers were asked by a creepy man on the school board: Do you have a secret tattoo? Do you have a secret piercing? Perturbed, none of the teens crossed the room.) Now, looking back, I don't recall any discussion of race at any Friendship Day I attended, except for a brief mention, at the beginning, that the event was founded in response to the "racially motivated" murder of Thong Hy Huynh on our very own campus. Perhaps it has changed in the years since. I would hope so.

Rob texts *me*. He invites "you and your boyfriend" to come over for a "small party/show" at his place. J lies on the couch watching YouTube videos of animal chiropractors cracking cat backs and readjusting dog hips. His new hobby that I do not allow him to practice on our animals. When I double- and triple-check on his attendance, he shakes his head. He's worked another long day. And in the hour since he's come home, he's not moved from the couch, not taken his eyes off the videos, not spoken more than a few sentences to me.

"But it would be good for you to do something fun," I say.

He finally looks up from his phone. "Going to a drug dealer's party doesn't sound fun."

"I told you he's not a drug dealer. That was just once."

"Sure, that's what he said to you." He looks back to the phone. "Sorry, I'm tired, I still don't want to go."

His lack of attendance never bothered me before, but now, our differences feel starker, like whatever is between us is stretching cavernously wide, a gorge cut away deeper and deeper, too dangerous to cross. And yet, it is also a relief to go without him.

Rob is offering me a beer. In preparation for this occasion, I took one pill of Pepcid AC on the walk. I pull another out of my pocket to take with the first drink.

"Does it actually help?" he asks.

"It does." I tell him about one of my Korean friends in college who carried an entire bottle in his pocket at all times. Pop 'em like candy, he'd say, and dole them out to the rest of us.

Rob laughs. The sound is full and genuine and a little bit frightening, like waves crashing to shore.

"I'm grateful I don't have to worry about that," he says. "Never had any issues. Must be an advantage of the white genes."

"Yes, one of many." Now I am laughing. It feels good.

He asks where my boyfriend's at. I say, Home. He's tired; he works a lot.

"Oh," says Rob. "Well, I'm glad you made it out."

Is it wrong in this moment to want to touch his face, to have that sudden urge to press yourself against another person?

This is the type of party where half the people have known each other since they were in diapers (they hug, they wrestle, they grope, they kiss one another) and the other half don't know anybody. ("How do you know Tom/Rob/Daniel/Yan?" "Oh,

I don't, really." "I'm here because a friend of a friend knows a guy in the band." "I'm here because I work with somebody who knows one of them.") It's a healthy party mix—there is a sense of camaraderie that the strangers can lean into, melded with a sense of the unknown for the old friends to feed off of. Everybody is comfortable or drunk. People exchange numbers. They make exclamations to hang out at a later date. But it is temporary. My voice sounds like another person's voice. I talk to hundreds of strangers with it. Then there is live music played by an energetic group of men in their midtwenties to late thirties, including Rob on bass. But it turns out I hate the music, which is mostly screaming and loud drums. It reminds me of high school. For a moment, I feel sad for them, these grown men holding on to their teenage years, but then I feel sad for myself, because I don't have anything that I am as excited about as they are about their band and its ear-piercing music. Carrying this sadness, which feels both delicate and heavy, like a big glass mirror, I decide it's time for me to go.

At the door, there appear to be nine hundred pairs of shoes. Mine are somewhere in the mass. It is astonishing that this many people would take their shoes off to enter a party. I remember a white friend who, when asked to please take off her shoes upon entering a no-shoes house, responded, No, I don't feel like it, and stomped in, boots on. I think of J, whom I often need to remind. What a mature party with mature people wanting to keep a place clean of immature dirt. Then there's that scream-singing from the living room. No, it doesn't make sense. People should keep their shoes on at parties to make for easier exits. I scan the pile, then sift, then dig. Finally, I find my black ankle boots beneath a pair of worn sneakers. I start to walk out. Except, no. My feet don't feel right. Something to do with the toes or the arch. I look closer. The shoes aren't mine. I take them off, disgusted. Then I reconsider. They do fit. I could put them back on. They look almost the same as my shoes, maybe even a little newer, slightly less scratched up. I could leave, as I had been intending to do, so, so long ago, it feels like. A sea of shoes. An eternity. The screaming continues. The vibrations of the drum pulse up through the floor.

The other woman's boots are nicer. That's why I can't take them. If they were worse off than my boots, I could. I would. In which case, whomever these shoes belong to could take my shoes as an upgrade. It's only okay to take someone's shoes without permission if you're leaving behind an upgrade. That's the rule. That's my rule. You must leave something better behind for those from whom you steal. I try on the worn sneakers. They're too big. Clearly belonging to a man. They smell sweaty. I shake them off. I try on a few pairs of flats. None have the right feel, the right vibe, the right aura. Then, just because I see them glimmering, I put on a pair of block-heeled midcalf boots made of pebbled gold leather. They're beautiful and strange, like a rare species of fish. I'd never wear them out. I'd never be able to pull them off. I can't pull them off. I truly can't pull them off. I've shoved my too-large feet into somebody else's too-small shoes. The music has stopped. Standard party sounds resume. My feet are suffocating. I sweat, worrying that the owner of the shoes will find me like this and press charges. What charges? Theft? Assault? Of shoes? She'll tell everyone of my disturbing, untrustworthy behavior—a fetish, they'll call it—and I'll be ostracized in this tiny town, even though, I'll swear again and again, cross-my-heart-hope-to-die, I've never done anything like this before, I'd give them back if I weren't trapped in them.

Somebody walks by but doesn't notice me in my plight. I pull and tug and pull and tug. And finally, the golden shoes come off. Never have I felt so relieved, so freed, so lucky! Then I remember I still haven't found my own pair. Everything is terrible again. The pile has doubled in size. It is an ever-growing hoard of shoes. This is purgatory. I am being punished for something I've done in a previous life. I jilted somebody, I stabbed somebody, I was a colonizer, I ruined lives. Another somebody asks me if I'm okay, and I tell them, in a voice so calm it surprises me, *Yes, just looking for my shoes*. Good luck, they say. I'm being punished for something I've done in this life, in this recent life. This is karma working against me. For all my secrets and my bad thoughts and bad behavior, for my not being good enough.

Rob and his bandmates walk toward the door. I look up at them and realize I've long grown out of my musician phase.

"We're going out for a smoke. A cigarette, specifically," Rob says. He waves the thing and smiles, like the first night. "Wanna join?"

"No, I'm okay. Just getting my shoes so I can go."

"Already?"

"This is what happens when you come into an Asian household," says the drummer, before walking out the door in a pair of fuzzy blue slippers. Thank you. Revelatory. Like I didn't already know.

"Do you want help? What do they look like?"

Rob crouches beside me and his leg touches my leg.

I look down at our touching legs. I move away. The bad karma is spreading.

"No, it's okay. I see them, I see them."

I snatch the boots, check them closely to make sure they're mine (they are), and put them on. I thank him for inviting me, say I had fun, and exit as quickly as possible.

Outside, it is freezing and the landscape is gray and lifeless. Children of the East Coast must understand mortality better than those on the West.

Since she is three hours behind, I call my mom on the walk home. We used to text each other every night before sleep: Good night, love you, then wait for the other's response. If she didn't reply within a certain time frame, I'd call until she picked up. She'd say, You're that worried about me? I was just in the bathroom. Or, I didn't hear my phone. I told her I needed to hear from her to feel comfortable going to sleep. But we've stopped doing that because of the time difference; the synced routine is broken. I'm sad we aren't doing it anymore. I needed it. Here is my philosophy: a natural response to chaos is the desire for control.

"What are you saying?" says my mom. "Are you drunk?"

"A little."

"Geez. I hope you're not drinking so much there."

"No." But I tell her both Daddy and J have a similar view on substances: in life, every person needs to be dependent on something, they've said on separate occasions.

She asks why I'm alone. She sounds worried. Where is J?

"At home," I say. I hiccup into the phone.

"What is it?" she says. "Are you fighting?" The sound of her voice makes me want to cry.

"I'm . . . I think . . . The problem is . . . I think I might love the cat and dog more than I love him!"

"What!" She laughs and laughs. I laugh, too. The hiccups grow wilder. "My crazy daughter. I miss you."

"Me too," I say. And then I do start crying.

At my door my phone buzzes with a text. It's from Rob: Did you make it home safe? I should've offered to walk you so you wouldn't have to go alone. Hope it wasn't too far . . .

I text back, Not murdered, and a thumbs-up emoji.

Inside, the dog and cat run down the stairs to greet me. I can hear the white noise machine running in the bedroom. "Hi, my babies, my sweet little babies," I say to the animals.

The phone buzzes with another text. He's replied, What a relief with a smiling-face emoji, the one with the sweat mark on its forehead.

My stomach ripples. What am I doing?

I run to the bathroom and crouch on the floor in front of the toilet.

J has not heard me over the white noise. I don't bother waking him. I am just a little sick.

To soothe my stomach, the ginger tea bag advises: *You don't need love, you are love.*

My brother on the phone. He's ordered a genetic test and analysis report to better understand his health and ancestry.

"I tested in the top percentile for Neanderthal! Who knew, I'm a fucking caveman!"

"Why doesn't that surprise me at all."

"You know it probably means you're caveman, too."

I order the same genetic test with the hope of getting answers. Instead, the company sends another kit with a note that I have not provided enough sample in the spit tube.

"Are these tests ever even accurate?" I ask J, the scientist.

He says, "Yes, I think so."

Still, I leave the tube on my desk.

It snows for the first time and J calls to ask if it's snowing at home. It is! A little! We are both excited, staring out of different windows, watching the same flakes birth from the sky. We make plans to take the dog to the park, to see if he'll like it. By then there is a thin layer on the grass, like sugar dusted on desserts, and the dog bounds in it, leaving his prints.

"It's like we're in a snow globe," he says.

"I was *just* thinking that," I say.

In that moment, I think, All we need is this. The happy dog, the snow. I wrap my arms around him.

In front of me, a man who says he's looking to do some genealogy research on a Tompkins County family by the name of Greene Young. I point him to the research room at the museum, which houses thousands of genealogy files—obituaries, marriage records, bound family trees, and cemetery listings.

"Wonderful." He turns to leave, but then decides against it, and turns back to me. "You're Chinese, aren't you? No? Japanese? Korean? Vietnamese? Oh, yes, Chinese? Ah, yes, I could tell right away. My wife is Chinese, you see. What region are you from? Where? Ah, Shanghai! I've been to Shanghai many times! What a wonderful place. My wife is from the Henan province. She's from a fairly large city called Zhengzhou. Are you familiar? No? Oh, well it's wonderful, too. Just a fraction of the size of Shanghai, but also incredibly metropolitan. We own some property over there, so we like to go back at least twice a year to stay for a few weeks and visit her family. I just love being there, the people, the food—you can't find anything like it over here, I'm sure you know. All of China is wonderful, if you ask me. I can tell you're a Shanghai girl though, just from the way you dress and your hair. A beautiful city girl. Are your parents still over there? Do you visit them often? Ah, that's too bad. You must miss him a lot. My wife misses her sisters. Her parents are long dead, of course. Hell, I'm getting there!"

He makes a disgusting warbling sound that is some diseased form of laughter.

"My wife sometimes gets very lonely here. Her English is subpar. Maybe you could teach her? I try, but she gets pretty angry when I correct her. You know how it is. But how can you be in this country and not speak English? It's a real embarrassment. She has to improve. I'm sure you can relate. I know she would be much more receptive to somebody like yourself, so young and vibrant."

The man tells me in Mandarin that I have a beautiful smile, but I pretend not to understand. "Oh, you don't speak? I said, 'You have a beautiful smile!' It's too bad you don't speak. Either way, your English is excellent, I'm sure it would be a great help to her. Here, take my card. Email me your information. We'll set up a time."

He patted my hand with both of his hands. After he walked away, I went to wash the contaminated limb. Repeat. I look in the mirror. Repeat.

I don't recall once smiling in front of him.

*

The roomful of guests looked up with some interest, for the little, dainty Chinese woman who glided up to the platform, clad in a native silken gown of gray, was at least picturesque. She looked as if she might have come out to sing an air from a comic opera or to do a geisha dance. As for a speech, the New Yorkers expected at best a graceful bow, a bland smile, a few gestures with the ever-active fan, and some perfunctory sentences in "pidgin" English.

—*New York Times,* 1904

The Chinese display wonderful aptitude in acquiring correct pronunciation; and it is generally understood that an educated Chinaman, owing to certain similarities of English and Chinese sounds, will pronounce English, after an equal amount of instruction, more perfectly than any other foreigner.

—L. T. Townsend, *The Chinese Problem,* 1876

AFONG MOY is at present under the care of the Lady of the conductor of the exhibition and is making rapid progress in acquiring the English language.

—*Afong Moy Playbill,* 1836

Why can't Asians speak English?

—Yahoo! Answers, 2013

Learning English proved to be much harder than I imagined. I still remember the first day of school when I wanted to know where the bathroom was. I shyly walked up to a teacher and whispered, "Do you know the toilet?" The teacher didn't even try to cover up her laughter as she pointed to the other direction. "The bathroom," she emphasized, "is right down the hallway." I was so embarrassed that I refused to try to speak English again.

—Jubilee Lau, 1996

Wellington Koo, the son of a Chinese mandarin, was Columbia's second speaker. He surprised the audience by his mastery of English.

—*New York Times*, 1908

Wallace shared her version of the Asian language (including several ching chongs and ling longs), urged Asians who come to UCLA to first adopt "American manners," and for good measure even managed to work in a reference to the tsunami in Japan.

—NPR, 2011

"They always are so surprised to see me reading American books and magazines and exclaim, 'Oh! Do you read English too?' They also are amazed at my fluent English. As if we could not speak, read or write. It gets my goat!"

—Pardee Lowe, "Pullman Stewardess," 1936

[Kin] speaks English with great fluency, and this, combined with her natural charm of manner, makes her a favorite with all who come in touch with her.

—*Boston Globe*, 1904

No matter how long we stay in this country, and no matter how "accent-free" our children learn to speak English, we are still regarded as foreigners, and as "foreigners" we are suspect as an enemy from overseas.

—Helen Zia, 1984

*

What am I doing? I write over and over again in a notebook with the seven mechanical pencils I am reviewing, testing each for balance, comfort, build, and whether one of them is capable enough to come up with an answer.

I consider telling J, but then I consider not. Instead I ask if he's had a chance to read the articles I sent. No, not yet, he says. Lots to do in lab.

Of course, some version of this has happened before. Too many times to count. And it is not its worst incarnation. But it is getting so old, so damn fucking old, it's boring.

My heart is tiring. As my mom would say.

I dream of the San Francisco hills. I crawl on my hands and knees, clawing my way up.

She wished to be a new woman.

The genetic testing company sends me a reminder: they still need my spit. But the stuff, I know now, won't provide any real results. J was wrong. I've done my research, so nobody can fool me. The company's tests aren't accurate. At least not when it comes to people like me. They don't have the data to pinpoint anything beyond broad categories. While it's possible to do a percentage break-down of a person's English versus Irish blood, the test's site states that those in the East Asia category might identify as any of the following (no breakdowns possible): "Russian, Chinese, North Korean, South Korean, Mongolian, Vietnamese, Burmese (from Myanmar), Japanese, Taiwanese, Filipino, Indonesian, Thai, Lao-tian, Cambodian, Singaporean, Bruneian, Palauan." What would be the point of taking a test that tells me nothing beyond what I already know and, worse, says, Hey, you're all the same anyway.

Invisibility can be protective and advantageous—like the animals that camouflage themselves to hunt or hide. When I was with that woman in the coffee shop, I wanted parts of me to be invisible to her. I wanted not to stand out. But on the other hand, back in San Francisco, I felt invisible to the editors, invisible in a way that suggested it did not matter how much I tried to stand out, I would not get their attention. Invisibility as harm, that of being over-looked and ignored. And now I'm thinking there is a third form of invisibility, of choice, of opting out, of going off into hiding, of separating off from the rest, so as not to exist.

Feels like I have a thousand paper cuts at the back of my head.

As long as the behavior or mode of thinking doesn't bring you pain, then it isn't a problem, says the self-help article. But if it does cause you pain, you should try to change it. It does not explain, though, how.

"Here's something to do: write a book based on my life," says my dad.

"I can't write a book about you! It's too hard, it's too close."

"I already have a title for you."

"Daddy, the book will be impossible to write!"

"It could be a very good book, considering my life."

"Fine. What's the title?"

"A Father without a Home."

"No! Don't say that. It's too sad!"

His laughter fills my ear.

Other snippets of my dad talking about who knows what:

"Before I was born I knew I would be American. Remember, you're American first."

"Am I cool or am I not? I'm cool in my own style. I'm one of a kind. It's like when you walk into a boutique and there's only one of a unique item."

"As far as I'm concerned all white people are thieves. There are some worse ones and some better ones, but they're all liars and thieves."

"Money is good but health and tranquility is better."

An Asian American celebrity is getting dragged online for speaking out about the lack of Asian American representation in media and the damaging stereotypes Asian Americans face in America, while simultaneously dating a white man. A sampling of the comments against her:

> well most of those white guys who obsess with AFs cannot get
> WFs that are equal in looks with them . . . Admit it, how many times
> have you seen a cute or attractive AF with a below average WM . . .
> and your mind is just blown . . . you assume he's rich, but then
> you see them get inside a cheap hatch and then it hits you . . . its
> because he's WHITE . . . pure and simple.

I have no interest in supporting Asian American women who just want to climb up the white social hierarchy (oftentimes at the expense of Asian American men).

I can't be who I want to be in the western world's view because of her! They will always view me as that stereotypical asian women who loves white . . . because of her. When will these brainless women learn that you can't speak for asians but sleep white? They need to accept that their choice of partner is the root of the problem and learn to stfu!

Problem is that our community is taken over by amy tan type of asian female "activists."

You think there aren't a lot of asian americans thinking what you are thinking? Our voices are just suppressed by accusations of "misogynistic asian man" when we point this out.

WMAW couples dont get to represent "asian struggles," and they dont get to be at the forefront. WMAW couples represent one of the, if not the most, toxic manisfestation of white worship within asian community. She can defend herself all she wants about how "we are different," that doesnt matter. She doesnt have the credibility to speak for asian americans, period.

I am sick reading the comments. Not because I agree with them, but because I hear where they are coming from, I can see how they got there, the hurt and shame and anger behind the words, the histories weighing them down. The questions are ones I've asked myself. Is it a betrayal? A betrayal to whom? And what is being erased in these comments?

It's as if being white is the one thing that defines me, J said.

But not all of us are lucky enough to get to choose how the world defines us.

We get into another fight, J and I. About what, who knows. The dog. Who's doing what. One of those fights where you look at the other person, a person you've known so well for so long (or so you thought), and go, aloud and inside, *Who are you? Who are you? Who are you?* So much so that the contours of their face begin to shift, like there are shapes and lines you've never seen before, and the face becomes a landscape of the unfamiliar. One of those fights. It takes a while to restore us back to one another.

Jasmine texts: Did you like the photos I took for the pencil roundup?

I didn't realize the story had gone live. I go online to look, and in rereading the first paragraph of the introduction, I begin to hate myself. Phrases like "geek cred" and "knurled metal," references to Ticonderoga and "grades of lead"—it's all a reminder of how little I know about what I do, how much I pretend and fake it, how much is edited in, not me.

The photos, however, are great. The pencils lie posed in different types of office plants—full leaves, pink flowers, thick succulents—with a harsh, direct light that gives them a somehow cool look, like skinny little rock stars. Jasmine is good at her job.

This isn't the first time I've heard from her since I told her I needed distance, but the other times I didn't respond. Disappointment, discomfort, resentment. The excuses don't make sense. But now all I want is to talk to her. I call. The phone rings for so long I think it will go to her voicemail, but right when I'm thinking we're no longer friends, I've been too distant, now she's going to avoid me forever, she picks up. Her voice is upbeat. I tell her what I think of the photos and she laughs. She says she has good news: She got a promotion. She's now the senior photo editor. I congratulate her.

"Sorry, I know you don't like talking about the office," she says.

"No, it's fine. This is about you, and you deserve it."

"Where have you been, anyway? How are you doing?"

I tell her everything. The disputes between J and me. My fears. My secrets. Even the boring shit. I tell her how I've been thinking more and more about what she said about dating white men.

"What did I say?"

"'Fuck dating white guys.'"

"Oh god, I wasn't talking about you," she says. "That was me."

"Well, it applies to me, doesn't it?"

"I mean, not really. You guys have been together, what, since high school?"

"No," I say. "We've only been together since college. We knew each other in high school."

"Whatever, same difference. You were always like, 'He's so sweet, I love him so much, I'm so lucky, blah blah blah,' when you were here." She tilts her voice up in a gross imitation, I realize, of me.

"That's not what I sounded like," I say.

"Um, yes," she says. "Honestly, it was annoying, you know, as a single person in the city. Which, by the way, I still am in case you're wondering."

I apologize. "That's not what I sound like anymore."

"Whatever. It's not like you were clueless back then. Is *he* kind of clueless from time to time? I bet so, yeah. But they all are. That's, like, the least of it."

"But what if he isn't trying enough? What if there's a cultural and experiential gap that can't be closed? What if there's something wrong with *me*? Like all these Asian men complain about on Reddit and stuff."

"Oh my fucking god, no. Do *not* listen to those MRAsian trolls."

"But I feel like there's something behind it. Obviously, the sexist shit is horrible. But like, haven't you thought about it, too? Why did I end up with a white guy? Why do so many of us end up with white guys?"

"Yeah, of course. One, there are fucking creepy-ass white guys with yellow fever. And there are some Asian women who don't care about that. Two, there are more white guys around, what do you expect?"

"Mmm," I say.

"Honestly, I think it's good to be asking those kinds of questions. But you're, like, asking them to the extreme. And it sounds like this has more to do with you having a hard time with the move and figuring out what you're doing with yourself than it has to do with him. Sure, it's valid—"

"Or maybe I have a new mind-set."

"Sure, sure. Maybe your feelings and perspective are really changing. I guess I'm surprised. You two were like—again, annoyingly so—but the most solid couple I'd ever known."

"Can relationships rest on laurels?"

"What I don't want is for one thing I said when I was upset to change how you feel."

"It's not just the thing you said," I say. "It's other stuff, too."

"Okay, well don't factor in what I said."

"Are you saying this now because you're in a good mood about your promotion?"

"No! I mean, to be honest, I'm still staying away from white guys. But that's me and my bad experiences. Hashtag boundaries. Hashtag self-care! But I'm staying away from psycho misogynists, too, whatever race. Only enlightened men for me. Which means maybe I'll be single forever!"

I laugh. Already I feel better. We talk about her for a while. She updates me on the office. She tells me her ex quit and is working at a startup, so much for creativity. This, we both find hilarious. She recounts her recent dates—none with enlightened men, according to her.

"Also, hey," she says. "I realize this is too little, too late, but I've been wanting to apologize for not backing you up with your letter idea. I was scared about losing my job and that was dumb."

"No," I say. "It's not dumb. I was kind of losing my mind at work."

"So what are you going to do now?" she says.

"I do need to do something, right?"

"Do something that's just for you and not him."

"Like a trip?"

"Sure, a trip. Where to?"

"China," I say.

"Oh, okay," she says. "Connect with your roots and have a revelation kind of trip."

"Ha, no, not really," I say. "To visit my dad."

I read some sections of what I've written to J.

He says, "Whoa, you really make it sound like a terrible relationship."

"Do I? There are sweet parts, too, where things are nice between them," I say.

"The J person comes off pretty badly, though," he says, with a hint of hurt.

"But so does the narrator, right?"

"Eh, less so," he says, and smiles, a small, mischievous smile, like he knows something.

"Oh, well! I'm still working on it. And besides, it's not really about him or even the relationship. It's about the narrator."

"Okay. But I want to go on the record saying that I don't think we fight, like, ever. And I'm home and we hang out more than you let on."

"Mmmm," I say. "Well, I'm not so sure about *that*."

This time it starts with the cat. I come home from the museum after a short Sunday shift and J is lying on the couch looking at his phone. A few minutes later I notice the cat hasn't greeted me as usual. Have you seen the cat? I ask. He says he doesn't remember. I call for the cat. I look in the basement, I go upstairs, look in the closets, in the bathtub, under the beds. I look in the kitchen. The window above the sink, the old one original to the house that pushes out and has no screen, the one I tell him to please not ever open because the cat could escape, is, well, open. I ask him why and for how long; it's so cold, why is it open? He is still on the couch, and has been telling me not to worry, that the cat is probably fine, just hiding somewhere. Now he stands up and says he was cooking and burned the pan. The window has been open for maybe a couple of hours. I close the window and go around the house calling the cat one last time, until I accept that he's gone.

We go out and look for the cat, but after five minutes he says, "Cats are fine outside. He'll just come back."

"Not our cat," I say. "He never goes out. And we're at the corner of four streets! Don't you see all those missing cat posters everywhere? If you want to stop looking, then just go back inside and leave me alone. I'll find him."

For many minutes, as I look desperately for the cat, whom I envision smashed flat on the side of the road, I blame J, I hate J. If the cat is dead, I will never forgive him. I will never speak to him again. And that will free me from this place. I can leave. I walk up and down and around the block shaking the bag of treats, clicking my tongue, calling for the cat. God, I hope this cat is not dead. Finally, he comes leaping and meowing out of somebody's backyard. I carry him back home so tightly he squirms.

"You found him, yay," J says from the couch, with his shoes on.

"No help from you."

"But see, he's fine, like I—"

"Don't," I say.

And I go from there. How his being so laid-back is, in reality, careless and selfish. How he wouldn't even help me look for the cat. How he never cleans the cat's litter. Doesn't take the dog out for long enough. How that stems from his having experienced no adversity in life—his whiteness, his maleness. Dishes, laundry, vacuuming, the dirtiness of the bathroom. The bills, all the bills. Does he know when they're due? Does he even know how to pay them? And how late he comes home, how when he says twenty minutes, it stretches into two hours, like time doesn't mean anything, and I end up sitting around like an idiot wondering why I'm even here. It's oppressive, I say. It's suffocating. I didn't come all this way to play housewife for him.

He says he doesn't expect that.

He says he has school and work.

He says he doesn't want to be the reason I'm unhappy.

He says he feels like I'm purposefully trying to create distance between us.

I go upstairs and close myself in the office. To be honest, I really do feel as though I hate him, or whatever feeling it is, it is a terrible, mean, and ugly one. Yamei Kin's portrait stares down at me.

Our women are supposed to be docile and childlike. Yet there is the story with us of the three hen-pecked husbands. They gathered in council when the village wag cried out that the women were coming for them with broomsticks. Two ran. When they returned, learning that they had been fooled, they marveled over the bravery of the one who had remained. They found that he had died of fright.

—Yamei Kin, 1905

The tea bag: *There is nothing like you, there was nothing like you, and there shall be nothing like you.*

An edit: There is nothing *exactly* like you, there was nothing *exactly* like you, and there shall be nothing *exactly* like you.

Otherwise, it just isn't exactly true.

He really *slams* the door when he leaves in the morning.

"I told my landlady about you," says my dad, excited. "She's having problems with her daughter, who is thirty-two. She has a daughter that is eleven. I mean the daughter of the landlady has a daughter, so this is the landlady's granddaughter. The landlady's daughter doesn't do anything, just sleeps in and then goes out to her boyfriend's bar, so the landlady and her husband take care of their granddaughter, who is also a little weird, like her mom. Maybe a disability. Something wrong with their brains. The landlady's daughter's boyfriend owns a bar that has no customers, so he lives with the landlady, too, and the two of them, the daughter and her boyfriend, now want to move out, but they have no money. She says her daughter is a bum, can't even take care of herself. Her and her boyfriend, neither of them make money. The landlady doesn't want them in her place, either, but she has no choice! I told her how good you are. You went to Berkeley. You live in your own house with your boyfriend. You have lots of jobs and take care of yourself. My landlady is looking forward to meeting you. She's jealous, you know. Having a loser daughter is sad. She doesn't even like to talk about her daughter. She wants to meet a good daughter."

We are that couple in the restaurant eating in silence. On occasion we look up from our food, at each other, and half smile. I never thought it would be like this. Now it seems like our new normal. I watch him beneath the dim yellow light. His mouth moves strangely as he chews.

"What?" he says.

"Nothing. I guess I should tell you," I say. He waits. "I'm going to go to China."

He chews some more. Say something. Say anything. Have a reaction. A piece of his hair on the left side of his head is distressingly displaced. From where do I know this person? What goes on inside of him?

"I'm going to go to China," I say, with firmness. "I found cheap tickets already, and I've had my visa ready for a while."

"When are you going?"

"In a couple weeks," I say.

"That's really soon. You're coming back, right?"

He looks confused and hurt. The question surprises me. I hadn't thought that far. But then, since he's asked, since he's suggested it, it occurs to me that there are other possibilities in leaving.

"Well, I have a ticket back, but I don't know about after."

"Oh. Okay," he says.

"We can talk about it later," I say.

We sit for an eternity of silence. I think about all of his flaws. The silence.

Now he's opening his mouth to end it. "I'm going to miss you."

For a moment, I feel it, too. Missing him, missing us. But then something inside me shuts off.

"Have you read the articles about race I sent you?"

He looks away guiltily. "I started, but then I got busy. They're pretty dense. I'm going to finish, though, I swear."

My mom thinks it's a wonderful idea. "Good, visit your father," she says. "He is your father."

In addition: "Bring me back some good tea. And silk scarves.

And my favorite candies, the white rabbit ones, but not the kind you can get here, there's special ones, with nuts too, only in China, do you know which?"

In the weeks leading up to my trip, we are cautious with one another. It's almost better that he's hardly around. From an outside perspective, if there were one, we might even appear to be a happy couple. We have polite sex a couple of times. (Though once, afterward, I feel like shit.) When he is home, we have conversations about his work, random things in the past, our pets. (I secretly apply to jobs in all the major acronym cities: SF and NYC and LA and DC.) We go out to eat when he can. We don't fight.

Until the day before I leave, when I tell him that we need to talk, seriously. I try to explain as much as I can of what I've been holding in—that I'm too unhappy here, and it doesn't seem to be getting better. That it's not his fault. It's just that our priorities and our lives are no longer aligned. I say a lot I don't expect to say, like that moving to Ithaca has felt both right and wrong, and I can't recognize anymore what is cause versus symptom. How am I supposed to know if I'm depressed due to the state of our relationship, or my lack of career, or the town? I'm afraid of waking up at thirty and being in the exact same position I'm in now. If I come to accept that I won't ever be totally satisfied, will I make different decisions? Will some other factors I'm not considering become more important? And isn't being satisfied a really shallow and egotistical motivation? But what if how I feel here does matter, every small deficiency amounting to a completely changed state? I don't feel like myself anymore.

He stares at me as I ramble. He says he thought things were getting better. He says he wants this to work. What if he tries harder? Can I try harder, too?

A text from Rob: Hey, how's it going? Somebody I know is leaving his job in the comms office next to mine. Would that be work you're into? Could put in a word if you want.

I tell him maybe, and that I'm going to China for the holidays, can I let him know later?

Yeah, no prob. Have a great trip!

There is more than one possibility in staying, too. But for now, I'm leaving.

"I love both America and China dearly," says the little, slender woman, sweet voiced and charming, who has earned unusual distinction in two lands and in two fields of learned and studious endeavor. "They both seem like home to me. I have spent almost as much time in America as in China, and I am sure I am thoroughly American in many things, although I am proud of the fact that I am a pure bred Chinese woman—a member of the literary class.

"In which country shall I eventually choose to make my permanent home? Well that would be hard to say. I think perhaps I shall take up more or less permanent residence in China by and by, but not for some years yet. Since I have never passed five consecutive years in a single place, or lived three years in a single house, however I don't feel that it would be advisable to say anything definite on this question."

—*Chicago Daily Tribune,* 1903

She wished to be a new woman. She wearied of him. She declined on the ground that she had engagements to fill in the East.

IV.

A FATHER WITHOUT A HOME

Knowing what desires we have had (some flaring, beautiful
    ambitions),
And have had to let go,
And knowing what questions we have put off answering,
Slurring over them, always,
Seeing double, gladly,
  (Fearful, unbigoted minds grasping at both sides of every
    question),
It is not surprising, only regrettable that we should have come
    to this.

      —Diana Chang, "Knowing What Desires We Have Had"

I take the bus from Ithaca to midtown New York, then the subway to the airport. The trip from my door to JFK's international terminal takes seven long hours. And in those hours I cycle through excitement, fear, relief, regret, and back again. I close my eyes and see nothing, try to feel nothing.

He's said before that if we broke up, he would join the military. He would need an incredibly regimented environment and routine to get over it. He would need to go away.

I have thought about that statement every so often and checked in with him. Would you still join the military? Would you quit your job? Yes. Yes.

Before I left, I thought this notion of his would surely have passed. He is in a Ph.D. program. He has at least five years of his life laid out, a schedule, before him. So I asked again.

He said, Yes. Nothing has changed. Didn't I understand? It wasn't about what was or was not going on in his life. He would join the military in response to the heartbreak.

I had always found the resolve sweet. But this was the first time I understood it, too, with a sliver of a threat.

"I've not made a single decision on my own in seven years," a former coworker once told me after her breakup. "It was always as a 'we.' For an 'us.' And now I hate making decisions by myself."

But look. I've done it. Not so hard, was it? I've made a decision, to go to China, completely on my own.

Already, several Chinese people have approached to ask, in various dialects, for directions or something to somewhere. They could have been asking if I knew of a good place to eat in this derelict airport, or whether I had an extra tampon to share, or if I could watch their suitcase for a while. Whatever it is, I don't understand. I try to make guesses, respond with points and nods and shakes and noises, like a dog performing tricks. There is always a look, whether it lasts on their faces for much longer (with those disappointed in me) or it comes and goes quickly (with those embarrassed for me), after discovering I'm one of *those*. Is this what China will be like, but times 1.3 billion?

Back when I was fluent in Mandarin, fifteen years ago, on a flight in China, an attendant asked my mother, "How do you have three kids? Do they have the same father?"

She explained we were American, not bound by the one-child policy.

"Yes, all the same father."

"They look like they have three different fathers," said the attendant. "This one"—pointing to my brother—"a Chinese father. This one"—pointing to my sister—"looks Japanese. And this one"—pointing to me—"looks mixed."

My mother laughed. "Do they really look that different from each other?"

The attendant nodded and said that she had already discussed it with her co-attendants. "But we agree that they are all very beautiful, especially this one," she said, and touched my shoulder.

I have brought that story up to my mom since.

"I don't look remotely white," I say. "And only Chinese people say that kind of thing. Are you mixed? Are you half?"

"It's just a compliment," she says. "Like, you have big eyes."

Miraculously, I am upgraded to business class. Perhaps the man behind the counter saw some admirable quality in me—like that attendant—or it could be this new joint credit card with travel perks I got for me and J (a reminder of our ties) doing its magic. Granted, it is a middle seat—"still much better, more space," the counter man assured me—between two middle-aged Chinese men. The one closest to the aisle through which I enter does not get up when I point at the seat next to him. Instead, he shifts his legs slightly to one side. I stare at him and wait for his next move. He says something quickly, annoyed, in Mandarin—*you, you* is all I catch—but I understand well and clear, as he points vigorously at my seat. I need to crawl over him to get there.

It's very crowded in China. They don't have same personal space as Westerners, texts my mom before we're told to turn our devices to airplane mode.

A flight attendant asks me a question. I apologize in English.

"You asked for vegetarian meals?" she translates herself to me.

I glance back down at the thick menu we'd all been handed, where we had a choice between teriyaki chicken and salmon, a choice I had been contemplating for nearly half an hour, excited at the prospect of eating the higher-end business-class food for the first time, food described in multiple languages on an embossed menu, which seemed to convey all the benefits of moving up in society.

"Oh," I say, regretfully. "Yes, but—"

She walks away after the confirmation.

I eat a bland tofu dish as my neighbors eat their sweet-smelling, steaming meat. The earlier version of myself had thought it was such a great idea to do this, to avoid the shitty airplane meat served in economy. I couldn't have known it would come to this.

At first I try again to read from Yamei Kin's biography. A *San Francisco Chronicle* article in 1904, too, details Yamei's divorce from her husband. She must have been quite famous by then to be getting so much attention in the papers, or else this was a common practice for the then-uncommon occurrence of divorce. Most of the details are the same, with a few additions:

No one appeared in court on Yamei Kin's behalf.

Da Silva is described as "a comely young man . . . born in China of Spanish and Chinese heritage" and Yamei Kin as "a full-blooded Chinese."

The article gives their San Francisco address on Broadway.

A full quote from Da Silva in court: "She obtained a doctor's diploma from an Eastern college, and is now practicing medicine in Boston. She wanted to be up to date and independent, and she felt she could not be if she were bound to a husband. Her chief reason for leaving me was that she was 'a new woman.'"

And a quote from a witness, William L. Ward, a Chinatown guide: "I got acquainted with these parties three hours after they hit San Francisco nearly ten years ago. She told me at Christmas 1902 that she was tired of living with her husband and shook him."

Apparently after "deserting" her husband in 1902 to go on her trip, Yamei Kin returned to California with difficulty due to the Chinese Exclusion Act. After helping to get her back into the country, Da Silva attempted and failed to get back together with her.

The summary of the article is quite funny: "Anxious to be a 'new' woman: Chinese wife adopts American customs and deserts her spouse to become a doctor. Now lives in Boston and supports herself. Man with an extensive name, who was married to her in Orient, gets a divorce—Other unhappy marriages."

Then I tire.

The rest of the flight, I fall in and out of sleep. Twice, I must climb over the man next to me to go to the toilet.

In the early morning hours of the empty Taipei airport, I wish, for a moment, that J were here. Is it that I miss him? Or is it that I want him to see these ridiculous and wonderful themed terminals, the one with gigantic Hello Kitty statues, the one set up like a movie theater, the one like a jungle, and the one, especially, with all the vintage bicycles. Him and his bicycles. No, this is not the same as missing. There must be a clear delineation between the two.

That's not cheap! My mom in reply to a photo of a pork bun for which I paid the equivalent of one U.S. dollar.

There he is waiting for me, physically real, however rail thin. UC Davis baseball cap, sunglasses, leather jacket, Wrangler jeans, and his familiar fifteen-year-old Lucchese calfskin cowboy boots, still looking polished and new. We hug. I feel the bones of his shoulders and back.

Now he's saying, "It's all Mickey Mouse. The best way to

describe it is as the biggest mafia in the world. It's just like the Godfather," about the Chinese government as we wait in line for the first bus that will take us from the Macau airport back to his apartment in Zhuhai, a city where he has no relatives or close friends, but a city that is smaller, cheaper, less crowded, and warmer than Shanghai.

"This isn't America, that's for sure," he says. "In America, you have freedom of speech. You think people can say whatever they want here? I can, because I'm me. Other people, not so lucky."

The air is heavy with moisture. Everywhere smells of a familiar mildew.

"The Zhuhai fisher girl." My dad points out the bus window. "Take a picture."

I take a few blurry, zoomed-in shots.

"There's a love story behind it, but I don't remember. She was an angel that came to earth and fell in love with a man, something like that. Now she's a symbol of Zhuhai. You can look it up later."

At another bus stop, a woman approaches and speaks to me. I look up at my dad for help. He talks to the woman, who, satisfied with the answers, walks away.

"It's time for you to learn Chinese," he says. "You're a writer. You're of Chinese background. You should know how to speak and read."

"Okay, okay. People are always asking me things anyway, even here," I say. "Do I look like somebody who has answers?"

"It could be. Or they think you look approachable. Maybe they think you're friendly and nice, and somebody who will help them. You don't look intimidating, like I do."

He wears sunglasses at all times, no matter the place or the time of day, yes, even in a dimly lit bar at night, sunglasses covering his eyes. It's better that way, to not let people see you entirely, to always be hidden, and to make others uneasy.

Remember, remember. In the bath, I used to trace Chinese characters on the water's surface. Horse. Love. Me. House. Family. I needed to memorize their strokes to make them useful. And to my mother I said, Wǒ de pǔtōnghuà bǐ wǒ de shànghǎihuà hǎo. *My Mandarin is better than my Shanghainese.*

He takes his time in the mornings. He walks from small room to small room, sweeping and wiping surfaces, moving items from one place to another. The apartment has a kitchen the size of a small bathroom and a bathroom the size of a closet—the toilet practically inside the wall- and curtain-less shower area. But the bedroom is bigger, with a queen-size bed and side table. The living room has a TV, a small couch, and a built-in desk with shelving, where he keeps his belongings lined up, neat. Two shelves are dedicated to empty bottles and cans, of beer, water, wine, and soda. ("I bring them down for recycling every few days.") Inside the mini fridge are the bottles of hot sauce, links of salami, and blocks of cheese he requested, and a container of old noodles. ("They might not be good to eat anymore. Smell them first.") By the looks of it, he subsists almost entirely on liquid. He puts away the rest of the stuff I've brought to him, then brings me a pair of kitchen scissors he bought on sale. ("Two for one and I figured you and your bonehead could use this.") The TV plays the news.

I sit, hungry, on the couch. I look at my phone. No signal. No Wi-Fi. Nothing from the outside.

My dad says I will have to go to the tea and coffee shop around the corner for internet. He hasn't bothered to get it installed in his apartment. What for? He has no use for it. But I've brought an old smartphone with me, so we can FaceTime once I go back.

("What's FaceTime?" "Okay, so you can see this old man's face each time?") But when I ask if he wants to join me at the coffee shop so we can get something to eat and I can show him how to use the phone, he replies, Later, there's plenty of time. Two planned weeks. He doesn't like to be rushed. ("You go. I'll meet you when I'm done with my morning routines.") He doesn't like to leave the house until after he's had a bowel movement. He shows me his daily planner, where he has documented the times of each morning shit. He holds up a water bottle I'd left on the living room's coffee table the night before, which he is now going to place on the bedroom's side table, the cap marked with my initials in black permanent marker: JJ. (The ones I share with J . . . "So we both know this one is yours," he says. "I have a certain way of doing things.")

When he's not paying attention, I take a photo of his back, his neck pitched forward, the lines of ribs visible through his worn, old shirt.

At the coffee shop I point at items on the menu, which is thankfully also printed in English, since the place caters to expats, but none of the waitresses speak English, or at least not to me, so we mime at each other like sad circus clowns, then they leave me alone with my pork bun and tea.

At first Gmail won't open, but when I sign into my VPN service and connect to a U.S. IP address, voilà, email access. Who knows what magic is going on in the ether. I just press the buttons.

J has sent a science news article about the biological origin of nose shapes, nostrils in particular. He is acting as though everything is fine. Or he really believes everything is fine. Or this is a gesture to make amends. The article poses and answers a question: Why are some nostrils wide and circular (like mine), while others are narrow and long (like his)? Something we've talked about before. A lab at Harvard has traced it back to ancestral climates. The hotter and more humid a climate, the wider the nostril.

What I don't understand is that there are different climates all over China, but most Chinese have a specific, particular, Chinese kind of nose, don't they? Isn't the nose at least half of what defines my face as especially Chinese? I'm typing this into an email draft and am about to hit send, but then something stops me. I think of the articles I sent to him that he never read.

Back to Yamei Kin. To the question of why she tired of and shook her husband. Here, a clue, an article published in the *San Francisco Call* one month after the one on their divorce: "Indict alleged slave trader: Federal Grand Jurors say Lee Toy illegally imported four Chinese women. Is arrested in city. Warrant may be out for Da Silva, agent for St. Louis Fair Concession Company."

Without Yamei, Hippolytus was busy with a new life of his own. He was fired from his job as an interpreter for the Chinese Bureau in San Francisco, and started working for a man named Lee Toy, who was the president of the Chinese concession at the St. Louis Exposition, a large fair held in the city. Toy was also connected with a major importer of Chinese goods, which, apparently, imported people, too.

The story goes: 207 Chinese acrobats and 12 Chinese women traveled by ship to St. Louis from the Canton region of China, just north of Macau. (That's where I am. Zhuhai borders Macau.) The women had been working as house servants in China, and been told that they would work as waitresses in the St. Louis Exposition's Chinese Village. Once aboard the ship, Toy revealed to the women that they would instead be kept as prostitutes. When four of the women objected, Hippolytus beat them into silence.

(And whom did he visualize when he beat them?) Their silence did not last long. Upon arriving at port, those same four women appealed to the immigration commissioner, reporting that they'd been purchased for $500 to $700 each, and intended for a "horrible fate."

Lee Toy denied the women's claims. "We had planned a very attractive village and wanted native Chinese to make a scene of realistic industrial activity," he stated. "I did not see any of the women until they were brought to the steamship the morning of our departure, Da Silva having picked them up. There is absolutely nothing in the allegations that our scheme was criminal in its nature."

Well, well, well, that's unquestionably bad.

My dad walks into the shop an hour later in his whole getup. He walks with bravado. He is doing better than I'd imagined, though his clothes hang loosely from his skinny frame and his face seems made of sharper angles. I am still getting used to seeing him in front of me.

"Did you look up the fisher girl's story?" he asks as he sits down, placing a giant black backpack by his feet.

"No, not yet. I'll look it up now," I say. "What do you carry around in that thing? It's huge. Is it heavy?"

"No, not heavy. I have maps, some guides, a long flashlight. Doubles as a weapon, just in case. Napkins, there's enough for the both of us—you know you need to carry around your own napkins and tissues here. My beer. And it can hold whatever we buy."

"Okay. Here, drink some of my tea," I say. "Eat the rest of the pork bun."

"I'll have a few zips."

"Sips," I say as I type Zhuhai fisher girl into the search bar.

He drinks, but does not eat the bun. "Not sips. *Zips*. That's my term for it."

The fisher girl was not quite an angel, like he'd said. She was the daughter of the Dragon King from the South China Sea. An immortal goddess-type entity. Drawn to the beauty of Zhuhai's Xianglu Bay, she morphed herself into an average fisher girl to live in the area. She met and fell in love with a mortal man who loved her in return. The man, however, motivated by (1) gossip and rumors against her or (2) a devil-type figure baiting him or (3) his own plain curiosity (depending on the source of the story), requested that the girl prove her love by giving him her bracelet. She confessed her origins to him, explaining that the bracelet tied her to her father and home. If it was removed, she would not only lose her immortality, she would die on the spot. The man did not believe her and walked away. So the girl, in love and despair, took off her bracelet. As she said she would, she died. The man felt immense regret and remorse and sorrow. An immortal elder, unrelated to the Dragon King, was moved by the couple's deep love. The elder decided to help the man locate an herb known to resurrect the dead. The herb, however, could only grow from the nutrients of human blood. The man used his own blood for days, weeks, years. When the herb was ready, he brought the once immortal goddess back to life as a mortal fisher girl. On the couple's wedding day, the fisher girl gave the helpful elder a giant pearl to express her gratitude. This is what the statue of her in the bay is holding above her head. The statue was built in 1982, and is the main tourist attraction along the path known as "Lovers' Road."

"Ah right, right," says my dad. "I knew it was something like that. One of the nicknames for Zhuhai is 'Romantic City.'"

"Doesn't sound like a very romantic story to me," I say. "Sounds like the man was selfish and made her die in the first place."

"That's one way to interpret it," he says. "But then he makes up for his mistake. And in the end, she could be a normal human, like she wanted. Sacrifice for sacrifice. Okay, enough of those stories, let's get going. Lots of places to see, people to meet."

He takes me to all of his spots. We walk all of his neighborhood walks. He introduces me to everyone. The market grandma and grandpa. The fruit stand lady and her son. The tea auntie. The trinkets stall uncle. The cold noodle couple. Each time, he talks and talks, showing me off. And each time, I stand up straight. ("This girl knows how to stand," the Chinese teachers used to say. But that was only for them. The rest of the time I hunched wildly.) I want to convey to these people, so badly: Look, this crazy old man has a decent, *high-functioning* daughter.

It is impossible for me to find shoes in China that fit. They are all either too narrow or too short. At a shoe store, I ask my dad to ask the owner if he has a pair of combat-style boots in one size up. The store owner shakes his head and says the ones I'm holding are the largest available.

"Try on the men's boots," says my dad, who then tells the store owner what I think is the equivalent in Cantonese, a language I understand none of.

I shake my head. "No, it's okay!" When I notice the store owner looking down at my feet, I try to cover them with my hands. It's a biological wonder that I can look so like everyone in China but have such average American limbs.

Maybe it was something I ate growing up. All that hormone-injected cow's milk and cheese, says my dad.

On the news, a landslide in a nearby city engulfs twenty-two buildings of an industrial park, the hopeless faces of those digging through the rubble with their hands, looking for what's gone missing. They toss aside pieces of fallen building. The reporter walks up to a section of wall and points out a structural problem. The camera zooms in and we can see that between the concrete of the walls are crushed food cans that have been used as support. I pick out a few words: "poor" and "people" and "sorry."

My dad translates:

"This world is fucked. Everybody is cutting corners. I'm just happy I won't be alive to see the troubles that will hit in your time."

At night, noise of clanging metal rises up into the room. I look outside, down below. Big light fixtures shining on the circular overpass. From nine stories above, I can see tiny people moving between tents and umbrellas, plus a thing or two that look like cameras. I check my phone; it says 3 A.M.

"Are you okay?"

I startle and turn around. My dad stands in the bedroom's doorway, a slender silhouette.

"You scared me. I think they're shooting a movie down there."

"Yeah, they do that at night when there's nobody walking around. Probably one of these low-budget TV shows."

"Is Zhuhai a popular set location?"

"Maybe. I've seen other things like this happen at night since I've been here. All sorts of activities here. Who knows what goes on at night."

"Are they always this loud?"

"They don't care. They're saving money, while the rest of us are losing sleep."

We stand at the window and watch silently together for a moment. Then he shuts the window and tells me to rest and get over my jet lag. We're going to do even more walking tomorrow.

Snores from the living room. His figure formed into a curve on the small couch, neck and back against one arm and legs up on the other. Didn't matter how many times I said I didn't need or want the bed, he wouldn't take it. "You're my guest," he said.

One of his apartment building's security guards comes running after us, an umbrella in hand. He gives the umbrella to my dad and the two of them talk, then we part ways.

"Nice guy, nice guy," says my dad. "You know, they all call me 'Big Boss' here. Not everyone treats these guys well. I bring them beer and chat with them when they're working their overnight shifts. They appreciate that."

"See those young guys on the street? The ones in the suits? They're trying to sell apartment units to all these new buildings. They're in college or just out of high school, nice kids, but their job is tough. They're out on the streets all day in the heat and rain, doesn't matter what weather, they have to go up to anybody who they think might be a buyer. That's how desperate these places are to fill units. They've approached me a lot of times. I even went inside for a tour—everything new and fancy, they let you customize features, counters and appliances and stuff like that. But to lease is three or four times what I'm paying at my place. At night, you only see a few lights on inside these buildings. They're empty, nobody actually lives there. These developers are trying to make a quick buck off of a growing city, but none of the people here can afford these fancy new places. My prediction is they're going to sit empty like that for years. Just watch. I'm always right about these things."

Now at a restaurant known for their congee. Soft Chinese music plays in the background. I want him to tell me about Sharon, so I say, "Remember when you told us that we're Jewish because Sharon was Jewish?"

"I said that?"

"Yes, one time when I was in high school and you were talking about her."

"Okay, I believe you. That's not why you're Jewish, though," he says. "You're Jewish because my grandmother was part Jewish. She was an orphan, but the orphanage told her she came to them from Mongolia or Russia, so it's very likely she was part Jewish. She didn't look Chinese. There were some Russian Jews who lived in the alley, too, and one time I heard her speaking to them in a language I didn't recognize. So how would she know how to speak that language unless she had learned it as a child?"

"She never told you anything?"

"No, she never said anything about her childhood. She didn't even tell me she was an orphan. I learned those things about her much later on."

"So she actually looked Russian? She looked white? Didn't you think that was weird?"

"Everyone just knew she was a little different, but we were her grandchildren. That's why I look the way I look. Different."

He asks a waitress for another beer.

"Here, eat more of this, since I'm not going to eat all of it." I spoon the spiced tripe he ordered onto his plate.

"Okay, okay. That's enough. I don't feel good when I eat too much. Not like you and your mother. So how's your mother these days?"

"Fine," I say. "Do you have a picture of your grandma I can look at?"

"Somewhere, I'll look for it . . . There's one somewhere."

Adorable, fat orange cat in the alley, rolling on her back, exposing her belly to me. I kneel down to pet her head. My hand comes back covered in filth. I wipe it on my jeans.

"Ah, what are you doing? Don't be a bonehead," my dad scolds. He takes a packet of wet wipes out of his backpack. "Here. Wipe your hand with this. These cats are cute, but that's the trouble. You never know what diseases they're carrying."

J sends a second email: How's it going? How's your dad? Tell him I say hi. The pets miss you. I miss you.

This might be the longest we've gone without talking since the day we got together, though it's only been a few days. I write back: Have you cleaned the litter box? Do they have enough water? Are they eating normally? Has the dog chewed anything up? Can you send pictures of them so I can know that they're OK?

On September 20, 1904, a couple of days after Lee Toy's arrest, the Associated Press reports that the U.S. Secret Service found and arrested Hippolytus in St. Louis and brought him back to San Francisco to face trial.

The *San Francisco Call* mentions the same, though the paper adds that Hippolytus was dismissed from his job in the Chinese Bureau "because he fell in love with one of the stenographers and neglected his duties." Which is fine, considering this would have been after Yamei Kin had left him (though they were still, technically, married).

What is not fine is that Hippolytus, too, denied bringing the

Chinese women over for prostitution. He said he knew nothing about the charges against him, except from what he had read in the paper.

And with the papers he had one major complaint:

Da Silva was very indignant because of the published statement that he was of mixed Chinese and Portuguese blood.

"I was born in China," he added, "but I am a full blooded Spaniard."

Spanish Interpreter Antonio de la Torre Jr. of the Immigration Bureau says that Da Silva does not speak good Spanish.

During this time, Yamei Kin traveled to upstate New York to enroll her adolescent son in St. John's Military School in Manlius, east of Syracuse. Her appearance there, as "a lady of remarkable literary attainments," was noteworthy enough for a write-up in their local paper, though they also refer to her in the headline as a "chink doctor." She booked lectures. She made plans for her career. She was becoming increasingly popular with women's clubs across the country. News circulated of her anticipated attendance as the sole Asian representative at an international peace conference in Boston. Whatever concern she may have had for her former husband, she expressed none. It seemed they had no attachments and were now simply two lives on far-diverging paths.

The TV or movie crew is back again. Again, I wake up and watch, though there is little action. Small specks of movement, lights on and off, a shout or two. I squint and think I can make out the cameras pointed at two people talking to one another on the overpass. Maybe they are staring off into the distance at the tall bright buildings lining both sides of the street, or maybe they are looking at each other. It could be a romance in the romantic city, since most TV shows and stories involve elements of romance, Chinese or American or otherwise, and the two characters are talking about their relationship, some struggle they are going through, which requires them to take a walk together outside of their home, or perhaps they are newly in love, having one of their first dates, or it could be that they are near the end, and this is their last encounter before they say a painful goodbye. It's possible one of them has fallen out of love, that one of them does not love the other as much as they are loved, that the love is too painful to carry on. It's possible they will decide to work on their relationship and it is not the end, but something in the middle, something to look back on and say, Those were our difficult days. They will laugh. What a funny time that was, they'll say, even if, right now, as they stand beside one another on the overpass, they don't find it funny at all. I watch them until the crew shuts it all down and leaves.

I haven't gotten used to sleeping here. Where I would expect a thick mattress, there is a board of plywood topped with a couple of blankets. I sleep on my side and my shoulders ache and crack as I move. The night noises disturb. Each time my dad coughs in the other room, I jolt awake and worry.

"Your father's grandmother doesn't look white. I've seen the photo. She is Chinese. If anyone looks white, it's your great-grandmother on *my* dad's side. She has huge eyes. Deep in the face and very straight nose," my mom says when I FaceTime her from the coffee shop.

"Why does everyone want to be white?"

"What? I don't want to be white! I just said your great-grandmother *looks* white. White people are selfish. Their parents are always telling them, 'Love yourself first.' What about love your family first? How's your father?"

"Good."

"Just good? How does he look?"

"Skinny."

"That's all you say? Why? You're tired?"

"Yeah."

"Geez, being around your father is that tiring, huh? All that negativity."

"No."

"Tell him you need to rest. Take a break. Can't run around all day. Australia is so nice, sunny and warm. I feel like I can really relax."

In China, my deskmate's mother pulled at my shirtsleeve. "Give my son more room," she said. "Mama! Stop!" he cried. The parents pressed up against the windows, their hands reaching in to pet hair, wipe dirt off faces, pull sleeves of competing children. What kind of day was this? All I can remember is the oppressiveness of those parents, how they would squash us all with their need and desire. My mother hadn't bothered to come. "These Chinese parents are crazy," she'd said. It was the same at judo practice. Jump higher!, the instructor yelled. Parents' faces crowded the door's small opening. When class ended, they bulldozed in. I pushed my way against them to find my mother waiting outside, distanced from the rest. Her Americanness had made her wary of the smothering. Was it Americanness, though? Or something else? Of no longer being a part of, but apart.

With this interactive death chart, you plug in your race, gender, and age, then it displays a chart of how and when you're most likely to die, based on CDC data. I plug in my stats: Asian, female, twenty-five. The chart whirls out its prediction. Most likely I will die of cancer or a circulatory disease. I plug in J's stats: white, male, twenty-six. Most likely he will die of cancer or a circulatory disease.

"Are you feeling lucky?" my dad asks.

The question is a trick, or an entrance to a vast, complicated maze I have no choice but to enter. The first days of bonding and reunion have given way to the old paths, the ingrained behaviors, the past pains and irritations. I am exhausted and snap at him.

"Not really. Why?"

"You better start feeling lucky, then. And watch your tone."

We walk farther, until he stops and says, "Here we go."

It is a small booth, the lower section a glass case full of various colored paper items decorated with Chinese faces and characters. The man inside sits on a plastic crate, a cat on his lap, listening to some sort of talk radio.

My dad says something in Cantonese, "Hello" or maybe "How's it going?" or quite possibly "Hey, old man, it's me." The man stands up; the cat scampers up and out of the booth, down the street. I watch it go.

"This is my buddy, the lotto man," my dad says. His buddy, the lotto man, nods carelessly in my direction. The man has yellow fingertips, which are now wrapped around a dark bottle with a gold cap.

"You see," my dad says. "Just like I told you. Every time I come here he makes me drink wine with him. These are my bars in Zhuhai." He sweeps his arm, which spans the entire booth. The lotto man pours amber liquid into three small cups, then gestures for me to pick one up. I do. He says something to my dad and laughs.

"What's he saying?"

"He says you don't look very happy. So drink!"

We clink our cups. Gom bui! The men pour their drinks down their throats, shot-style. I sniff at the stuff and take a sip. It is bitter and strong and I wince. It is definitely not wine as I understand wine, but my dad has called it wine. Another trick.

"It's liquor," I say.

"This is Chinese medicinal wine, that's the name," he says. "You don't have to finish." So I do, and I feel the heat rise inside me.

The lotto man's mouth moves. I watch his body closely, desperate to glean meaning out of where his toes point, how far he leans forward, the placement of his arms, the twitch of his eyebrow. After a few minutes, I'm certain he's tired of my dad's constant talking. I forgot, or did not remember fully, how much he truly talks. I don't think five minutes of silence have passed without him telling another story from his past, complaining about something or another, going over the mundane details of this or that. He's always talking, to anybody and everybody, even if they don't want to hear it.

"Let's go," I say. "I'm hungry."

I pull at my dad's elbow, but the two men exchange a few more words, the lotto man laughs and slaps my dad on the shoulder—so maybe I'm wrong, maybe he wants to keep chatting, maybe he likes my dad, maybe they really are buddies.

"The lotto man says it's too bad you can't understand or speak. But it's okay. You can pick it up in a couple weeks. You'll remember. Chinese is inside you."

"That's what people keep saying, but where exactly is it?"

Before he can answer, another man walks up with a small toddler. This new man lifts the boy onto a chair in front of the lotto booth. The boy stares at me with the sullen expression of a tired child I understand well. My dad reaches for the boy's face and pats his cheek several times while saying something in a stern voice. The boy's eyes widen and he half opens his mouth, showing his tiny white teeth and pink tongue. He glances toward his own father, for reassurance or for guidance or to tattle, but his father is not paying attention. I pull my dad away from the booth, away from the poor boy.

"Why did you do that?" I ask, when we are far away enough not to be heard, though I'm not sure why I worry. It's so unlikely here that anyone will understand our exchange.

"Hey, stop pulling me. Watch it, young lady," he says. "It's fine to pat a child's cheek. It's the head you can't pat, like a dog. That's bad luck. The cheek is okay. It's good. He understands. Kids, everywhere I go, they stare at me. So I tell them, I told this one. I told him to behave. Be a good boy. If he's a good boy, he'll have good fortune and success. He knows now. He's lucky. Think about that. Get it?"

The last time we spent this much time together was when I was thirteen and he took me to Europe. On what money, I'm not sure. During the trip, we were always interacting with strangers, late into the nights. He never had a hard time finding locals who would take us around. He was glamorous and in control, while I often felt awkward and ugly. And the whole trip, he was giving me lessons and testing me, as though each challenge would make me stronger. Go buy the train tickets, ask that woman for a restaurant recommendation, play checkers with this man at the park, pick a hotel and book the room.

Once, at a bar in Barcelona, after I returned from the bathroom, he and our guides of the night were gone. I walked around the place in search of him, panicking. I went outside, but he wasn't there. "What will you do if you find yourself alone?" I could hear him saying. "How will you handle the situation?" I went around the crowded block a few times; concerned people spoke to me in Spanish, but I shook my head and kept walking. It occurred to me that he may have truly abandoned or forgotten me. Or that something terrible had happened to him. Or that I'd entered an alternate reality. But when I returned to the bar, there he was outside, calm and casual, chatting with the strangers. He waved me over.

"Did you have a nice walk?" he asked.

"Where were you? Why'd you leave me alone?"

"I didn't leave you alone. I knew where you were the whole time. I was watching you."

"No, you weren't. I didn't see you."

The group of them laughed. "Oh yes, we followed you as you marched around the streets," one stranger said, doing a drunken impression of my stride. "Your papa is a funny man."

I felt idiotic and crazed, but held back my tears.

"My daughter is very mature and independent, though, isn't she?" he said to the strangers and wrapped his arm around my shoulder.

Yes, they all said. She handled herself very well, like an adult.

We finally get into a big argument. It begins with my telling him about a friend of mine he knows whose boyfriend cheated on her. He says to tell her these wise words from an old-timer: She should date more mature men, older men, even somebody closer to his age. What? I ask. That's gross. What's gross about it? he asks. And then we go at it, standing in his living room, an hour-long, weaving debate that goes from the virtues and deficiencies of women versus men, to generational differences, to the absurd and nonsensical.

"You think you know more than me? I've been around much longer than you," he says. "Let's see if you can make it as far as I have."

"Maybe I won't! Maybe I'll die in early age, and you'll get to live to be right!"

"I would never hope for that," he says. "That's a very unintelligent thing to say."

I fall to the couch and stare at the blank TV. He walks off to the kitchen. I can hear him cleaning and tidying.

After we've cooled, I say, "I don't like us to have conflict."

He comes back into the living room. "This isn't conflict," he says. "Don't use that word between us. What that was, that wasn't conflict. That was just a speck of dust or pollen, it floats above our heads, it's there, then it's gone. You can't even see it anymore. You and me, there's never conflict. Listen to me and listen carefully. There are two words that describe what we have and they are, one: trust. Do you know what the other is?"

". . . Love?"

"No, love is too basic. Love is tossed around for all sorts of people. It's meaningless."

"Not for me."

"Okay, but it's not love. There's trust, and?"

"And?"

"Counting."

"Counting?"

"Trust and counting."

"What does 'counting' mean?"

"It means we can always count on each other. You can count on me and vice versa."

"Oh, like, dependability."

"Right. Trust and dependability, or counting, whichever one you want to use. Okay, Jing Jing?"

"Mmm, okay."

"Come, let's get going. I forgive you. You forgive me, too. Okay, give me a hug. All good now. Lots more to show you in Hong Kong."

What feels the worst is when a white person speaks Mandarin. Like the businessman in line in front of me at the ferry building Starbucks. The barista asks the white man in English what he'd like and he responds in unhalting, very good Mandarin, that much I can tell—that his accent is well practiced. The barista doesn't pause or look impressed; she must encounter people like this all the time, catching the ferry to and from Hong Kong. She replies to the man in Mandarin, takes his money, and puts in his order. Next, the barista asks me, in Mandarin, what I'd like. I wish briefly to be another person, either one who can speak or one expected not to speak. Then I respond in English that I want a soy green tea latte. And there it is, that small glance, the minor grimace, the disconnect. The barista nods and replies in English to tell me how much the drink costs, though I can see the amount on the display, I am not that unintelligent and inept, however inadequate I am in this moment. And yet, while I wait, why do I try to make eye contact with the white man, as though to signal something to him? I stop. I stare down at my shoes instead.

On the ferry, my father falls asleep. I pull out my computer.

Hippolytus's story continued to unfold in grand dramatics, as documented by the *Call*. He, too, was becoming a local sensation. The Secret Service found a love letter in his possession, addressed to Agnita Burbank, a stenographer at the Chinese Bureau office, his former place of employment. The woman with whom he fell in love, which, as the newspapers claimed, caused him to lose his job ("neglected and failed his duties"). In Agnita's possession, the authorities found more letters from Hippolytus (addressed to "My Dearest Ami" and "My Onliest Pretzel). The letters promised marriage and a life together; they expressed his plans for the Chinese women he brought over to St. Louis; they lamented the case against him. Agnita Burbank therefore became an important witness, somebody with information that, if shared, could be used against Hippolytus.

Meanwhile, reporters found a second lover, seventeen-year-old Carmen Averreto, to whom Hippolytus had also promised marriage. Carmen, after reading about Agnita in the papers, said, "Now that he has another girl, I want him no more. . . . He was nice to me and gave me this piano and this ring. It was pretty. It had five stones, but they have all fallen out but one, just as his love for me has fallen away. I will care for him no longer. But I thought I loved—he played music, he sang and he talked, oh, so fine." Days later, to further clarify how far she'd moved on: "Life is too short to bother much over men anyway. I'm all for myself when it comes to love matches, Da Silva is out of my life and I am not worrying." Another mystery: a photo of an unidentified woman in his possession. "He has his local sweethearts guessing how many young women have fallen victim to his blandishments," states the *Call*.

The paper goes on to speculate:

What Burbank knows will be of value to the secret service men. If she can be induced to believe that all has not been exactly fair in Da Silva's professed love for her, she may tell everything. . . .

Upon a woman's whims and caprices rest important developments in the case. The query is, will she remain true to the man who once said he worshipped her, or will she say "Revenge is sweet," and tell all she knows when called upon to testify?

And what was Yamei thinking of all this? Was she thinking of him at all? Did she ever wonder if her leaving him had anything to do with his downward spiral, a once-promising musician and linguist turned human trafficker and playboy? Had she so successfully distanced herself from him that the news meant nothing to her at all? Did she ever think back on their shared memories, wonder where they had gone astray? Or had he exhibited these disturbing qualities early on? Had she known something like this was coming? Why, then, had she married him? And what was their breaking point? The moment that made her decide to shake him?

My dad experiences hiraeth in Hong Kong when he returns after this ten-year absence. He points out places where his family lived and died. There's the pier where he first docked by ferry from Macau. This was after the two-night train journey from Shanghai to Guangzhou, the boat from Guangzhou to Macau, then the three-month wait in Macau. He was sixteen. He learned to take cold showers—not showers really, more like splashing cold water from the faucet onto his body—since the room where he and his brother stayed didn't have hot water. But it was worth it. The communists couldn't reach you in Hong Kong—that sixty or so kilometers of sea, and the British, acted as a protective barrier. There's the hotel where an uncle and his lover killed themselves together, because she already had a husband and this was the '50s, when there was so much shame. I believe it was a room on the fourth floor, which would be appropriate, he says. In Mandarin, "four" and "death" are just an inflection away from one another. The mint-green exterior peels with age, but once it was one of the best, most expensive hotels in the city. There are many suicides in this family, did you know? Another uncle killed himself in Shanghai around the same time, but at home, not in a hotel, and the reason was less apparent. He was just an emotional man. In Hong Kong my dad bought an American car, a Mustang. He worked in a camera shop and lived in a three-story apartment in Kowloon. Down the street was a great dim sum spot, and around the block, a noodle shop where an old man hand-pulled the noodles to perfection. Everything is different now. Gone are the dim sum spot and the noodle shop. In their place is the expensive pet district where tiny purebred puppies sit in window displays, pressing their small bodies and noses against the glass. I take a hundred photos of the puppies, and two of my dad on a street corner where he used to live, the little apartment building long ago demolished and replaced with a gigantic pink tower more than ten times the height. In the photos, he stands there beneath the street sign, pointing up at the words that signify he is where he once was.

This is the same place, although nothing looks the same, except maybe those thick, tall trees in the background.

Here, we are constantly getting lost. He asks shopkeepers for directions. We walk up and down blocks, and end up farther away, with no sense of return, and then somehow, are back where we started, without having reached our intended destination. He asks again for directions. In one of his backpack bottle pockets is a tall can of German beer. In the other, a small glass bottle of medicinal Chinese liquor. He walks with another can in his hand, drinking along the way, and only when he runs out do we stop walking, so that he can go to the nearest market to buy more.

"Can you drink less, please?"

"Nobody minds if you drink in public," he says. "It's all the same here. Inside, outside."

"Well, can we stop somewhere with Wi-Fi so I can figure out how to go wherever we're trying to go?"

"What would you do if you didn't have that little gizmo, that little gadget? In the old days we just walked around and asked for directions and stumbled upon things. You think I was born yesterday? You're tired? I'm almost seventy years old and can walk all day, and you're tired? This is your first time here and I'm showing you around."

My feet are sore. The pain pulses up toward my head. I suppress it.

"My parents were never married. They just had the three of us, my brothers and me. My father's family didn't like my mother. She was a ballroom dancer and my father's family was bourgeoisie. They always looked down on us, so when we went to Hong Kong, I had to prove myself, and I surprised them all by surpassing my cousins in business. Did I tell you my grandfather died before my middle brother and I got to Hong Kong? He died in the casino after losing all of his money. He brought everything he had to the casino in Macau, the Grand Lisboa. I'll take you there later. He thought he could make a lot in time for our arrival, so he could provide for us when we arrived from Shanghai. But he lost it all. He was friendly with everyone at the casino, he knew the manager, so they let him borrow money to keep playing. He kept borrowing and losing, borrowing and losing, until the manager decided to finally cut him off. My grandfather didn't want to leave, he was headstrong, so when security tried to escort him out, he yelled at them. Then they got into a little fight, they started shoving and pushing him out. He was a pretty old man by then. It was 1965, he was born in 1897, so he was . . . sixty-eight. Around the same age as me now. He started to cough up blood and he fell over and died right there on the casino floor. The manager felt so bad about it, he wiped the entire debt and bought the most expensive casket he could find in Macau to send my grandfather back to Hong Kong. My brother and I got to Hong Kong soon after, and my grandmother spent years blaming the death of her husband on us, the outcast grandsons."

The business district is crowded with men and women in suits. They take their lunch breaks in little alleys. My dad talks about one of my many possible futures, and in this one, I live in Hong Kong. J could teach at one of the universities. I could get a job writing at a newspaper or in an ad agency or wherever—I am very capable, according to him. Maybe I could even go back to school and then teach, and then J and I could become university professors. Academia is safe; it will always be there. I've heard this so many times in my life that I instinctually say, Okay. But then the more he considers this hypothetical, the more intricate it becomes, to the point where he's detailing the customs process for shipping the dog and the cat.

"No," I say. "I wouldn't want to deal with that."

"It's not a big deal," he says. "People move all the time and bring their pets."

"Okay, well, I don't think he would want to move here anyway. He doesn't like crowded cities."

"It will grow on him. He'll love all the food. Your bonehead loves Chinese food. Even more than you do! Ha ha. The science departments at University of Hong Kong are ranked very high. Look up the rankings next time you're at the coffee shop, and tell him."

"We're not moving here, okay? And we definitely wouldn't move here together. I don't even know if I still want to be with him. We're having problems. I can't even think about something like that, so please just stop, okay?"

"Stop shouting. People are looking. They all understand English here."

He is right. Our lunch neighbors glance disapprovingly at me, a grown woman throwing a fit at her old dad. A shame.

A teenage boy behind the register mumbles something and smiles sheepishly.

"What did he say?" I ask.

My dad says something back to the boy, to which the boy responds and shrugs.

They talk some more. I grow impatient.

"What did he say?"

"He says you look like an actress."

"What did you say back to him?"

"I asked him which actress, but he didn't have anybody in particular in mind. He says you look like somebody who could be in a movie."

"Tell him thanks. I've never heard that before."

"I get it all the time, here and back in the States," he says. "Your uncle was a famous actor here. He was part of the Hong Kong Rat Pack, that's what they called themselves. It might be people are able to see some resemblance. For me, it's that I'm very cool, and they think that I must be an actor by my demeanor. That's the word, right? Demeanor? For how someone behaves and holds themselves?"

"Yes, that's right."

That night, my nerves frayed from his company, after he is finally tired, I go out alone. ("Be careful," he says. "Watch your surroundings. You could get mugged, or worse. Call the hotel if anything happens. I'll wake up.") I say I'll be fine, even though I am nervous to walk around without him, despite knowing that plenty of travelers do this, including a white acquaintance of mine who recently posted photos on Instagram of her #solovacay to HK! But that is a different story. There is no accommodation to my foreignness. Nothing marks me as different—I even dress Chinese, my dad says, after I buy and won't take off a puffy blue jacket from a street vendor. ("People can tell I'm not from here, by my leather jacket and cowboy boots," he said. "You blend in. You look like everyone else.")

I walk out of the hotel. The chandeliers in the tearoom across the street glimmer through the windows. I test myself by walking around this quieter block. I put on the face of someone who has somewhere to go. I survive. I relax a little. I go toward Mong Kok, toward the businesses and shops, the bustling narrow streets crowded with people. I push my way through.

Inside a cosmetics store, where I think I will find products made for a face like mine, there are large billboards for skin brightening, lightening, whitening creams. In them, the models look like ghostly dolls. I pick up items from bins, spray and smell perfumes, try product samples on the backs of my hands. The actions of consumerism are familiar; I become one with the other buyers. I pick out an eyeliner and lipstick, wait in the long line, and once the transaction has taken place, feel like I've accomplished a major feat. Blending in can feel good, or at least satisfyingly comfortable.

At Portland Street, a fixture in Hong Kong movies and now the city's most popular red-light district. We came during the day, when it was quiet and shut down, but at night it is entirely different. The neon lights cast a bright, chaotic topography above the people below. I consider walking down the hill, experiencing what it has to offer, going through the doors to be like the men and women inside. I wonder what men like Hippolytus thought of this place, the particular use Chinese women could have. Then a man bumps into me from behind. He scowls, mumbles something, and walks off. I stare at his back as he goes down the street and into a building. I turn back.

In the middle of the night, my phone buzzes, notifying me of a memory from one year ago: Northstar, December 2012. The algorithms have created an album and video of our trip to Tahoe, a series of photos of J smiling over a plate of food, of me proudly holding a snowball, of steam rising from our legs in a hot tub, of our faces pressed together, flecks of white dotting our hair and eyelashes. The soundtrack to the video is of violin and piano, with long, low notes that crescendo into high, quick notes, and it almost makes me cry, until I see that the music is literally titled "sentimental." I change it to "chill," and a quick beat drops, with a woman's voice *ooh*ing and *ahh*ing in Auto-Tune. I watch the video of my life one year ago to each soundtrack—gentle, happy, uplifting, epic, extreme, dreamy, club—and each evokes a different atmosphere to my—or the phone's—memory. I can't decide which one feels the most true.

My dad lets me pick the next restaurant, so I choose a sushi place that shows up with high ratings on TripAdvisor. When we get there, the service is slow, my dad's sake tastes wrong (according to him), and he complains the whole time. "What kind of place did you choose? None of these new restaurants know anything about good service. This fish doesn't look fresh. You shouldn't eat so much raw fish; you can get worms. Where's the waiter? I'm going to give him a piece of my mind. We've been waiting here for fucking half an hour for the check."

The trick now is to stop speaking. To go absolutely mute.

"My grandmother on my mother's side, the best woman I've ever known, made a big fucking scene, so big, the whole neighborhood was there at our apartment. Have you ever watched that movie called *The Ten Commandments*? Uh, what's the actor's name, an old actor, he's gone now, he was always in these biblical movies, acted as Moses. I try to think of his name. You can look it up later and tell me . . .

"So my grandmother is yelling and then the police came. They have these neighborhood police taking care of all these things, they know everybody and their dirty laundry, even back in those days. First, of course, she burst out like a lot of women do, going wild for a while, then she calmed down and finally she said, very loudly, 'Let my people go.' Back then I didn't understand what that meant, now I think back and that's exactly what Moses said to the pharaoh because there were a lot of Jewish slaves in Egypt at the time. In other words, she said, I will stay, but let my people, my family, go. My uncle was a political prisoner. Stubbornness. He was in jail for five-year terms, the first, second, third time. He spent more time in jail as a mature man than he was outside of jail. This was my mother's younger brother. I don't know if he's still alive. Every time I see Didi, somehow he comes to mind, my grandmother's son, the one in prison. Then it also comes to my mind, it's because they are both the same sign, doggies. Not just looks, also how they are inside, their nature.

"The same year Zhou Enlai died and Mao Zedong died, then that summer there was a big earthquake in Tangshan between Beijing and Manchuria territory, a huge earthquake. Basically the whole city was gone. They could not possibly rebuild, so what they did was bulldoze everything. Nineteen seventy-six. That year my grandmother died, then Mao died on September ninth, all that happened in the same year, and then my uncle was let go and he went back to Shanghai to collect my grandmother's ashes and a few belongings. I don't know how much was left after the Cultural Revolution. My grandmother was born in the year of the rooster, 1909, so when she died in 1976 she was not that old, she was sixty-seven or something. Around my age right now. But she suffered a lot, she had cancer, well, she was smoker, that did not help . . .

"Look up the actor from the movie, he's an old actor, I don't know if he's alive anymore. But my grandmother said the same thing as Moses: Let my people go! And then soon after, me and my brother got our exit visas to escape the Cultural Revolution in China and go to Macau."

Is it possible to die of emotional overdose and jet lag?

At the Hong Kong Museum of History, I ask if he'd mind if I walked off alone.

"Sure," he says. "I already know all of this Hong Kong history. I don't need to see it again."

To have a break from him is a huge relief. I go through slowly, reading plaques, taking photos.

> The Boat Dwellers segregated themselves from land-based people. . . . When on shore they were extremely careful not to get into trouble with the land inhabitants.

> . . . Bun mountains (bun towers) . . . are erected for the Bun Festival on Cheung Chau Island. . . . People climbed the towers and made a grab for the "lucky" buns, which were said to bring protection and good fortune. Unfortunately, a tower collapsed during the scramble in 1978, causing many injuries, and the practice was suspended.

> To provide temporary housing for these "coolie" laborers in transit, many cramped and unsanitary lodgings sprang up in Hong Kong, being widely referred to as "pigsties."

> Hong Kong's cultural life was significantly enriched by the flourishing screen industry in the 1960s and 1970s as evidenced by the professional production of Cantonese and Mandarin movies of different genres that catered to the varying tastes of the populace.

> When the technique of perming hair was introduced in Shanghai, the city's hairdressing trade flourished. After World War II, many Shanghainese barbers settled in Hong Kong and established Shanghainese-style barbershops.

Hours later, when I am done, I find him asleep, his chin on his chest and his mouth open, in a lobby chair. Seeing him there, tired and vulnerable, floods me with guilt.

"Daddy, wake up," I say, tapping him. "Let's take a cab back to the hotel so you can nap."

"I'm fine, I'm fine," he says, jolting up. "No cab. The bus costs practically nothing."

"I'll pay for it," I say.

"No. It's a waste of money. And you don't even have a job right now."

He knows which words leave the worst sting.

The cigarettes here come with labels like SMOKING KILLS and SMOKERS DIE YOUNGER and SMOKING CAUSES MOUTH CANCER and QUITTING WILL IMPROVE YOUR HEALTH, accompanied by gruesome images. This does not appear to have any effect whatsoever on the people in line with their many cartons.

Back in Zhuhai, an ad on TV:

A Chinese woman doing laundry. A black man with paint on his face comes into her home and whistles at her and winks. She curls her finger to gesture him over. They are standing close, face-to-face. When he moves in toward her she pops a laundry detergent capsule into his mouth, then shoves him into her washing machine, headfirst. The camera pans to containers of the laundry detergent while noises of a full, clanky machine play in the background. Pan back to the washing machine, now quiet, presumably done with its cleaning cycle. The lid opens and out of the machine rises a pale Chinese man. The woman looks googly-eyed at him, almost swooning. The Chinese man winks. They live happily ever after.

"What was that?" I ask.

"Oh, typical Chinese racist stuff," says my dad.

"I never had any problems with black people in America," he says. "Always got along great. I get along with anybody, though, unless *I* don't want to. You know your daddy. Wherever I go, I fit in. Without the black community we'd have no civil rights movement. Asians in America followed their lead. I've said it before and I'll say it again. We wouldn't have what we have today without the black movements. We owe a lot to them. Remember that."

I nod and nod, happy to hear it.

"So many Chinese and other Asians in America today don't even know history. They just want money. Money, money, money."

"Okay . . ." I say. "Not all of them, though."

"A lot of them. Point is, these new Chinese, they don't know shit. Have you heard of Peter Yew?"

"No."

"You need to do more research! Ah! Those gizmos. What are they for? Okay, Peter Yew. This was a few years after I'd gotten to New York. In 1973 or 1974 or 1975, one of those. There was a car accident in Chinatown between a white lady and a Chinese kid, and the cops get there and start beating on the Chinese kid. And this Peter, he sees the cop beating on the kid and he tries to stop it. And you know what happens? The cop starts beating on him! Chinatown wasn't too happy about that. They complained to the NYPD. Nobody listened. A lot of groups got together and started organizing a big march to city hall. They were protesting police brutality against Asian Americans in New York. This was around the same time that lots of Asians were getting together and calling themselves Asian American, instead of Chinese or Vietnamese or Japanese. You've heard of Vincent Chin? Okay. So you know something you should know. All these people were organizing in Chinatown for a long time because of bad police treatment in their neighborhoods, so when Peter Yew gets beat up, it sparks a big protest, and I marched, you know, I walked to city hall with all of them. I knew a couple of police officers, too, from the camera shop, so I asked them for information. How many officers would they have at city hall? How were they preparing? They were buddies of mine. And see, this black cop I knew, he told me, 'Be careful,' and he gave me this brown paper bag. Guess what was inside? A piece. What, you don't believe me? It's true. And you know what I did? I gave that information straight to the organizers. I kept the gun for myself, though, ha! Luckily I didn't need to use it. The captain at the time, I don't remember his name, but he was greased real well. Took all the red envelopes, still didn't do shit for Chinatown. After the protest, he was removed. Probably transferred to a crappy position, to who knows where. The cops that beat up on the guy got indicted for assault. It made a difference back then. All these Chinese today, they don't know. They live in their bubbles. They don't know history. You need to know your history."

"Another problem is all these lazy immigrants. All these Chinese taking advantage of the system, like my cousin's mom, taking disability money for years, for what? She never worked once. She didn't even try to learn English. You think she knows any of this history? There are a lot of them like that. I'm just proud that even when things got bad, I never took handouts. Never. Then you have people coming from these places just to terrorize America, so yeah, do I think we need some stronger immigration laws? Maybe we do."

"What? That makes no sense. How can you say that when you came illegally, too? How can you—"

"I've lived through a lot. I have more experience. I've lived this long, haven't I? I worked hard. I wanted to be American. Remember, you're American first."

The year was 1971. He jumped ship with fifty dollars in his pocket and little English on his tongue. Of course it sounds like your stereotypical immigrant story. There he is, walking to the Seamen's Church Institute, asking for a room and a job, and since there is a small window of post-anti-Chinese-immigration era and pre-anti-all-immigration era, they accept him, offer him a room for ten dollars per night, and write down the address for the office where he can pick up his social security card—what he needs to be able to work—the next day. That easy!

An email from J: hi, I'm looking up coats for you. It's getting so cold here and I think you could use a warm one. Let me know if you like any of these, or if you don't want a coat.

I like all of the coats, but I don't say so, because I still don't know whether I will need one.

In China these days, the children behave terribly, my dad has concluded after two years of living there.

"They scream and cry when they don't get what they want," he says. "And the parents just spoil them, acting like their servants. This country's going to have a lot of trouble when these kids grow up."

We go to a market. First floor: fish. Second floor: dried goods and vegetables. Third floor: clothing and accessories. Three little girls on fake Razor scooters zoom by us, nearly running over our feet and knocking our ankles.

"Where're their parents?" I ask.

"Probably store owners here. These kids think this market is their home. They don't pay attention."

As we walk along the corridors, I can hear the girls approaching behind us again, the sound of their scooter wheels bumping against the uneven tiles. This time as they zoom by, my dad points at them and says, "Stop it! Stop it right now! You slow down!" in English. The girls slow down and stare, open-mouthed. Then they recover. They giggle. They follow us for a while, which I point out.

"They're fine. They're going slow now. They just need somebody to tell them what's okay and not okay," he says.

As we look at some scarves, the girls approach. The leader of the crew has pigtails and missing front teeth. She looks up and smiles. Her friends beside her smile, too, their young faces sweet and mischievous. Pigtails leader asks where we've come from, in a demanding, clear voice. (After a week of watching Chinese TV and listening to my dad talk to people, I can understand her, albeit simple, sentence, as though the Chinese really was dormant somewhere inside me, now revived through immersion.) I am surprised the girls aren't scared of my dad after he scolded them. And too, I am surprised at my father's calm.

Meiguo, he says, smiling.

"She's American?" the little girl asks, pointing at me. "She speaks English?"

"That's right," he says in a steady, sweet tone. "Study English"—I miss a string of his words—"you can go to America. Do you hear?"

All of the little girls nod vigorously and chirp like baby birds being fed. They look so hopeful. Do they know what they're hoping for? Is there really a future for them away from these market stalls? Is that future any better than the life they have here among the cheap clothes and good food? Surely, it must be, most think. But what will they lose? Will they be as bold in a place they can't call home?

They wave goodbye as they ride slowly away.

"Did you understand what I said to them?" my dad asks.

"Yeah. Study English and you can go to America," I say.

He laughs. "Not quite. I told them if they work very hard, then they can go study in America, where they can learn English and be as good as you. I reminded them to ride slowly in the market. Also, I told them to spend more time doing schoolwork instead of having fun all day."

"I was close!"

"Yeah, close enough." He pats my shoulder, then he adds, "See, they'll remember today forever. They'll remember to be better kids."

Now on the TV is a multihour special on Charlie Soong, a businessman who had close ties to Sun Yat-sen.

"There were lots of Charlies back then; whenever an American saw a Chinese face, they called them Charlie."

"Why?"

"Well, there was a lot of frustration toward the Chinese. They were hardworking and took jobs from—"

"No, I mean, why were there so many Charlies?"

"Oh. I guess it was a name that was easy for Chinese people to remember."

Which brings me back to the question: What was it like to be with a white woman in the '70s?

"People used to be so upset if they saw an Asian man with a white woman. But by the time Sharon and I were together it wasn't a problem."

"Really? Not at all?"

"One time we were driving through Georgia, and we went to a Laundromat to wash our clothes. When we got back, all of our clothes were folded so neatly. We get there and the owner says, politely, 'Here are your clothes.'"

"So what does that mean?"

"He was a bit of a hippie guy, an older hippie man."

"So why do you think he folded your clothes?"

"Well, he was a nice guy. He saw I had a BMW, too. Maybe that's why. And I gave him a generous tip."

"But what does that have to do with you being Chinese? Do you think he wanted to be nice because he knew other people around there didn't like that you were with a white woman? Was he compensating for something else?"

"Well, that's possible. I don't know. Another time, we had to get the car fixed, and we pull up to a mechanic's place, and a young guy came out, and he goes, 'Hey, boy,' when he saw me."

"What did you say back?"

"I just said the same thing back to him. 'Hey, boy,' and so he was a little surprised and started taking me seriously. Next thing he says, 'What can I do for you?' And so I told him exactly what we needed, but this was before I was a mechanic, so I didn't understand as much as I do now."

"Okay . . . So? What does it mean?"

"What do you mean, what does it mean?"

"What did Sharon think?"

"Oh, Sharon would get mad."

"About what?"

"My white friends, they would introduce me as 'my Chinese friend' or 'my Asian friend' to people. She would get so mad when they said that. She was very sensitive about that. I said, So what? I'm Chinese, I'm Asian."

"But people don't introduce their white friends as 'my white friend so-and-so.'"

"Yes, that's true, but it never bothered me. But oh, Sharon would be so mad."

"So she fought for you?"

"Oh, yes. She fought for me, hard."

The one time I thought I saw his ex-wife, we were walking up a long flight of stairs that connected our old San Francisco cul-de-sac to the street above. We were going to the doughnut shop and Burger King in the nearby shopping plaza, and planned to bring the feast back to my brother, sister, and mom. Then he said, "That was Sharon." I spun around and saw a woman's back, her long, frizzy brown hair, and the butts of two giant dogs, Great Danes, walking ahead of her. The image could be made up, could be conjured from other images he'd shown me in years since, but the incident was not.

I asked him again if it had happened, and he said yes. Sharon had asked to see me. Why? She hadn't even said anything. Why had she just walked by if she wanted to meet me? He said Sharon didn't want to meet me, only to see me, to know that he was happy, that he had a family, something they could not have had together.

It was difficult to believe that this woman, whom I had thought of, strangely, as a would-be mother (what if I had been born a different child) could appear and disappear so quickly. I had so many questions for this white specter from his past, and it was only much later that I'd realize they might never be answered.

"Her parents weren't happy at first," he says. "But then they met me and they accepted me into their family. They were old-school, East Coast Jews. Sharon was their JAP. They were very protective. They liked me, though. Her dad especially."

"Why did you separate again?"

"It's complicated," he says. "For one, I told you she couldn't have children."

"Was that it, though? You just said she was the love of your life."

"Yes, she was. Not my first love, and not my last—that's your mother. But of my life."

"So?"

"Later, later. Why so many questions all of a sudden?"

"Just curious," I say.

Cobbled streets. Ruins of St. Paul's. Bright yellow and pink Portuguese-style buildings. Bible shops run by old Chinese women in religious habits. Gold shimmering casinos. The Vegas of the East. Egg tarts—pasteis de nata—with brown caramelized tops and layered, flaky crusts. Colonialism looking and tasting better than it should. And should I be enjoying it as much as I am?

There are many beautiful, stylish men and women here. I stare at them, make eye contact with anyone who will look back. I envision what could have been had I been somebody else, or even if I had been a different version of myself, a self who had "returned" to China or Hong Kong, if I'd ever had the interest to do a year abroad in college, if I'd never begun a relationship with J, fallen in love, if I hadn't been so intent on distancing myself from this place in my adolescent years (*I look too Asian . . . I don't want to be so Chinese . . . I'm not one of those Asians . . .*), if I had been a self who had known more than I knew then, or know now, then what could have been? Would I have been happier? Would this have been a better fit?

When we first started dating I had a dream where we were on a bus, in the back, where the seats face one another. Across the aisle from us sat a few teenage girls, all white, not unlike my friends from high school. They began taunting us, at first in even voices, then in loud screams. *Why would you date a girl like that? She looks like a dog! He's gonna leave you, he'd never stay with a girl like you.* I woke up deeply upset. I told J, and he laughed it off, said that he would never leave me and that I looked nothing like a dog.

Recently, after getting the dog and the cat, I had a dream where I was the one screaming. I was the one leaving. *The dog and cat are coming with me. They're mine!*

I told J. He looked hurt, and said, Why are you having dreams like that?

What changes got me from one to the other, and how much change, and in what direction, is still possible?

After reading that on February 3, 1905, the jury in Lee Toy and Hippolytus Eca da Silva's trial decided in a mere fifteen minutes on a verdict of not guilty, I stop caring about his fate in life. Of course she left him.

No surprise that Yamei once told a reporter that she had been unhappily married to a man and that she had finally moved on from that former life after her husband had died, though he hadn't. But it hardly mattered—he was dead to her. If they ever loved one another, it was definitively lost to history. All that was recorded and left was a shadow of their end.

Now we're sitting at the Grand Lisboa's bar. My dad orders a Guinness. I request water. One of us needs to stay sober in this glittering landscape of money and desperation and false luck. Since it is eleven in the morning, the bar is slow, and my dad chats up the bartender, who has tattoos on his forearms and some peeking up beyond the collar of his shirt. He winks, quick and subtle, when he brings the glasses. My dad tells the bartender the story of his grandfather's death on the casino's floor. In this telling, my dad switches between Cantonese, Mandarin, and English, and I wonder if there are certain parts, certain emotions and images that are easier for him in one language over another.

"He needs to practice English, too," my dad explains. "If you want to move up, bartend in America, you'll need to speak English. My daughter's a writer. If you have any questions, any at all, about the English language, she has the answers."

The bartender—his name tag says BOBBY and three Chinese characters beneath it—nods and says, "Ah, yes."

"No, no, I don't. Does he even want to bartend in America? This seems like a really good place to bartend."

"I want travel to Europe," Bobby says, slowly, carefully, in a deep tone. "Berlin. London. Paris."

"You'll need to know English in those places, too," my dad says.

They speak Cantonese for a while.

"I asked him what he thinks of my Cantonese. He says that it sounds like his Cantonese. That's because I'm natural at languages. You know, some people have that talent. My mom said I started speaking in full sentences when I was one. People like that can hear and repeat. I didn't learn Cantonese until I was in my twenties, but nobody, not even these native speakers, can tell. Not a trace of an accent. It's the same for my English, right?"

"Yeah, you only have a tiny accent, and it's really unique to you."

"That's a New York accent!"

"Your father speaks very good," says Bobby. And he brings another glass of beer.

"Last one, okay? Last one, right, Daddy?"

"She's always worrying about me. Always telling me not to drink too much."

Bobby smiles. "Good daughter."

I fall in love for a moment, but then it is time to go.

Yamei Kin's legacy was larger than lost love.

She mentored dozens of Chinese women who went on to study medicine at American universities. She designed, built, and established the first medical college in China for women. She traveled the world lecturing on topics from international relations to fashion to tofu. During World War I, she worked at the USDA, the first Chinese woman to hold such a position. "My boy is at the front doing his bit," she said. "I want to do mine, too." She lived an intensely full life, the kind you read about and wonder, How can one person do this much? After her son, Alexander, died fighting in France at twenty-three ("What did he die for? What did we have to do with that sickening war?" she cried), she continued to work and lecture. Eventually she retired, to a quieter—though certainly not quiet by most standards—intellectual and social life in Beijing. She invited actors and singers and writers into her home. She held parties where guests discussed art and politics. She employed a woman to read Chinese novels aloud to her, and spent her last years translating those books into English. She never remarried. She was a new woman until the end.

"This restaurant is called Fat, Ugly Auntie's House," says my dad. "Named after that woman over there."

"That can't be right. She's not either."

"It's not about what she is or isn't," he says. "It's her nickname."

I try again to ask him about Sharon. I think it will shed light on my relationship. These are the lessons I want, but he keeps avoiding. He repeats what he's said before, and nothing new.

"Remember when I got upset in Hong Kong?"

"When? When you were always grumpy and hungry? When you complained about walking? When you didn't want to go out and stayed in the hotel and I had to go walk to the noodle shop by myself, even though I'm an old man and you're young?"

"No." I clench the spoon in my hand. "When I said that I didn't know if I wanted to be in Ithaca anymore."

"Oh, that, yes."

I ask if he thinks I should have dated more people, if I should have met more people, to which he replies that he used to think so. Is that a reason why he left Sharon for Mommy? Was it because Sharon didn't understand some things that Mommy did, since they were both from the same place? Were there emotional disconnects, and things Sharon and he couldn't talk about?

"No, not at all," he says. "I didn't leave Sharon for your mother. That was later."

"Okay, well, was there a cultural gap?"

"I do think most Asian people are big eaters. Like your mother is one. I didn't know because I hadn't been with a Chinese girl in a while. Everything she cooked in the morning would be gone by the end of the day, and this was before you were born, so you know she was the only one eating. I didn't mind, though. I just had my coffee and toast. Americans, I think, are more weight conscious. This trip, I watch you and remember, you're a big eater like your mom." He laughs.

I laugh, too, for the first time in a while. "Okay, that's not exactly what I meant by cultural gap."

"What? That's what I think! I did get Sharon into Asian foods, though. She learned to make sashimi and seafood dishes. She liked it because she doesn't gain weight eating them. Jellyfish. It's impossible to gain weight from jellyfish. Mapo tofu. You go to the bathroom four hours later and it's all flushed out."

What I wanted were answers and all I'm getting is food commentary.

I try again: But why did you and Sharon get divorced?

"I told you it was very complicated."

"Complicated how, though? I feel like my relationship is complicated."

He pauses and takes a sip of his beer.

"Your relationship isn't complicated," he says. "Actually, your bonehead is very simple. You know, he's easygoing. And I know he's an honest person, which you can't say for most people."

"But what about you and Sharon?"

"You want stories from your old man now, huh? I guess you're old enough to hear it."

It was one thing on top of another. First, she wanted him to go to AA meetings. He went, but he didn't like it. A lot of mumbo jumbo, jibber-jabber. Second, she was going through her own issues. Sharon said her father had abused her, but none of her family believed her, not even her sisters. What was there to do? He believed Sharon, he was on her side, he did everything he thought he should do at the time, even went to therapy with her and her family. Maybe he shouldn't have drunk so much, and maybe he could have supported her more. They were both stressed. They fought a lot. One night, when things got heated, the cops came. And one of those cops making the call, well, he doesn't know how exactly it happened, but Sharon had an affair with the cop. The cop probably comforted her, saw his opportunity with this woman who was weak, at a bad spot in her life. It wasn't entirely her fault. The cop likely pursued her. But he couldn't forgive her, he couldn't get over that. And even the therapist, whom he went to on his own once, told him, I wouldn't know what to do, either, it's a really tough situation. So he left.

"Oh," I say. Though it does not surprise me, it is far from what I imagined, and its lessons hazy and inapplicable. A melodramatic and loud series of events—what else was I expecting from him?

"You wanted to hear about my life, didn't you?" He takes a few sips of tea. "I wasn't the best dad, I know that. But I was a pretty good dad, right? And after Sharon, I was very cautious. I never wanted you and Ling Ling to ever think I did something like that to you. I wouldn't even wipe your butts after you turned three. I told your mother, 'You do it.' With Didi, it was fine."

"Okay, okay, I don't need those details."

He laughs. "But I was a pretty good dad, right?"

"Yes," I say.

"You don't have problems like that in your relationship, do you?"

"No, not at all."

"As for your question. Did I want you to date more people? I think it would have been good for you to be with a nice Jewish boy. Or go travel and have more experiences by yourself. But your bonehead, I like him. I like the Irish. They're hardworking and genuine, not like most people. Definitely not like most of the Chinese."

"Sometimes I think it would be better to be alone."

"There's a Chinese saying about this. What do you think is the most important quality to having a good connection with another person?"

"That you get along with them?"

"Well, of course. You have to have something in common. You can talk to them. You get along, that's just a basic thing. An obvious thing. What is the next step? Even more important than that?"

"I don't know."

"You have to be able to reflect each other's hearts."

"Where did that saying come from?"

"It's my saying, a Chinese saying, ha ha! I heard something like it when I was a kid, but this is the way I put it. Heart to heart. That's the most important. Without that, there isn't a real, true relationship. Am I right?"

"Yeah, I guess that's true."

"Right, your dad knows a thing or two."

He drinks more beer and we sit silently for a while.

"Did you ever think about going to AA again?" I ask.

"No," he says. "That shit didn't work for me. And look, I think I'm fine. I stay in control. I also believe I'm one of those human beings that doesn't die easily."

I nod. I eat. I hope so.

In high school, J said at a party, I could throw a rock from my house to yours. I said he couldn't. The next day, he called me to come over. We stood on the pathway that led from the back of his house to the back of mine, but it curved to the right and was so overgrown with trees and bushes that we couldn't see my house from where we stood. He threw rocks as far as he could, and they flew a great distance, much farther than I thought they would. He had a great throwing arm, and still does. They're at your house, he said. No they aren't, I said. But neither of us really knew the answer, because it was beyond our line of vision.

My mom calls; she's back in Davis. She asks how I'm doing. Fine, I say.

"You don't sound fine," she says.

"I'm just tired. We walk around a lot. Daddy is more active here than I thought he'd be."

"You worry so much. You think he's that old he can't do anything? I always tell you, he's fine. You always think the worst. Just like him."

"I just said everything is fine," I say.

My father has come up beside me and says, "Let me talk to your mother."

"Daddy wants to talk to you."

"Why? I don't want to talk to him."

"Just let me talk to your mother."

He waves his hand, impatient.

So I give him the phone and go into the bedroom and close the door behind me. I lie on the hard bed and stare up at the ceiling.

He comes into the room and hands me back the phone.

"Hello?" I say.

"Yeah."

"What?"

"Don't talk to your father about bad stuff in your relationship. He doesn't like to hear about that."

"What?"

"He says it's hard for him to listen, because he won't forget. If you say something bad about your boyfriend, then that will be all he can think about. So only talk bad stuff if you really think it's bad and you want it to end. Otherwise, he won't like your boyfriend anymore and then you both suffer."

"Why didn't he just tell me that?"

"I don't know. Ask him."

"No. I don't want to."

"Okay. I don't want to talk to him again, either. Don't make me talk to him again."

"He made *me*."

"Whatever. I don't want to talk to him again. He make me crazy."

"Okay, fine, bye . . . Love you."

"Love you, too."

The last days in Zhuhai are tense. Our frustrations can't be hidden or buried any longer, and we flare up into several arguments. So much for no conflict. If I had to chart our relationship, it would look like tall skinny mountains dropping into deep gorges, over and over. Am I replicating this pattern in my relationship? I confirm my suspicions as I scroll through hundreds of photos of J, swinging between high and low emotional states.

At the coffee shop again, an email from Rob, with the subject line: Job at Cornell.

> Hope you're having fun in China. Here's the link to the job listing I
> was talking about. Think you'd be a shoe in.

It occurs to me that I never gave him my email address. Then I remember it is available on a site I use to get freelance work. The thought of him putting my name into Google creeps me out a little. Also, it isn't "shoe in," it's "shoo-in" as in to shoo somebody in a certain direction. But maybe he meant the shoe thing on purpose. Who knows.

I look again at the job listing and I think, Fuck it. I spend hours writing a cover letter, then submit my application.

On the bus, after a long day of my dad's drinking. My last full day. We ride without speaking, and as we near our stop, he walks down the stairs from the upper level to the lower level, trips, grabs a pole with one hand, and it seems everything is fine, but then his body swings from one side of the stairs to the other and he smashes his knee against a hand rail. Rail against rail. I help him onto the street. When I ask about getting a cab, he brushes me off. He wobbles home. I walk slowly beside him.

Back at the apartment, we nap until dinner, when we have to meet his landlady and her family at a nearby restaurant. He has put off having this promised dinner with them until my last night, for reasons I don't comprehend.

I wake up from the sound of his phone ringing in the other room. I lie there, waiting to hear if he picks it up. He doesn't. There is snoring. I don't want to spend this last night with strangers, random people, in a language I can't understand. I am tired of it. I tell myself that I should have made my trip shorter, to have avoided souring our interactions to this extent. My dad's phone rings again, and this time I hear him waking up, coughing, moving. I stay where I am. He talks on the phone, clears his throat, speaks in an upbeat voice.

My dad walks in and says, Come on, get ready. They're waiting for us.

I don't move. I'm tired. I'm drained. Can't we cancel?

He tells me to stop being a child.

I don't move.

Quit it. Get moving!

And my whole body recoils with resentment, then springs alive.

At the restaurant, the landlady's granddaughter stares at me, but when I look back, the girl hides her face in her hands or in the landlady's chest and squeals incomprehensibly. Then the girl starts running around the restaurant clapping her hands, making noises at people. It would be cute, except that she is twelve, and seems too grown up for the behavior. She is wild and they yell at her to stop. Next to her, the landlady's mother puts up a fight with her nanny—or her aide—who is trying to tie a bib around her neck. The old woman slaps more and more hands away. The landlady makes an attempt, scolding her mother, who shakes her head violently and yells what are not words in any language, but painful utterances incomprehensible to anyone. The landlady tells my dad that her daughter, the mother of the child, who is not present, is not only a bad daughter, she is a bad mother, and look at how her child has turned out. Then she turns back to her own mother and tries again to put on the bib, but at this point, my father, who has been translating for me and giving me looks, his eyebrows bouncing above his sunglasses, interjects and says to stop. No bib for auntie. The family quietly acquiesces to this outside patriarch, and the old woman pats my father's hands in thanks and smiles at him with her mouth of missing teeth.

The landlady's husband says something, and looks profoundly at me.

"He says, 'The Chinese smile at their duties, even if their duties make them suffer,'" my dad says.

My suffering is regular and small, and I want to suffer stoically and quietly, which perhaps then is the most Chinese quality about me.

At dinner, my father and I do this. We continue to smile. We eat and talk, we have our private conversations, I tell him to eat more, he tells me to drink more tea, have the lamb, we reminisce about earlier times, and we smile and we look at one another like we have never spoken an ill word, never raised our voices, never seen a day of turmoil. At first it seems we are pretending and performing for our hosts, but then, since we are so practiced, we forget we are pretending, and as the night goes on, it becomes real through the action, the living.

J writes to say he's read the articles I sent him. He says he's very sorry for not reading them sooner. He says he realizes how he's been a generic, typical white person in many ways. He wants to pick me up from the airport.

I smile at the computer screen. But I am hesitant.

Are you sure you want to drive all that way?

He says yes, he'll be there.

I have caused J suffering by coming here. And J, too, suffers quietly.

It is the nature of relationships that they are impossible to fully understand from the outside, their inner workings built both from memories and habits and histories made up from the exterior world, and from those known only between the two involved, that exist only through them and are lost when they are lost to each other. A relationship is particular in the way people are particular. Whatever lessons one can glean from other people's relationships can only be taken in pieces, assembled into bare, minimal instructions. Yamei and Hippolytus had no further contact or longing. My dad and Sharon, the same with a hint of longing. My dad and my mom, of that, he says, "We have the three of you, so we will all always have each other."

The next morning, early, he says we should take a cab, instead of the bus, to the border of Zhuhai and Macau. During the ride, he is quiet. I stare out the window at the trees and the bay; we pass the fisher girl again. At the Gongbei Port of Entry, he asks if I want a photo of myself in front of the big building and its sign. "You don't have any photos of yourself here," he says. I have taken many photos of him and the landscape, but he has not taken any of me. I show him how to use the camera on my phone. He tells me to move a little to the left, so he can get the Chinese flag in the frame.

Across the border in Macau, we go for tea at a big dim sum place. We get only a little lost trying to find it. While he's in the bathroom—he says he's not feeling well, he didn't sleep well the night before—I request his favorite dishes: the tripe, the chicken feet, the duck tongue with peanuts. When he returns, he says, "Wow, you know how to order by yourself now?"

"Yeah, but I still only point and make sounds," I say.

"Whatever works."

We chat about random things. The topic of my mom visiting Australia comes up and he mentions a movie with an Australian actor I should watch when I get home, a comedy, which he begins to describe, though it's hard for me to pick up what he's saying. In the middle of detailing, according to him, one of the funnier scenes, he begins to laugh between his words.

"You should, ha ha, really watch it, heh heh heh, the man in it, ha, so funny," he says, and lifts his sunglasses to wipe at his eyes.

"Okay, I will," I say.

"It's really, ha, worth checking out." Tears run down his face and he continues to wipe at them.

"Daddy? Are you okay?"

"I'm fine. Just thinking about it. Makes me laugh."

At the airport, we walk around. We look at posters on the walls. He goes to the bathroom again and does not come back for some time. I worry I will have to go through the security line before he returns, but just as I'm thinking it's fine to run a little behind our intended schedule, the plane doesn't leave for another hour, he reappears.

"Time for you to go in," he says.

I nod. "When will you move back home?"

"Oh, I don't know. We'll see. I don't have a place to go yet."

"I'll find you an apartment in Davis, or you can come to Ithaca."

"Yeah, maybe. Let's talk about it later. Don't worry about me. Go on."

At the end of the line, he hugs me. He pats me on the back and says, "Don't worry, Jing Jing. Focus on yourself. You'll figure things out. You get it from me. You're my daughter."

I go through the line. I have no coherent thoughts, just a rush of feeling, like oversaturated, garish bursts of color. I look back and see my dad standing in the same spot, watching me go. He waves. I wave back. I used to see them, the criers, in the security line, and even though it was an acceptable place for public displays of grief and sadness, where everybody blatantly ignored and allowed for them, I had judged. What was wrong with those people? My guesses had been shallow. They were sad to leave vacation. They were scared of flying. They were drunk or high. They were the type of emotional people who cried all the time. They didn't want to go home. They were upset to leave home. But these are none of the reasons I am crying in the security line, and when the Macau airport agent checks my passport I can barely say thank you. He nods, expressionless.

After the bags and I are scanned through various machines (can they see what might explain this?), I jog to the nearest bathroom, where I am surprised to find large, pristine, individual toilet rooms, totally enclosed, perfectly private. I open the door to one and lock myself in, then rest my forehead against the cool wall, finally alone for a moment.

V.

RETURN

He drove through snow for five hours to the airport. It was dark, just around midnight, that jarring juncture stuck between the days. Then he turned around and drove us another five hours back into the dark.

He asked if I was tired. I was. It had been an unusually turbulent flight, and I had not slept during it. Then I'd gotten confused going through customs and followed the people ahead of me, joined a long line, waited there unmoving for half an hour until a staff member saw my blue U.S. passport and directed me to a grid of self-serve kiosks. I stood before one of the machines. Its camera took my photo and showed it back to me. A ghostly version of myself. I tapped at the screen, answered its questions in a daze, and then it was over in a matter of minutes. I could leave. I was allowed back in. I glanced at the people I'd left behind in line. I'd grown attached to them. It seemed they hadn't moved an inch forward. I felt bad about going ahead without them. I explained this haphazardly to J and apologized that he'd had to wait.

"It's okay," he said. "You can sleep while I drive."

Mostly, I did sleep, or existed in the space between.

A few times, I woke up and it was pitch black outside except for the car's headlights and the falling snow against the window, and when I looked beside me, he, too, resembled a ghost, cast in the dark gray of night, and yet I wasn't scared, half dreaming, half awake; he was preciously familiar, like a memory come alive, and it felt in that moving car, for those moments, like we were entirely alone on the road and in the world, wherever we were, that there was nothing outside but the dark and the snow, and to simply watch him, driving, rubbing his eyes, yawning, I was calm and inexplicably content; I could see pieces of our lives floating among the snowflakes, melting on the windshield, and for those brief moments I was living with the certainty that I was exactly where I should be, where everything was deeply quiet yet deeply alive. I thought about the many aspects in this life that I could not control or understand, despite how much I wanted to or tried, how my father's life, my mother's life, the lives around me and the figures from the past, they were not mine to determine, not mine to map out, no matter how much they shaped what I had become, however much we were connected, I could only help in small ways, I could listen and piece together and recount, but what was truly mine was only a little, no, a minuscule speck of it all, and while this was a sort of devastation to me, one I knew it would take some time to fully accept, it felt nice, at least, to be on the way, in spite of not knowing exactly how far I had come nor how far I had left to go.

ACKNOWLEDGMENTS

Thanks so much to: Jeff Jorgensen, for always believing in me and for supporting me in too many ways to count; Vt Hung, whose thorough notes and many conversations sustained me while writing this book; Alexander Sammartino, for reading an early draft and for his invaluable perspective over the years; C Pam Zhang and Jonathan Dee, who read drafts and provided helpful advice; George and Paula Saunders, for all of their guidance and support, and the beautiful space to write; Dana Spiotta, Arthur Flowers, and Eleanor Henderson, for teaching me along the way; Sarah Neundorfer, Meghann Lilley, and Sylvie Lee, whose friendship and creativity inspire me; Alexa Stark and Ellen Levine, for seeing potential in those early pages and for their hard work in shepherding this book into the world; Megan Lynch, whose excellent editorial insights and feedback gave me the necessary push to make this story better; Sara Birmingham, for keeping everything beautifully on track; everyone at Ecco who helped make this book a reality; and Jeff's family, especially Mary Ryan, constant champion of my work.

I am indebted to William Shurtleff and Akiko Aoyagi at Soy-Info Center for compiling an extensive biography of Yamei Kin; Judy Yung, Gordon H. Chang, and Him Mark Lai, who edited *Chinese American Voices: From the Gold Rush to the Present;* and to the *New York Times* for their amazing archival TimesMachine.

And to my family—my mom, Leslie; my dad, Karl; my siblings, Aileen and Angus—I am beyond grateful. They give me life to draw on and the freedom to do with it what I want. Thank you especially to my sister, who read the book when I most needed it and kept me sane. And finally, again, to Jeff, who can't be thanked enough, and because he reminded me to acknowledge Irving and AJ—all three, great loves of my life.